"Is he really that good, or is he trying to impress you?" Esme demanded.

Dafydd hesitated. "I think it's genuine. And I think Mr. Williams and Dai do, too. He's working hard enough at present, anyway, and he's had enough chances to run away if he was going to. We prayed for him last night. Dai rang his mother and told her he was all right, and apparently she didn't seem all that bothered."

"Welcome to my world," Esme muttered.

Dafydd was not sure whether he was supposed to have heard and could think of nothing to say, but James responded, very quietly but clearly: "And mine. There's a lot of us, Esme . . . "

There was a long silence. Cars passed outside and Dafydd repressed a guiltily gleeful smirk as he heard a very subdued thump thump thump start up in the next house. "You'd better go and get that final cache," he suggested. "And as I know you're coming back tomorrow night, I'll make welshcakes."

Esme scooped up her crutches. "Yes please! And you've got a treasure-hunt to write, don't forget! I can't wait, if it's as good as this one! Come on, Jay!"

Dafydd watched them go down the path and get into the car. He put two cups away, made a pot of tea for himself, made sure the kitchen doors were shut and let Sky out. He sat in the living-room with the tea tray, his notebook and a pile of scrap paper, and prayed for Aled, for James and Esme. Then he poured a cup of tea, picked up a pen and wrote BORTH at the top of a sheet of paper.

He had a treasure-hunt to write.

"You ought to do a proper puzzle cache, Mr. Williams; those were really good clues!" James joined in.

"Thank you!" He grinned. "Paned? I've just had Mrs. Ellis on the phone from the Carnival Committee; Siân's told her about it, and she wants me to do another treasure-hunt for the carnival weekend."

"Oh, you must!" Esme said immediately, sitting down in his armchair. "I won't have a drink, if you don't mind; I'd like to go down to Dol Wen as soon as possible and annoy Siân. Does she know where it is, or do we have to be stealthy?"

"I had to ask her permission, but go ahead and be stealthy if you like, just don't get arrested." Dafydd wondered what Siân's neighbours would think; wondered if Donald and Sandy would notice.

"Not for me, thanks, we've had a coffee already." James hesitated. "But can we come back tomorrow evening and see the kits? And what happened about Aled? The sheep-shearer?"

"I don't really know. At least that recording did work, and she's on it as well as him. Dai's still talking to the police at Aber; the craft shop company's head office wants Sophie Marston found because apparently she was fiddling the accounting. The shop's closed, and likely to stay that way from what I can gather. Aled's still at the farm with Evan Williams, working there officially now. He's made a list of all the places where he sheared sheep and Dai says he wants to offer to shear for them next year or do some sort of work to make amends."

"We'll be straight over," James said, and rang off.

"You, young lady," Dafydd said to Sky, "are going to be shut in again, I'm afraid. We're having visitors." He carried her upstairs, shooed the kittens back into the spare bedroom and closed the door on all five of them, went down and filled the kettle and set a tray with three cups and saucers. He sat in the living-room, watching as James' car drew up outside and Esme got out. She looked at the railings, at the array of socks and other small articles which Rheidol had brought back, examining one or two more closely. She looked at the pavement in front of the railings and then began to feel along the underside of the horizontal bar which held the uprights together.

This is how James felt, watching people find his cache, Dafydd realised. Has he guessed where it is and isn't telling her, or does he not know either?

Suddenly, with a cry of delight, Esme noticed the button thread and pulled up the plastic bag. One of her crutches clattered to the ground but she hooked an elbow round the decorative spikes to keep her balance and waved the bag at James. "It is! It does say O.L.—I know where it is!"

Dafydd opened the front door. "You'd better come in, both of you. Pity I haven't got any cake."

James collected the stray crutch and handed it to Esme, and they came up the path together.

"That was a really fiendish hide!" Esme protested. "I've been here twice and just never thought to look for thread, but I'd guessed where the final cache was from the rest of the letters."

Dafydd hesitated. "Can I drop it in at yours? I don't mind you coming here, but there's been a tom-cat in, and the house *stinks* of cat. Yes, a small black one with white socks . . . Oh dear. Poor little Tom Socks. That's almost how I got Sky, but they didn't just abandon her, they left her with someone and never came back. I'm glad you've taken him in. And I should think your place must smell as bad as mine, so please come round, you'll be very welcome!"

When she had rung off he lifted Sky onto the stairs and replaced the receiver. Well, well. The stately Mrs. Ellis was not only sound on cats, but had taken charge of Tom Socks—and was no doubt spending much of her spare time trying to deal with the smell. He grinned. Siân was still working on the puzzle, and he'd heard nothing from Esme about it either: it was taking them far longer than he'd anticipated. Maybe he should give them a hint . . .

The telephone rang again. Mrs. Ellis with further ideas? He lifted the receiver.

"Mr. Williams?" a familiar voice began, with a background of conversations and clattering china. "It's James here. There's one Esme just can't get, and she's done the anagram without it and thinks she knows where the final cache is, but she's insisting on finishing it properly. Could you check the cache is still there, please?"

"Which one is it?" Dafydd asked. "Wait a minute, I'll just have a look. . . " He laid the receiver on the telephone directory, went into the living-room, and lifted the net curtain. The edge of the plastic bag was poking out behind the marguerites. He hurried back. "Yes, it's still there."

reach down to one or two of the items, and I think it's a marvellous idea. Would you be willing to set up a similar treasure-hunt for the carnival weekend?"

Without pausing to think, Dafydd responded with horrified honesty. "I don't have to be there for it, do I?"

He heard Mrs. Ellis catch her breath, but then she laughed, a genuine and most un-ladylike yelp of merriment. "Of course not! And to tell you the truth, every year at this stage of the planning I start feeling exactly the same! But it's such a good idea and your clues are so clever that I felt I must ask you if you'd be prepared to share it with us. We'd have to change the place where the final prize is hidden, of course, because Mrs. Gilchrist won't want hordes of people poking around in her geraniums, but would you let us?"

Dafydd took a deep breath. "Well, as long as the prize is not alcohol, I don't see why not. But if there are to be many people looking for the items, we'll have to ask all the local people if they object to having items hidden by their houses. Oh, and I'd like it still to be wheelchair-friendly; I planned it originally because Miss Davies wanted to go geocaching and there were so few in the immediate area which were accessible. But we could certainly expand the area covered. I'd like to put one at the church, and possibly the golf club; even up at the Animalarium, if they don't mind."

Mrs. Ellis said that she thought that was a good idea, and she'd leave it with him until Friday when there was another Carnival Committee meeting; was two days enough, and could she pop round to pick up what he'd done by then?

Chapter 17

ON WEDNESDAY MORNING the phone rang and he went to answer it, expecting the caller to be Siân or Esme, asking for help with the clues.

"Dafydd M. Williams sy'n siarad . . . hallo! Are you sure you've got the right person?"

Mrs. Ellis said rather pompously that yes, she was quite sure, she was phoning about the treasure-hunt he'd set up.

Dafydd sat down on the bottom stair and was immediately joined by Sky, purring loudly. "I'm sorry if I've offended anyone, Mrs. Ellis, but I made sure all the items were hidden on the public highway—apart from two, and one's in my garden and the other's behind the Davies' drainpipe . . . "

"No, no, I've not rung to make a complaint. Mrs. Gilchrist told me what she was doing and I helped her to

The Metamorphosis of Dafydd M. Williams, Detective

Parts 1-3

Malinda Law

William Congreve & Co., Publishers,
Manor Farm,
Congreve,
STAFFORD.
ST19 5QG
(07549) 952396
Email: marchell@williamcongreve.co.uk
Web: www.williamcongreve.co.uk

ISBN 978-1-7385110-3-7

British Library Cataloguing in Publication Data.
A catalogue record for this book is available from the British Library.
Printed and bound in Great Britain by Panda Press Ltd, 1 Newcastle Street, STONE, Staffordshire. ST15 8JU
Typeset body of text in 12pt Garamond, title and chapter headings Jokerman, by William Congreve & Co., Publishers.

Biography

Malinda Law was born and brought up in Shropshire, a descendant of Huguenot weavers who fled to England in 1572 and Somerset miners who moved to South Wales in the 1850s. Having discovered the work of Dorothy L. Sayers, Agatha Christie, and Monica Edwards at an early age, her ambition from then on was to write stories, live in Wales and own a cat; since then she has been writing, knitting, and amassing the raw material for her thrillers. Her experience of living in Wales amounts to three years at Aberystwyth University and a fortnight or so each year in self-catering accommodation on the Welsh coast. She and her long-suffering husband are currently owned by their son's two cats.

Preface

When younger I was often disappointed by stories supposedly set in Wales, as the country they portrayed bore no resemblance to that which I had experienced. I was similarly disappointed by my suburban existence which was singularly lacking in drama. Exciting things happened to people in books: why not to me? This yearning for adventure stayed with me as I grew older, though my expectations became more realistic.

Meanwhile, I devoured all the detective stories and thrillers I could find. When I had exhausted my parents' book collection I turned to the local library, only to discover that many of the modern thrillers were (unnecessarily, in my opinion) extremely gory, violent and sexually explicit. I also noticed that characters who were church/chapelgoers or clergy had ceased to be well-meaning but largely ineffectual, and had become hypocrites, and, in some cases, particularly unpleasant villains.

Once my children had left home I began to spend more time writing stories of the type I wanted to read, and in 2014 I decided to write a thriller set in Wales with a basically good, moral, ordinary person as the main character, who when faced with increasingly challenging situations would have to overcome his own inadequacies in order to win through, as any reader might. Thus was Dafydd M. Williams created. For the benefit of the English-only reader 'Dafydd' is pronounced 'Davv-ith', the 'th' as in 'the'.

All characters, events and incidents are either the products of my imagination or I have used my imagination to adjust them to suit the story. Although the setting is genuine (and worth visiting!), I have taken liberties with a few of the places. Dafydd's house is an amalgamation of at least two local properties. The Chapel has, alas, been closed for many years, as has the Tourist Information Office; and the Grand Hotel is now flats, but Stretton and the Min-y-mor guest-house exist, though not under those names; as do Miss Smith's house next to the Victoria, Siân's bungalow in Dol Wen and Dai's house in Cliff Road, along with the Spar (now the Premier), the little supermarket by the Lifeboat Station, the Friendship Inn, the Golf Club, and the Railway Station with its museum. There is no manse in Borth, nor is there a vicarage, and I have moved Tynyllechwedd wood. You will not find Richard's house among those on the hill above Borth, or a piano teacher at a farm near Rhydyfelin, though the Borth Carnival takes place each summer as it has done for many years.

Similarly, when geocaches are described, there is/has been a cache like this somewhere . . . but not necessarily where I have placed it for the purposes of the story. As Dafydd discovers, geocaching is a form of treasure-hunt. Thousands of containers of various sizes and shapes have been hidden all over the world, with clues to their position provided on the geocaching website on the internet*. Geocachers use G.P.S. co-ordinates to find these containers,

* www.geocaching.com/play

signing the enclosed logbook and also logging the find on-line; the caches are often placed in areas of historical or geological interest.

Finally, as Dafydd and many of his friends are Welsh-speaking Welsh, I have included a small amount of that ancient and beautiful language. Many thanks to M.A.P. and others who have assisted with this: any errors are entirely my own.

Malinda Law,
Staffordshire, 2024

For M.A.P.

Contents

Part 1:

The Dreaded Batter Pudding-Hurler of Borth

Chapter 1

IT WAS AT 7.27 p.m. on the Wednesday after St. David's day in 2014 that Dafydd M. Williams came stumping past the Friendship Inn in Borth and was hit in the face with a batter pudding.

He did not initially realise what had struck him. Staggering back and wiping his face, he was too surprised to react with more intelligence and simply looked around for the perpetrator of the attack, saw no one and went on his way to the Baptist chapel. He arrived a few minutes after seven-thirty, collapsed onto a vacant chair in the side room and apologised for being late.

"Marged isn't here yet," Siân smiled, "and the Minister is photocopying, so you're all right . . . Are you all right? You look flustered."

Dafydd wiped his face again with his handkerchief and inspected it. It was slightly greasy.

"Well, I've had rather a shock," he admitted. Siân and three other elderly ladies leaned closer. One adjusted her hearing aid.

"On my way here, it was; by the Friendship. There must have been someone behind the dustbins in the alley. And when I came past, whoosh, something straight in my face! I thought it was a seagull, but then I saw a big piece of pudding on the ground. Batter pudding, if you please, and still warm!"

The ladies twittered condolences which he acknowledged sheepishly, realising the mistakes he had made. For a start he should have picked up the missile as proof—to himself, let alone anyone else—that he had not simply imagined the whole thing. If it wasn't too dark on the way home he would have to look for clues . . . What clues could there be, apart from the pudding itself? Footprints? If only he'd thought to have a closer look while he was out there: now he was stuck at the chapel until the end of Bible study. He ground his teeth. Still, at least he'd not been any later, so that everyone stared at him as he came in and found a seat—but if he'd been that late he wouldn't have bothered to go in at all and could have gone back to have a look round by the bins . . .

He scowled into the cloth bag as he took out his Bible. Who had attacked him and why had they done such an odd thing? Was it personal, or had he simply been in the wrong place at the wrong time?

Marged and the Minister arrived simultaneously through different doors to be met with the report that Mr. Williams had been attacked on his way there; only a batter pudding, but you never knew, did you, and it was probably students and something ought to be done . . .

Dafydd felt obliged to speak up at this point. "Well, if that's the worst they can think of to do it's a good thing, and we've no proof it was students. It might have been a mistake. Which chapter is it tonight?"

"How can anyone attack someone with a batter pudding by mistake?" Marged demanded, seating herself opposite him with a smile and smoothing her rather short skirt over her knees. As usual, Dafydd concentrated on her slim and shapely ankles and the capacious shoulder-bag she had dumped beside the chair . . . Very capacious, it was. Suspiciously so, in the circumstances. But the Minister was taking a plastic folder of handouts and a Bible, both of which were held together with sticky tape, out of an old shopping-bag which was even bigger.

"You ought to tell the police," one of the ladies suggested.

"No!" Dafydd snarled before he could stop himself, and shrank back into his seat as everyone stared. Not the police, and absolutely never Dai the P.C.S.O.: even if he'd ended up in an ambulance, he'd die sooner.

"Why not?" someone asked. "Mr. Williams——?"

"Oh, he wouldn't be bothered," he mumbled, wishing he'd kept his mouth shut. "Wasting police time, that'd be. I'm not hurt."

Someone made further remarks about students, but the Minister glanced at the clock and started to hand out pages of notes, asking if Dafydd was sure he was all right and then announcing the twelfth chapter of Jeremiah.

"What do you think, Mr. Williams?" One of the ladies leaned towards him, her Bible beginning to slip off her lap.

Dafydd blinked at her. He'd never bothered to remember any of their names except Siân Gilchrist's, and then there was Marged Pugh the Inevitable . . . What did he think about what? He should have been paying attention.

"Mair means, was God being fair to Jeremiah?" Siân smiled at him.

"It probably didn't feel like it," Dafydd muttered, and, having participated, immediately lost interest in any response there might have been. Why do I bother to come, he thought. I don't get anything out of it: most of what he says I know already, it's just something to do on a Wednesday evening, the only thing I do in the week—I really am a hypocrite . . . That sounds like one of those mythical heraldic things: is a hippogriff the half-lion half-eagle? Or the dragon-looking one? Hippo means horse, so that's one half, but what's a griffin? I need to look that up when I get home . . .

Evan Jenkins was saying something about God's purposes being beyond human comprehension.

Dafydd scowled. Good, that lets me off the hook. If humans aren't meant to understand it . . .

He realised he was being smiled at again, this time by Evan himself, and composed his features hastily before the scowl was noticed. As usual the Minister was wearing his week-day uniform of grey trousers left over from the previous decade's Sunday suit and the beige jumper with pills of acrylic under the arms; he had two, which he wore in alternate weeks. The other had a carefully-mended pluck in one sleeve. If Evan decided one day to wear jeans and a red sweatshirt, would anyone in the village recognise him? If I shut my eyes, can I remember his face? Better not . . .

"It's possible to survive without human friendship; Jeremiah is proof of that," the Minister remarked. "But Elijah cried out in the wilderness: 'I have had enough, Lord: take my life.' And God answers: 'Yet I reserve seven thousand who have not bowed down to Baal'."

And that's supposed to help? Dafydd glowered at the younger man and to his disquiet Evan grimaced and turned to his next page of notes.

Noticing the hiatus, Siân leapt briskly in.

"That's why it's so important for everyone to be friendly to people! Especially people who're on their own."

Dafydd studied the notice board. There goes Siân, doing her 'Minister's Widow' act again: we should all be nice to people and then the world would be a better place. I don't think it says that anywhere in the Bible; what it does say is 'Do not trust them, though they speak well of you'; we've just done that bit! At least Evan doesn't go round being worthy and positive all the time, he's not as bad as some of them . . .Oh, why do I bother? I don't enjoy this, but it gets me out of the house: everything else in the village is either exercise or for women—and I can't get to Aberystwyth or Machynlleth for things like lectures on industrial archaeology. Well, I could, but it'd mean walking back to the station in the dark, and I'm too old to go out at night. I wouldn't feel safe in a big place like Aber, or even in Mach, not in the dark. Like tonight: no one threw a batter pudding at any of *them* . . . Isn't a hippogriff the one with a beak and wings? Or is that wyverns? I ought to concentrate . . . Why does Dai annoy me so much? Popping up all over the place in that yellow high-viz jacket, like a—a fungus! And it's not only me that objects to him, I've heard people saying things in the Spar. Hanner-Heddwas, they call him; half-policeman . . . which is at least more polite than some of the things people call P.C.S.O.s. I know he's only doing his job, but it's how he does it . . . Even so, I'm not usually rude to people. Even people like him. I bet he's not forgotten that any more than I have. Oh dear . . .

On his way home, having refused offer of an escort—"Thank you, Mrs Pugh, but I have my stick and I shall be fine," (not to mention being six years younger than any of them except the Minister, he thought wryly)—he marched resolutely up to the alley by the Friendship, almost expecting another attack.

Nothing happened. There was no sign of the batter pudding, and no sign that anyone had hidden. Muted sounds of conviviality drifted from within the building. With a shrug Dafydd plodded towards home, beginning to think about a pot of tea and the crossword puzzle he had left unfinished. As he opened the wrought-iron gate his ginger cat trotted down the path, tail up in greeting.

"Hylo, Rheidol bach," he responded. "Ble roeddet ti heddiw? Where were you today? Yn hela llygod yn y cae? If you were hunting mice in the field, I hope you've not brought any indoors and let them go."

He continued to talk to the cat as he opened a packet of cat food, switched on the kettle, fetched the tea-caddy from the cupboard and the milk jug from the fridge, and put a cup and saucer on the tray along with the tea-strainer. The kettle was nearly boiling so he warmed the teapot and measured in the leaves. At last he sat down by the front window with his paned. He could hear Rheidol eating in the kitchen.

It had definitely been a batter pudding. Slightly warm, slightly greasy. Brown at the edges and yellow, nicely risen. Big, too; about the size of a meat tin, ten inches by twelve. Not too heavy or it would have hurt more . . .He went to the hall mirror and checked his reflection for damage. There was a faint smear of something adhering to one eyebrow; he rubbed it off. He also noticed a grease mark on the front of his coat where the thing had slipped downwards.

He shivered suddenly. Marged had been right: it had not been a mistake. He was a creature of habit and anyone in Borth could have known he would be coming past that alley on his way to the chapel at that time on a Wednesday evening. Someone in Borth had used that information; they had intended him as their target. Dafydd drew the curtains and sat nursing his cup of tea, wondering who could have had a motive to attack him and how they had intended him to respond; after all, if he had somehow made a genuine enemy, a half-brick would have been a better missile. Had he insulted anyone's cooking? Not that he could remember; the last time he had eaten out had been in autumn, at The Treehouse in Aberystwyth, and he had no complaints about the food there . . .

Maybe it was something to do with the railway. Some unsuccessful traveller with a grudge? He had never lived in Borth while he was working for the rail companies, had never told anyone there about his job. No, it had to be someone from the village, and he'd had very little to do with any of them, even the people at Chapel. He couldn't imagine Evan Jenkins bothering with batter puddings and the others had all arrived before him—except Marged.

He got up again and went back to the kitchen to top up the teapot with hot water.

It could have been Marged. She had a strange sense of humour, but he couldn't think of a motive although she had certainly had the opportunity and presumably the means of doing so . . . Maybe it was Marged—or another woman, because Marged was married—in love with him and trying to attract his attention.

He stared at Rheidol in consternation. "O diar, pws, be' fyddwn ni'n wneud? Or, rather, what shall *I* do, puss; it's not you she'll be after!"

The cat flicked an ear towards him briefly and continued to wash.

Dafydd grinned at this patent rejection of his theory, took the teapot back to his living-room, and poured another cup. It was probably students after all. Someone being silly. Let's get the old man who goes to Chapel every Wednesday night . . .

If only he'd not been so startled! He need not have said anything at all, but he'd told people: they'd remember and it'd be all round the Chapel. They'd talk about it until something else happened, and not much ever did happen in Borth. He couldn't stop going to Chapel, to the Bible study, or they'd come round to see if he was all right . . . and what could he tell them?

It needn't just be Chapel either: what if it got out and the whole village knew? He should never have let Siân talk him into going to Bible study that first Sunday when he'd just moved in. "Come along on Wednesday at half past seven and make friends," she'd instructed, standing in the doorway after the service so he couldn't escape without giving some sort of answer . . .and he never had answered: Evan Jenkins had come up at that moment, to be told by Siân that Mr. Williams was new in Borth and he was going to come to Bible study, wasn't that nice—and the look on the Minister's face had been so surprising that the polite refusal he'd been formulating had remained unspoken.

Even now he was sure Evan Jenkins' expression had been one of relief. More than that: the gratitude of a man who finally sees the Seventh Cavalry coming over the hill. What on earth had Evan expected of him?

Dafydd poured himself another paned, uncomfortably aware that if the Minister had been hoping for more than the attendance of a male not yet seventy he had been disappointed. He had dutifully turned up every Wednesday at half past seven and every Sunday at the services, but he had made sure that he never got involved. He'd deflected most of their questions and offered no opinions, and after three years still no one at the chapel knew any more about him than they could see by looking. They only knew his middle name began with M because he had obediently signed up to a direct debit and there were already three D. Williamses on the list, one of whom was another Dafydd.

What had Evan expected? And why did he now feel so guilty about not having done it, whatever it was?

He could not concentrate on the crossword, and gave up. Before he went to bed he checked that he had locked both doors.

There was no sign of Rheidol in the kitchen when Dafydd came downstairs next morning. As usual he made toast and tea, washed, shaved, raked a comb through his dark curls and was out of the house by six-thirty, heading north along the sea wall in the mist of early morning. There were two dog-walkers out on the beach in the distance, gulls flapping up from the water's edge as the intruders came closer. A ringed plover sprinted across the shingle and he wondered if they would nest again this year.

At the edge of the golf course he went down onto the beach and walked back along the strand-line, picking up a few items which caught his eye: a small plastic football, a skate's egg case, a piece of driftwood. He collected his *Daily Telegraph* from the Spar before returning home, went into the kitchen to make more tea and found Rheidol waiting by an empty food bowl. There was a single sock on the doormat, pale green with a pink ribbon bow.

"At it again, are we?" Dafydd said sternly to the cat and went out to hang the sock on the dark green Victorian railings by his gate. The mist had cleared and the sun was coming out but it was still cold. One of the paper-boys swooped past with an empty bag flapping behind him.

So at least they didn't know. Not yet. Why had he told anyone about the attack? He shuddered at the idea of people staring at him, pointing and laughing . . .He went in and closed the dark green door firmly behind him. He had not expected to feel so angry. He hadn't at the time, but now . . . Why do something so senseless? Why do it to him? Why was it always him? Just because he was short? And why on earth had he told the Bible study ladies? Marged would talk. Siân wouldn't if she guessed he didn't want her to; she wasn't too bad, just persistently more friendly than he wanted, but he could well imagine that Marged was at this very moment telling an attentive bus queue how someone had flung a batter pudding at the old man who came to their Bible study—and then that Dai Hanner-Heddwas would be on the doorstep with his notebook asking impertinent questions, asking who he'd annoyed—who he'd annoyed *this time,* even . . . Well, he wasn't going to give Dai the satisfaction of finding out. He'd do it himself. Realising that he had clenched his fists, he laid his hands carefully flat on the Formica-topped kitchen table. Whoever it was, they were going to regret having ever heard of batter puddings.

When he finally remembered that he had been making a cup of tea the kettle had long since switched itself off. He turned it on again, toyed with the quick crossword and then after a second cup of tea reached for one of the two cookery books on the dresser. Flour, milk, eggs, fat. It seemed simple enough and he had all the ingredients. He tied a striped apron round his waist, wiped cat hairs off the kitchen table, and set the oven.

"As I said, the temperature of the fat and the nature of the fat is the secret," Mrs Taylor informed him, unfolding her spectacles and placing them on her nose with the air of a surgeon scrubbing up before an operation. "Now then: are these what you've made? Oh dear . . . "

For a few long seconds she regarded the collection of Yorkshire puddings in Doric Ware saucers laid out across her kitchen worktop. Dafydd squirmed in anticipation of ridicule.

Mrs Taylor shook her head sadly and selected two samples for particular comment. "This one clearly stuck to the pan, the middle is still very wet and uncooked, and this one is very heavy and sad. I take it the others are later attempts?"

Dafydd nodded. "The book was not sufficiently specific. I shall annotate it once I've achieved something edible."

"Ah, the scientific approach. My Herbert was a scientist." She sighed. "These modern books are no use at all. All glossy pictures and no technique. What brought you to me, young man?"

"Well now, I'm sorry to have troubled you, but I once heard from Siân that you used to teach cookery and I was sure you'd know where I was going wrong. I shouldn't have bothered you." Dafydd was gathering up the saucers. Siân had also mentioned Mrs. Taylor's love of hydrangeas, which was how he had identified her bungalow.

"I hope I've been of help. It's many years since I've taught. I admire you for trying, Mr. Williams, and not just going into a shop and buying them frozen in packets. Too many people expect everything done for them. They have these great big kitchens full of fancy gadgets, and barely the skill to open a tin!"

By now she had climbed onto what was clearly her favourite soapbox and he wished he'd continued to experiment unaided.

"They don't know eggs are laid by hens, half of them, and think meat comes from factories; they don't have any idea about nutrition or how to cook. If they had to live on a ration like we did in the War they'd starve for lack of sense!"

Dafydd agreed. It seemed safest.

When he finally escaped from Mrs. Taylor, who lived near the Manse on the hillside at the south end of the village, he made his way slowly up the steep track to the monument at the top which was the local war memorial. There were small boats in the bay, a train crawling across the fields by the golf course, a few hikers on the coastal path. The village seemed very small and dull; a string of houses along the main road, a few side streets and then the caravan sites and the houses on the hillside. There had been even less of Borth when the railway came: no caravans, no golf course, no hotels, no ice-cream parlour or amusement arcade . . . but there had probably been a grocer's, a butcher or two, a greengrocer, a blacksmith, a wheelwright and a carrier's cart which went to Aberystwyth once or twice a week.

Siân would know. She was an incomer like himself but had looked further into the history of the place. She seemed to know everyone too, even distinguishing between the many Chapel ladies with similar perms and raincoats. How did she do it? After three years he recognised a few of the locals: Mrs. Howell and Miss Bevan the tourist information ladies who provided him with bus timetables; the Vicar; Evan Jenkins the Minister; Bill who was another ex-railwayman, and his talkative wife Babs; Miss Smith who lived next to the Victoria Inn and dressed rather oddly; Malcolm Edwards (when accompanied by the horse) . . . and Dai, of course. Dai Hanner-Heddwas the P.C.S.O. One of the most provoking people he'd ever met.

Dafydd looked down at the rooftops. That was the Baptist chapel and there was the road to the railway crossing; there was Dol Wen, one of the side streets. The roofs were tiled, not slated, and stood out from the others. One was Siân's house. That was the hotel on the corner by the station, and over the back on a green hillock rising out of the brown flat fields around it was the church, with the pens of the Animalarium visible beyond that if you knew where to look.

It was growing colder and the wind was freshening, and when he glanced at his watch it was ten to four. He picked up the bag of saucers and set off down the track. If he dropped in at the shop he could buy sausages if they had any and have a go at making toad in the hole.

Chapter 2

THE NEW SLATE-SHINY miniature supermarket had sausages in stock. However, Marged was there too, talking to the woman at the till and looking as though she was good for another hour or so.

"Here he is!" she called cheerfully, noticing him. "Dafydd, tell Gwenan what happened!"

Dafydd's heart sank.

"Oh, it was nothing to worry about, Mrs. Pugh. People playing the fool, most likely." He began to sort out the right change for the sausages in hope of dropping it onto the counter and escaping, but remembered that he was short of milk too.

"It might be important." The shop assistant gazed admiringly at him. "You see, Ellie at the Spar's been attacked too—and it might be us next."

"Is Ellie all right?" He was trying to visualise the women at the Spar, which was his paper shop. Was Ellie the tall dark one, or the smaller, greying one?

"Oh, yes. Really cross because she'd just had her hair done, but she's not hurt. Are you all right?"

Dafydd mumbled that he was fine, hurried across to the fridge for a plastic carton of milk and pushed a five pound note across the counter. Marged stepped back into his bag, which clinked alarmingly.

"What have you got in there?" she asked. "Have you been drinking, Dafydd M. Williams? And what does that M stand for?"

"Meindiwch Eich Busnes. As I keep telling you."

He heard Gwenan stifle a giggle; had no one but him ever told Marged to mind her own business? There were times when he could be magnanimous and cope with her curiosity, but this wasn't one of them. He dumped the bag on the counter.

"I have been researching," he said firmly. "Finding out how it is that you make a batter pudding. And I've made enquiries from an expert, who was not the attacker, and it is not easy at all, not even with a recipe. Now, the item which hit me was a very good specimen so whoever cooked it was either very fortunate or knew exactly what they were doing."

"Or they'd had it from someone who knew," Marged suggested.

"I doubt that: it was still warm, and my source says they don't re-heat well." He took his change and the receipt. "Thank you. So I shall speak to Ellie now, and find out what quality the missile was with which she was attacked, and if it was equally good then we are looking at a professional."

"You mean, Darren at the Victoria? Or Lucy at the Friendship? I've never known Phil at the hotel make Yorkshires——" Gwenan began.

"No, no. Not a professional chef, necessarily, but someone who has had years of experience and turns out lovely light batter puddings every Sunday for dinner."

"Well, that lets me out," Marged grinned. "Robert always reckons mine are more like paving slabs. Good luck with your detective work, Dafydd; we must let you know if we hear that anyone else has been puddinged."

He bade them a grave farewell and left. Cars went up the road past him: cars went down. He raised a hand to acknowledge Malcolm Edwards who was taking his horse for a walk, stopped to read a couple of new posters on the board by the phone box (more Council cuts, this time to the library and the tourist information service), remembered he was supposed to be buying lard for the next batter pudding, bought some at the butcher's (no sausages left, as he had suspected), and wondered what clues Ellie at the Spar would be able to give him.

The Spar seemed full of people. Ellie was the elder of the two staff; she was telling an eager knot of women about the attack, with several men and children loitering and pretending not to be interested. She broke off on seeing him.

"Mr. Williams! Is it true you're looking for the criminal?"

He would have to be cautious about what he said, because not only might the perpetrator be listening, but word would eventually get back to Dai and he'd probably be in trouble for withholding information . . .

"Well, not properly looking, but the pudding which hit me was not bad at all; like a picture it was, the little I saw of it, and I was thinking, could anyone make one? How hard is it to make batter pudding? So I got out the book and had a go, and it is not easy at all, ladies; well, not for an old railwayman, though you may find it simpler. And I wish I had kept the pudding which hit me, to know the size of the tin, and—and whether there was salt in it or not and such-like, because someone who can make good batter puddings is being silly and it seems a wicked waste to let them carry on. Ellie! The pudding they hit you with: was it a good one?"

Ellie admitted that she hadn't noticed, being too shocked to do more than run back into the shop shrieking. However, her hair had needed to be washed because of the grease.

"Was it lard or oil?" Dafydd asked, but received no sensible reply. He bought a bag of flour and set off for home. He still had eggs left; he would have another go, and this time he would cover the batter while it was standing. In the last batch there had been a couple of ginger hairs floating.

He placed the measuring-jug on the table and checked the list of ingredients and equipment. Yes, that was everything. Now then. What had she said . . . ?

Little bits of lard in the tin.

Tin in the oven set at 230 degrees . . . No, not yet, he reminded himself. The batter has to stand.

Batter. He closed his eyes, trying to remember the former Domestic Science teacher's words. He should have made notes.

Sieve the plain flour into a basin. Make a well in the centre and drop in the egg. With a metal spoon, because it's colder, stir gently, bringing a little bit of flour into the well with the egg 'til it's all mixed. It'll be very thick and lumpy. Add a little milk and stir, add a little and stir, breaking up all the lumps, until you have two thirds to three quarters of the milk mixed in. Add the rest, turn the basin partly on its side, and with the spoon held flat, whisk . . .

He tried. The spoon clattered on the basin and Rheidol appeared hopefully.

. . . until the air starts bubbling out and making a sound like horses galloping. Very few people can do this: I had one child who could do it beautifully and we all stopped and listened. You do need to whisk it thoroughly, it's only the air that raises the pudding.

Then leave it in a cool place for at least half an hour.

Then get your fat piping hot and when you drop your pudding in it should start cooking immediately.

Half an hour, first. He covered the basin carefully with a plate.

Leave to stand, which softens the gluten in the flour. Gluten is the stretchy stuff which gives it the shape.

He set his alarm clock and had another go at the quick crossword.

Part way through, he remembered the sausages. Bother. Oh well, apply basic principles . . . He separated the sausages into individual links, put the oven on at 200°, pricked the sausage-skins, scraped the lard carefully out of the tin and onto a saucer (his last clean one) covered with a bowl, and put the sausages in the tin to cook. Back to the crossword . . .

When the sausages seemed to be almost done he carefully tipped the fat out into an empty tin, wiped the dregs up with kitchen paper, put the lard back in and turned up the oven to 230°. Five minutes for the lard to heat and the oven to come up to temperature, and test it with a little bit of mixture . . .

Yes, the test blob was beautifully golden and puffed. He scooped it out, poured in the rest of the batter and closed the oven door.

He had made toad in the hole. He felt inordinately proud, given that it hadn't finished cooking yet and he ought to do something about vegetables . . .

Half an hour later he sat down to toad in the hole, carrots and cabbage, still feeling very smug. The batter was perfect even though the sausages were definitely overcooked. Next time he would do better . . . and he remembered his mother making something similar with apples and blackberries instead of sausages. Blackberries would not be possible for another six months but he could try with apples or maybe pineapple chunks.

After the meal he washed up, scraping all the saucers onto one and leaving the resultant mess for Rheidol to investigate if he chose, then made a pot of tea and sat annotating the cookery book. It had been a very successful attempt, thanks to Mrs. Taylor.

He fetched his writing case and addressed an envelope, put his address at the top of a sheet of blue Basildon Bond and hesitated.

Dear Mrs. Taylor, he wrote, having considered the matter.

Thank you for your excellent instructions for making a batter pudding. I have, by using them, compiled a passable toad in the hole, and felt I should inform you of this success.

Thanking you again, yours sincerely,

Dafydd M. Williams.

It seemed rather a waste of a stamp to send it by post so he decided to deliver it by hand early next morning. He would have to make sure he was really early or she might think he was angling for another cookery lesson and invite him in, which he didn't want. Besides, she had seemed the sort of person who might well be an early riser like himself. It would make more sense to deliver it at night, he thought. Once he had finished the cup of tea . . .

Rheidol appeared beside the chair, mewed, jumped up and made himself comfortable on Dafydd's lap. It seemed unfair to disturb him and it was late to be skulking round front gardens, even to deliver a letter. Dafydd sighed and reached carefully for the crossword, wincing as Rheidol's claws sank into his leg despite his caution.

Nine o'clock came and went; Rheidol still asleep. Dafydd could not work out the last three clues, and could not reach the thesaurus. He yawned and leaned back, eyes closed, thinking about the possibilities.

Either it was students being silly at random or it was someone from the village being specific. He now suspected that the attack on himself had been a trial run, to find out what would happen; he couldn't think of anyone apart from Dai whom he might have annoyed. And he'd been the ideal candidate for that trial run, hadn't he? A short, elderly, respectable chapel-goer, slow-moving and slow to react. If he'd done something—anything at all—then quite possibly that would have been the last of it. It was all his fault.

Well, at least he was trying to do something about it now. No doubt that jumped-up P.C.S.O. would think it was students larking about, if he bothered to think at all, but after his own research he was beginning to wonder if the pudding-thrower was a local adult with scores to settle. Whoever it was, they wouldn't be worried about him. He had been just a guineapig for the first attempt . . . A guineapig. Short and fat, and if you hold it up by its tail its eyes fall out. You chose me because you knew I walk with a stick—I had my stick with me! That makes it even more of an insult, because you knew I still wasn't a threat even with a stick! I could have retaliated and I didn't, I was too surprised, I never expected—— If I ever find out who did this, they'll find out that guineapigs bite . . .

He moved, felt Rheidol's claws again and very nearly shoved the animal off his lap but sighed and stroked the short smooth fur.

So if he'd not been a genuine target, what had Ellie done? Short-changed someone? Unlikely. Thrown children out of the shop for being a nuisance? Possibly, but how would children have got hold of a batter pudding?

He woke with a start as Rheidol leapt off his lap. It was two a.m. and the light was still on, as was the electric fire; the empty cup at his elbow and the envelope addressed to Mrs. Taylor were still on the table beside it. Bother. Well, at least no one had come knocking at the door to find out if he was still alive, or maybe they had and he'd not heard them.

"Mae hen bryd i mi fynd i'r gwely," he announced sternly in the vague direction of the departing Rheidol. "It's high time I went to bed. A phaid â tyrd nôl â rhagor o sanau, 'te!"

He smiled, hearing the cat-flap thud shut. If Rheidol did bring back more socks, at least they weren't going to get away and start chewing through electric cables as a mouse might. It could be worse.

He got up stiffly, took the tea tray into the kitchen and left the cup on the draining board, put the milk away, locked the back door, turned off the fire and the lights, locked the front door and went up to bed. He paused before starting to undress. Dratted cat; he now felt thoroughly awake, though he'd probably sleep late in the morning, and he still had the letter to deliver . . .

Why not? Not bothering to put lights on, he found his thickest coat, put the letter in the left hand pocket and his keys in the right hand one, and set off.

The village was eerily quiet except for the sea behind the houses. Partly from habit, and partly in case of inquisitive

P.C.S.O.s and others, he went through one of the gaps between buildings and onto the beach, and made his way carefully along the shingle under the light of the half-moon until he reached the next litter of large boulders which were part of the new sea defences. Inland again, past the shuttered lifeboat station, the sky prickling with stars in gaps between clouds. On up the hill, frost beginning to sparkle on the grass, in at Mrs. Taylor's front gate, cautiously down her smooth and probably icy path past the hydrangeas . . . the last thing he wanted was a broken hip in such circumstances . . . letter through the letterbox and the flap eased down so as not to make a noise, back down the path, closing the gate softly, down the hill before anyone noticed—and why so many lights were still on at nearly three in the morning he couldn't imagine . . . back down the long road and home. Lock the door. Upstairs.

Bother, once more. He still wasn't tired. He went to bed and lay in the dark with the curtains half-open, listening to the night. Oystercatchers flew over, calling as they went, easily audible over the constant rumble of the sea. He should have looked to see if the green sock had been claimed. Usually Rheidol's gifts were, if they weren't the scuttling and squeaking sort. He would have to check tomorrow.

Chapter 3

DETERMINED NOT TO become nocturnal (which was a waste of electricity), he had set his alarm clock for six a.m. When it rang he crawled out of bed unenthusiastically but as usual the walk on the beach was invigorating. He came back with the newspaper to find a new offering on the doormat.

"O Rheidol bach, ti'n ofnadwy . . . Dreadful animal you are! O ble wyt ti wedi cael y peth hwn? On second thoughts, I don't think I *do* want to know where you got this . . ."

He picked up the item with great caution and dropped it in a brown paper bag, then put that in a plastic bag which had contained potatoes, hung it on the railings and went indoors to wash his hands and make a restorative cup of tea.

"Cath ddrwg," he said sternly. Rheidol looked back, smugly placid. "Very bad cat. Dim caws i ti heno! No, don't look at me like that. I said no cheese tonight, and I mean it."

He was grateful for the net curtains in the front window when the paperboy came past. On seeing the bag the boy halted abruptly, peered inside, hung the bag back on the railings so carelessly that Dafydd feared it would fall off, and shot off down the road grinning all over his face.

Before he had recovered from this embarrassment the telephone rang: it was not Marged, as he had feared, but Siân, announcing that the pharmacist at the Health Centre had been attacked as she arrived for work and fortunately she had kept the evidence: would he like to see it?

What with Rheidol and puddings, he reflected, his life was becoming far too exciting. He set off for the Health Centre, wondering what he was supposed to do with the clue now he had one. Measure it, presumably; he had brought a ruler and a notebook. Weigh it? Taste it? Surely not; maybe the pharmacist would know how to test a batter pudding for salt and for the type of fat used. Perhaps he could guess that from the smell . . .

The pharmacy was busy, as usual. He stood meekly in line behind mothers with small children and a man in a suit who kept fiddling with a mobile phone, but then the assistant recognised him and waved him through to the back premises.

"Good morning, Mr. Williams." The pharmacist sounded English and wore a badge giving her name as

Elspeth Fraser. She was about his height, slim with her white hair cut in a neat short bob, and she showed no sign of having been hit by a batter pudding. He realised he was staring and hastily said good morning, Mrs. Gilchrist had told him what had happened and if it wasn't too much trouble . . .

"No, not at all. You're here before Special Constable Laffan. This is it." She put down a tray on the table between them.

Dafydd tried to look as though he knew what he was doing, worried that he would be reprimanded for meddling with evidence if Dai Hanner-Heddwas arrived before he could get away. He measured, wrote, sniffed, wrote again. He dared not touch the evidence in case they somehow managed to prove he'd been the attacker.

"Where did it happen, Miss?" he asked, pen poised. "I see. And it would have been light then; did you see anyone?"

"Just someone in dark clothes. Trousers, a long anorak sort of coat, I think a hat . . . A woolly hat. Not much help, I'm afraid. They must have been waiting for me to lock the car. I always park against those bushes because then I can leave the window open a crack if I got wet opening the gates; it clears the condensation." She grimaced. "Sorry: I'm rambling. It was just such a surprise—I feel a bit silly about calling the police now, I'm not hurt at all. Anyhow, I screamed, and when I'd recovered I rushed over to the Centre, and the people queuing were very concerned and Mrs. Gilchrist told me about the other incidents and that you were looking for clues, so I rushed back and shooed the seagulls away. That's why it looks a bit tatty."

"I see." Dafydd heard raised voices outside in the shop. He would have to be quick. "Mrs. Gilchrist; what was she wearing? And what was she here for?"

"Her green anorak with a pink hat and gloves," Elspeth Fraser said promptly. "None of them was sufficiently young and fit enough to have thrown something at me and then run round to be in the queue. And I can't legally tell you why she was here, but it was genuine."

"Thank you very much, Miss. I appreciate your help." He glanced at the door. "I'm not meant to be this side of the counter, am I now?"

Elspeth Fraser smiled. "I'll let you out the back way. Then you can look in the car park before Mr. Laffan gets there."

This was worse and worse. Dafydd checked very carefully for footprints around the car nearest to the bramble thicket, but the ground was still hard with frost and apart from a few scuff-marks he could see no sign that anyone had lain in wait. At least he'd tried . . .

He hurried down the road, put several hundred yards between himself and the Health Centre, and felt safer. He was almost sure the most recent pudding had been cooked in lard. Definitely a professional job, then. He passed the chapel and the Friendship Inn and was nearing the Victoria when, glancing back, he saw the sight he had been dreading: Dai Hanner-Heddwas in the distance, pedalling towards him at top speed.

He'd never make it home in time.

Dafydd looked round for help and saw movement: Miss Smith, drawing her front-room curtains. He'd never even said good morning to her, but Siân knew her. He hurried across the road and rang the doorbell.

Miss Smith opened her front door, saw Dafydd, and to his amazement and before he could begin to try to explain, shooed him in and locked the door behind him.

"Come in." She smiled, pushing back long grey-brown hair. "Or rather, as you're in already, come and sit down and tell me just what you've been up to."

She led him to the kitchen, produced two folding chairs and clicked the kettle on. "I'd put you in the parlour," she explained, "but Dai Hanner-Heddwas might look in. He's already seen you come here, he must have done, but there's no sense making his job any easier. So who are you and what have you done, Mr.——?"

"Williams." Dafydd sat, cautiously, in case the chair collapsed. "Dafydd M. Williams. Yes, tea, please."

The walls were white-painted and there were grey lino tiles on the floor, rather sandy; the cupboard doors were pine on which at least two different varnishes had been used over the years. There were plants on the windowsill and pieces of driftwood and a bottle of eco-friendly washing up liquid, along with a bar of no-nonsense yellow soap in a soap-dish; rather to his surprise, there was also a microwave oven beside the kettle.

"I'm Sue Smith. Susan Elizabeth. What does your M stand for?"

She was making the tea. Teabags, in mugs. Oh well, he thought, you can't have everything.

"Minnesota," he admitted. "After an uncle. Miss Smith, where were you on Wednesday evening at twenty three minutes past seven?"

She frowned at him. "In New Quay, probably. Peter and Marjorie gave me a lift back, but we stopped for chips in Bow Street on the way and they were on the point of closing, so that must have been about ten. Why?"

"So it wasn't you, then. Someone threw a batter pudding at me on my way to Chapel that night. And then someone did the same to Ellie at the Spar——"

He froze as the doorbell rang.

"Ignore it." Miss Smith handed him his tea in a mug with a picture of the Cofiwch Dryweryn graffiti on the side. He had seen it once from a bus on his way down to Caerfyrddin, painted on an old wall in a lay-by. It was fifty years since Capel Celyn village had been drowned by the Tryweryn reservoir. Did she know the history behind the graffiti, or had she just chosen a colourful mug? Her tea was in a tall white mug with an overall pattern of dragonflies, and they each had a spoon which Dafydd realised was intended for the purpose of removing the teabag; he watched her to see what he was supposed to do with his and dropped it beside hers in what he had feared was an ash-tray.

"It might be double glazing," she continued, smiling. "It often is. Mr. Williams—all right, then, Dafydd—if you didn't throw a pudding at Ellie, why are you on the run from the police?"

He found her easy to talk to, sitting calmly opposite him in an army surplus jacket with moccasin slippers visible under several layers of long skirts and her hair escaping from a badly-made bun. He told her all of it, even down to his brief suspicions of Marged and the Minister, and his cookery lesson with Mrs. Taylor. She laughed from time to time but when he had finished sat looking intrigued.

"So as far as you know there have been three attacks, all with batter puddings, at least two of which were about ten-by-twelve, all very good specimens, so made by someone who was good at it. You decided to do some detecting but now you're afraid you've fallen foul of Dai Hanner-Heddwas, or at least trodden on his toes by getting to the pharmacy first. If you didn't touch anything and you didn't destroy any footprints then I don't think he can actually do anything to you, but he might decide to be very unpleasant. I'm ambivalent about the police, generally; I always get the impression they see me and assume I must've done something illegal. Have you had altercations with Dai in the past?"

Dafydd avoided that question. "I don't like the man. Even if he was a grocer or a guard; it's not the uniform. It's the way he is. Rubs me up the wrong way, even saying good morning. I know I shouldn't feel like that, he can't help it I'm sure, but—— Ach a fi!"

Miss Smith nodded. "I do like that expression. So much more emphatic than 'ugh'. Anyhow, back to the anonymous pudding-thrower. Can you see any sort of link between the victims?"

Dafydd had been considering this.

"No." He sighed. "Not all women; not all Welsh, not all incomers. Not—well, I suppose we might all be older than the pudding-thrower, and that would make sense because he or she needs to get away, faster than us. And we all live here in Borth, or work here: I don't know where Miss Fraser lives, but she was talking about getting wet opening gates."

"She might live up in the hills on a back road, or simply in a house with gates to the drive."

"Or the other side of a farm crossing on the railway . . . Is this cat yours?"

It was a large, sleek, pure black cat, which had materialised at their feet.

"Yes, this is Konrad. Er—the way you said it, has he been being a nuisance?"

"Not recently, no." Dafydd grimaced. "Had Rheidol's food regularly 'til I waited one night with a bucket of water . . . But that's cats; I dare say you've similar tales to tell of mine. Big ginger lad, silvery collar . . . "

She nodded. "Yes, he's come in a few times. And had stuff, too: I found one of my gloves on your railings a few weeks ago. Has everything out there been brought in by Rheidol? However did he manage the football?"

"Oh, that I found on the beach. As long as it was only a glove. Today, I am ashamed to say, he brought in a pair of very—er—skimpy—pink knickers."

"No!" Miss Smith laughed and stopped guiltily. "Oh dear, not at all funny for you or for the owner . . . Surely you didn't hang those on the railings?"

"I did. In a brown paper bag. And the paper-boy had a look, saw what it was, and off he went grinning his head off!"

"Oh dear! As long as that wasn't what Dai wants you for . . . If he does take you in, they can't hold you more than twenty-four hours without charging you. Ninety-six if it's serious. Fourteen days for terrorism. Do you have a solicitor?"

Dafydd stared at her in consternation.

"Well, ring me, and I'll sort one out for you. You learn things like that at Greenham." She reached over and put her mug in the aluminium sink, carefully avoiding a heap of yogurt pots which were draining on a wooden rack, and picked up a shopping-list pad. "Back to the original problem. I do wonder if the pudding-thrower wants publicity. You were first; you'd go and tell your Chapel people. Why didn't you go into the Friendship first? They might have seen something; someone slipping out just before it happened, even."

"Into a public house?" Dafydd was aghast. "I never even considered it!"

"H'm . . . Maybe whoever it was knew you well enough, knew they'd be safe if they nipped straight back inside. Do you want me to go in there and ask if anyone saw or heard anything, if you don't want to?"

Dafydd opened his mouth to say no, firmly, and hesitated. "If you must. If you think it's necessary."

"I think it is." Miss Smith made a note and continued. "So you were first . . . And then Ellie; she and Pauline would tell everyone that uses the Spar. And then Miss Fraser; she tells—or someone does—everyone at the Health Centre. What do you think?"

Dafydd nodded. It made sense.

"So next," he said slowly, "should be someone from the church, just before a service, and the other shopkeepers, and the lifeboatmen . . . I wonder, now. It's a certain sort of person wants publicity, isn't it? Not just being silly, but more than that. Like a challenge: get all the village knowing about it, and still no one catches you. And the more people that know, the cleverer you think you are and the more risks you take . . . Oh dear. As long as it stops at batter puddings."

She looked at him, long and hard, without speaking. Konrad was eating biscuits loudly under a small table piled high with plastic boxes and plant pots. "Dafydd Minnesota Williams, just what did you do as a job?"

"Worked on the railway," he said promptly.

"You do surprise me. Or maybe not . . . Please keep me up to date with your detective work; I'm fascinated. This is my number, but if the curtains are open just drop in, I'm usually here."

Dafydd accepted the scrap of paper gravely.

"You're the only person who knows I'm Minnesota," he admitted, suddenly filled with dread. "Please keep it to yourself."

Miss Smith nodded. 'Of course. Do you want to go out onto the beach through the back gate? I'll go first and check he's not lurking."

Chapter 4

ALTHOUGH DAFYDD WAS dreading a visit from the Community Policeman and had gone so far as to memorise Miss Smith's telephone number, nothing happened. Aware that he would be found more easily if he followed his usual routine, he decided to do his washing three days early, then, leaving shirts and underwear to flap on the clothesline, he went for a good long walk along the shore, all the way to Ynyslas and back. It was cold and he was wishing he had taken sandwiches and a thermos by the time he was back at the edge of the village. A familiar yellow Labrador came bounding towards him, followed by Bill.

"Hallo, Sherlock, how's things? Caught anyone yet?"

Dafydd grimaced. "Still investigating, Bill. How's your wife?"

"Cleaning the oven. So we came out. Rosie!" He whistled to the dog, which abandoned whatever it was barking at and dashed back up the beach scattering pebbles. "Seriously, lad, it's a good thing you're looking into it. Some of the women are afraid to go out, wondering if there's someone hiding round corners, and knowing you're on the job . . . well, they feel safer. Not just Babs, either. I've been talking to some of the boys in the Railway . . . "

Dafydd barely heard the rest of it, half-honoured, half-appalled by the responsibility he had so lightly assumed. He stammered something about the police, and Bill laughed.

"Dai? He's gone up to the caravan park, trouble there or so we heard from Tony. By the way, young Aled reckons he saw a hen harrier out on the marsh last night."

"Marsh harrier, maybe. How close was he? Wouldn't mind seeing a hen harrier . . . "

When he finally got home his fingers were so numb despite his gloves that he had trouble unlocking the front door. Inside, kettle on, defrost for a few minutes, make tea, out into the back garden and fetch in the washing, shut the door on the cold, set up the clotheshorse, hang up the washing, cut some bread and cheese . . .

His feet had just about thawed when he remembered that he hadn't told Siân what had happened since her phone call. He checked the newspaper to make sure she was unlikely to be watching something, and dialled. Engaged. Oh well; it was probably one of her children or grandchildren.

He started the quick crossword, but his mind wandered. Had Rheidol's latest offering been claimed? He should have checked . . . For the last clue he had to resort to Roget's Thesaurus, but it was finally completed and he tried to ring Siân again.

This time she answered. Yes, she was fine; wasn't it cold; oh good, Miss Fraser was a nice young lady (Dafydd grinned, but then, Siân was eighty-six) and was he any nearer finding the suspect? Maybe if he arranged to see Miss Fraser after work she'd be able to tell him more; they could have a nice long chat . . .

More than a little irritated, he informed Siân in the English accent he usually kept for ringing complaints departments that he'd not only made extensive enquiries but also examined the car park and felt certain that he had extracted all the available information. Regrettably, none of the additional clues as yet pointed to anyone in particular, but no doubt in due course they'd find out who was to blame.

Siân seemed so disappointed by this response that he hurriedly added that he was grateful to her for having informed him of the incident, although he was now worried about what Dai Hanner-Heddwas might do in retaliation for his attempts at detecting.

"It's irrational, Siân, that's what annoys me. There's something about him that sets my teeth on edge, and today because I'd been at the pharmacy—I didn't touch anything, I was very careful about that, and it wasn't my fault I got there before him—he came chasing after me on his bike and I actually took refuge in Miss Smith's!"

"Goodness me. What did you make of her?" Siân enquired. "I've asked her to come to Chapel, several times, and she's always said outright that she won't. Maybe you should ask her."

"Oh, if she won't turn up for you I don't suppose she'd change her tune for anyone else." Dafydd was trying not to grin at Siân's persistence. "It's such a pity that people don't appreciate all the effort people go to, trying to do them good . . . "

Siân was silent for a long few seconds, but just as he was about to apologise for such a pointed remark he heard her sigh.

"She's nice enough, but a bit . . . difficult." Another sigh. "*Different* . . . And how's that kitten of hers?"

"Kitten? If you mean Konrad, he's bigger than Rheidol. She's very easy to talk to."

Help, he thought, why did I say that? Now she'll start trying to pair me off with Miss Smith . . . Is that what she says about me to people, that I'm difficult? I wouldn't be surprised . . . and I am difficult, but they all seem to want me to find the batter pudding-thrower so they'll have to put up with it!

"Miss Smith," he continued solemnly, "has an alibi. The other thing I rang up about: I've the dentist tomorrow in Aber. Do you need anything while I'm over there?"

As usually happened, Siân told a few of her friends of his expedition. Two notes were dropped through his letter-box that evening by passing dog-walkers, one asking if he could collect knitting wool someone had ordered, the other with a sketch and dimensions of a fire-grate and suggestions as to where he might be able to get one, along with a cheque for 'not more than' a sum which made Dafydd wince. Like the Drovers in the old days, he thought, to-ing and fro-ing with lists of things for people who weren't going there themselves . . .

He tucked the requests into his wallet with Siân's shopping-list, brought the bag of things intended for a charity shop out of the cupboard under the stairs and left it ready by the front door, found a sandwich box and put the remaining portion of toad in the hole in it, wrapped in greaseproof paper. Should he bother with a thermos? Not if he managed to get that grate: he'd have more than enough to carry . . .

He lay in bed looking at the stars through the gap in the curtains. Miss Smith . . . He'd seen Konrad, of course, and he'd seen her striding around the village, always in a long skirt and walking boots even in summer, her hair pinned up and sometimes a shawl round her instead of a coat, looking a little like his grandmother.

He wondered how old she was, whether she knew Welsh. She'd spoken with an English accent but there had been an old copy of *Y Tincer* under the cat's dish, so she read the Welsh-language local news-sheet, and he was sure it had been a Welsh-language calendar which hung above the telephone in the hall.

"Efallai mi fydd hi'n siarad Cymraeg efo Konrad," he said aloud. "Speaks Welsh to her cat, maybe, as I do to mine." It was a good thing she didn't mind that Rheidol had brought in one of her gloves. Where had she come from? Somewhere in England. What had she been doing in New Quay? What had she done as a job? None of his business, but she had found out so much about him, and he had only her word for it that she had not been in Borth when he was attacked.

He tried to remember the details of her kitchen; clean enough but very different from Mrs. Taylor's, which could have doubled as an operating theatre. Could she have made a batter pudding?

He couldn't sleep. In the end he put the light on and read the Bible for an hour or two, working his way through the first book of Chronicles. As long as he caught the 9.06 train . . .

His day in Aberystwyth felt like a holiday. He caught the train, showed his B.R. pass to the guard and sat back, gazing out as the countryside slid past. Up over the top at Llanfihangel, down to Bow Street, up again and finally down through Llanbadarn, past the new supermarkets and offices and into the terminus, a shadow of its former self. He remembered it with all the platforms in use and a bookstall behind the buffer stops . . . He joined the crowd at the pedestrian crossing and stumped off up Terrace Road towards the seafront, pausing at a charity shop to drop off his bag of white elephants.

His appointment was not until 11.50. He collected the knitting-wool, bought Siân's oatcakes, and then sat for a while watching the sea, the workmen busy with the repairs still in progress after the winter storms. It had been bad this time; even now there were stretches of the promenade without railings and in some cases without a proper surface at all, but the hotels seemed to be recovering and the halls of residence showed signs of exuberant inhabitation.

Only too soon it was time for his appointment, but the dentist found nothing wrong and released him to go down to the harbour where he looked at the boats for a while and ate the rest of the toad in the hole before making his way back slowly via the fire-grate, Siân's measuring-jug and elastic, and his own shopping which included honey from the health-food shop Maeth y Meysydd and fresh fish. Hoping he wouldn't regret the extra weight he also bought a bag of oatmeal and a huge Savoy cabbage, which proved to be more trouble than the oatmeal because of its sheer size.

Waiting to cross the road opposite the Salvation Army Citadel, he glanced at the poster on the wayside pulpit notice board. 'If you were on trial for being a Christian, would there be enough evidence to convict you?'

Endless, endless traffic: he ought to go down to the pedestrian crossing . . . and another dozen cars . . . Would there be enough evidence—well, is there? Of course there is, I go to both services on Sundays, and Bible study; I always have, all my life, even after Mam died and I didn't have to any more—and I read the Bible; mostly when I can't sleep, but I read it, and I give via a direct debit, they can't get me on *any* of that . . .

Still traffic and traffic and traffic. And a perfectly good pedestrian crossing further down the road which he was *not* going to use.

I do all this stuff, he thought, as the cars streamed past. Why hasn't it worked yet? Why am I so angry about being the first person who was hit by a pudding? Why am I so angry, full stop? Like a bad-tempered dragon . . . Or something with wings and a beak.

You can't say I'm a hypocrite for not being a proper Christian! It obviously doesn't work for everyone, and I'm one of the ones it doesn't work for, I've *tried*—I've done *my* bit of it . . .

He stepped off the pavement into a gap in the traffic, got halfway across, charged in front of a bus because it seemed to be going quite slowly and probably wouldn't dare hit anyone, and got to the opposite pavement feeling ruffled and defiant.

I *am* a Christian! I was baptised in London, properly, when I was—oh, about twenty-six; I've never smoked or drunk alcohol and I never went dancing and I don't go to the cinema . . .

He realised he had walked down past the pedestrian crossing and felt worse, went into one of the new shops by the station and bought a cake, almost at random. Then, avoiding the ladies' fashions, he spent a while studying a rack of polo shirts. Would they wash? The logos weren't too obtrusive and might unpick. Did they have one in his size? He took a 'small' in mid-blue from the rack and held it up, saw the price and put it back. It was probably too big anyway.

He went back to the station still feeling angry. Why had he done that? He'd got plenty of clothes: the Aertex shirts he'd worn in the office were still perfectly good, most of them. There was no point spending money on himself just because he felt down. The cake was an unnecessary extravagance, too: he'd have to make it last a good long time . . . and he wouldn't have a paned in the station cafe, either; he'd go and sit on the platform. He'd already wasted enough money.

He found a bench, checked the various lists, re-packed his rucksack and four sturdy cloth shopping-bags (the cabbage had one to itself) and sat back to wait.

The hum of other people's conversations remained in the background until someone mentioned Borth. He listened intently, dreading that he would hear the words 'batter pudding', but the women were talking about a film crew. As far as he could tell, they had been filming in and around Aberystwyth but on Monday were moving on to Borth. A detective series, the women agreed, but modern; not Hercule Poirot.

Dafydd had been vaguely aware that something of the sort was to happen; Bill had mentioned it, but he hadn't been paying much attention. Well, it wouldn't concern him. He had no television and was unlikely to be invited to watch it by anyone he knew except perhaps Siân, and it didn't sound like her sort of programme. He checked his watch and moved off down the platform to wait where he knew from experience one of the train's doors would be: the one which on arriving at Borth would be opposite the exit from the platform. As he put down his bags again the announcer's voice crackled over the loudspeakers and a few minutes later the train came ticking gently across the points, gliding to a halt exactly where he had expected.

Passengers seethed out of it.

When the rush had died down Dafydd got in, chose a seat, and settled comfortably to wait until the train went back the way it had come.

Owen Thomas, 'Conductor', according to his badge, but still considering himself to be a Guard, sat down at the other side of the gangway.

"Bill tells me you're detecting for the Yorkshire pudding-thrower." He leaned closer. "Reckons there's a lunatic at large in your village, lying in wait for unsuspecting pensioners."

"The pharmacist wasn't a pensioner." Dafydd moved the bag containing the fish onto the overhead rack: the heating was on. "And I doubt if it's a lunatic, but if so, they're a very good cook."

"So what's it all about, then, if it isn't a lunatic? It'll be some old woman gone off her head . . . "

"Still pretty quick on her feet, if it is an old woman. And they'd worked out where and when to hide to get each of us. That'd take a psychopath, surely? And would a psychopath bother to make batter puddings?"

Owen shook his head, considering it.

"Well, if she had a grudge against people, that involved Yorkshire puddings . . . "

Dafydd nearly said that he'd thought of that but it couldn't be right because he'd never criticised anyone's cooking, then realised that Owen was trying to get information from him. Maybe he was the culprit. No, probably not, as he would have been working. Which shifts was he on? But he could never have had a still-warm batter pudding with him if he was at work, and he lived over beyond Machynlleth . . .

"How's your son going on?" he asked. "Australia, was it?"

"New Zealand." Owen fumbled for his wallet and produced a photo. "That's him with Hollie and the little 'un. Meryl wants to go out there to see them, but we can't go this year, at least. Cerys says if we come to hers she has this Skype thing on her computer and we can see them on that . . . "

At last the train left, clattering over the crossing at Llanbadarn, through Bow Street, finally into Borth. Dafydd had been considering the weight distribution. He decided to take his own shopping home first (remembering the fish, which needed to go into the fridge) and leave the grate there too; he had carted it quite far enough.

He was thinking about fish, and batter puddings, and barely noticed there was something different about his front garden. As he pushed the front door open it caught on something: post. It could wait. He dumped the cabbage on the kitchen table, put the fish in the fridge and the other things in the cupboard, gathered Siân's shopping and the knitting-wool into the largest bag and went to put the grate by the front door, handy for when it was collected. On top of the pile of junk mail was a brown envelope.

Dafydd scooped everything up and sorted it on the kitchen table. Most went straight into the recycling bag. The brown envelope was addressed by hand to 'The Occupier', with 'D. Williams' added in angular capitals. He opened it, wondering if it was another clue, and stared. Then, incandescent with fury, he stuffed the sheet of paper into his pocket, collected two bags and stormed off to see Siân.

Chapter 5

" . . . AND DOREEN'S WOOL. Thank you: I'll give it to her on Tuesday if I don't see her at Chapel."

Siân pushed the paper bag into her shopping trolley and looked at his other bag, a dustbin sack. "Now then, young Dafydd, you'd better sit down and tell me all about it. The tea will have brewed by now."

The social necessities had given him time to recover a little and although he was still angry he felt defensive about admitting it.

"That Dai Heddwas," he mumbled, collecting the tray and following her into the sitting-room. The predominant colour was mustard-yellow and the wall above the fireplace was a mosaic of framed pictures of Siân's many children and grandchildren. He put down the tray on the glass-topped coffee table and settled into an uncomfortably low armchair. "The stuff off the railings —yes, I know I was out and he could have just thrown it all away, but—— Oh, I could smack his face!"

Siân put a cup of tea in front of him and perched on the sofa. "So what's he done, exactly?"

Dafydd passed her the letter and was ridiculously pleased to see her lips purse angrily as she read it.

"Hm," she said at last. "So, because of the film crew coming on Monday, and everyone—'everyone' being Dai Hanner-Heddwas—wanting Borth to look its best, he has taken it upon himself to take your bits and pieces off your own railings—and expects you to understand the reason for this action, if you please! The cheek of it!"

"He did leave everything in this bag. By my front door. I assume that's what's in here . . . "

"Is it all there?" Siân asked. "Oh, don't mind the carpet. It'll brush off."

"Even if it isn't, it might have been claimed . . ." He was investigating the contents of the sack, and suddenly laughed out loud.

"Well?" Siân prompted.

"Oh dear. Just a very wicked thought I had. On Friday morning my cat brought me a pair of—of rather small ladies' underwear, which I put out in a brown paper bag. And it isn't here! It might have been claimed at any time yesterday or today, but I could just see Dai Hanner-Heddwas finding out what was in the brown paper and taking it away to be burned as not suitable to be worn in Borth in the presence of a film crew!"

"Or maybe they were his girlfriend's!" Siân quipped.

"Siân Gilchrist! Really! I shall tell the elders!"

He shook his head at her and they sat chuckling. Siân offered cake and asked if that was the worst thing Rheidol had brought home.

"Oh, very much so. Apart from a live grass snake, which was a different problem entirely. So what do you suggest? I could put everything back, but that would be asking for trouble, or I could just throw everything away, which would be giving in. What else can I do with the things? I could put up a card in the Spar . . ."

"There's that gift shop that only opens in high season," Siân suggested. "If you ask Mrs. Evans to put things in the window . . . "

"Would she do it, do you think? And sometimes it's a new item every morning; that's a lot to ask unless she trusted me with the key."

"I know! I'd have to make sure, but I expect she'd be pleased to do it. Edith and Mike opposite the Victoria! They've got a big windowsill and the front door opens straight onto the pavement, so anyone could look in, and they have their niece staying; Esme."

"The young lady in the wheelchair? I know the people you mean. Yes, if they wouldn't mind taking those model ships down for a week or two. Once this film nonsense is over I shall go back to using the railings whether Dai likes it or not!"

Siân said that if he left the sack she would see what Edith said about it, and she'd almost forgotten, what with that policeman, but had he heard about the latest pudding incident?

Dafydd sat up sharply, dropping crumbs onto the carpet. "Another incident?"

Yes; Siân had had it third or fourth hand, so there might well be more to it than she knew (probably less, depending on her sources, thought Dafydd cynically), but one of the golfers had been attacked early that morning as he arrived at the Club House. Not being local he hadn't been aware of the possibility, so he had been too surprised to notice much, but apparently the criminal had run off round the building and vanished.

"And he did say that he remembered seeing a stripy jumper. Black and white stripes, so Marged says."

"And a bag with 'swag' written on it?" Dafydd enquired sarcastically. "That's how he—or she—disappeared. I dare say he just took off the stripy thing and bundled it out of sight somewhere. All he has to do then is come round the corner in a plain dark top and be someone completely different who happened to be passing—or even just walk off and get in a car and drive away slowly. You wouldn't look at someone who wasn't hurrying."

"Oh! We should have thought of that! We could have gone and looked for where he hid it!" Siân's eyes sparkled. "Will you go and look tonight?"

Dafydd shook his head. "That Dai will have got it by now, and if he hasn't then I'm interfering with evidence, aren't I?"

Siân looked disappointed. "Marged and I might go for a walk down to the Golf Club on Monday, just to see. And may we call for you on the way past?"

"You are incorrigible," Dafydd said sternly, trying to keep a straight face. "And then we all get arrested for Unlawful Assembly!"

Rheidol's Sunday morning offering was a large chunk of moss, so big that for a moment Dafydd thought it must be a mouse. He set off for Chapel a little later than usual in hope of avoiding anyone who wanted to talk to him before the service, was pleased to find that he forgot all about policemen and batter puddings in the face of a really challenging sermon, and escaped before anyone could talk to him afterwards.

As he passed Miss Smith's house she opened the door and beckoned him inside.

"I saw that Dai Hanner-Heddwas taking the things off your railings," she began indignantly. "Coffee? Yes, tea if you prefer . . . What on earth makes him think——?"

"Because of the filming," Dafydd explained.

She was unimpressed. "Who does he think he is? He's not even on the Carnival Committee. Well, Mr. Williams, that wasn't the only reason I waylaid you. I have a proposition to put to you."

Dafydd boggled, gathered his wits hastily and stammered something about not conducting business on a Sunday.

"Not a business proposition. Look, go and sit in the parlour while I make the tea."

He obeyed, wishing Siân was with him. Even Marged would do; Miss Smith was still very much an unknown quantity. The parlour was small, filled with a hard black shiny sofa and a table, the windowsill crowded with pot plants; and, as he belatedly realised, was made smaller by having most of three walls lined top to bottom with books. In spite of his disquiet he moved closer to read titles. The first bookcase seemed to be all folklore, the second natural history; and not all the titles were in English.

"Interested?" she asked quietly, putting a tray down on the table. Two mugs, each with a saucer and spoon for the teabag, and a milk jug.

Dafydd nodded.

"Do you read much?"

He nodded again. "Historical mostly. Railways, ships, mining history . . . "

She gestured at him to sit down and passed a mug. This time she had 'Cofiwch Dryweryn'; he had a pattern of seahorses.

To his surprise she asked: "What does 'Prifysgol Anweledig' mean to you?"

Dafydd fished out the teabag and dropped it neatly into the saucer. Maybe she didn't have a teapot. "Invisible University," he said, and waited to see if there would be an explanation.

"Beth am fod yn Adran Gludo? Llyfrgellydd yr Adran yn unig, efo cyfle i ddarllen llyfrau o'r adrannau eraill."

Dafydd stared. He hadn't realised she knew Welsh so fluently. He'd better speak it to her, then . . .

"You are asking me to run a library department? Of transport books, for this Invisible University? Who are the students?"

"All of us. There are all the departments you'd expect, which is why I said you'd have the opportunity to read their books. I have natural history and domestic science and some of the literature; if you tell me what you're interested in I'll introduce you to the other librarians. You must know what it's like, trying to get a specific book from the local libraries. Half the time it's reference only, like everything at the National Library in Aber is, and it costs so much by the time you've travelled to fetch it or read it that you might as well just buy it on Amazon."

Dafydd was vaguely aware that Amazon was a vast bookshop for people with computers. He seldom used libraries now, content with the books he already owned and occasionally adding new items on expeditions to Machynlleth, Aberystwyth, or Shrewsbury, but supposed that she knew what she was talking about.

"And we do have some actual students: Donald and Sandy from Dol Wen. He's doing a thesis and he's been using my collection here. Sandy not so much, but she's had some cookery books."

Donald and Sandy . . . Dol Wen was where Siân lived, so they must be the students she talked about occasionally. They seemed to be quite civilised compared with some he had heard of. And Donald was writing a thesis . . .

"Donald is the tall lad who visits you?" he asked, realising that it must sound as though he spied on her callers.

"Yes, and his friend Tim is the red-haired one. Lives in Aber, but uses the department here." She grinned. "And now you, not to mention a few others who drop in for bird-books and so forth. I've got the reputation of a scarlet woman without any of the complications that would accompany actually being one, and it's great; no 'respectable' people bother me, so I can get on with things without having people constantly trying to sell me raffle tickets or sign me up for committees. Have I shocked you?"

Dafydd hesitated. "Not really. I can sympathise. So what do you do? As a job, I mean."

Miss Smith had been an academic, forced to take early retirement when her department closed, and was writing a definitive work on plants in folklore.

With footnotes, Dafydd thought, wondering why she had chosen to live in Borth. There again, why had any of them ended up here? Siân and her late husband Ieuan, Evan Jenkins the Minister, Bill and Babs, himself; very few of the people he knew had been born in the area. He finished his mug of (now cold) tea, wondering who had seen him going into her house, and what they might think he had been doing for well over an hour. Let them speculate.

"It sounds like a very good idea," he announced, trying not to let his pleasure at having been taken into her confidence show in his voice. "I'll go home and think of questions—like, do people borrow books to take away, and what if they don't bring them back?—and come back to discuss it, but yes, it would be sensible to share the resources we have between us. How many people do you have so far?"

"Four who store books. Five with you. And two or three more who are just readers, apart from the students.

It's quite secret: it has to be only people we can trust to respect the books, people who'd mind if they lost or damaged one, so we can't advertise. It's all on personal recommendation. Yes, please go away and think about it, but don't tell anyone. Even if you decide not to. Especially if you decide not to."

Chapter 6

THERE WAS FAR too much going on, Dafydd decided, peeling a cooking apple and wondering how thinly to slice it. Cats and policemen and secret libraries and batter puddings—and if he didn't start heating the fat he wouldn't have a batter pudding, at least not for this meal.

He closed the oven door on the tin and took the apple peelings and cores down to the compost heap. As he came out of the shelter of the buildings the wind hit him, cold and penetrating. The sky was a mass of heavy grey-brown clouds. Surely it wouldn't snow? It looked as though it might . . . Over on the marshes the reeds were blown almost flat in the sharp gusts, and the donkeys turned their backs in patient stoicism. Why didn't they go into their shed, he wondered as he often did, closing the back door gratefully. What a day; any fences left standing after the winter might well come down in this lot, and what it would do to the railway service . . . It was not surprising that the up train was late.

He took a plate of boiled fish, peas and carrots into the living-room and sat down by the window. In the shelter of the wall under the railings there were daffodil shoots and a few crocuses. He ought to get that ground elder dug out: maybe this year once the bulbs had finished he would lift them all, dig over the border and put some of the compost heap to good use, if it was ever fine enough to do it. It had taken him all his time last year to keep three small rectangles of lawn mown, and vegetable gardening simply hadn't happened . . . He sighed. He couldn't do anything today; it was Sunday. And tomorrow he had to be polite and wait for Siân before he could go to the Golf Club—there was so much he wanted to get on with and he couldn't do any of it. So much for the Minister's sermon on doing things immediately . . .

The wind thrummed and whistled in the window-frame, the sound lost in a rumble of thunder. Here it comes, he thought, and went to look out as rain spattered across the glass. Someone's car alarm went off in the distance, and suddenly there was a flash of lightning and hailstones the size of peas were bouncing off the windowsill. If the donkeys don't go under cover in *this*, he thought; then hurried to the front door and leaned out.

"Come in! Come in here until it stops!"

The two figures hunched against the now horizontal hail straightened up with alacrity and sprinted for the house, leaving the gate ajar, dripping and panting on the doormat.

“Wow! Thanks, Mr. er——?” the girl began, shaking hail off her purple knitted hat. “Do you have a dustpan, before it melts?”

He fetched the brush and dustpan and his supply of spare kitchen towels, set the kettle to boil, whisked the last few damp items of underwear off the clotheshorse and offered to hang up their wet coats.

“This is Sandy, I’m Donald,” the boy informed him. Sandy was busily sweeping up hailstones. “Thanks very much. Er——diolch yn fawr. Tywydd diflas!”

“Croeso; you’re welcome.” Dafydd was drying his hair, soaked from just leaning over the doorstep. Miserable weather indeed; he grinned at Donald. “I’m Dafydd Williams. Tywydd ofnadwy, wir.”

It was, completely dreadful. There were white drifts of hail against kerbs and lamp posts, the thunder continued to grumble overhead, and though the hail had turned to rain it was blowing down the street like curtains. Dafydd ushered them into the living-room, folded the newspaper, put the fire on, invited them to sit down and offered tea. He smiled when he noticed Donald studying his bookcase.

“Prifysgol Anweledig.” He held out his hand. “Miss Smith recruited me today. Transport department.”

Donald shook his hand, grinning. “So that’s why you invited us in!”

“No, no; that was basic humanitarianism. But as it’s you, we at least have a subject of conversation.”

“You haven’t finished your meal! Oh, do carry on!” Sandy was looking at his plate.

Dafydd said it was fine, not to worry, took it into the kitchen, ate the fish quickly (where was Rheidol? Not like him to miss a trick), and called through: "I've an apple pudding in the oven, if you'd like. Plenty for all of us, warm you up after that soaking. Do you take sugar in tea?"

Fortunately neither did, so he didn't have to look for the sugar bowl. He took in a tray, asked Sandy if she would pour out— "and it's leaf tea, fach, so mind you use the strainer" —and went in to dish up the batter pudding. Custard? No, it would take a while to make and he hadn't allowed for so much milk. He cut generous slices and passed spoons and forks to Donald who had come to help.

"Mm! This is better than yours, Sandy!" Donald grinned at her. "Thanks, Mr. Williams. Not had one with apple in before. Is it a traditional Welsh recipe?"

"I doubt it." Dafydd had brought in a chair from the kitchen for himself, placing his cup and saucer on top of the bookcase on a copy of L.M.S. Branch Lines. "Could have done with a bit longer, the middle is still damp . . . Mam used to make this with blackberries and apples when I was a lad. Flintshire, we lived then. Over the back of Minera. But her mam had no oven, brought up five cooking over an open fire with an iron bakestone and a pot on a crane."

Donald showed great interest. "Do you know much about that? Because I'm writing a thesis on the history and traditions of——"

"—farinaceous products." Sandy pulled a face at him. "He means pancakes."

"Well, it was pancakes to start with," Donald agreed. "The traditions of Shrove Tuesday, but all that's been researched to death, so I branched out into welshcakes and other things you can cook on a bakestone, but there doesn't seem to be much superstition about them, not like with pancakes."

"That is because of the religious heritage of the people who were making them," Dafydd said, rather proudly. "Most of the poorest people in Wales who would be having to cook on a bakestone would be Nonconformists, and there was no truck with superstition among them, I can assure you. All this business of stone circles and holy wells has come back in because of the historians and the incomers, and it has been taken up by people who have turned their backs on the God of their forefathers . . . Sorry if I have offended you, but that is my opinion and you are welcome to yours."

There was a slightly uncomfortable silence.

"Good for you!" Sandy said, unexpectedly, and licked her spoon. "I don't think you're a hundred percent right, but it's interesting to know how you see it. That was a wonderful pudding. I simply can't do Yorkshires: how do you get it to rise like that?"

On Monday morning the street was wet and the sky was grey. Dafydd went out for his walk and his paper, came back to find that Rheidol had deposited a very wet toy rabbit on the doormat, left it to dry out on a newspaper from the recycling box, and wondered what he should do instead of his washing while he waited for Siân to arrive. Change the bed-sheets? Sort out the small box of paper-work to be filed? It was too chilly to move far from the fire, so he dealt with the paperwork, and then, on the backs of some circulars, began to list his book collection.

After ten minutes he fetched a ruler and more paper, and drew out a table with columns for title, author, publisher, date, condition and notes. He should have asked Miss Smith for the P.A. standard for cataloguing . . .

As he was in no hurry he enjoyed the experience, renewing acquaintance with old friends and finding some books he had forgotten he had, as well as at least one duplicate. He also discovered that if he put them tidily in the bookcase they no longer all fitted.

At twelve, remembering Donald, he went out to the kitchen and made slapan, cooking less than half of the recipe quantity and putting the remaining mixture into the fridge in the measuring-jug.

He sat in his chair in the window, eating it warm with the new honey. Not a sensible midday meal, but he could have bacon and cabbage in the evening. A large grey van drove past, followed by another. The film crew? They didn't seem to be doing anything of interest. He went to wash the honey off his hands, finished the last shelf of transport and mining and shuffled the papers together. He would drop that in for Miss Smith next time he passed.

For perhaps ten minutes he sat gazing out of the window at the wet grey afternoon. Then he got up, resolutely turned off the fire and went upstairs. It was high time he did something about the spare room.

Wearing an extra sweater because of the cold, he piled cardboard boxes in a corner, added a suitcase, Rheidol's carrying-basket and the packaging for the most recent kettle, moved his old bicycle and uncovered another bookcase. How wide was it? It might fit in his living-room (which was probably bigger than Miss Smith's parlour), and if people were going to borrow things he didn't want them traipsing up and down the stairs. He began to pile books on the floor.

He had got the bookcase out onto the tiny landing when the doorbell rang. Although he had expected it to be Dai Hanner-Heddwas or Siân, it was Iwan for the fire-grate. He handed over the receipt and the parcel, informed him that no, he wasn't any nearer finding the batter pudding-thrower, and went back up to deal with the bookcase.

At least it didn't have glass doors, which would have meant more journeys up and down the stairs. Having considered the problem for a while he slid it down on one end, squashing his fingers and denting the hall paintwork in at least one place. If it doesn't fit I am not taking it up again, he thought grimly, finding Rheidol suddenly underfoot as he manœuvred it into the living-room. Good thing there's no one to fuss about what happens if I do myself a mischief, and it isn't heavy, as such, only awkward . . .

It fitted, not where he had originally thought it might, but at right angles to the other, by the door. He pulled it out into the middle of the room again, fetched a duster and a brush. Once it was filled he didn't intend to move it for several years, if ever, so the floor might as well be clean first. He shoved the bookcase back into place, moved the second chair and surveyed the room. Not bad. Now for the books.

There were a few more railway books, some old working timetables, a D.I.Y. manual from the 1960s, a novel which he remembered guiltily that someone now dead had lent him about twenty years ago, and three shelves of religious books which had been his father's.

He put the D.I.Y. book and the novel into a carrier bag in the cupboard under the stairs for the next time he went to anywhere with charity shops, and set about listing the rest.

Chapter 7

THE NEXT INTERRUPTION was Siân and Marged, with Bill's dog which Marged had borrowed as an excuse to be going for a walk. Dafydd said that yes, he would come too, he'd catch them up; and five minutes later was plodding up the road fastening his coat as he went. It had stopped raining.

"Nothing yet today," Siân informed him, neat in her pink woolly hat. "But I've spoken to Edith and she says yes, it won't do any harm, and Esme can give things back to people if she's out or taking Mike to Bronglais. Esme said you ought to put up a notice in case people don't realise; she said she'd print something off for you. Wasn't that storm dreadful yesterday? There's trees down, and no wonder: it was on the television."

"I noticed the trains have been late." He looked across at the distant hills beyond Ynyslas. "Your roof's all right?"

"Yes, thanks. Marged, how do you think we should approach the golf buildings? Can we just walk up to the place and start looking, or do we need someone to be a distraction? Or should we go and explain? What do you think, Dafydd?"

Before Marged could suggest anything likely to get them all arrested, Dafydd leapt in.

"I think I had better go and explain that I am researching the incidents and ask to be shown where it happened, lay it on thick about putting paid to it before they lose custom, then we can say we'll go and look for clues. You must keep Rosie very close to you, Marged; she might be hit by a golf ball."

"Oh, you are a practical man, Dafydd," Marged sighed, towing the Labrador away from someone's gatepost. "I was hoping to fake a twisted ankle and get all the golfers buzzing round me being solicitous. I've been practising fainting gracefully without showing too much leg."

"That would be so suspicious they would probably send for the police straight away. Or the men in white coats," he said, straight-faced. Siân giggled.

"Trust you to take all the fun out of it," Marged pouted. "Practical and boring you are, Dafydd M. Williams . . . What does the M. stand for?"

"Meindiwch eich busnes." He grinned back. "Is that a hen harrier? There's supposed to be one about."

They all watched the bird swoop low over the field on the other side of the railway, but no one had binoculars with them and it was too far away for a definite identification.

"You shot off very quickly after Chapel, Dafydd," Siân commented. "What did you think of the sermon?"

"Woke me up." He realised what he had said and amended it quickly. "Not being actually asleep; it was what he said about doing things immediately. The disciples leaving their fishing immediately when Jesus called them to follow Him; like the lifeboat crew when they're called out. Not stopping to worry about it. Made me realise I've spent my life being cautious, and yes, Marged, sensible. So I'm doing things more immediately now."

"I thought that." Marged was solemn, for once. "I've missed so much by not taking risks. You lie there at night and think, if only . . . and it's too late."

"God doesn't give you just one chance, ever." Siân informed them. "You have to jump at all the opportunities."

You can tell her husband was a Minister, Dafydd thought irritably. Why couldn't they have come first thing this morning? I've wasted a whole day—well, not wasted, but I've just—done stuff. *Irrelevant* stuff . . .

Marged muttered something about having also jumped at quite a few opportunities and fallen flat on her face.

Siân smiled. "Me too, fach, and Ieuan told me once that he must've spent half his life looking stupid. But as Mr. Jenkins said, there's lots of chances God gives us to do things. Not all of them looking anywhere near important. But the more opportunities you do take, the easier you find it to recognise the next one and what to do about it."

Remembering Miss Smith and the students, Dafydd nodded. "The Lord mixes you up with people and situations you never imagined you'd ever be involved with. And believe me, that's putting it mildly."

"Yes—people who go round throwing batter puddings at people!" Marged was trying to reel in the dog again. "We're nearly there; do you want us to make ourselves scarce, or would you like moral support?"

Leaving Rosie tied outside, they came in with him. Dafydd was not sure that this was a good idea. He asked to speak to the person in charge, not knowing anything about golf clubs, and was finally introduced to the Secretary.

"Do you have a complaint?" the man asked, eying the deputation with apprehension.

"No, no! The incident yesterday; I am attempting to discover who was responsible, and we'd like to examine the place where it happened, to look for evidence." Dafydd took a deep breath, aware that again he was speaking with an English accent. Why was he so nervous? "As long as we won't be causing any trouble. Have the police finished?"

The police, the Secretary told them, had been sympathetic but not particularly helpful, and yes, he had finished with them on Saturday. The pudding—a big rectangular one—had been gobbled by gulls, but Dai had interviewed the victim, Mr. Reynolds, then poked around and found a garment which he had taken away with him.

"Aha! You were right!" Siân nudged Dafydd.

"A stripy jumper, was it? We worked out that was how the culprit disappeared so quickly. Where was it?" he asked.

"Stuffed in a litter bin by the path." The Secretary smiled, suddenly informal. "And yes, we'd guessed that too, and Dai was not at all pleased that we told him! But at least we'd not touched it, so off he went with it in a plastic bag, for DnA tests, perhaps: Morgan says they only need one hair."

Dafydd saw Marged shiver. He too felt an unexpected sympathy for the assailant if Dai got to him—or her—first.

"Do you have any thoughts about who it might have been?" he asked. "Nothing to prove, just intuition."

"Someone young. Not a child, a young adult. Maybe someone older, but quite fit, the speed they ran off. And I'd say local or a frequent visitor. But I'll tell you one thing: it's done wonders for us! The bar first of all, and today people are ringing up, wanting to come over and see where it happened. Mr. Reynolds is quite a celebrity now, and he loves it."

"We could do tours, like the murder tours in London!" Marged suggested. "Your alley, Dafydd; behind the Spar; the car park at the Pharmacy, the Golf Club . . . "

"Corners of Borth with dustbins?" Dafydd was unconvinced. "People are really wanting to visit because of the man being attacked? What is the world coming to?"

"Quite." The Secretary cocked his head as a telephone began to ring in another room. "But Reynolds' lady friend is a journalist . . . If you'll excuse me?"

They thanked him quickly and left, retrieving the Labrador. Long before they reached Dafydd's house it became clear that Siân was tiring, so they sat in a row on a bench on the sea wall and shared a bar of chocolate cream which Marged happened to have in her pocket; she had also brought biscuits for Rosie, but after crunching them up the dog still came and sat at their feet, drooling hopefully.

"Fancy that man's friend being a journalist!" Siân commented. "A coincidence, do you think, or did the pudding-thrower know?"

"Miss Smith said she thought it was someone wanting publicity." Dafydd could have kicked himself: no one knew about his visits.

"Oh, that's what you were doing round at hers!" Marged grinned. "Is she Watson or Hastings? According to Celia you were there ages—and she said she'd never thought of you as her type!"

Who on earth was Celia? Dafydd took a deep breath. "Yes, and I also complained about her cat which has been coming in and stealing Rheidol's food. Siân, I have a toy rabbit looking for its owner. It ought to be dry by now, if you could take it to Edith on your way back?"

They all walked down to Edith and Mike's, Dafydd retrieving the rabbit on his way past. Marged went on to Bill's to return the dog, but came back to find them still admiring Esme's quilting over tea and cake, and discussing where the film crew might have got to and what they might be doing. She was offered cake and Edith went to make a fresh pot of tea.

"Here you are!" Esme announced suddenly, turning her laptop half-round to show them. "We're famous!"

They gathered round, and found it was a website of local news. There was a very brief, jocular article headed *Yorkshire Pudding Mystery*.

"It's by Mari Lwyd." Siân peered at the screen. "So that must be who Mr. Reynolds' lady friend is . . . "

For Marged's benefit they discussed their visit to the Golf Club again, Mike holding to his theory that the latest episode might have been a copycat attack to bring people to the club. Eventually Edith apologetically asked if they minded her watching a quiz show, the visitors realised how late it was getting and made their excuses, and after seeing Siân home Dafydd hurried back to feed Rheidol.

He had forgotten the books which were still stacked all over his living-room. While Rheidol ate he moved the most obvious hazards, then prepared bacon, cabbage and cold potato slices, fried. Esme had given him a cardboard folder with a notice in it. He would have to find the drawing-pins.

Having eaten his meal, he washed up and pinned Esme's notice in the front window ('Mae'r pethau ar goll yn Stretton, yn cyferbyn Y Victoria'; and underneath, 'The lost items are at Stretton, opposite the Victoria'). Really, it should have been pethau *colledig*, and *gyf*erbyn *i'r* Victoria, but it was kind of her to have printed it out and it would look messy if he corrected it. Would anyone would be able to read it without coming into the garden? He made a pot of tea and sat by the window. Someone called Celia had reported to Marged at least one of his visits to Miss Smith. A pity Celia hadn't been on the lookout when the pudding-thrower was at work. Maybe it was Celia herself, whoever she was. Had Miss Smith been to the Friendship yet? If she had, she couldn't have discovered anything relevant or she would surely have put a note through his letterbox.

He realised how tired he was. The books could wait until tomorrow.

He went back to the kitchen with the tray, put the milk jug in the fridge—and saw the cake he had bought. Bother; he should have offered that to the students. He ought not to have any now; he'd had a meal and it was late. Another day . . . Why had he chosen something with icing? It'd be horribly sickly. He sighed and went to lock up. Why did nothing ever work out right?

Chapter 8

THAT NIGHT HE slept soundly. When he rose at six it was raining and the sea sucked at the pebbles with sullen hunger, but only a dozen yards from the shore a few dark shapes were floating. At first sight they could have been tufted ducks, but after three winters in the area he knew what to look for and recognised them as scaup. There was a spring in his step as he went home, nodding to Malcolm Edwards and his horse, pushing the newspaper inside his coat to keep it dry, and swinging the milk carton.

His first job was to catalogue the religious books. He shelved them tidily in alphabetical order by author, leaving a gap for *The Pilgrim's Progress*, which had been a favourite of his father's and which he had decided to read.

Clean the bathroom, next. While he worked, he mulled over the problem of identifying the pudding-thrower.

It wasn't someone with a grudge against individuals, or Welsh or English people or males or females. It had to be someone who wanted publicity for their actions, among the people of Borth at first and then beyond. Had anything happened on Sunday or Monday? Quite proper for no attacks to take place on a Sunday, but that might not mean that the culprit was a Christian (albeit a very confused one); maybe the person had no excuse to be in Borth on a Sunday.

Despite attacking local people, the pudding-thrower needed their approval—or maybe sympathy would be a better word. Why would someone do something as complicated as making and throwing batter puddings? A water-pistol would have been easier . . .

But a water-pistol attack would have been more readily forgotten; and, with the weather as it had been, you might well be able to shoot someone without their particularly noticing . . .

Round and round went the reasoning, and every time he came back to the idea that someone wanted people to notice, to laugh at the eccentricity of the attacks, to tell people. Why? So people would notice Borth?

Surely not; it wasn't the holiday season yet—and why would people come just because of batter puddings?

Yet they were coming. The Secretary of the Golf Club had said as much.

So the attacker knew how people—modern, visiting people—thought. And once they'd come to Borth, what did he or she hope they'd do? Spend money, presumably, as short-term visitors weren't likely to provide children for the local school or drivers for the voluntary car scheme.

It was someone with a house for sale! He very nearly went straight downstairs to ring Miss Smith, Siân and Marged, but as there wasn't much left to do in the bathroom he made himself finish the job.

If it was someone selling a house, surely it would be near the site of at least one attack, so people visiting—touring the locations, as Marged had suggested—would see it. He couldn't remember any houses for sale in the right areas, so maybe that wasn't it after all.

He sat back on his heels next to the bath, glad he'd not rung anyone. You fool, why did you think that? It obviously isn't the answer. Why would anyone think throwing things at people in Borth would make other people want to live there? What a stupid idea.

At least he'd dealt with the bathroom. He went downstairs with the cloths, dropped them by the washing-machine, washed his hands thoroughly and made a pot of tea.

There was the cake in the fridge.

He got it out, looked at the best-before date. Bother. I should have started that earlier; I dare say it will keep beyond tomorrow, but I'd better at least open it. If only I'd remembered it when the students were here . . .

He cut a slice and sat at the kitchen table. I'm glad I didn't get it out for Donald and Sandy, it tastes like a shop cake and they were so pleased to have real food; home-made apple pudding. I don't even particularly like it myself or I'd have eaten it already; I've finished the slapan. Why did I buy it? I didn't really want it. I just wanted a treat, I suppose. Only it isn't a treat. Not now I've started eating it. Ach a fi . . . But it'd be a waste to throw it away so I'll have to eat it.

He cut himself another slice.

Oh, why am I like this? It's all the fault of whoever threw that batter pudding. I was all right 'til that started. Good thing I didn't buy a shirt: I didn't want it, but if I'd bought it I would have had to keep it 'til it wore out, and I wouldn't have ever worn it because I didn't want it, and it would've just sat there looking at me for years, unless I put it away in the spare room . . . with the other things like that that I've bought.

Why am I so useless? I've tried finding out who did it but I'm no further forward for learning to make the things and interviewing people and—and running away from Dai; at least he can't exactly sneak up on me unnoticed, in all that high-viz stuff . . . And Bill's told everyone I'm looking for the culprit and I wish he'd kept his mouth shut because now I've got to, and Siân and the rest of them seem to think it's wildly exciting, but it was *me* they threw it at . . .

He realised there was one piece of cake left, and ate it. He felt slightly sick, and guilty, and a failure, and still angry.

Now even God's started getting at me. Telling me I'm not good enough. Just like the rest of them: I'm never going to be any use, except as a *target.* If anyone tries anything, I'll—I'll—I don't know what. But at least this time I'll be *ready* !

Immediately, like Evan said in his sermon . . . Druan iddo; poor bloke, if Siân keeps trying to pair him up with every spinster she meets. I wonder if she's suggested to him that he should have a long chat with Miss Smith and ask her to Chapel?

He found himself grinning. No wonder Evan had looked so relieved when he arrived in Borth: he was another single male to share the burden of Siân's match-making! Maybe they should join forces and begin earnestly suggesting to Siân that she should remarry. Was Dai Hanner-Heddwas available? That would annoy her!

He got up and went into the hall, pulled his coat aside from the mirror and stood in front of it, caught himself standing up straighter and then leaning forward a little so he didn't look quite as tubby. Portly: that sounded a little better . . . No, he was definitely tubby. He put out his tongue at his reflection. Rheidol rubbed against his legs hopefully, having learned that uncovering the mirror was usually followed by opening the fridge where the cheese was kept.

"Dw i'n ddiog," he told the cat. "I'm lazy. Fat and lazy, and today hasn't helped. I'll have to go for a long walk. See if I get any inspiration about these puddings. There must be someone out there doing it, wanting publicity . . . "

He went back into the kitchen, cut a very small sliver of cheese for Rheidol and stood gazing out of the window across the garden and the railway to the fields and hills beyond.

Who else in Borth would want visitors?

The hotel, the pubs, the guest-houses and holiday lets, the golf course . . . what if Mike was right, and it was the Secretary! The local shops . . .

There were so many of them, and in theory all the owners and tenants were suspects, but at least half were simply too old or too unfit to be considered. He poured the last half-cup of tea from the pot and squinted unseeing at his back garden, trying to picture all the local shopkeepers and guest-house owners. It was no good. He rinsed the tea things, pegged the wet cleaning-cloths on the clothesline to get them out of the way and went back indoors for his notebook. It was going to be a long, long walk.

"So I listed all the places, and the people if I knew them, and this is it. I've put an X against the people I think are too old or couldn't run."

Miss Smith took the notebook. There were four or five closely written pages.

"I did have a word with the landlord at the Friendship and some of the bar staff," she began, "but they don't remember anything happening that night . . . which doesn't necessarily mean anything, of course! Now then. Shanklyn guest-house: you don't know them, but I do; he's a big fat jolly man, people would recognise him instantly, and his wife's just had her ingrowing toenails done." She shuddered. "He was telling Gwenan about it in the shop. We can cross them off. Lyndhurst: Joan's tiny, only about five foot one. Again, people would know her at once, and even if they didn't they'd notice her height. I see you've put down the Vicar and his wife and Kim, and the Minister."

Dafydd nodded. "And the people at the Animalarium and the Tourist Information ladies. And Dai Hanner-Heddwas."

"And yourself? You could have invented that first attack."

He looked steadily back at her. "I'm not that quick on my feet. And I was at the station in plenty of time to catch the 9.06 to Aberystwyth on Saturday, with two other people waiting who saw me there, and the golfer was attacked at 8.55. Yes, you're on the list, and the students: I've only your word for it that you went to New Quay."

He wondered how Miss Smith would react but she seemed quite pleased that he was taking things so seriously. She went through the list annotating it, then looked up.

"We need to visit a few places to check up on people we don't know. Would your friends know them? Then we won't alert anyone before we're sure." She glanced towards the window. "I do wish we knew if there'd been more episodes on Sunday and Monday. Because if someone's been attacked in Clarach or Bow Street, that's your theory gone."

"I'll ask Siân." Dafydd gazed unseeing at the natural history books. "There are only about a dozen people it could be, that we know of so far . . . But it could be a relative of someone with a shop; I didn't think of that."

"I did," Miss Smith interjected. "And unless they work for the person I doubt it's a relative. All the attacks have been before or after office hours. At first I thought it might be because it was dark then, and easier to escape, but now I'm sure it's someone who works."

"That might cut out some more people, then," Dafydd suggested. "The butcher and his lads are in before eight, before seven some days, and they go early too."

"Well, realistically, tourists aren't likely to make much difference to the butcher's turnover, are they? Not directly. Nor the bridal wear shop. It's more likely to be someone at a gallery or a chip shop . . . "

At that point the phone rang. Miss Smith went out to the hall to answer it.

"Yes. What? Okay. Don't say anything to anyone. I'll come straight over. Don't worry, Sandy. He'll be fine."

"What's happened?" Dafydd asked as she came back, rising to his feet.

"The film crew's been attacked. And Dai has taken Donald in for questioning."

It was the first time Dafydd—or possibly anyone—had seen Miss Smith run. He followed her up the road more slowly, not quite sure where she was going, but intending to visit Siân and learn more about the latest attack. A car drew up beside him and Marged's husband Robert gestured at him to get in.

"Sent me to find you, they did," he explained, accelerating. "There's been three more puddings, one at the school and one at the caravan park; and then the film people were up by the station last night and one of the engineers looked up from twiddling knobs, and—splat!"

"Oh dear, oh dear."

Dafydd finished fastening his seatbelt and sat still. He wanted to run round inspecting the various puddings, but there was no chance of that. He would have to be patient.

They found Miss Smith, Sandy and Marged in Siân's kitchen, all talking at once.

"Donald can't have done it, because he was on the computer to his sister when it happened, so unless the police think he did the others——"

"The caravan site: Doreen says it was a woman who'd been having rows with the neighbours for ages about her dog barking, she threw a bottle at someone last week, so no one thinks that her being puddinged could possibly be connected with the other ones, it's just someone copying the idea——"

"And the teacher who was done outside the school, he said himself that he knew which children it was——"

"They were filming in the museum at the station; well, on the platform——"

"And the cables all coming out of the back window and down to their vans, so Aled says——"

"It was dark by then, and they had those big lamps, it was really dark where the light wasn't because the lamps were so bright——"

"All right!" Dafydd put his hands over his ears. "So the station attack was the genuine one. And it was dark and no one saw who did it, but it couldn't have been Donald and you know that. Have you thought, Sandy, that Dai might know that too, and he's holding onto Donald in hope of making the real culprit own up?"

Sandy's mouth fell open and her face brightened. Miss Smith frowned at him.

"Has that got into the papers?" Dafydd continued. "Or onto the computer news Esme had?"

Robert silently produced a national daily and held it out. They pounced, spreading it over Siân's kitchen table.

"There! Bottom of the second page. 'Film team hit in pud riddle!' "

Dafydd thought it sounded more like a cryptic clue than a headline, but there it was. Borth, in the national press.

"They won't dare do anything to Donald now," Miss Smith announced gleefully. "There'll be reporters down here tomorrow and Dai will have to let him go or the negative publicity will do so much harm . . . "

Siân was offering tea. Dafydd refused; he told them he had to buy food for Rheidol, but once he was out of Dol Wen he made straight for the Grand Hotel and rang the bell at reception.

"I'd like to speak to the man who was attacked last night," he told the young woman who came out of a back room and was clearly surprised to see him. "I wasn't expecting them to be here now, but do you know where they are?"

She said that she thought they had gone up towards Ynyslas, and did he want to leave a message?

Dafydd considered. "Yes, I will. Thank you."

He crossed the road and read the notices in the window of the Tourist Information Office. It was Mrs. Howell on duty, the younger of the two staff. He went in and asked if they had a timetable for buses to Aberaeron, leaned casually over the desk and noted the information he wanted while she went to find it for him, thanked her, and went home. He looked up a telephone number and rang it. No reply.

He tried again at half-hourly intervals, and eventually a voice said: "Hallo?"

"Dafydd M. Williams here. I think you know why I've rung you."

There was absolute silence from the other end of the line.

"So I'm right, then. Don't worry, I won't talk to any reporters. But I think we need to discuss things. As soon as possible."

Another, shorter silence. Then: "You don't have a car, do you? I'll come to Borth. See you by the fire station in twenty minutes."

He fed Rheidol, cut the quick crossword out of Monday's paper and put it in his pocket with a pen in case his contact was late, and set off. He wondered if Miss Smith was back yet, but her parlour curtains were still open and no lights were visible. He could not have involved her, anyway. He had to do this himself and he had to get it right . . . Siân, saying: "The more opportunities you do take, the easier you find it to recognise the next one . . . "

"O Lord," he whispered into the night, "Give me the words. Please. Don't let me muck it up . . . "

Beyond the fire station was the disused chapel which had for a while been used as a Catholic church, and beyond that a house which had been the crossing-keeper's cottage. He found a place to wait sufficiently close to a street lamp and started the crossword.

A car went past across the crossing, turned, and came back; drew up on the opposite side of the road. A dark figure emerged.

"Hallo, Mr. Dafydd M. Williams."

"Hallo, Miss Bevan. Before you ask, I don't bear any grudges."

"Thanks." She moved into a patch of deep shadow. "I hoped people wouldn't."

"It's Mrs. Howell, isn't it? As much as yourself, if not more so."

Miss Bevan nodded, all but invisible. "I thought it had to be worth trying. If they close the Borth office they'll cut our hours even if they keep us on, and she and Tom have just bought a flat . . . "

Silence, broken eventually by Dafydd.

"I'm hoping to talk to the film engineer tomorrow morning before the reporters get here, if they do. He's the only one who might cause trouble, I think, especially if we pay for Ellie's hairdo."

She wiped her eyes.

"I'm so sorry. Really I am—I hope I didn't hurt you. I didn't mean to hurt anyone; I thought it couldn't do any damage, but I'd forgotten about the fat. . . Oh, I am such a fool! I never imagined that anyone could be afraid—— Mr. Williams, what on earth can I do? I wanted people to talk about it and come to Borth, but I never meant anyone to get arrested!"

"I don't think Donald's been arrested, as such." He hoped his voice sounded warm and comforting. "And I doubt you will be, either, if no one wants to cause trouble. I don't."

"The film people jolly well shouldn't, all the extra publicity!" She moved into the pool of light and scrubbed her face with her sleeve. "Eh, I'm a right mess. Good thing you're not a reporter. What are you going to do? I suppose you'll have to tell P.C.S.O. Laffan, and I ought to tell him first."

"If the other—er—targets choose not to make a fuss, there's no point him doing anything. There's no need for him to know who you are if he's not guessed." He added: "And you make an excellent batter pudding: they might take you on at a restaurant, if you want."

She smiled at that, and he smiled back. She was younger than he'd thought, around half his age at most.

"Laffan is one of us, Miss Bevan, if only from working here. What you've done is good for this place, on balance, and if he has any sense he'll realise that if he wants to work with us here he needs to be sympathetic, not against us for the sake of it. There's no sense identifying you if he doesn't know. Let me have a word with him. Now, I've been wondering since Wednesday, so please put me out of my misery: *why* is it batter puddings?"

Chapter 9

LLINOS BEVAN HAD OFFERED to give him a lift but Dafydd had said he'd rather walk, for which he was grateful because as he reached the hotel a group of men were coming out. The film crew, in search of a pub? There was no time to be lost.

"Excuse me," he began hopefully, stepping out in front of them, "may I have a word with one of you, please? The sound engineer . . . ?"

"Someone else? Someone wants to see me first thing tomorrow morning." One of the older men stopped. The rest hung about a little further down the street, waiting for him.

"That's me, Dafydd M. Williams. But would it be more convenient now? As we're here . . . ?"

The man shrugged. "Come with us and you can buy me a pint."

Dafydd had no idea how much a pint was likely to cost but agreed and let them sweep him along with them to the Victoria. It was the first time he had ever crossed the threshold of a public house and he was glad his mother was no longer alive in case anyone recognised him. The bar was brightly-lit and tiny, full of tables, and people who were all talking at the tops of their voices to be heard above the sound of a blaring television: the noise was overwhelming. One of the men pushed through to the bar and began to order drinks. Dafydd offered the sound engineer a ten-pound note.

"You get what you want, bach," he shouted above the racket.

"Okay. What are you having?"

"I don't drink!" He failed to keep the panic out of his voice. Had anyone noticed?

"Orange juice? Okay. Go an' sit over the back, it's quieter there."

Dafydd went in the direction indicated and found a shadowy back room which in daylight would have a sea view. He sat with his back to a wall, feeling apprehensive. How was one supposed to behave in a place like this? What if someone spoke to him?

"One orange juice." It was plonked in front of him along with a handful of change, and the sound engineer sat down at the other side of the table with a pint glass. "So why, Mr. Williams? You can't be a journalist if you don't drink . . . "

"Oh, definitely not a journalist, Mr. . . . ?"

"Barry Ryan. Call me Barry. What's this about?"

"Batter puddings." Dafydd took a cautious sip of orange juice. It had ice in it. In March! "You were attacked last night; I was the first, almost a week ago. Er—how do you feel about it?"

Barry considered for a few long seconds.

"Angry. No, annoyed more than angry. And puzzled. Why on earth would anyone go to the trouble of doing that?"

"That is exactly how I felt. So I started to try to find out who was doing it, and why. Well, I was on my way to Chapel and told them there, and Ellie at the Spar told all her customers, and Miss Fraser's attack was all round the Health Centre, so by then we'd worked out it was someone wanting publicity. And when the golfer with a journalist lady friend was next, there was publicity beyond Borth itself, right out as far as the local news goes. And then they attack you, and that gets into the national dailies."

"Go on." Barry was studying him solemnly. "I'm with you so far."

Dafydd took a deep breath. "We thought about it. Who would need publicity for Borth? The Golf Club Secretary said people were ringing up to visit, to see where it happened. Maybe it was a shopkeeper, or someone who lets lodgings. So we looked for people young enough and quick enough to have got away, and . . . well, we were right."

"We?"

"Oh, just a few of us. People with time on our hands. Nothing official. Not David Laffan the Community Policeman!"

"I see. So what are you going to do about it? And why was it Yorkshire puddings?"

"It had to be something silly." Dafydd had been thinking this out while waiting for Miss Bevan to answer the phone. "Something too silly to be seen as a real attack, something that wouldn't do any damage, but which people would talk about."

"Like being hit with a sockful of custard," Barry offered unexpectedly. "Only that does hurt; my brother tried it on me when we were kids. The pudding didn't hurt, but 'til I knew what it was and I'd checked none of the equipment was damaged I was ready to break someone's neck. It could have been acid, or ink; we've had people attack us for real because they haven't wanted us there filming."

"How do you feel about it now?" Dafydd asked. This was the crux of the whole conversation.

"How do *you* feel? Persecuted? Used?"

Dafydd hung his head.

"Used," he admitted. "But now I know *why*, I don't see what else might have worked so well. And I would have liked to have had the—the courage, the *daftness*—to have done that when I was a young man going to lose my job!"

Barry roared with laughter. "You win, Mr. Williams! So who was it?"

Dafydd hesitated. "Not 'til we know the police aren't bothered any more. It's not that I don't trust you, but what you don't know you can't be made to tell."

Silence. The sound of cheerfully raucous voices came from the bar. The sooner he could escape, the better . . .

"Are you being melodramatic, or are the police round here that bad?"

"I hope I'm being melodramatic, but there was a student in for questioning for it this afternoon. It wasn't him, and I hope P.C.S.O. Laffan would not do anything illegal, but there are others . . . "

Barry whistled softly. "Here too? Even here? If you're going to try to keep your attacker anonymous and you get journalists crawling all over the place, you're going to have trouble. The police are going to have to be seen to have succeeded in doing something about it."

"Bricks, yes. Batter puddings, surely not? Tomorrow I'm going to speak to Dai and suggest he make an official report that it was just local people getting carried away with reviving an old local custom, and there's no need for anyone to be afraid or take it seriously."

"An old local custom? He'll never buy that, will he?"

"Oh, yes." Inspiration had come from somewhere and Dafydd was gratefully inventing the story as he went along, feeling he must stay on top of the conversation, hoping he wouldn't suddenly lose the awen, the muse, and be unable to extricate himself. "Of course, in the old days it was a pikelet made on a bakestone, but as people got ovens they found a batter pudding was just as good. A local lady found references to it when she was researching, and someone obviously thought it would be a good idea to revive the custom. You see, when St. David was born, he was baptised by the Bishop of Munster in a spring of water which came newly from the ground for that purpose, and at the baptism there was a monk who had been born disfigured, with no features to speak of, and some of the water splashed on him and miraculously healed him. They say all this happened; clearly it could be an old tale with no more than one grain of truth in it, but the tradition was that on Dydd Gŵyl Ddewi—St. David's Day—people threw pikelets at the faces of people they wished the saint's blessing on, to remind the saint of the monk healed at his baptism."

"You've just made that up." Barry grinned as Dafydd's face fell. "You *did* just make that up? It sounded quite as credible as most traditions. I should think he might fall for it if you can get your researcher to sound genuine. You're living dangerously, aren't you, Mr. Williams? A good Welsh Chapel bloke telling tall stories to Irishmen in pubs . . . But you seem to have taken to it like a duck to water. Just don't go too far."

Chapter 10

THIS TIME HE did need to see Miss Smith before he went any further. He'd got up at five, waited until a respectable eight-forty and rung P.C.S.O. Laffan, making an appointment with him for ten; now at twenty-five past nine he was on Miss Smith's doorstep, ringing the bell and wondering if she would be awake.

She was awake, dressed completely in army surplus with an apron over the top. "Mr. Williams! Come in."

"What's happened? What are you cooking?"

"Guess," Miss Smith said between clenched teeth. "It's about time someone did something about that policeman."

Dafydd stared at her in disbelief.

"Donald hadn't come back by ten. Siân said Sandy could stay at hers overnight, and Robert brought me home. Those poor kids . . . "

Dafydd silently held out his shopping bag.

"You've made a batter pudding too?" she exclaimed.

"I'm going to see Dai Laffan," he said, very quietly. "I've got an appointment."

"Where? At the police station in Aber?"

"At his house. Yes, I thought that was rather odd, but he said he was off duty today and he was busy."

"He's the sort of person who *would* be busy." She pulled a face. "Officious little blighter. Tried to turn me out of here when we had that storm last winter and the sea came over the wall down your end; sending us up to the school, if you please! I shut the door on him."

"Me, too," Dafydd admitted. "Evacuating vulnerable people! I wouldn't go, and he would not take no for an answer, so I lost my temper. In fact, I was very rude to him." He sighed.

"I'm not surprised; he'd try the patience of a saint. You're meeting him at his house? I hope it's not a trap; it'll be your word against his if anything happens, and I bet the police would believe him."

"*If* anything happens?" Dafydd patted the shopping-bag.

"But he'll arrest you too!" Her voice rose.

Dafydd shrugged. "I'm going, anyway. If he thinks it was me, it can't have been Donald. Er—do you have a spare army jacket to fit me?"

She gathered her wits, rescued her pudding before it burned and produced a camouflage jacket from somewhere in the upper reaches of the house.

"Thanks." He hung his own coat over the collection of aprons and tea towels and bags on the back of the kitchen door, having removed his door keys from the pocket, and buttoned up the jacket. He unclipped his back door key from the ring and handed it to her. "I can take your pudding too; I might miss the first time. You'll be more use mobilising support if I don't come back. And if you could feed Rheidol . . . "

"Oh, Minnesota——"

To his amazement she threw her arms round him and hugged, hard, then stepped back and looked him up and down critically. "You need a hat . . . try this one. Yes, that'll do."

It was a dark brown Australian waterproof hat with a wide brim. Dafydd glanced at himself in the mirror she held up and was vaguely reminded of cowboy films. He certainly didn't look like a retired railwayman.

"There." She slid her batter pudding into the bag on top of his own. "Good luck, Minnesota Williams!"

After this send-off he felt he should have a pair of six-guns in his belt as he advanced up the main street, weaving between the wheelie-bins put out for collection.

Dai lived in one of the Victorian semi-detached houses on the road up to the monument, not as far up as Mrs. Taylor's bungalow. Dafydd was feeling cold by the time he reached it; the camouflage jacket was not as warm as his own coat, but that was not the only reason.

He latched the gate behind himself and went up the narrow tiled path. There were borders beside the path and under the bay window which had been tidied by someone who knew very little about gardening, and the lawn had bare patches in it. He stood in the porch. There were patterns of stylised flowers on the tiled walls at either side of the white front door from which the paint was peeling. It was too late to back down now . . . He looked for a door-bell, saw two possibilities and a corroded brass knocker shaped like a dolphin, and knocked firmly.

"Come in," someone shouted.

He pushed the door open and stepped into a damp, cold, dimly-lit hall with paint-splashed parquet underfoot. "Mr. Laffan?" he called.

A man in jeans and a dark jersey who was presumably Dai Hanner-Heddwas came out of a back room carrying two mugs.

"Good morning, Mr. Williams. You are Mr. Williams?"

That ridiculous hat; he took it off quickly. "Yes, I am. And I have come to offer you a proposition, Mr. Laffan."

"Eh? Would you like a cup of tea? I'm just making one."

"Er—can that wait for a minute?"

He put the hat down on a convenient small table. There were wires sticking out of the woodchip-papered wall above it, ending in a ball of duct tape. "Mr. Laffan, I challenge you to a duel. Choose your weapon!"

David Laffan's jaw dropped.

Dafydd held out the shopping bag, vaguely aware of someone in the doorway behind Dai. "Go on," he said, steadily. "Take one."

Dai put down the mugs next to the hat, reached into the bag and gingerly lifted Miss Smith's pudding. His face was pallid and Dafydd could hear him breathing.

He took his own pudding, weighed it thoughtfully in his hand.

"After three. One. Two. Three!"

Dai launched his pudding a split second before Dafydd. It hit him on the side of the face, stinging his ear. (It was quite heavy and solid: Miss Smith couldn't have had much practice at batter puddings.) With a satisfaction verging on glee he saw his own pudding plaster itself over Dai's face and he tried not to grin too broadly as the man reeled back against the wall.

"It was you, was it?" Dai whispered.

"That one certainly was!" Dafydd scooped up the pieces and put them tidily back into the bag. He felt as though his whole body was fizzing with excitement. Round one to Minnesota Williams.

"Good grief, was that why you wanted to see me?" Dai rubbed his face, and picked up the mugs again. "Well, I'm still going to make tea. We've been working since eight. Do you want one?"

"Yes, please . . . Donald! What on earth——?"

"Hi, Mr. Williams. I've been helping Mr. Laffan with his central heating. Dad's a Corgi registered plumber, which helped. Whoever put this system in made a right mess of it."

"Miss Smith thinks you're handcuffed in a dungeon somewhere." Dafydd sat down on the bottom step, suddenly weak at the knees. "And you've been plumbing."

"I told Sandy when I got back last night." Donald had smears of plaster dust down his sweatshirt. "And he's told me loads of stuff about Staffordshire oatcakes. It's been a weird couple of days. Hey, d'you think I could have a go with one of those Yorkshires? I've wanted to since we first heard about it."

"It's not my wallpaper." Dafydd struggled stiffly to his feet again as Dai returned with a tray. "Thank you. No sugar, thanks. Er—Donald would like to try throwing a pudding."

"Go ahead," Dai offered recklessly, passing him a mug. "It all needs redecorating. Must say I wouldn't mind another go, myself !"

In the end they threw batter pudding at each other until they were weak with laughter and there was nothing left that was big enough to throw.

"So was it you?" Dai asked, when they had retired to the back room with digestive biscuits and further cups of tea.

"No, it wasn't." Dafydd paused, wondering why he was surprised to find that Dai had bookcases too: two tall ones, crammed untidily with books on a wide variety of subjects, a commentary on Mark's Gospel flanked by *The Guns of Navarone* and a collection of Garfield cartoons. Beyond the table littered with books and paper and crockery there was a large window overlooking the back garden and the houses beyond; the green velvet curtains had faded at the edges as though they had come with the house, like the oddly-textured carpet. "And it wasn't Donald either. Or his young lady."

"He guessed it wasn't me," Donald put in. "He wanted to find out if it was someone trying to get us into trouble. Just because we're students. But he took some persuading once he found out about my thesis!"

"Do you know who it was?" Dai persisted.

Dafydd hesitated. "What will be done, when you do know?"

Dai shrugged. "Possibly breach of the peace or assault, if anyone wants to take it further. Probably just a verbal warning. Depends how people feel about it."

"The local people mostly feel embarrassed about having made a fuss. Reynolds the golfer is enjoying his five minutes of fame and I told Barry Ryan a story about it being an old Borth tradition. He didn't seem bothered."

"An old Borth tradition?" Dai stared at him.

"Oh, completely fictitious. You see, the story goes that when St. David was baptised by the Bishop of Munster, a spring opened up for the Bishop to use. One of the monks at the ceremony was disfigured, with a misshapen face, but when some of the water splashed on him he was healed. That far it's a genuine legend. So on St. David's day, people throw pikelets or batter puddings at each other; it's supposed to bring the saint's blessing because of what happened to the monk. Even if I hadn't made it up I wouldn't believe it, but it's an explanation to give the newspapers."

"I wish you hadn't made it up," Donald said wistfully. "It'd be perfect for my thesis."

Dai frowned. "I don't think you ought to mislead people deliberately like that."

"Nor do I!" Dafydd was Minnesota Williams again, facing down the sheriff with tumbleweed blowing past the saloon. "But what's been happening needs to have an explanation, and you cannot simply tell national newspapers that it was someone worried about losing their livelihood and having an idea to bring more tourists into Borth! That is the truth but it's not what the newspapers will want to hear, so they will make something up, and what they make up . . . is it likely to be in our favour? If more tourists do come, not just in high summer, but now, it's good for the whole community. So here is an explanation which is not quite true but which does no one any harm and may keep a lot of small businesses afloat. If no one makes a formal complaint, surely you don't have to have an official investigation?"

"Hm. But it isn't the *truth*."

There was a long silence. Dafydd read *Christian Ethics* on a spine in the bookcase, and squirmed, but retaliated.

"David Laffan, you have been P.C.S.O. here for not quite a year now, and you are not liked. You are truthful, you try to speak Welsh, you are painstaking, you mean well, but you rub us up the wrong way. I'm sure that comes of being new and careful and having superior officers looking through your reports, but people think you are a high and mighty reflection of the police bureaucracy with no courage to take decisions, a tell-tale out to stop people doing things. We're not asking you to connive at fraud or turn a blind eye to deliberate law-breaking, but there are ways of getting people to do things without antagonising them."

Dai glowered at him. "You think I'm useless, you call me names behind my back——"

"Yes, we do. Dai Hanner-Heddwas. Dai half-policeman, you being a P.C.S.O., not a P.C. Would you *want* us to call you Dai Laffan?"

Donald smothered a snigger.

"Making fun of someone's name, which they can't help, is really disgraceful . . . " Dai began primly.

"That's why we haven't!" Dafydd exploded. "You think it's just you—— You try being Minnesota!"

Donald choked back another snigger and went red as they both glared at him.

"Okay, okay. I can't believe it but I really hadn't spotted 'Dai Laffan'," Dai groaned. "I suppose Borth couldn't just call me David? Dave, even?"

"Not those who see just the uniform and the rulebook." Dafydd sighed. "But they might if Borth comes out of this well—and if they'd seen us pelting each other with batter puddings!"

Dai opened his mouth to respond but the telephone rang. He swung round irritably and went to answer it.

Dafydd looked unhappily at Donald. He'd done his best, and he wasn't at all sure he'd not made things worse.

Chapter 11

"YES, INSPECTOR BOWEN," DAI said, into the telephone. "Yes, but . . . Yes, sir. Quite. Very well, sir. Goodbye."

There was a long silence, followed by a double click and the sound of dialling.

"Miss Bacon, David Laffan sy 'ma. Ga'i defnyddio'r Neuadd am hanner awr wedi naw o'r gloch yfory? I hanner dydd, dw i'n meddwl. Da iawn. Beth am heno, hefyd? Am saith o'r gloch, am awr neu dwy . . . Diolch yn fawr. Ydw, fi sy'n talu . . . Diolch."

"What's he saying?" Donald demanded.

"Wanting to use the Community Hall tomorrow. Nine thirty 'til midday—and tonight at seven for an hour or so. Paying for it himself, so it can't be anything to do with the police," Dafydd whispered back.

Click. More dialling.

"May I speak to Mari Lwyd please? Ah, good morning. David Laffan here, about the Borth incidents."

Dafydd and Donald stared at each other in horror. The lad moved towards the door, but Dafydd grabbed his shoulder. "Wait! Listen!"

"—A meeting at ten tomorrow, in the Community Hall," Dai was saying. "With you present, as sole representative of the Press . . . Yes, an exclusive. For . . . may I suggest at least a non-hostile report?"

Donald's eyes were wide. "What's he going to do?" he whispered indignantly.

"Shush!" Dafydd was straining his ears to catch the words.

"—Yes, one colleague if you wish, on the same terms. Understood, Miss Lwyd? Non-hostile . . . Good. See you at ten tomorrow. Goodbye."

Dai came back into the room and stood holding onto a chair-back, his face pallid, trying to breathe normally. He's afraid, Dafydd realised. Afraid or angry. Or both.

"I don't suppose you heard any of that." Dai took a deep breath. "That was the D.I., telling me to get off the case before the West Wales force becomes a laughing-stock. I tried to explain but he wouldn't listen. He wants it—and me—buried."

He paused again, fingers clenched on the chair-back. "He said he's taking it on himself, I'm to send him all the notes I've got and I'm on a written warning. Can't blame him; he's got enough on his plate with a robbery in Aber and he doesn't need to be tripping over reporters."

Another deep breath. "Anyhow, I'm already in trouble so I thought what the heck, booked the Community Hall for two sessions, and rang Mari Lwyd. She's coming to the meeting tomorrow at ten with one colleague, no other Press admitted, and I hope it'll be a sympathetic report they do for us."

"So what's the meeting about?" Donald demanded. "And what's happening tonight at seven?"

David Laffan looked at Dafydd, at Donald.

"Another meeting. I'd like your help with both, if you would, and I hope it works . . . "

"Okay, bach, we're in." Dafydd sat down at the table and took out his notebook. "What do you want us to do?"

They sketched out a plan of action, refined it over sausage and ketchup sandwiches, made lists, argued about who to involve and how to word the message, and then Dai typed it out on his computer and printed a hundred and fifty copies while Dafydd and Donald cut each sheet into six and piled them on the table among the empty plates.

At last they were ready. Dai fetched his car and they got in.

"I'll drop you at Cae Gwylan, Donald, and you by the boatyard, if you're sure?"

Dafydd nodded.

"And then I'll come back, start at the southernmost caravan sites and work north until I run out of letters. If you get any opposition don't argue, just try the next place. Good luck!"

He let in the clutch and the silver Vauxhall moved away down the hill.

At Cae Gwylan Donald leapt out with his bag of letters. Soon they reached the boatyard by the Leri and it was Dafydd's turn. He clambered out, jammed the hat more firmly on his head and saluted. "I'll do my best, David."

"Good man," Dai grinned. "Sock it to 'em, Minnesota!"

"Sure thing!"

On the way down the main street with the last few letters he stopped at his house to put out food for Rheidol, then went upstairs for his Bible in case the meeting finished in time for him to get to Chapel. Maybe he should ring the Minister and ask him to delay the Bible study . . . Something Dai perhaps had forgotten was refreshments; he added his packet of tea leaves, then took it out again and fetched his rucksack.

He dropped in at the Spar for a box of teabags, four pints of milk and five pounds'-worth of cheap biscuits. The chapel could have any left over.

He dumped the rucksack on Dai's dining table and collected plates.

"Oh, just stick them in the kitchen somewhere. Thanks." Dai, typing at lightning speed, turned briefly to look at what he had brought. "I'll reimburse you for those; well done. Is Don back yet?"

He wasn't. Dafydd left Dai to type and tackled what looked like several meals'-worth of washing up, left it to drain, and noticed a cookery book open at the recipe for Yorkshire puddings.

"Are you using this recipe?" he asked, when the typing paused.

"Yes, in case people don't have one. Why?"

"It doesn't make it obvious that the fat has to be a type with a high haze point, and it must be smoking hot when the batter goes in. Or you get a sad wet brick of a thing."

"Ah. I'll add that, then." Print scrolled rapidly down the screen, and the typing recommenced. "And . . . save. There; if we run out we can email it, or copy it at the Hall if I take a master copy. Thanks, Dafydd. I owe you a lot, you know. If it hadn't been for your detective work . . . "

Dafydd said modestly that it hadn't just been him, there'd been half the village involved one way and another, and it hadn't worked yet. He noticed that Dai was still unnaturally pale, his face shadowed.

"It'll be all right, bach," he murmured.

Silence. Dafydd found himself looking at the book-shelves. Christian books, more than one of them looking well-used. *Immediately* . . .

He cleared his throat. "Might help if we prayed," he suggested.

Dai sat up straight. "Yes. Yes; should have thought of that first, before we did anything. Thank you, Dafydd."

He got up and stood beside him, nearly a foot taller. "You first," he mumbled.

Dafydd took a deep breath. "O Lord, forgive us. That we forget You. That we do so much in our own strength, or try to. Look favourably on David Your servant, because he's chosen a hard road. Give him Your words. Let us have the grace to give him a hearing . . ."

Dai was shaking. He held onto the doorframe and spoke so quietly Dafydd could barely hear him.

"Father God, I'm afraid. I'm proud and I'm afraid to be laughed at, to be despised . . . Give me Your strength to admit my faults, to humble myself before people who hate me . . . I can't do it without You. It's not about me, Lord. Not now. It's about You. I want to see this place thriving, hopeful, thanking You. If Your plan involves me losing my job, so be it. If I have to tell everyone I've been arrogant and lacking compassion, that's a small price to pay, and it's true. Thank You for showing me my faults."

Silence. Dafydd wanted to pat the younger man on the shoulder.

I've got to walk this lonesome valley . . .

They smiled tentatively at each other.

"Thanks." Dai cleared his throat and blinked a few times. "You're a Welsh speaker, aren't you? Could you read through these, please, and do a translation? I'll make us some tea."

Dafydd took the sheaf of printouts. "I'll do my best. Er——" He hesitated. "Sorry I was rude to you. Last winter. When the sea came over."

Dai looked back at him. "You weren't the worst, by far. They told me to get everyone evacuated in case the sea wall went; there was all that damage in Aber, but almost no one would leave, they didn't seem to understand how dangerous it was. They just wouldn't *listen.* And then it didn't break, after all."

Dafydd nodded. "That's not the point. You were doing your job. I shouldn't have been rude to you."

Dai drew a deep breath. "Thanks. I forgive you . . . but will you forgive me? By the end, I was so frustrated I was really hoping the wall *would* go just so you'd all have to admit I was right!"

Dafydd grinned. "I'm not surprised. Of course I forgive you. Let's get at this translation."

Dai grinned back. "I'll put the kettle on."

Chapter 12

THEY HAD PUT the chairs out in the Community Hall, found a box for Dai to stand on—he said he was not going to go up on the stage for anyone—and put a small pile of translations near the door for anyone who preferred to use Welsh. Sandy and Marged were in the kitchen and Donald was trying to mend one of the blinds which had jammed. Dafydd wandered down the aisle straightening chairs and saw Dai and Siân discussing something. After a while Dai beckoned him over, looking as though he would pass out at any moment.

"There are people queuing outside," Dafydd informed him. "Can we open the doors?"

"It's a quarter to . . . Okay, tell Don he can open up when he's ready. Do you mind if we pray again? I was telling Siân . . . "

"Of course we can." Dafydd looked round for somewhere private. "Donald! You can let them in now, when you're ready. Shall we go into the store room for a few minutes?"

They stood among stacks of chairs and surplus tea-urns, with the door pulled to.

Siân looked at the two men and nudged Dai.

"No; Dafydd. Thanks . . . "

For a few seconds Dafydd's mind went completely blank. He could hear people coming in, talking. With an effort he remembered Dai's bookcases, the green curtains, the cluttered dining table.

"Help," he whispered. "Help, Lord . . . In Your name. Your will."

Silence. Something Dai had said: "It's not about me, Lord. It's not about any of us. It's not what we want, our plans, our lives, our comfort. It's about You . . . "

Siân the Minister's widow took over. " 'I have plans for you, declares the Lord. Plans to prosper you and not to harm you. Plans to give you hope and a future.' Off you go, bach. God is with you."

"Thanks." Dai squared his shoulders and led them out into the hall.

He couldn't be more nervous if he'd been the batter pudding-thrower, Dafydd thought compassionately. Why did he take a job where he would have to talk to people? But I marched up to a policeman and challenged him to a duel because I was wearing a hat and an army jacket, so maybe it's the uniform gives him the courage. Yes; we never saw him out of it, and Bill reckoned he must sleep in it . . .

He's not wearing uniform tonight.

Oh, Lord, look after him, poor dab.

At five past seven Dai stepped up onto the box and coughed.

"Ladies and gentlemen, I apologise for disturbing your evening, but this is an important time for our village. As you know, a week ago tonight a batter pudding was thrown at Dafydd M. Williams—and I'll let him tell it from there."

Dafydd clambered onto the box and was temporarily silenced by terror at seeing so many people looking at him. Pull yourself together, bach! He noticed the Minister in the second row and addressed himself to him, explaining his attempts at detection and giving a précis of the conclusions he had come to "with the help of others", as he put it. Miss Smith had declined to be named, though he had seen her come in.

"So we collected a list of anyone young and quick enough, whose livelihood depended on tourists. And I thought, if this person has thrown puddings rather than paint and is trying to save their own job, tourists who spend money in one shop may well spend money in another, may take lodgings, may come back. So I began to think that maybe we should not look at this person as a criminal, or at least see them as not wholly bad."

He sat down and Dai took his place.

"It was at this point that I gave up my own attempts at detection, and, making the dangerous and incorrect assumption that any horseplay had to be down to students, asked Mr. McBain to help with my enquiries. I soon found out that he had an unbreakable alibi for the attack on the sound engineer from the film crew. More to the point, he assured me that neither he nor Miss Pickering his friend could make batter puddings of a suitable quality.

"I must apologise to anyone who was alarmed by Mr. McBain's disappearance. I did not arrest him, but I did ask him to stay on my premises in the hope that his absence might bring the true culprit into the open. I was fully expecting another pudding incident during that day or the early evening, and when this did not happen I was at a loss as to what to do with Mr. McBain. At eight p.m. I told him he was welcome to leave, and apologised for detaining him."

"Shame!" came from the back of the hall. Dafydd suspected Miss Smith.

Donald hopped up onto the box.

"He's not a bad sort, Mr. Laffan," he announced cheerfully. "Once he knew it wasn't me he tried to find out about the other students round here, if I knew anything that might suggest someone in particular. Well, none of the lads I know can cook, so I couldn't help him. And he said would I mind staying to see if there was another attack. I'd not realised Sandy would get so worried, and I didn't mind, but his place was freezing and he said his central heating didn't work, an' that's what my Dad does so I had a look at it, bled the radiators and so on, an' looked at the boiler . . . "

He referred to his script. "Anyhow, we got chatting about my thesis and he told me lots about Staffordshire oatcakes and lent me a book because I'm researching the folklore of pancakes and things. And then he said his theory hadn't worked and I ought to go, but I'd got the boiler apart and I stayed there 'til ten and went home and emailed Dad, and went back in the morning and checked some things I'd missed. Anyhow, it's your turn now, Mr. Williams."

Dafydd stood up again.

"Well, that night I had a word with the person I suspected, and I was right. And I heard all about why they were doing it, trying to get people into Borth. Horrified about your ruined hairdo, Ellie, and your 'arrest', Donald, and sorry not to have been able to think of a better way to the same result."

He was aware that the audience was restless, becoming hostile. He must not let it frighten him. "So I went home, and on the way I met the film people. And I spoke to Mr. Ryan who was the victim in their group. Yes, I went into the Victoria with him and I bought him a drink because that was how he wanted to talk. And I am not likely to turn into a drinker of alcohol from that one incident, and I do not condemn those of you who do drink! Mr. Ryan, of all the victims, was the one I thought most likely to insist on a prosecution, so I wanted to persuade him to consider the incident to be nothing but an unexpected experience, to be laughed about afterwards . . . And Mr. Ryan, who is a very patient man, agreed that it would be a good tale to tell, but then he asked me why it should be a batter pudding that was the missile chosen."

Dafydd paused, feeling himself hot with embarrassment. This was the worst part of his own confession.

"Now, I'd drunk nothing but orange juice, but oh, my tongue! Ran away with me completely it did, and I told him it was an old Welsh custom to throw batter puddings, took it back to the baptism of St. David and the tale of the disfigured monk cured by a splash of the water. Well, that is one of the legends, but I made up a tale that it was a custom to throw a pikelet, or a pancake, or a batter pudding, at someone to call the saint's blessing on them—and that was a pack of lies, and I am sorry for it, for trying to mislead Mr. Ryan."

He was speaking through people's laughter now, and gave up until they became quieter.

"And then the next day, not having heard that Donald had been mending a boiler and thinking he was in custody, I made an appointment to see P.C.S.O. Laffan. To have words, because I knew who was the culprit, and it wasn't Donald."

He looked at Dai, who grinned and took his place.

"Mr. Williams arrived looking like thunder, with a very suspicious shopping bag. I asked him in and he challenged me to a duel. With—you've guessed it. Batter puddings. And he can't half throw straight!"

There was a burst of hilarity from the audience. Someone began to applaud; Dafydd was pushed to his feet and stood blushing next to Dai while people hooted and stamped and cheered. He'd not realised just how many people had longed to do something of the sort to the unpopular policeman. Poor Dai. He grimaced up at him apologetically. Dai was shaking visibly but managed to smile.

At last the noise died down and Dai continued.

"Well, once we'd—er—run out of ammunition, and had a cuppa, and Mr. Williams had seen Donald up to his eyes in bits of plumbing, we discussed the problem. I hadn't realised just how officious and arrogant I must have seemed to you, and I am very sorry. Feel free to throw as many batter puddings at me as you like: I deserve it."

Silence. You could have heard a pin drop in the hall.

"If you are kind enough to give me a chance, I will try to be a nicer person to have around. I will do my best for this community. And if I start being obnoxious, somebody please *tell* me!"

Silence again, Dai still shaking like a leaf. Then Sandy came out of the kitchen and started to clap, and more people joined in. It was a more subdued response than before, but Dafydd was pleased that they had acknowledged the man's courage.

When they were silent, Dai carried on.

"This is where it gets serious, and where Borth needs your help. All of our help. The batter puddings have got into the local paper, and at least one national paper. People are turning up at the Golf Club to see where it happened, and so far, all well and good. It was done to bring tourists in and they have begun to arrive.

"But the problem is the batter puddings. Mr. Ryan won't be the only one to ask, why batter puddings? It seems that the culprit had the idea from The Goon Show, an old radio programme, but that is not the sort of explanation that sells newspapers or brings tourists to Borth!

"Mr. Williams told us his tall tale, and Mr. McBain said that he wished it was true, it would be ideal for inclusion in his thesis. But there is no old Welsh custom of throwing batter puddings, for any reason, so at first we were no further forward with finding an explanation to tell the reporters. I believe there have been two in the village today: only two so far?"

Someone called back that yes, they were staying with her.

"Good," Dai grinned. "But two reporters aren't enough to bring in all the tourists we need. We need more, and a good tale to tell them—a tale that will stand up to all their scrutiny, because it is true! So we discussed it further and then we thought, why must a tradition be an old one? Why don't we start a tradition? We don't have to bring St. David into it, except that Dydd Gŵyl Ddewi is near the day it started on. Go on, Mr. McBain. This is your moment."

Donald got up on the box and referred to his script.

"Many cultures have a tradition of a day for mischief: punkie night, oakapple day, Saturnalia and so on. We suggest to you that Borth should begin a similar tradition, as of this year, that on St. David's day and for a week following, people should work off a year's frustrations, boredom, and desire to be silly, by making batter puddings and throwing them at anyone they choose—preferably only locals, or at least people who are forewarned. It must be only batter puddings, and no harm must be done, and people not prepared to join in or risk an attack should wear suitable protective clothing—please, we can discuss the details later, this was just my idea—and we also suggest that we should have a big festival of batter pudding-throwing tomorrow, here, at ten o'clock, when Mari Lwyd and a colleague from the Cambrian News will be here to witness it. No other reporters. And if anyone asks why we're doing it, it's because A) it improves our cookery skills, B) we need some excitement after the winter, and C) it might be a tourist attraction. What do you reckon?"

There was a buzz of laughter and discussion.

"One minute!" Dai shouted. "There's tea and biscuits now, and in a quarter of an hour we'd like to hold a vote, when you've had time to discuss it. Okay, that's me finished."

By the time the fifteen minutes were up, the meeting had split eighty-twenty in favour of the new tradition, a committee to finalise the details and rules of combat had sprung up from nowhere like the spring at St. David's baptism, and there were so many promises of batter puddings for the ten o'clock meeting that Dafydd wondered if they should also provide plates and knives and forks. The Minister came up to Dafydd and informed him that he had rung all the usual attendees and moved the Bible study to Thursday night for once; he was followed by Marged who handed them both tea towels and said they might as well be useful for a change.

At last all the audience had gone, the hall was tidy, and Dai was locking up.

"Come back to my place for a bit?" Dafydd suggested. They were the last two left.

Dai looked grateful for the invitation and led the way across the dark car park to his Vauxhall.

"Was the real culprit there tonight?" he asked.

"I don't know. I don't think so." Dafydd was glad that he could not remember seeing her. "Do you need to know?"

"Not really. Just for my own records, so to speak. Not to tell anyone."

He's still a policeman . . . But if you don't trust him now, who will ever trust him?

"One of the Tourist Information ladies," Dafydd murmured. "I told her you wouldn't need to know, not if no one was going to go to court. So if anyone does, it's me you'd better arrest for it, seeing that everyone in Borth knows I threw one at you."

Dai shook his head. "I hope it won't come to that. I do hope not . . . "

They sat in Dafydd's living-room with the tea tray on the table between them. Rheidol had appeared and been introduced, and was now curled up in front of the fire.

"I respect you," Dafydd informed Dai, handing him a cup of tea. "Apologising in front of everyone like that, and without your uniform."

Dai shivered. "You noticed . . . It was like being naked, standing up there as *me*, not as a P.C.S.O., I felt so horribly vulnerable. Thanks for praying; it made a difference."

"That's all right, bach. Tell you the truth, now, that's the first time I've ever prayed in front of anyone else, not all together like in Chapel. She's a lot to answer for, with her batter puddings."

Chapter 13

BY TWENTY TO ten on Thursday morning the Community Hall was filling up. Most of the local shops had either closed for the occasion or left one person in charge, there were three young men on the door to keep out the journalists, and the hall blinds were drawn. Everything was going according to plan, and Tîm Pwdin, Team Pudding as Mari Lwyd had christened them, were putting the last few tables out.

"I was there last night," someone said shyly from behind them. "Thanks for not giving me away, Mr. Williams. I threw those puddings, Mr. Laffan. I didn't mean any harm, but I'm sorry for all the trouble I've caused."

Dai held out a rather grimy hand. "Well, you did it for the best, and I doubt if you'll do it again . . . not unofficially, anyhow!" He grinned. "Fun, isn't it? Would you let Ellie throw one at you? And Miss Fraser? Dafydd here? All of them, if they come?"

Llinos Bevan shook hands, gulped and said that yes, she could see that would be helpful to them, and she deserved it . . .

"I'll get more than you," Dai murmured. "The people I've upset in the time I've been here . . . I never realised what a complete little—oh, what was his name? The A.R.P. man from Dad's Army?"

She smiled suddenly. "Hodges! Yes, *exactly* . . . Poor Mr. Laffan. That's the man from the film crew just coming in. I'm ashamed to say I went for him because he didn't swear as much as the others and I hoped he'd be kinder if he caught me! Oh dear . . . "

"Are you sure you want to admit it publicly?" Dafydd asked. "You're Council; won't they see to it that you lose your job for being awkward?"

"They're going to close the Borth office. Oh, they say it isn't decided yet, but we all know it is. And most of the offices not closing will have opening hours cut, so I don't see my job lasting much longer anyway. I don't want to pretend it was for the greater good of Borth, either; it was our jobs I was thinking of, mine and Meredith Howell's. Not that everyone won't be pleased if we get hundreds of tourists . . . "

"You're very honest, Mrs. Bevan. Ah, Miss Bevan." Dai pushed his hair back and left dusty smears on his forehead. "Now, one suggestion which Dafydd made last night after the meeting is that the new tradition ought to be less of a retaliation and more of a reconciliation. That's why we put the tables out. We hope everyone will accept it . . . Fortunately both the Vicar and the Minister are on the Committee, so there shouldn't be any trouble. The idea is that when you go to pudding someone, you also take a second pudding. You throw the first one, get it out of your system, then sit down with your pudding-ee and eat the second one. Hence the vat of stewed apple in the kitchen, donated by Mrs. Gilchrist, and the equally huge vat of gravy, donated by Marged Pugh. What do you reckon?"

Llinos nodded. "Yes. It won't be as popular, I shouldn't think, as just throwing and running away, but it should help. I'm glad I brought some puddings. Right, what can I do to be useful?"

Mari Lwyd's companion was a photographer, Deanna Bradshaw, who prowled around the hall working out angles and lighting, then pulled a chair in front of a fire exit and sat waiting. The doors closed, the audience found seats or stood at the back, and an expectant hush fell over the room. Rain drummed on the roof.

They had decided to ask the chairman of the Carnival Committee to announce the new tradition; as she was also part of the Pudding Committee this caused no problems. She welcomed everyone, explained that Borth had decided to 'embrace the challenge' and create a new tradition out of the 'recent incidents', read out the draft rules of combat (including Dafydd's amendment, which drew some disappointed heckling), and asked for a show of hands.

"In favour?" A forest of hands.

"Against?" A few hands went up; were counted.

"Over one hundred for, six against," she announced. "If you sign up according to how you voted as the sheet comes round, we'll know exact numbers for the minutes. Now, Mr. Laffan!"

Dai had washed his face and hands but there were still streaks of dirt on his sweatshirt from the tables at the very back of the store room.

"Hallo, everyone," he began. "Firstly, before we get carried away, if people with edible puddings can leave them at the kitchen hatch, then there'll be some to eat that haven't been on the floor. Don't worry: we'll make sure there are plenty to throw!"

Dafydd saw a wicked grin spread across Mari Lwyd's face and hoped that Dai had seen it too.

"Secondly, we've agreed with the Animalarium that they will have the leftovers for their pigs, so no waste. Now then. I know, because Dafydd here told me yesterday, that I've been an absolute pain in the whatever for the last ten months. I apologise to you all and will try to be less annoying in future, but I can quite understand that some of you—probably most of you!—will want to throw puddings at me. I do hope you'll also feel able to sit down with me afterwards and eat some." (Cheers and cat-calls.)

"This morning, the batter pudding-thrower of Borth unmasked herself—metaphorically. She's very bravely agreed to be puddinged by her victims and hopes that tourists will flock to Borth as a result. Can we have a round of applause please for Miss Bevan!"

Llinos, blushing like a beetroot, went to join Dai on the stage as the hall erupted, cheering, booing, clapping. Deanna was taking photographs.

"I was trying to think how to get people to visit, to save our jobs," she explained, when the noise had died down. "All I could think of was to do something silly . . . I'm very sorry for frightening anyone, especially the people I threw them at. Ellie, Dafydd, Miss Fraser, Mr. Reynolds, Mr. Ryan, I'd feel much happier if you threw one at me, and I hope too that you'll feel able to join me in a slice of pudding afterwards."

Dafydd saw Dai put his arm round her. They came down off the stage together and stood on a sheet of tarpaulin in a corner. Dafydd followed, beckoning to Ellie and Miss Fraser, took a batter pudding from Siân and let fly, fairly gently.

Llinos' gasp was lost in the general upheaval as the audience realised they actually meant it. People surged forward to throw puddings at Dai; at Llinos, who was laughing with tears and grease running down her face. Small fights broke out in the crowd.

Marged's voice rang out: "Some to the kitchen, if you please . . . I didn't mean like that, young Aled! Oh, you just wait!"

The air was full of laughter and batter pudding, with an undercurrent of old scores being settled.

Dafydd heard someone saying "Excuse me," behind him and turned to see Mrs. Taylor facing a large man in overalls.

"I shan't throw anything at you," Mrs. Taylor was explaining carefully, "because it's a wicked waste to throw food, but I do wish you'd cut back your buddleia. It's right across the pavement, and when it rains people can't get past. We have to walk in the road."

"You mean that big thing, has purple flowers? Our Damian's supposed to be taking that out as soon as we get a fine Saturday . . . "

Dafydd moved past them and saw a batter pudding land across the Vicar's face. He held his breath, but the man simply wiped his spectacles, retrieved the largest portion of the missile and returned it.

When things had calmed down a little Miss Smith announced food, and people began to queue at the hatch. Dafydd collected pudding and gravy and sat down between Siân and Barry Ryan, who was talking rugby with Bill. Mari Lwyd was interviewing Llinos further down the table with Dai and Malcolm Edwards beyond them. Deanna took a few more pictures and accepted a bowl of pudding with stewed apple.

"There's quite a bit of pudding left," Siân told Dafydd. "And those persistent newspaper men are still lurking outside. It seems a shame not to let them have some of it."

"Siân!"

"What? Oh, on plates, you silly man, you should know me by now."

"Dai did say he'd give Mari an exclusive. I'll go and have a word with her."

Mari agreed that it did seem a shame to leave them outside in the rain.

"Look, you do three plates and I'll go out and have a word. If they agree we could sit in the Landrover and eat there. In the spirit of the Borth Batter Pudding Festival."

After a few more words with Llinos she pulled up her hood and went out. Dafydd went back to tell Siân, and they made up a tray: three plates of pudding, cutlery, a jug of gravy and another of stewed apple.

"Look at David and Llinos," Siân murmured as they crossed the hall. "It would do him good to have a wife, and she's a nice lass . . . "

Dafydd jammed the hat on, not only because it was raining, and held the door open for her. "Really, Siân! But yes, now you've said it . . . Here you are, gentlemen, and would you like tea or coffee?"

Tîm Pwdin finished tidying the hall, left a bin bag of scraps outside for the Animalarium, and stood exhausted in the porch as Dai locked up.

"Come back to mine?" he suggested. "Derek Edwards fitted a new thingummy last night, so the place is warming up again, and he said Donald did a good job. Unfortunate that those two had lectures this morning."

They piled into his car and Llinos'. At the bottom of the hill they passed Mrs. Taylor, walking. Llinos stopped and offered her a lift. After a few seconds of hesitation she accepted and sat beside Siân, and was dropped at her front gate.

"Tea or coffee? Te neu goffi?" Dai asked, gathering paper off chairs and dropping it into a washing basket. "There should be enough mugs, Dafydd was kind enough to wash up for me yesterday so they're all clean. Er—roedd Dafydd yn golchi'r llestri neithiwr, a mae'r cwpanau i gyd yn glân rŵan . . . Is that right?"

"Yn lân," Miss Smith corrected. "Glân mutates after yn."

They sat eating digestive biscuits and drinking tea. Dafydd looked round at them: Siân and Marged, Llinos, Dai, Miss Smith; all of them greasy and smeary. He'd have to have a thorough wash as soon as he got home, and wash his clothes, but despite his misgivings it had all worked out. A pity the students hadn't been there.

"Now they've organised it, it won't be half as much fun," Marged complained.

"Things seldom are," Siân said darkly. "I wonder what Mari Lwyd will put in her article, and what the other reporters will put in theirs?"

"I suppose it depends how long it takes them to get that Welsh handout translated," Llinos remarked. "And how accurately they translate it . . . "

Dafydd smiled across the room at the hat, which he'd taken off at the threshold and abandoned on the window-sill, and remembered guiltily that both the hat and the jacket he was wearing were borrowed. The jacket should be all right in the washing-machine, but how about the hat? How on earth had that got greasy, as he'd not worn it in the hall? Maybe it would come clean if he wiped it over with washing-up liquid and left it outside in the rain. He told Miss Smith that he'd return them once they'd dried. "I'll wash them first."

"Oh, I'll do the washing. I'd forgotten I still have your coat and your key. On second thoughts, you can have them back if you like, once they're clean. The jacket's a bit small for me and the hat suits you, Minnesota!"

The telephone began to ring. Dai excused himself and went to answer it.

"What did you call him?" Marged leapt like a terrier at the information. "Is that his middle name?"

Miss Smith stared, horrified. "Oh! Sorry!"

Dafydd shrugged. "Yes, I am Dafydd Minnesota Williams. Named for an uncle born out there. Minnesota Emrys Williams, he was. And what is wrong with the name Minnesota?"

"It goes well with the hat," Siân said tactfully, looking daggers at Marged.

Their host came back and flopped onto a chair.

"What's happened?" Llinos demanded anxiously.

Dai pushed his hair back. "That was Martyn Gough. Chief Superintendent. Asking if I want to carry on in Borth. Apparently Mari Lwyd emailed him her report, to be approved before it went to the editor to go online."

"And you said——?" Miss Smith prompted.

"If the people would have me. Yes."

"And he said . . . ?" Siân smiled.

" 'You'll do.' " Dai rubbed his face. "I suppose that's good. I'm just a bit stunned . . . Well, thank you, Llinos. If you'd not thought of batter puddings . . . "

"If the Goons hadn't once made a show entitled *The Dreaded Batter Pudding Hurler* . . . " Llinos grinned. "And if you hadn't turned to detection, Minnesota Williams . . . !"

"Minnesota——?" Dai began, turning to Dafydd. "I thought——"

"Dafydd Minnesota Williams," Marged explained airily. "So it looks as though we're stuck with you, Dai Pwdin. Things could be worse."

"What?" Miss Smith spluttered. "Oh yes! Dai Pwdin! You couldn't be anything else!"

"Oh, all right then . . .I suppose it's better than Dai Laffan." Dai lay back in the chair, grinning broadly. "Well, here's to Llinos—Llinos Pwdin! And the Goons, and most importantly here's to Borth. May God bless her and all who sail in her!"

Part 2:

Napoleon Powell's Piano

Chapter 1

DAFYDD M. WILLIAMS LOOKED OUT into the darkness, saw no one around, and pushed his bicycle down the path to the back gate. Keys into right hand pocket of the camouflage jacket. Padlock and chain already in left hand pocket. Back gate, pre-oiled so it wouldn't squeak. He opened the gate and checked again for late dog-walkers. No one visible.

He took a deep breath, turned on the bicycle lights, jammed the hat onto his head more firmly, and, using the stack of bricks he had placed in readiness that afternoon, boarded the bicycle. He pedalled out of the back lane and away down the road towards Ynyslas.

As he had expected he hadn't forgotten how to ride the machine, but as it had been shoved into his spare bedroom three years previously when he moved in, to emerge two weeks ago in dire need of an overhaul, he was breathless and aching before he reached the Golf Club. At least no one was watching him: he was determined to get back into training but equally determined to get through the earlier stages without spectators. He wasn't sure if he'd be able to dismount properly, either: in the old days he'd leapt on and off bicycles without thinking about it, but now he was on the lookout for a bench or a suitably sturdy, non-spiky fence which he could use as a ladder.

The half-moon illuminated the flat landscape, grey fields and hills in the distance to his right and grey dunes to his left with only the golf course in between. It was too late for rabbits but an owl was screeching out on the marsh. He cautiously let go with one hand and pulled the hat down further. If it blew off he would be in no condition to chase it across the road, let alone through the rough grass beyond the fence . . . Stupid to have worn it, really; it would offer no protection if he fell off, and it had a broad brim which caught the wind, but like the camouflage jacket it gave him confidence. In the hat and jacket he was Minnesota Williams, detective, gunslinger, freedom-fighter and diplomat; in his usual clothes he was just Dafydd, the retired railwayman who lived in Borth with his cat and went to Chapel twice a week.

Ridiculous, to put so much meaning into clothes. As bad as the women who made up their faces for the same reason, his mother would have said . . . No, he wasn't hiding behind the hat and jacket; simply reminding himself that only a month ago he had surprised himself with his own temerity and tact. He hadn't been the only person surprised. He grinned suddenly, remembering the look on P.C.S.O. Laffan's face.

He couldn't see a suitable fence. At this rate he'd be at Ynyslas before he found somewhere to stop, so it would be sensible to turn round and go back. Start with a short journey . . . He listened intently, heard no traffic and wobbled across the road in a wide arc. Back towards Borth. His hands were numb with cold and his thighs ached. It really was time he did something about getting fit.

Twenty minutes later he was filling the kettle to make a pot of tea, the bicycle leaning against the cooker. He would have to find a better place to keep it. Maybe he could put a hook in the cupboard under the stairs if the ceiling was high enough, which was doubtful. Maybe he should buy a shed; the lawnmower could go into it too.

The cat-flap banged shut behind his ginger cat Rheidol who went to his empty dish, waving his tail.

"Wyt ti wedi cael bwyd yn barod," Dafydd said sternly, but went to the fridge, cut himself a sliver of cheese and dropped half into the dish. It vanished instantly. "Yes, you've had lots of food and I watched you eat it, so don't tell me that big grey cat came in and had it all."

He bent to stroke the ginger head. Rheidol rubbed hopefully against his hand.

"Ti'n dew, pws. You're fat. And so am I; we eat too much cheese. Ydym; ti a fi, pws, yn bwyta gormod o gaws. Beth ddylwn ni yn wneud? What should we do about it? Oh, I know what I *should* do; I just keep not doing it."

He sighed and clicked the kettle off again. It was part of his homecoming ritual to make himself a paned, but it would be stupid to drink tea so late at night. He shouldn't have had the cheese, either: he didn't want to have nightmares . . . He locked the door and went up to bed.

The next day he began to make a list of things he wanted to achieve.

Shed/storage for bicycle and mower
Lose weight and get fit
Read more
Tidy spare room
Garden
Watch birds at Ynys Hir

He had at least read *The Pilgrim's Progress* now, something else which had come out of the spare bedroom. Next time he went into Aberystwyth he would look at sheds and when the weather improved he would get going in the garden.

He was about to make a paned when the telephone rang. It was Siân, asking if he would come over because one of her friends wanted a word.

"Has your friend a batter pudding or two with her?" he enquired cautiously.

Siân laughed. "No, no. You're quite safe. You can come over now? I'll put the kettle on."

Siân's friend proved to be Edith, who lived on the main street opposite the Victoria. She began by asking what Rheidol had brought him recently (a pink bootee, a frog and a sock), then after a pause while Siân issued tea and jam tarts, got to the point.

"It seems awfully rude, but please say if you'd rather not. I have to go to London on Tuesday. Mike would come but he really isn't fit to travel, and I don't know London at all, and as it's a railway you'd be ideal to come and look at it; I was telling Siân and she said you get free rail travel still, so at least you wouldn't have to pay . . . "

Dafydd blinked, having foreseen several completely different requests.

"To where in London are you going?" he enquired. "From Borth we would be arriving at Euston, going via Shrewsbury and Birmingham New Street."

Edith fished an envelope out of her shopping bag and studied a letter. "It doesn't say. It's one of Esme's friends. His father has died and his mother wants to sell the house. Jonathan told Esme about the railway and she thought of the museum here at the station. And Jon's mother says we can have it all if we can take it away."

"A model railway?"

Edith nodded. "Jon says he'll pick us up near the station. He wants us to see it. There's track and everything, apparently, and his father made quite a few of the models. He used to take them to open days but there's no one left who can do it and Esme says the mother would rather it went to a museum where it would be used than disappearing into somebody's garage."

Dafydd could understand this. He had no problem with escorting Edith to London, as long as Mike didn't object, and it would be an interesting day out. He wrote 'Tuesday.

Edith—London' in his notebook and said that he would look up the train times.

That night he studied his collection of timetables. If they left Borth at 7.43 a.m. they would be at Birmingham for 10.28 and there was a train from Birmingham, if they caught it, which reached Euston at 11.24. Then they would have until 16.43 before starting the journey back, arriving at 21.07. Maybe that would be late for Edith: it depended on how long Jonathan would take to show them the railway. Was it on a base-board? How would they transport it? A van? A car? He certainly couldn't help with that . . .

He put away the timetables, lifted the corner of the curtain and looked out into the dark garden. Time he went out.

If anything, he was even clumsier and more ungainly on his second outing, but he pedalled grimly as far as the fork in the road at Ynyslas before turning back. This time he had not worn the hat, which was one thing less to worry about, but he still wobbled alarmingly when he cornered, not daring to ride faster in case he crashed. It would come with practice. Two cars passed him, both from the rear, and he hoped that he had not been recognised.

He sat in his armchair rubbing his knuckles into his leg muscles, annoyed that he had let himself get so unfit. There was no need for it: it wasn't as though he took no exercise at all, but walking down to the shop for his newspaper on weekdays and to Chapel on Sundays and Wednesdays didn't compare with cycling. He would persist: once he was fit, he'd ride down to Ynys Hir and watch birds; he could take the bicycle on the train to Machynlleth or Aberystwyth, or Tywyn, and explore . . .

He ought to eat properly too; not that he ate chips for every meal, but he certainly didn't manage the five-a-day people went on about, sometimes not even three of them. Well, summer was coming, when both cycling and salads would be more palatable. He was tired. Tomorrow after Chapel he would look at his food supplies and work out a sensible menu.

Chapter 2

HE WALKED BACK from Chapel feeling annoyed and guilty, not because he had almost forgotten to deliver Edith's train times, but because of the sermon. Guilty because there was no escaping the fact that refugees all over the world were getting a raw deal now, just as in Old Testament times, and annoyed because he didn't see what he could do about it. You could pray, and he certainly would: you could donate to various charities, and he already did when the opportunity presented itself to do so anonymously. He was not going to let any charity have his address, being pestered with too much junk mail already.

Was it ethical to buy a shed when people were starving? Well, it gave shed-makers and shed-sellers a wage . . . He sighed. If he was meant to do something about it, he would look for hints as to how he was meant to proceed.

After a couple of bacon sandwiches he cleared his kitchen table and emptied the cupboard onto it and under it.

Flour, eggs, vegetable rack, dried fruit, baking powder, bicarbonate, apple rings, stock cubes, salt, tinned vegetables, tinned fish, tinned fruit, jam, honey, vinegar, Worcester sauce, mustard powder, pasta, rice, cereal, oatmeal, tea, sugar, pickled onions, pasta sauce; there seemed to be an awful lot of it. Under the table was a bag of plastic boxes, a thermos, two plastic plates, an old frying pan with a loose handle, a biscuit tin of bicycle spares and another two identical biscuit tins, one of which contained biscuits (they all rattled differently); a Tilley lamp, washing-powder, a mop bucket, a brush and dustpan, a pair of walking boots, matches, a box of candles, a few garden tools, the downstairs clotheshorse, a stack of old newspapers to go under food dishes and the litter tray, the lawn-mower, and last but not least, what looked like a year's worth of cat food, cat biscuits and cat litter, which might last for a month at a pinch.

Sort out the dates . . . No. First check whether you could hang up the bicycle in there . . . Thought not.

Right. Now look at the dates on things. He began to make a list.

Use lasagne
Use stock cubes

Good thing salt didn't have a use-by date, as it had come from his previous house and was possibly even older.

Peach slices a month after the best before should be fine, but he didn't fancy the jar of fish paste which had been behind the lasagne and was four years out of date. It smelt all right when he removed the lid but, just in case, he scraped it into the bin rather than the compost bucket and put the jar to soak.

He started a second list.

Don't buy:
sardines (Rheidol preferred pilchards)
lasagne
stock cubes

And while he was trying to get fit, no more jam, honey, fruit in syrup or sweet biscuits either. And no more candles: they had been in the third biscuit tin, and he'd bought more because he'd forgotten where he'd put the first lot. He ought to use the candles up instead of using electricity. What if he stood them where Rheidol couldn't knock them over . . .

Back to menus. Tomorrow he was in; Tuesday he would be out all day. That meant sandwiches, and something quick when he got home. Pasta and sauce and cheese? Wednesday and so forth, in all day as far as he knew.

Monday. Two meals, at least one with some sort of leafy green vegetable for vitamins. Which vitamins? Mrs. Taylor would know, but he wasn't going to go and ask. Maybe Miss Smith would have a suitable book in her library. More to the point, what was fresh and needed using up? He had tonight's meal to make, too . . .

In the end he ate mashed potato with sardines and celery. He also peeled and chopped carrots, leeks, half a swede and a rubbery parsnip, and made a vegetable lasagne, using up a tin of tomatoes for the sauce, which would reheat for Monday along with the rest of the mashed potato. He found a half-packet of lentils and put them in hot water to soften, boiled a couple of beetroot which he had bought with good intentions a fortnight previously, and left them to cool overnight, then cleaned the cupboard (on Sunday! but he shouldn't have done any of it on a Sunday, really, and at least it was clean), put back the tins and packets, hid the jam and honey at the back until he felt healthier, and left the pickled onions at the front of the middle shelf. Sometimes he bought a chicken breast, cooked it and left it to go cold: it was good sliced in sandwiches and tasted better than some of the stuff in packets, but was even nicer with a pickled onion.

He stacked cat food next to the lawn-mower, stood the mop bucket on the newspapers and two biscuit tins on that, then in a fit of silliness added the washing powder, plates, brush and dustpan. It was as precarious as a house of cards, so he took the last few items off the stack, hung up the brush and dustpan, and dithered about whether to dispose of the plates.

The telephone rang. Whoever was that, this time of night? To his surprise it was Marged.

"Dafydd," she began, "Siân says you're in need of a shed. Would a Wendy-house be any use? Eirian's just been on the phone and they're disposing of theirs tomorrow to make room for a trampoline, so I thought I'd better ring you straight away."

"Hallo, Marged. Thank you, but what exactly is a—a what?"

"Wendy-house. For children. It's wooden, like a little shed with a door and a window, only not as tall."

"Could a lawnmower fit in it? And a bicycle?"

"I assume so. Definitely the mower would."

"Well, I can have a go . . . What do they want for it and how do we transport it?"

"It's already in sections in the back of Gareth's van. I've no idea about paying but I dare say a batch of welshcakes would be perfectly adequate; save them taking it to the tip at Machynlleth. I'll get back to her, then. If you're out, can they leave it round the back?"

Dafydd said that he wasn't intending to be out, thanked her, and put the phone down.

What was the time? Nine-thirty. Yes, he'd have plenty of time to make welshcakes in the morning and work out where to put the Wendy-house. (Supposing it was pink with curtains? Well, the mower wouldn't care.) It sounded as though he was going to have a full day, and he was tired; he would go to bed and see what time he woke up. He might well manage a bicycle ride in the early hours of the morning.

As he had hoped, he woke at five and organised himself ruthlessly into getting up and going out on the bicycle before breakfast. The dawn chorus was unexpectedly loud, given the dearth of local trees: he wondered which species were singing. Some he could recognise, but not all.

However loud must it be over in the oak woods at Ynys Hir, the R.S.P.B. reserve?

Although he rode as far as he had on his previous trip and was still inclined to wobble when turning, he felt far less creaky as he returned: he managed to dismount properly and wheeled the machine triumphantly up the path thinking about breakfast and welshcakes.

By 8.30 a.m. he had made two batches of the flat curranty cakes, eaten porridge, washed and shaved. He collected Rheidol's latest offering (another single sock) and hung it on the front garden railings. There were daffodils out in the long narrow flowerbed and tulips in bud. He nipped the head off a dandelion and wondered how long he could get away with not cutting the grass. Having collected a few pieces of litter he went back inside, dropped them in the bin and went through to study the back garden.

There was a slate wall with a wooden gate, and a gap in the wall filled rather untidily with fence panels beside a patch of hard standing covered in slate chippings, presumably where former inhabitants had kept a car. There was also a slate-pebble path which bisected a tiny rectangle of lawn and an embarrassingly weed-covered vegetable patch.

The new shed would have to go on the hard standing, which wasn't very flat but was at least solid. He heard the cat-flap and Rheidol came down the path, jumped onto the wall and trotted away down the back lane. In the garden of the next house there was a derelict tŷ-bach, disused now people had indoor sanitation. Maybe that was what had been where the hard standing was in his garden . . .

A vehicle drew up somewhere nearby and a door slammed. Marged's son?

He hurried back indoors, glanced quickly through the front window, and opened the door.

"Gareth? Yes, Dafydd ydw i. Thanks for bringing it. Diolch yn fawr."

Gareth told him there was no need to thank him, it would have been a pity to throw it away and where did he want it put?

"Where? Yn yr ardd gefn, os gwelwch yn dda . . . " Dafydd gestured towards the house and realised he'd have to show the man how you got round to the back garden. "Mi fydda' i'n ei dangos i chi. I'll show you."

He patted his right hand pocket for door keys and hurried past the van and along the pavement to the lane which led to the various back gardens and yards. Gareth followed in the van, reversing up to the gate. Between them they got the four walls unloaded (one very heavy, with a glazed window and door), one floor, two roof panels, a roll of spare roofing felt and a bundle of long square-section pieces like fence posts, which apparently went down first with the floor on top. Some of the pieces had been painted dark brown and some were greyish weathered wood.

"Diolch yn fawr," Dafydd said, when they had finished. "Thanks very much. What do you want for it? Pres petrol, neu beth?"

Gareth brushed away the offer of petrol money. "Does dim ots. It doesn't matter; it was only going to the tip."

"Os dach chi'n siwr . . . Well, if you *are* sure, have these anyway. I made them this morning."

Dafydd handed over a packet of welshcakes and waved as Gareth drove away.

It took him most of the morning to put the Wendy-house together and when Marged arrived to see how he was getting on he was grateful for her assistance. At last they finished nailing a new ridge-strip of felt onto the roof and went indoors for a rest.

"Yes, there's more welshcakes." He grinned at her. "I made plenty. Paned?"

They sat in the front room and recovered slowly.

"It shouldn't blow away, at least," Marged commented. "Those roof panels were heavier than they looked."

"Getting the ground flat under the floor-beams was worst." Dafydd offered more tea. "But it will be useful to have it to keep the mower in. And I shall try to fit in the bicycle, but at least the bwthyn is big enough for the mower. Thank you, Marged."

"Don't thank me." She took another welshcake. "If Siân hadn't mentioned it . . . So you're spring-cleaning; any particular reason?"

Dafydd looked solemnly at her over his teacup. Her previous visit had been two autumns ago when in a weak moment he had accepted her offer of a bag of windfall apples. She had disconcerted him by carrying them straight through the front door and into his kitchen, whereupon he had felt obliged to respond by offering a paned and what little stilted small talk he could muster. As she was the first person from the village who had entered his house he had assumed she was being nosy, but now he had heard both Pughs conversing with other people and knew that while her husband Robert was succinct and to the point, Marged was insatiably curious about anything and everything which might provide an excuse to talk. It was no wonder that they always seemed to have grandchildren staying during the school holidays.

"I'd like to have a good reason, an interesting one," he told her, "but there is none. I just thought, why is the mower in the cwtsh" —he looked at her to make sure she understood that he meant the cupboard under the stairs—"and the bicycle in the spare bedroom? And I was looking at advertisements for sheds, new, and they were so expensive I thought I would see if anyone had an old one to be disposed of."

"Well, I think you're taking up pigeon-racing." Marged crossed neat ankles and leaned back in the chair. "That, or you're taking in a lodger. A student, maybe."

"It would have to be a very small student, to fit in the bwthyn." He grinned.

"No, in your spare room! That bookcase is new: was that upstairs?"

He nodded. "I'd not touched the spare room since I moved in, not to speak of, so it was about time. Marged, do you know about cooking? Vitamins? If I start eating five fruit or veg a day, I'd like to be sure I get a good mixture."

Marged knew vitamin D was sunlight and vitamin A was carrots, and vitamin C was oranges; beyond that, she suggested he tried eating as many different colours as he could find. "And potatoes don't count as vegetables, and nor does tomato ketchup!"

"How about tomatoes and cucumbers and all the other fruits? Do they count as vegetables? Why *are* some fruits fruit and some vegetables?"

Marged's theory was typically and memorably daft: if you could put it on a trifle and still eat the trifle, it was a fruit. Dafydd wondered where this left grapefruit and lemons but did not argue, and after a few more minutes Marged announced that she'd better be going, she'd only nipped out for a loaf.

He gave her ten minutes before fetching the mower and introducing it to its new home. Then, without much hope of success, he fetched the bicycle.

To his surprise, it fitted: rear wheel first, diagonally. At last! Even two weeks of having it propped against the sink had been too many. Without it the kitchen seemed vast.

Having completed one job he went upstairs and looked round the spare bedroom. The wallpaper had rabbits and teddy bears on it and the lino was pale grey-blue with rust marks where something had once stood. The curtains were red patterned with white geometric shapes, made from a thick soft cotton now beginning to develop holes, and had once hung at his mother's kitchen window.

What was left? Cardboard boxes, cat-basket, suitcase, the rucksack he took on serious shopping expeditions, packaging from things and a chest of drawers which contained spare bedding, a few pieces of clothing and oddments from his parents' house. The room had been listed by the estate agent as a single bedroom but he doubted if you could fit a full-size single bed in and have space for anything else at all. This room looked out over the street; his own bedroom had a good view of the railway line which was partly why he had chosen the house.

The bathroom had been shoe-horned in as an afterthought, with a tiny window in the gable end which looked out onto next door's back garden. Presumably that was why the front bedroom was so tiny; if you added the bathroom as well . . .

He tidied the most recent packaging into a cardboard box, in case the kettle stopped working while it was still under guarantee and could be returned, took the rest to the top of the stairs and realised that it was two p.m.

What was he going to take to London? Sandwiches, mackintosh, railway atlas—he would be interested to see what they had been doing at Rugby—some cash for emergencies, though it would probably be easier to find a cash-point in London. Rucksack or shopping bag? Bag: you never knew who was standing behind you in a crowded Tube train.

It had sounded as though they might not be going on the Tube, which would be easier for Edith. She had seemed very apprehensive, as though setting out for Africa or the Antarctic; and he wondered whether Esme and Jonathan, who presumably thought nothing of travelling, had realised what an adventure it would be for an elderly woman whose longest journey in the last five years had been to the hospital at Shrewsbury with her husband. It would be quite an adventure for him, too. Maybe he could help her to enjoy it more, because he had worked for a short time in London and could point things out: the L.N.W.R. lodges with the destinations carved on the sides, and the statues representing the eight cities served by the railway; remnants of the original Euston station which had been replaced in the 1960s by the modern concourse with its huge screens and—that was something he ought to warn her about, very tactfully: the public toilets which were quite decent, all things considered, but which required a 20p coin to operate the turnstile.

He went back into his bedroom and rooted around in a battered cocoa-tin for a selection of change, just in case.

Chapter 3

DAFYDD HELPED EDITH up into the train, found seats, and sat opposite her.

"Do we change at Machynlleth?" she asked.

"No, this goes straight through to Birmingham. Birmingham International."

"That's good. Thanks."

She took off her coat and folded it onto the seat beside her, took a cloth bag from her large handbag and from it produced some knitting: grey, and clearly a sock.

She settled down with it, looking out of the window, pointing out shelducks and a cormorant as they drew near Dovey Junction. Dafydd was looking out too, studying the scenery, the new wall where the roadworks had been at Glandyfi; wondering if the house at the far end of the bridge was still inhabited; when and if the ospreys would come back this year . . . As they sat at Machynlleth waiting for the other train to come down the coast, he turned his attention to the knitting. How had she done the heel? The back of it looked reinforced.

"It's a sock for Mike," she explained. "Bought ones are too tight round his ankles now."

Dafydd admitted that he had been studying the heel and she expressed surprise.

"Mam did hers another way," he explained. "She tried teaching me to knit, but I never did socks. I used to take a scarf round with me to work at if I had a long wait. A scarf and a pair of mittens. Still got them somewhere."

Edith smiled. "Well, if you like you can cast on for the other one. I brought the needles because I reckon to finish this foot before the day's out. Can you cast on?"

Dafydd took the wool and the second set of needles and tried to remember. After a minute or two Edith showed him, slowly, and he tried again with more success.

"That's good," she acknowledged. "Now pull that out, start with nearly two yards of wool and cast on two hundred and twenty stitches."

"Two hundred and twenty?" Dafydd stared.

"Only for this round. I make the cuffs extra loose by casting on double the amount of stitches and knitting two together for each stitch on the next round, but I still do the ribbing on needles a size smaller, or it goes baggy."

By Shrewsbury he had successfully cast on, reduced the number of stitches to a hundred and ten (having arrived initially at a hundred and thirteen, but Edith told him gravely that it was quite all right to cheat sometimes) and begun the four inches of knit one purl one rib.

Knitting stopped as they neared Birmingham International where their train terminated. They emerged into rather grey daylight. Dafydd checked the departure board, found the lift, and took Edith over to the correct platform; the train arrived, and once more he helped her in and found seats.

"People could do this for a living," she commented. "Escorting people on train journeys."

Dafydd shook his head. "I think they do . . . I don't mind doing it today, of course I don't, but it shouldn't be necessary. There used to be porters and people to help, people to ask. You can ring in advance and arrange for someone, but . . . it's the way things are. Most people can manage, so you have to make special arrangements if you can't. You can't rely on there being someone around to ask, and sometimes even if there is they don't know. And it's all extra palaver before you go anywhere, so I expect some people just don't bother. And of course that means that even more of the people who do travel *don't* need help."

"Esme says that. The staff are willing enough but sometimes they don't know where the ramp is or it's been moved, and she can't use certain buses because of the access, and some people with pushchairs get quite nasty when they're asked to move for a wheelchair. She says she'll be glad when they get her leg made up. She's been to be measured . . . Right, how far are you on with that rib? Not bad; you'll be done before I am at this rate. I shall have to speed up."

She took out the sock and set to. Dafydd got out his rail atlas.

"You'll catch up a bit round Rugby," he remarked. "I've not been over this way for years; I want to see what they've been doing to the junctions and the station."

They emerged at Euston and made their way outside. Edith produced a bright orange headscarf and tied it on for identification purposes, and they walked down towards the British Library.

"Is that him?" Dafydd asked, as a car drew up a little ahead of them.

Edith quickened her pace. "Yes, a blue Fiesta, and he said he'd put a penguin on the dashboard so we knew. Hallo, Jonathan."

The young man leaned across and opened the door. "Hop in quick: you must be Edith and Dafydd. Pleased to meet you. Your train must've been nearly on time, I've only gone round once."

Dafydd pulled the door further open for Edith and hurriedly got into the back seat. The car moved off as the doors closed. He leaned forward and guided Edith's seatbelt clip into the socket and dealt with his own. Jonathan was a brisk slim young man with oddly-styled hair, clad in jeans and a black sweatshirt with the name of a rock band on it, which seemed to be the uniform of his generation. No doubt he was wearing trainers too . . . But why shouldn't he? Dafydd advised himself sternly to keep an open mind, and sat back, wondering where they were going.

It proved to be quite an ordinary large house, built in the thirties or forties, in a suburban street of quite ordinary large houses. Jonathan drew up on the tarmac drive and went round to help Edith out. Dafydd extricated himself stiffly and noticed two parallel strips of metal, flush with the surface of the drive, running from under the garage doors and curving away into the back garden.

They were introduced to Jonathan's mother Kay, who was younger than Dafydd had expected, as brisk and slim as her son and also wearing jeans, trainers and a dark sweatshirt, only her face betraying that she was past middle age. She showed them where the cloakroom was, offered coffee, and led them out onto a patio which looked out over borders of well-kept shrubs and perennials. Dafydd noticed a finial poking up from behind rosebushes and stood up briefly. It was a small home signal, about three feet high. He sat down again quickly and received a conspiratorial smile from Kay, who was relaxing visibly. Dafydd dreaded to think how Esme had described them, but they were obviously approved.

He sipped at the rather strong coffee. Edith was admiring a scarlet camellia and asking Kay if they got much frost. Jonathan asked him if they'd had a good journey down and what it had been like in the storms they had seen on the television, and then when they had finished the coffee (or in Dafydd's case, as much as he was prepared to drink) Kay told Jon firmly to show Edith the garden, and sat watching as they walked slowly away.

"It's got to go." She picked up her empty cup, put it down again, and turned suddenly to him. "I really can't keep such a big place on; I might manage for a few years, but sooner or later . . . I'd rather choose to let it go now, than wait and be forced to. Kenneth and I discussed it when he was first diagnosed."

There was nothing Dafydd could say, so he said nothing.

"I'm sure people think I'm callous or making a big mistake, but I can't bear to be in this house without Kenneth. I spend as much time as I can outdoors. Jon and Petra are having most of what I won't be taking with me, but none of us could sensibly have the railway, or the piano, or the organ, or his aunt's dresser . . . Come and look."

Kay ushered him indoors. He noticed how neat the rooms were, as though no one lived in them already, and felt a pang of sympathy for the woman who was clearly making a great effort to appear calm and sensible. He wanted to say something comforting but dared not in case she broke down.

"One grand piano." She indicated it, and it took him a second or two to realise that it only looked wrong because he had never seen one with the lid closed before. "I play, but I'm going to a cottage—a real cottage, not one of those so-called cottages with two double garages—in Wiltshire, in the grounds of my school-friend's riding-school. She does a lot of work with disabled children. Ideally, I'd like to swap with someone who's got a decent old upright and needs something better."

Out of the pale blue-carpeted lounge, Kay closing the door carefully behind them, and into the dining-room; pale green with dark furniture including a huge solid dresser black with age and polish, on which a dozen or so Portmeirion plates were displayed.

"That's Aunt Phyllis Morgan's dresser. Petra's having the china. I'm keeping the Spode 'Lavender' we had when we were first married. There's enough left for what I'll need. Come upstairs."

Out of the dining-room, closing the door again, and up past the stair-lift with the seat folded back out of the way. Glimpses of closed doors. It was all as tidy and impersonal as a hotel. Into—to his initial horror—a bedroom which was obviously in use, tidy, but with a jersey folded over the back of a chair, and maroon flowery slippers on the floor by the double bed.

"This is the organ." She gestured at the short arm of the L-shaped room, filled with a large electronic organ in a wooden case. "Do you play? It was Kenneth's father's. I always meant to learn properly, but as someone told me once, an organ is just a kist of whistles. It's not a *musical* instrument, not like the piano. You can put feeling into playing a piano, but with the organ no matter how hard you thump or don't thump, it comes out the same . . . I offered it to a local church but they were going to get back to me yesterday and they haven't. Jon looked on eBay but they only fetch about fifty pounds, and while I'm not bothered about the money it means they aren't particularly wanted." She sighed. "It'd be a shame to break it up, but the children don't play and if I took anything it'd be the piano . . . Now then. If you look out of the window you'll see the railway. Most of it. The stock's in the garage . . . Oh, bother, I shall have to answer it, it might be the church. If it's Herring-dancer I shall give him a piece of my mind . . . Come down when you're ready."

Dafydd went to the window as instructed while Kay hurried downstairs to answer the telephone. There was a loop of track round the garden with a wooden signal box and at least three signals, a brick platform among grape hyacinths and tulips, and an enticing view of points and sidings behind a trellis. Ten and a half inch gauge? Seven? He made his way slowly downstairs, but could not help hearing part of the telephone conversation.

"—I've told you. Stop waving money at me, or I shall get very angry. And you can leave me alone because I've found it a good home and the people are here today for it! Good day!" She slammed the receiver back and turned, catching her breath and fumbling for a handkerchief.

"Sorry, I didn't mean to . . . " Dafydd began, producing a clean, folded handkerchief and offering it. "No offence?"

"Thanks." She accepted it and wiped her eyes. "It's that man—he wants to buy the railway. I said no, because Kenneth made it to run on open days at the care home where he used to work. And then the place closed, oh, back in the eighties, and it all came back here and we used to take it to fêtes and all his friends used to come and help. But Petra's family aren't interested—well, the youngest girl would love it but there'd be no one to run it for her, and Jon isn't settled yet and he says himself he doesn't love trains the way Dad did, and if I kept it, it would be because it was his, and I wouldn't run it and it'd just fall to bits like the house and the garden . . . " She wiped her eyes again, and took a deep breath. "Esme said there's a museum in your village and you could run it on open days, and you could take it to fêtes and raise money for charities."

Dafydd nodded. "Yes. I can see that'd be what you'd like it to do. You said there was stock . . . ?"

She smiled suddenly and pulled aside coats which were hanging on a rail under the stairs, displaying a small open truck lined with a cushion. A tabby cat blinked reproachfully at them and stretched.

"That's one of the trucks. Minnie won't mind it going: she's quite happy in a cardboard box, as long as it's raised out of the draught."

They went out through the kitchen this time, the only room he had seen which looked as though it was lived in. Collecting Edith and Jon, Kay went to the back door of the garage, turned off a complicated alarm system and invited them in.

"Oh my word, there's a lot of it," Edith said nervously.

Dafydd was trying to stop himself grinning from ear to ear like a schoolboy. Did modern schoolboys dream of this sort of thing? Probably not.

"Go and look, by all means." Kay pushed him gently towards the sheeted bulk of the largest item and switched on the lights. "He made that. It took him years. The boiler certificate's okay for another six months."

Jon helped him to lift the canvas off and he stared in admiration: it was a model 0-4-0, with a side-tanks and a tall chimney. The name-plate on the side read JULIET. He peered into the cab. Miniature controls gleamed faintly.

"It's beautiful," he said quietly. "And your husband made it . . . "

"Yes. From diagrams in magazines. But the trucks he designed himself: did all the drawings himself from real ones."

Jon was lifting more covers off: an electric loco you sat in like a bath, several long carriages which the passengers sat astride; more trucks. Beyond them was a workbench with a lathe and other pieces of equipment which Dafydd did not recognise.

Kay smiled gently at Edith. "Have you had lunch? I did some salad in case you hadn't, and there's ham, or would you prefer cheese?"

Chapter 4

DAFYDD SAT BACK in his seat opposite Edith and closed his eyes. Four or five little trucks. Carriages. Electric loco. And Juliet. And the track, the signals, the signal box. Apparently most of the infrastructure was designed to be moved easily from one place to another, but even so . . . They'd need a lorry. It was all right to put things in a van to take them three miles; twenty miles, even, but to take things like that over two hundred miles they'd have to be packed carefully.

Furniture removals company?

How much would that cost?

And Kay had said they could have the railway for nothing, if it was going to be used, but did that include the tools and spares, and if it went wrong who would mend it, and however much would it cost for the insurance to run it?

He opened his eyes and realised that a young man in a zipped black jacket was watching him. The man looked away quickly, but Dafydd was sure he seemed familiar from somewhere . . . He'd been at Euston, in the crowd waiting for the train to come in and the gates to open, standing close behind Edith: Dafydd had wondered if he was a pickpocket, but it seemed he was simply another traveller.

Edith was decreasing for the toe of her sock. Dafydd took the knitting out of his bag and got on with it.

"I don't see how we can have it," she said wistfully, drawing the yarn through the last six stitches and folding it away in her bag. "It's just too big. I was expecting a little Hornby one."

Dafydd offered the knitting back to her. He had almost finished the ribbing. "We could transport it and probably store it. It's the driving and maintenance and insurance we couldn't deal with. But we could start by having it on view in the museum and people would probably come out of the woodwork, the way they usually do. While you were going round the garden she took me to see some of the other problems: she's got a big Welsh dresser, and an organ, and a grand piano. I got the impression they'd been handed down her husband's family."

"Jon said she was his second wife," Edith confided. "The first died young; never had children. And he was allergic to animals."

"There was a cat called Minnie."

"Petra's idea. She's a rescue cat: they took Kay to choose her after the funeral. Company for her, Jon said. And so there'd be a reason for 'noises off ', which I think is very sensible: the things I've heard when Mike's been in hospital: creaks and bumps and all sorts . . . Esme says it's a pity I'm not deaf ! I know, but I know how she means it."

"Kay said she was moving to help a friend at a riding school. Disabled children."

They considered this for a while.

"He must have been a nice man," Edith remarked obliquely. "She's found something to do with herself, at least. But she's young enough to do it."

Dafydd remembered Mike and suspected that Edith was looking towards her own impending widowhood, wondering what she could do once she was alone. Come to that, how was he using his retirement? Not wholly selfishly, but sufficiently so to make him feel guilty . . .

For a long while neither spoke. People moved up and down the carriage; got in and out at stations. A girl with a ponytail sat beside Edith between Rugby and Coventry, and asked about the knitting. The young man in the zipped jacket was still there.

They changed trains successfully. The train filled up considerably at Wolverhampton and Dafydd stood until Shrewsbury, where the mother and children who had joined them got out. He was pleased to see that the young man was standing too. The train stopped in the bay at Shrewsbury, waiting to go down past the castle and out onto the Welsh Coast line. Edith produced a small, rather soft bar of chocolate and shared it with him, asking about the castle. Dafydd told her what he knew, adding that the football ground had for many years been close to the station; right next to the river, with a man in a coracle to rescue the ball if it was kicked out of the ground.

"They used to walk the fans down the side of the tracks to the ground sometimes." He was gazing out into the glare of the electric lights. "There were sidings all across there, and the bay platform under the castle used to be where the Vale of Rheidol locos were kept when they were on the way to be mended . . . And over there by the Abbey, that was the Abbey station, big goods yard there with a crane; and where the supermarket is was the old Potts line: the Staffordshire Potteries line that went up through Market Drayton. They used to keep an oil train in the siding there sometimes, years back."

"It's that Chinese man!" Edith murmured urgently. "Don't look!"

"I've seen him," Dafydd whispered. Sure enough, it was the young man in the zipped jacket, hurrying back along the platform and jumping in as though the train might go without him. Had he been to the cafe? The toilets, not fancying the one on the train? Trying to find a place to smoke?

"I think we're being followed!" Edith continued. "Or someone is . . . Do you think he's a policeman?" Then, suddenly worried: "*Is there someone with a rucksack?*"

Dafydd realised that she was afraid of a terrorist attack. On a tube train, perhaps, but surely not here . . . He needed to calm her down.

"Well, there's lots of people with rucksacks; I have one myself, though I didn't bring it. I expect he's just going to Aber to see his girlfriend."

"He doesn't look like a student," Edith protested. "Or a policeman."

"Don't stare at him!" Dafydd was Minnesota Williams, detective. "We'll keep him under observation, very carefully, and see where he gets out."

"Yes, we might be able to give the police all sorts of information." She smiled. "He doesn't look very dangerous; rather a quiet young man, really."

"He's probably a confidence trickster." Dafydd heard himself say it and added hastily: "Only because of looking so harmless. He might be a librarian. Or a curate."

"Oh, no. Not clever enough. He doesn't look very brainy . . . quite probably a shop assistant or a garage hand; a wizard with motors, but can't spell, like Marged's Gareth."

"I think we ought to stop there, before we assassinate his character altogether," Dafydd said sternly, "but I know just what you mean. Mam and I used to try to guess what people did as jobs while we waited for the bus in Wrexham. She used to come up with wonderful examples, like 'making the holes in buttons', or 'making spouts for teapots', and she kidded me that bricklayers worked in twos, one to put in the bricks that went one way round, and one to put in the bricks that went the other way round . . . We waited by a wall that was Flemish bond, you see."

He found a pencil and drew a sample in his notebook. "Flemish bond is alternate headers and stretchers, longways and endways, in the same row. English bond is a row of one, then a row of the other."

Edith studied the sketches. "Well, I never knew that."

They were half an hour late into Borth, and by then Edith was almost asleep on her feet. Dafydd saw her home, had a brief chat with Marged who had been keeping Mike company, and accepted a lift to his house though he could well have walked.

He thought he saw a familiar figure from the car window but the man hurried up the steps of the Victoria and vanished. Probably a coincidence . . .

He stood in his kitchen and looked at the bag of pasta and jar of sauce he had left out. Why was he so tired? He'd sat down almost all day. No, pasta could wait. He fed Rheidol and made himself cheese on toast and a pot of tea. The lentils were still soaking . . . Suddenly, he felt completely worn out.

He left his plate in the sink and took the second cup of tea up to bed with him. So much for healthy eating. At least Kay had given them salad.

He went for a cycle ride the next morning at five-thirty. It was a fine, windy morning with gulls and jackdaws being blown around the sky, and he found himself being pushed sideways as he rode. He did not go beyond the end of the golf course but made his way back at full speed, determined to get on with some gardening. After a hasty breakfast he collected a spade and went out into the back garden.

The lawn was too damp to cut but might dry off later, especially with the wind. As he hadn't even finished digging the vegetable plot the previous year, he would have to take it slowly . . . not double-digging, not yet; turn it all over and maybe come back to it for another go later, if the weather held . . .

He managed one row of neat, crumbling spadefuls, straightened his back consciously and went back indoors to take Rheidol's latest offering out to the front railings. As he opened the front door with a plastic bag in his hand he saw someone walking swiftly away up the street. The bag contained a doll's hairbrush: he fixed it to the railings with an elastic band and was pleased to notice that the bootee and one of the socks had gone. One harassed mother had told him that he should control his cat better, but most of the 'victims' acknowledged that cats would be cats, and at least the stolen items were offered for collection.

He went back to his digging and completed another row. Broad beans, perhaps? Not potatoes: he didn't have enough space. Carrots. Maybe another try at kohlrabi: they were funny things, like turnips. Maybe he could get a grow-bag and try tomatoes . . .

What he really wanted to do was mend the wall; the fence panels were flapping loose again. He kept shoring them up with oddments, but that was because he didn't like the fence: it ought to be a proper slate wall all the way along. Most of the rubble seemed to be lying around still, in the lane and in his garden.

He stretched once more and began to dig again. He needed mortar, which was why it hadn't happened: he could get sand from the beach in small quantities simply by sweeping it up off his kitchen floor and storing it, rather than throwing it out into the garden, but cement would have to be carried, from the railway station at least. Maybe Gareth could fetch some for him when he visited Marged.

He was startled when a voice said cheerfully: "Mae'n braf heddiw, nac ydy?"

"Dai!" He shoved the spade into the earth and went to greet the P.C.S.O. "Yes, it's lovely weather. How's things? Sut mae?"

"Oh, 'n iawn." Dai changed to English. "All okay, as far as I know. How did you get on in London? And why is someone following you?"

Dafydd's eyes narrowed. "So he is . . . I did wonder. You'd better come in and I'll explain what I know."

"Are you sure she said 'Herring-dancer?' " Dai grinned in disbelief. "Yes, I can see you might remember the name. Wonder what she meant? And you think this man who's following you is Herring-dancer?"

"Is, or works for him. I got the impression that the man had been offering more and more money for the railway, and the young man on the train didn't look . . . Well, he didn't look rich, though I must say I don't know what a rich man that age does look like." He hesitated. "I've met people in my time; properly important people and also people who thought themselves important, people my grandmother would have called 'crachach'. This Herring-dancer man; to me he seems to be one of the latter."

Dai drank his tea thoughtfully. There was a tiny clink as he put the cup back in the saucer. "Your Kay; did she seem afraid when she answered the telephone? Do you think she might be in danger from him?"

"Oh, not afraid. She was angry; she said he should leave her alone because it was too late; we were having it."

"Ah. So that's why he was following you; because she'd told him she was giving the railway to you. He wanted to know who you are and where you live, and now he does know. The young man who was asking questions in the Victoria last night left this morning, probably going back to London: I asked at the station. How are you going to bring the railway back here?"

Dafydd finished his tea. He smiled. "I think that might be a job for the people who dealt with the Dreaded Batter Pudding Hurler."

Dai grinned. "Team Pudding, in other words?"

Dafydd nodded. "Tîm Pwdin."

Chapter 5

LATER THAT DAY Dafydd decided to go into Aberystwyth. He turned off the pan of lentils which should have been more than ready but still felt a bit solid, caught the 13.06 train, and went to a charity shop in Terrace Road, looked through boxes, and in the end asked the assistant if she had any knitting patterns. She produced three: none was suitable. He bought a cone of dark green four-ply yarn which looked about right, thanked her and went towards the next shop.

There were cyclists in Aberystwyth. There always had been, but now that he was cycling again he noticed them: people like himself with baskets full of shopping, students in jeans and sweatshirts and a surprising number of young middle-aged people, mostly male, many seal-slick in Lycra with aerodynamic helmets. He was too old for that. Too old, too flabby. You couldn't wear Lycra, at least not in public, unless you were slim and fit: well, obviously you could, but it wasn't fair on people: they didn't need such an aesthetically unpleasing sight added to all the other horrors of modern life. However, he did venture into a cycle shop, thinking that a helmet at least might be worth having, but everything seemed to be ridiculously expensive and he left quickly.

After failing to find any sock patterns in the next two charity shops he was directed to Aberdashery, where the assistant was very helpful: there was a selection of sock patterns, including one which came free if you bought a ball of some rather vibrant wool. Dafydd scrutinised this carefully, found that it offered four different styles of sock, one of which was completely plain, and bought it, along with a ball of wool in the least exotic combination of colours available (shades of green and yellow). He also bought a set of five double-ended needles made from bamboo, in the correct size for the pattern, and went back to the charity shops in search of more double-ended needles in case he broke or lost any. Having acquired a total of eleven in different sizes and lengths and some more four-ply wool including a bag of odd part-balls for 50p, he went back to the station and sat in the cafe working out how the heel was done on the plain sock; it seemed to be different not only from his mother's method but also from Edith's.

That evening he solemnly knitted a tension square, saw the time and did something hastily with the beetroot and lentils, and after Bible study came home and, using the dark green wool, cast on for a sock.

They managed to collect all the members of Tîm Pwdin, including the students Donald and Sandy, for a meeting on Thursday evening at Dai's house on Cliff Road. Although he had made an effort to tidy up there were still papers piled on the floor and on the windowsills. He brought in a tray of tea for them and Llinos followed with a plate of biscuits.

They discussed the size and probable weight of the railway, the circumstances in which it had been offered to the village and whether the museum would want it. Dafydd had been to see the trustees and received a conditional agreement, providing that they could find someone to drive the locomotives and that they could get sponsorship, at least initially, for the insurance.

"We need to be able to get it from London without paying too much," Siân reminded them.

"And without Herring-dancer realising, and hijacking it *en route*," Donald added.

"Napoleon's piano!" Llinos grinned. 'It's another Goon show. The Harry Secombe character agrees to help move a piano from one room to another, and then he finds out that it's Napoleon's piano, and one of the rooms is in the Louvre . . . "

"I thought it was a railway, not a piano," Marged grumbled.

"There is a piano!" Dafydd said abruptly. "Kay—I do wish we'd asked her surname—also wants to swap her grand piano for an upright. I got the impression that any upright piano would do, if it could be tuned, so if we can find a local piano-owner who wants to do a swap the other way, we have a van going from Borth or wherever to London and back, quite legitimately, without the railway being involved."

"Wouldn't Herring-dancer guess?" Miss Smith frowned.

"Maybe not, if the piano van didn't come from Borth."

"You'd need a proper piano-moving company. They specialise. I can ask who the Arts Centre in Aber use." Sandy was making notes. "How about local schools? Or is it too nice a piano for risking in a school?"

Dafydd grimaced. "It looked very genteel to me. Nicely polished. And we also need a piano-removals company who would be happy to take a railway as well."

Llinos went out and put the kettle on for another pot of tea. She came back and stood in the doorway. "I'm sure if we ask around, we'll find someone who'd like a grand piano."

"Yes, but what about her mother?" Marged murmured.

"Well, we can work on that," Miss Smith said briskly. "We need to make sure we have somewhere to keep the railway when it gets here, before it arrives in a rainstorm at five p.m. and they want to unload it and go home. What storage is there at the museum?"

"Not much that's suitable," Dafydd admitted. "There's a ground-floor store, but it opens onto the yard and the door's just padlocked through a staple. Not secure enough to keep Herring-dancer out."

"So where can we keep it? Is there anyone on the Carnival Committee who has a barn?"

"This is going to sound silly," said Edith, speaking for the first time in twenty minutes, "but you said, Dafydd, that

Kay had one of the trucks under her stairs, just loose on the floor under the coat-rack with a cat asleep in it. Could we keep—well, not all of it, obviously, but some of it—in our houses? At least until the museum decides what to do with it. He couldn't burgle all of us."

The idea appealed to some people; Siân said she'd rather like one of the little trucks herself, and Dafydd felt similarly, but Dai pointed out that Juliet would be the worst to find space for, as it was so heavy, and the removals people probably wouldn't want to drop individual items at a dozen different houses. They discussed it for another half-hour without coming to any useful conclusion, agreed to meet in a week's time or when someone had any news, and departed.

"When d'you think they'll get married?" Marged asked cheerfully. She was giving Siân, Dafydd and Edith a lift. Miss Smith and the students had opted to walk, and Llinos had stayed to wash up with Dai, politely refusing all offers of help.

Dafydd and Siân exchanged grins. Siân said, with a straight face: "Are you hoping they'll ask you to be a bridesmaid?"

Dafydd's knitting progressed steadily, as did the digging and raking of the vegetable patch. He found a box of seed packets which were mostly at least a year out of date and started some off in plastic trays in the spare room, well away from inquisitive paws. He managed to cycle at least once a day, even on Sunday, though one morning a sudden shower caught him just as he turned for home and he ended up soaked to the skin. Sandy provided a list of removals firms, Marged's husband Robert found someone with an empty lock-up garage they were willing to lend, and Miss Smith found someone who, it seemed, would be overjoyed to receive a grand piano in exchange for an upright.

It was the first time the former lecturer had visited Dafydd and she watched with barely concealed incredulity as he brought in a tea tray: tray-cloth, cups and saucers, teapot, tea-strainer, milk jug.

"She teaches, and her house is listed as an exam venue as well. She asked what make it was, and a lot of other questions which I've passed on to Edith to ask Esme to ask Jonathan . . . Oh, isn't it complicated! I really ought to get Esme's email address. Anyhow, Mrs. Powell lives in one of the farms at the back of Rhydyfelin; it's up a narrow lane with grass growing down the middle. One of my readers has a daughter who goes there for lessons. And as long as the grand arrives intact and isn't worse than her existing piano, she'll be only too pleased."

Dafydd passed her a cup of tea. "That's good. But how long will it take to travel with it? At least a day each way, I'd think, possibly more. Is there a day when she doesn't have pupils? Apart from Sunday, when the removals people wouldn't be working anyway?"

"I think you'll find that they do work Sundays, nowadays." Miss Smith repressed a smile. "But moreover, if we do manage to find a van and they can fit through her lane—it can't be as narrow as it looks, her husband takes a tractor through it regularly—they have an outbuilding where the removals people could put the railway until we can fetch it. And that way Herring-dancer wouldn't see it arrive, not if it came into Borth one piece at a time."

"You'd need to warn the piano teacher about him, in case they followed the removals van there and broke in overnight."

"It's a farm; they have dogs. They'd know if there were people about."

"H'm. We don't know how ruthless this man might be if he thought it was his only chance. If he sends a man to follow us all the way to Borth from London, and to stay overnight . . ."

They considered this.

"We could have been going back to Scotland." Dafydd was still coming to terms with the situation. "To anywhere. He sent someone to follow us. Do you know how much it costs, buying tickets on the day if you're full-fare? If you buy them on the train? Herring-dancer has money to throw around. If he's really determined to have the railway, he might do anything. And if he's based in London, presumably it's easier to find people there to do things than it is out here. I wish Edith and Kay weren't mixed up in this . . ."

There was a long silence. Rheidol snored on the green rug by the hearth.

"Why do you suppose he's called Herring-dancer, anyway?" Miss Smith put her empty cup back on the saucer. "Yes, please."

Dafydd poured them each another cup. "I think it's an anagram," he suggested, "but I'm not sure. I've got

'Richard' and 'Darren' out of it, but the surnames are a bit strange: Greenn, with two Ns, and Chinger."

"Richard N. Green . . ." Miss Smith considered this. "Possibly. The other piece of news is that according to Brenda at the wholefood shop in Aber there's going to be a big sponsored walk organised by the churches and the other organisations in the town, in aid of the Syrian refugees. And a sponsored cycle ride, a sponsored toddle, presumably for small children, a baking competition and a craft competition. Well, I wondered if you could suggest that at your chapel. I've spoken to Kim, the vicar's daughter, and she said it sounded like a good idea and she'd ask her father: do you think your minister would get involved?"

"Well, we've just had a sermon about refugees." Dafydd frowned. "Years ago, when Mam was alive, there was a flower festival at the church in Minera. And they wanted the Women's Meeting from our chapel to do an arrangement, which meant Mam doing it: and she said no, she didn't have the patience for fiddling about, but if they wanted she'd run a craft display for them. Get people to bring things they'd made and pay a pound or two for the privilege. And she made a fruit cake—a big one, like a Christmas cake—to be a prize for the item the visitors liked best, and put a book out so visitors could write comments, and they put boards over some of the pews and displayed it all nicely. Well, they had all sorts entered. Model ships, patchwork bedspreads, knitted tea cosies, some pottery, a rug, someone's embroidered fire-screen, paintings . . . "

"What won?"

"A little girl's nightie, all white cotton embroidered in white with holes in. Flowers and such. And the lady who made it was bedridden and that was how she passed her days, but no one knew except the family until that craft display . . ." He nodded slowly, remembering. "Mam took a rag rug she was making and sat guarding the exhibits, in case anyone tried to walk off with something!"

"Well, that's a good idea. We ought to have it during a school holiday when there are visitors here, but it's too late for Easter. It'll have to be Whitsun. And an exhibition gets away from the 'sponsored' element; I know most people with schoolchildren are at their wits' end for sponsors, because you can't just keep asking your relatives for money. Anyway, the whole point used to be that you sponsored so much per lap or per mile, and that encouraged the children to make an effort, but now most people just hand over an amount 'for the lot', so there's no incentive to do more than the bare minimum." She grinned. "I'm sure we could get plenty of people involved, simply because they'll be so grateful they don't have to sponsor anyone!"

In order to suggest the idea to the Minister before Bible study, on Tuesday afternoon Dafydd went up to see him at home, where he found him mowing the lawn.

"Yes, lovely weather. Good thing, too: the birds are starting to build and the cowl blew off the chimney in the winter; grate full of sticks this morning and I suppose there'll be more lodged in the chimney, so I don't want to light the fire 'til I know it's clear . . . " He sighed. "Mind if

I finish this? Only another couple of yards to go, then we can go in and talk."

Dafydd perched on the wall and waited. "Anything I can do?"

"You can trim the edge, if you like."

Nothing loth, Dafydd took the long-handled shears and had a go.

"I'm sure there's a sermon to be found in dandelions," the Minister said wryly, having taken the mower away and come back with a kneeling mat and a trowel. "I dug over two hundred roots out last year, but it only seems to have encouraged them. Do you want to leave that now? I'll put the kettle on."

They sat in the man's neat beige living-room. The carpet was wearing thin by the sofa where generations of visiting feet had scuffed.

"It's about refugees." Dafydd accepted a cup of tea. "Miss Smith came round and told me that Aber are doing all sorts of events to raise money, and she says why shouldn't Borth? She's spoken to Kim, and asked me to speak to you. Now, I know we can't do anything big, but I did wonder about a craft competition—well, an exhibition, all stuff made by amateurs locally, with a book for visitors to comment, and a prize—a cake or something—for the item they liked best. Miss Smith said it might be best not to try doing a sponsored event."

"Yes, I think she's quite right. A craft competition? You mean, like a sale of work?"

Dafydd explained about the Minera flower festival, and that he hadn't considered selling the exhibits. "It might be an idea, though. Have some things for sale, in a separate place so there're no mistakes."

The Minister considered. "My sister took me round a church in Staffordshire a few years ago where they were doing something similar with quilts. They had—oh, two dozen, easily, displayed all round the church, hanging up on poles between the pillars, and a moneybox next to each one for donations. The idea was that you donated whatever you liked to your favourite quilt and the winner was the one which raised the most money. The Davieses' niece quilts, doesn't she?"

That was Esme; Dafydd nodded.

"Quilting seems to be in at the moment; there's the museum at Lampeter and another at Llanidloes, and then there's the 'Quilts in the garden' competition at Cae Hir. We don't want to steal their ideas, but ours will probably be very different . . . especially if Marged gets involved!" The Minister grinned suddenly. "You know, I can just see Marged arranging a fashion parade of people wearing tea cosies."

Dafydd grinned back. "That might be an idea. They'd be quick to knit, at least!"

"Well, thank you for letting me know. I'll mention it on Sunday, and I'm sure people will come up with more suggestions. I've been meaning to speak to you for a while, myself. How do you feel about running a prayer meeting?"

Dafydd opened his mouth, and closed it again. After a few seconds he said: "I'm not—I mean, I don't, not often enough by myself; I don't even read the Scriptures every night, and when I do it's not much, unless I can't sleep."

"I didn't say, are you perfect enough to run a prayer meeting? I said, will you be the person with the key who comes in first and sits there and prays with whoever comes—if anyone does, but you'll probably get Siân at least—and locks up afterwards? I've known for a few months that this chapel needs something of the sort, but I'm not the one to run it. If nothing else, because I would very much appreciate it if people prayed for *me*, what with taking on Furnace as well."

Silence.

"Dafydd, when you walk on the beach in the mornings and you look at the wildlife, how do you feel?"

He frowned. "Content . . . I think I know what you're getting at. Honoured. Honoured to be allowed to be there, to enjoy it. Even when it's raining, sometimes. But worshipping Nature is wrong . . . "

"You aren't, though, are you? You're worshipping the Creator. And you know exactly who that Creator is, and why it all happened as it has—at least, as much as any mortal can know. Prayer doesn't have to be words. Well, not formal words. Words help . . . a heartfelt 'Wow!' means more to the Creator than any amount of saying Amen to someone else's 'Thank-you-for-the-world-around-us' in Chapel with your mind on something else. When I was a young man training for the Ministry, I'd been writing an essay on some very complex and convoluted point of doctrine, to the point that I wasn't sure what I thought about anything any more. I remember distinctly; it was about this time of year and I'd been writing it all night. And I stood up and realised it was getting light outside, and opened the curtains . . . and then I slipped out of the house, with the sun coming up and dew on the grass and birds singing, and I stood on the lawn just listening, letting it happen all round me. And I knew God was in charge, and God was just and merciful and far too big for anyone to describe adequately . . . and He liked me. I may even have danced a little: does that shock you? It would shock some of them."

He stood up, reached for a book, found the page. "Read that."

Dafydd took the book, a collected edition of W.B. Yeats' poetry, and after a brief debate with himself as to how he should pronounce 'Cruachan', read it aloud.

There was a long silence. The Minister continued.

"Yes, I know Yeats was not a Baptist, but I like the concept of all Creation 'Acclaiming, proclaiming, declaiming Him' . . . When my sister's children were quite young I was staying with the family and there was a thunderstorm. Now, Mother always used to cover the mirrors and hide under the stairs, in the cwtsh. But Sally and Michael and I took the children up to a bedroom and watched the lightning with them, and we sang Francis of Assisi's *The Canticle of the Sun*: 'Let all things their Creator bless' . . . "

"Thank you," Dafydd said, very quietly. "And thank you for asking me to run the prayer meeting. I'll be pleased to."

Chapter 6

IF THERE WAS going to be a sponsored cycle in Aberystwyth, there was no harm finding out about it. Dafydd went down to the Community Hall on Wednesday morning and found that there was a batch of sponsor forms and details among the racks of leaflets. As he had suspected it was going to be a long ride: ten miles, starting on the Prom and ending at the football ground. There were a few hills on the route. Well, if necessary he could get off and walk. He might as well try to get into training; it wasn't a race, but he'd be happy just to finish, and he could put a donation in instead of getting sponsors. Why not? It was something to work towards, and he'd been managing a bit more distance over the last few mornings; he'd got right up past the boatyard to the railway crossing. He ought to be able to manage ten miles by the date of the event . . .

On his way home he saw Dai and flagged him down, told him about Miss Smith's idea and mentioned shyly that he'd been asked to run a prayer group.

"If I'm free I'll come," Dai said promptly. "Or would you rather I didn't, in case it puts people off?"

Dafydd shrugged. "I don't suppose it'll make much difference—not meaning to be rude, but I have no idea who'll turn up. It might be just me and Siân . . . and if it is we could hold it at hers, at least in winter, to save her the walk."

"You'll get who you're meant to get," Dai said sagely. "Quantity isn't necessarily a good thing. Not with something like this. Any more ideas about transport for the railway?"

"Looks as though it might have to be a horsebox. Specialist piano-movers charge the earth. Gareth says his mate'll drive it for us and he'll take the day off to help. He says if you put bales of hay round the upright it should be okay, and the grand shouldn't fall over, it might just roll about a bit." Dafydd grimaced. "We can wrap them in blankets and so on before the hay goes in, it's just moving the weight. And how we fit the railway in round the grand I can't imagine; at least the rails and so on should be light enough to go on top of things, but how we get Juliet in I don't know. Though they must have managed to move it, to get it to fêtes. Wish I'd asked her for details like that, but Miss Smith has Esme's email address now, which helps."

"Remember the congestion charge if you're going into central London. Where does she live, exactly? Ah, that shouldn't be a problem, then. Have to warn Gareth and his mate to stay well clear of the centre: they might not have thought of it . . . ”

With the challenge of cycling ten miles in front of him, Dafydd was even more determined to eat properly. He’d collected a ‘Healthy Heart’ leaflet at the Community Hall which went on about oily fish and lots of fruit and vegetables, so he went into the supermarket and bought tomatoes, pilchards, grapes, bananas and a lettuce. The tomatoes were reduced for quick sale, being rather soft, so he added a couple of green peppers to his basket and was pleased that he kept a cloth bag in his pocket for impulse purchases.

He took this collection home and tried to work out how to use it. Of course, he should have gone out with a meal plan and bought stuff accordingly, but it shouldn’t be impossible.

Grapes and bananas were easy: you just ate them. He nipped off a couple of grapes, rinsed them, and munched. Pilchards would go in a salad or in the bright orange variant on shepherd’s pie which he had invented in his first week of cooking for himself, many years ago. Tomatoes and peppers would make ratatouille, which he liked. They’d not had an aubergine in the supermarket; for exotica like that he’d have to go to Aber or Mach; somewhere big.

Aberystwyth, then. He should have thought of getting vegetables last time he’d been there. He went up and collected his rucksack and a few more cloth bags. There was a train in forty minutes, and he could work out a few sensible meals on the station.

He went into the Aberystwyth branch of Lidl, hoping for at least an aubergine and rollmops. He collected a good selection of vegetables, and found that the week's special offers were cycling equipment. Why not? He rooted through the piles of packages, picking out things in his size: a sensible red zipped jacket, padded black leggings and a black vest top, all with reflective trims of various thicknesses. Gloves, a suspiciously cheap pair of black trainers and a red and white helmet were added to his basket, and he hesitated before making his way to the tills. How much would all that come to? Less than the sheds he'd seen, but did he really need any of it?

He did need a helmet. Gloves would be useful because his woollen ones just got wet and slippery when it rained, and leggings because cycling in sodden cotton trousers was horrible, though whether he'd ever dare wear them in daylight was another matter . . . Also, because he always went out at dusk or dawn, anything with reflective stripes was going to give him that much more chance of being seen. It was going to be expensive, but if he was going to get the stuff at all, he'd never see it cheaper anywhere else unless he was very fortunate in a charity shop.

Stop dithering and make a decision!

He took a deep breath and went towards the checkouts.

He packed his rucksack with carrots, celery, two aubergines and the helmet, picked up two cloth bags with the rest of the things in and went out onto the pavement, where he paused to adjust a strap on the rucksack which had twisted.

It still felt like a dreadful extravagance. And he'd wasted money on knitting-wool too: what on earth had got into him? He'd have to be vegetarian until he felt he'd paid for everything.

He sighed and turned abruptly towards the station, cannoning into a woman who had just come out of the same shop. They both staggered, regaining their balance, and to his horror one of her bags split and cans rolled across the pavement.

Apologising, he grovelled to collect them, realised the plastic bag was too far gone to be of any further use and offered one of his own spare bags. The woman had dumped her shopping in a heap and was kneeling on the pavement stuffing tins into her coat pockets. She protested that she'd be okay, but it was clear that her other bags would not cope with any more weight.

"It's fine; I have others." He pressed the hessian bag into her hand and began to collect tins of dog food. "Have you got far to go?"

She lived in Penparcau, and said she'd be all right once she was on the bus. No, not to worry . . .

"That's good. Sorry to have walked into you. I wasn't looking where I was going." He noticed with alarm that the mishap seemed to have been the last straw for her and she was close to tears. "What sort of dog have you got?"

"Cats. My two boys and Shaun's kitten, an' little Sky."

"Sky?" He wondered how you spelt it, like the shade of blue or the island, retrieved the last can (tomatoes), and thought that if she'd let him he might see her to the bus stop. Some of the other bags looked close to disintegrating.

"She's a lovely cat, pretty little tortie. We'd love to keep her but the others don't get on with her at all, an' I don't know what to do; you see we had her while they went to a wedding and then they came back and never fetched her, and they won't have 'er back, and I don't wanna put 'er in a cats' home, she's a sweet little girl, but she won't eat . . . "

"I might be able to have her," Dafydd found himself saying.

The woman stared, scrutinising his face closely. She nodded. "You look kind. D'you mean it?"

"I've got a cat. She might not get on with him, either, but he's pretty good with other cats. Usually."

In the end he went with her on the bus and met the family. Shaun was a wiry, scruffy schoolboy and his kitten was a half-grown male tabby, while Becky's 'boys' were black tomcats. Becky opened tins, tipped dog food into a clean litter tray and put it down on the kitchen tiles. Three cats instantly started to gobble. Becky climbed onto a chair, crooning soothingly, grabbed Sky from the top of one of the kitchen cupboards and handed her down to Shaun who plonked her by the food dish. She snatched a mouthful as the others began to hiss at her and leapt back to the worktop, onto the fridge and back onto the cupboard.

"Isn't she pretty?" Becky demanded, grabbing her again and cuddling her.

Dafydd had to agree. She was a neat, painfully thin animal with short blotched tortoiseshell fur and a white shirtfront and paws.

"I live in Borth," he told them. "If you'd like me to have her, I'll see if she can cope with Rheidol, my cat."

"Oh, that's so kind of you." Becky was stroking the brown and yellow head, very gently. "Shaun, get her box—an' there's her litter tray too . . . "

He was well-laden when he caught the bus: his own shopping, Sky in her box (which he had insisted on strapping with parcel tape, as the fastening looked likely to jolt open) and the hastily-emptied litter tray in a bin bag. He got off the bus, hurried to catch the train and found a seat. Sky mewed piteously on his lap and people showed interest.

"I'm looking after her for someone," he explained. "Yes, tortoiseshell."

A white paw appeared in a gap, then a brown ear and a yellow eye. He spoke soothingly in Welsh, wondering if she had ever heard that language before. What did she eat? Presumably anything she could snatch before she was attacked. He'd have to keep her in . . . Where? Have to be the spare bedroom. Have to get her to a vet; Becky hadn't known whether she'd had any inoculations, and he suspected that her own cats weren't immunised. They certainly hadn't been neutered. However did she cope with three male cats in a tiny council house, especially as she kept them in because the neighbours didn't like cats?

The train slowed for the crossing, then again for the station, and stopped. Dafydd gathered his personal belongings as instructed, and got out, planning. Good thing he had litter for Rheidol. He could find a couple of saucers for food and water. Presumably she'd sleep anywhere she felt safe; he'd find an old jersey or something. Have to leave her in the box while he prepared her room . . .

"Dyna di, fach. Here you are, little one. Dy gartre newydd. Your new home." He snipped the parcel tape, opened the box, and stood back.

Sky stepped out onto the lino, stretching, ears and whiskers quivering; sniffing at the chair, the pile of boxes, the suitcase. She found the apple-box he'd folded an old pullover into, got into it, sniffed around, paddled with her paws a few times, stepped out.

He opened a pouch of cat food and tipped it onto a saucer, put it down and watched with satisfaction as she ate, cautiously at first, then nose-down in the saucer gobbling until not a speck remained. She looked up hopefully.

"H'm." He opened a second pouch, which was devoured almost before it was on the saucer. Yellow eyes looked up at him and the string-thin tail waved.

"Not yet, little one. Digest that lot first."

The second saucer contained water. The litter tray was on a couple of newspapers up a corner. The window was firmly closed.

He slipped out and left her to it.

Rheidol was anxious to go upstairs and couldn't understand why Dafydd shut him in the kitchen. After half an hour Dafydd went back up. Sky was on the windowsill but jumped down and came to him, rolling over in front of his feet. She was so thin . . . He put down another pouch of food and left her eating.

In all, she ate seven pouches of food before curling up in the box to sleep. He tiptoed out of the room, smiling. There was no doubt at all in his mind that he'd done the right thing in bringing her home.

He went to see Miss Smith the next day, as soon as her curtains opened (which was, that day, at ten-twenty).

" . . . So I got an appointment with the vet this morning, took a taxi out there, and he said they can't give her any injections 'til she's had the kittens!"

"What?!"

"Exactly! And I said, surely not, she looks like a coat-hanger, poor little thing, and he said feed her well and keep her in, give her a big box with towels or papers in for a nest, and wait." He hesitated. "He said they might not live, depending on how starved she's been. But I don't think Becky'd had her long, or her stomach would have shrunk and she couldn't have eaten so much yesterday. Becky did her best, but there just wasn't the space in her house."

"Poor little thing." Miss Smith sighed. "I won't visit because of Konrad; she'll already be aware that Rheidol's about, even if they don't meet, and it'll be more stress for her. Dafydd? You're mad. Absolutely crazy. But I'm glad you are."

Chapter 7

MOST OF DAFYDD'S spare time was now spent up in the spare room, sitting on a kitchen chair knitting, working out menus or doing the crossword, talking to Sky while she padded around or washed herself or simply lay beside him in her box purring, often with one little white paw extended. On Friday afternoon he reached down and held the paw gently, to see what she would do; to his surprise she closed her eyes and purred more loudly, as though she enjoyed it. She was eating well, though still seemed far too thin to be expecting kittens.

In an attempt to be fair to Rheidol Dafydd tried to give him extra attention, while still keeping the two cats apart. On Friday night Rheidol slipped past him and curled up very firmly on Dafydd's bed. Dafydd gave in and let him stay there, with the bedroom door closed, but forgot about

Sky when Rheidol scratched at the door during the night, wanting to go out, and simply opened the door. Rheidol went straight to the spare bedroom door and sniffed inquisitively, but trotted off down the stairs and went out within a few seconds and Dafydd went back to sleep.

On Saturday morning he woke at five, early enough to wear the leggings. He was very self-conscious about them, but they were so much more comfortable than ordinary trousers that he wore them whenever he cycled at a time when few people were about. By now he had begun to cycle around the village during the day too, taking the rucksack if he was on a shopping expedition and wearing normal clothes, and so far no one seemed to have noticed, though admittedly he had not seen Marged.

As the bicycle bumped across the railway crossing by the boatyard he wondered when they would be able to collect the model railway from London. So many pieces of the jigsaw had been fitted into place already: apparently they were simply waiting for Gareth's mate to be able to use the horsebox on a Monday, the day Mrs. Powell had the least pupils. She had magnanimously agreed to offer to teach in her pupils' own houses during Monday and Tuesday, if they didn't want to rearrange the lessons . . .

Surely that was a swallow, swooping across the road ahead of him? He'd already seen house martins, a few days ago. He began to sing quietly: "Let all things their Creator bless . . ."

When he got back, to his surprise and consternation Miss Smith came round the corner as he was putting the bicycle back into the shed.

"You are taking this seriously, aren't you!" was all the comment she made about his appearance, for which he was grateful. Apparently Gareth had rung her at nine-thirty on Friday night with the news that if they could get everything organised in time his mate was free to drive the horsebox for them on Bank Holiday Monday and the following Tuesday if they needed it. "I thought I'd better tell you as soon as possible, because of it being Easter Day on Sunday. I'll ring Mrs. Powell and tell her, and I've emailed Esme and Dai, but can you tell Donald and Sandy, and Siân? Oh, and Edith; apparently they're all determined to be in on it if at all possible, so it looks as though we'll have a car going to London as well as the horsebox."

"Whose car?" Dafydd asked, leading the way up the path and wondering if he should offer her breakfast; he was going to have some himself, whether she did or not, because he was ravenous after the long ride.

"Llinos', we think. Dai will probably have to work, but Kay wants you—and Edith if she'd like—to come back and help oversee them loading the stuff, and I do see that we can't just send Gareth and Glyn; they could be absolutely anyone, though of course they'll have Napoleon Powell's piano."

"Tea? Toast? Bacon?"

Miss Smith was a vegetarian, but she accepted the offer of toast and tea and said don't be silly, of course she didn't mind if he said grace, or ate bacon as long as he didn't try to make her have any, and would he be all right to go to London because of Sky and Rheidol; she was leaving Konrad extra biscuits.

Dafydd made wholemeal toast, poured the tea and put the bacon to grill, and said that he didn't see why not, his cats both ate dry food as well as the pouches, he'd give Sky extra water too and draw the curtains part-way across in her room to keep some warmth in, in case he was back very late, and what were they going to pay Glyn for use of the horsebox?

"I think part of the attraction is the possibility of meeting Herring-dancer," Miss Smith said wryly. "Glyn thinks he could deal with anyone who tried to hijack the vehicle, though what condition the piano would be in afterwards is another matter . . . and Gareth says they'd like a go on the railway when it's set up."

"Fair enough. Have we found a driver yet?"

"Donald's emailed the Seven and a Quarter Inch Gauge Society, or whatever it's called, and asked for a list of members within range; they said they'd pass his message on and it was up to individual members to contact him, rather than *vice versa.* Don't know if he's had any replies yet."

Dafydd turned the bacon over and remembered that the new prayer meeting was to start on Tuesday evening at seven-thirty. The Minister had solemnly issued him with a key to the chapel after Wednesday's Bible study. He hoped he would be back in time.

In the end Edith decided that she'd better not go to London because her husband was reacting badly to a new sort of medication. Donald had gone home for the Easter weekend and taken Sandy with him, Dai had to work as he had expected, and Llinos was unhappy about the thought of such a long journey with no one else insured to share the driving, so they told Kay that Dafydd, Miss Smith, Gareth and Glyn would be coming. There were three seats in the front of the horsebox for two passengers and a driver. This meant that someone would have to travel in the back, which was apparently legal because there was a built-in passage between the two and a seatbelt for whoever it was. Dafydd had the feeling that he'd end up in the back, and wondered if he should go by rail, but realised that would mean someone having to collect him from a tube station. Presumably there would be enough light in the back to knit by.

He sat considering the possibilities, absently stroking Sky's head. At least she didn't look as though there were kittens due in the very immediate future, but he hoped she wouldn't feel she'd been abandoned when she was left alone for so long. If only you could explain things to animals . . .

Easter Day was a very welcome break from planning and trying to second-guess Herring-dancer. Dafydd rode to Chapel for the first time, locking his bicycle securely to the railings. They sang joyful hymns and celebrated the Lord's Supper, there were chocolate biscuits with the tea or coffee afterwards, and the flower arrangements which had adorned the windowsills were gathered up to be distributed among elderly people who hadn't managed to attend. Dafydd asked if there would be one to spare for Edith and

Mike although they weren't chapel-goers, and delivered it himself, in a carrier bag slung from his handlebars.

Lunch was salad and a piece of cold chicken which he'd cooked on Saturday, with a small plateful of diced meat for each cat; Sky rolled over in ecstasy at his feet when he took it upstairs to her, and gobbled it in seconds. Rheidol's vanished almost as fast.

He went for a sedate walk after the meal, out along the shore beyond the last houses, and sat among the sand dunes enjoying the sounds of it all: the waves on the beach, the gulls and oystercatchers, the wind in the marram grass and the shouts of children wrestling with a kite in the distance. The day of the Resurrection had been the modern equivalent of Monday, with everyday life going on as normal all round the disciples. How had they felt, realising that the man cooking fish on the beach was the man they had seen die only a few days earlier . . . ?

The Minister had explained that the Romans counted days and hours differently, including any part of a day as though it was the whole day, while to the Jews days began and ended at sunset. Jesus rose on the third day, not seventy-six modern hours after His death, but after about nine modern hours of Friday, all twenty-four hours of Saturday and the first few hours of Sunday, until possibly only a split second after sunrise. That was an aspect that Dafydd had seldom considered; as far as he was concerned, no matter how long you were dead it was still a miracle if you came back to life.

We don't understand the sheer unbelievability of it, Dafydd thought soberly. I grew up knowing that Jesus died and rose again on the third day, and it was like knowing that the King was George the Sixth and the last real Prince of Wales, Llywelyn Ein Llyw Olaf, was killed in 1282. I never, ever realised that it was something really illogically incredible that had happened, something that was more important to me than anything else I could ever learn; not until I was about thirty or forty and actually thought about it.

Death can't hold onto people any more, not for ever. They'll all escape one day: when God says it's the right time they'll all come back to life. Jesus had to die because that was part of the solution to the problem, and He had to stop being dead because that was the rest of the solution . . .

A blue butterfly caught his eye as it fluttered past and he watched it until it vanished beyond the next dune. Imagine being a caterpillar, then having to turn into a chrysalis without knowing what would happen next. Do they try to stay as caterpillars for as long as possible? Do they somehow understand that they will be butterflies in the end? Or do they just feel they *have* to do whatever it is they do to become a chrysalis?

Suddenly he remembered the Korean children who had drowned only a few days before, and felt a pang of guilt for being so much older and being still alive. O Lord, let them have heard about You. Let them call on You, and answer them as You promised. Give them an escape from death, the only one that matters in the end . . . O Lord, their families . . . Comfort them, Lord. Things do happen;

horrible things, accidentally, deliberately . . . It isn't You that do it, Lord, but You let it happen. You use what happens and bring good out of it, but I know You, a little, and I love You, and I don't understand, so how can people who don't know You cope with a God who lets children die? Their children?

We'll all die, one day. We might all die on the way to or from London, Gareth and Glyn and Sue Smith and me, for the sake of a model railway . . . but if you don't do things in case it might be dangerous no one'd ever do anything. Don't let anyone mourn me, Lord. I don't want to die, but I'm not frightened of death, only of dying . . .

'Teach me to live, that I may dread
The grave as little as my bed . . . '

Who had written that? Not the person who'd called death 'the last taboo' . . .

The children were still trying to get their kite to fly. It would soar, briefly, then cartwheel into a dune. At last an adult came and adjusted something, threw the kite up and played it carefully until it was flying, and handed over the string to a child.

Dafydd got up, stiffly, and brushed sand off his best trousers. He turned towards Borth with the sun in his eyes and started to walk, singing as he went.

"He arose! He arose! Halleluia, Christ arose!"

Chapter 8

IN THE END he quite enjoyed the journey to London in the horsebox. Glyn and Gareth collected Dafydd and Miss Smith at seven as they had arranged, and set off to Aberystwyth to pick up the piano. Miss Smith sat in the back to start with, but by the time they reached the farm at Rhydyfelin she was pallid and monosyllabic, and did not argue when Dafydd offered to let her sit up front for the next part of the journey.

They loaded Mrs. Powell's piano very carefully, swathing it in old sheets once it was in position, then packing it round with bales to stop it falling over. Mrs. Powell asked them to text her as soon as they knew when they were likely to be arriving with the grand, so that she could contact the piano tuner; apparently one was already standing by for instructions.

The horsebox pulled out onto the main road and Glyn began to sing a folk-song, quite unselfconsciously:

"Mi sydd fachgen ieuanc ffôl, yn byw yn ôl fy ffansi" … 'A simple youthful swain am I, who loves at fancy's pleasure … ' Dafydd had been taught that song in English at school, but now he joined in with the Welsh words. They sang the sailors' songs *Fflat Huw Puw* and *Harbwr Corc*, and then Gareth began 'Ble rwyt ti'n myned, fy eneth ffein i?', which Dafydd now knew was also the English nursery rhyme *Where are you going to, my pretty maid?* Possibly to everyone's surprise Miss Smith sang the reply 'Myned i odro, o Syr, mynte hi'; 'I'm going milking, Sir, she said'. The two sang the whole song antiphonally, Miss Smith clearly enjoying her final retort.

On the long road up to Llangurig Glyn drew into a lay-by to get rid of an impatient Audi, joined the back of the tail that had built up behind them, and started a hymn, *Yr Arglwydd yw fy Mugail da, The Lord is my Shepherd*, which went to the tune Crimond.

Glyn took them down the A470 to Abergavenny, crossed the Severn at Gloucester to avoid the tailbacks around the toll bridges and went down the A417 to the M4 where they stopped at a service station.

They all got out. Gareth bought coffee, Glyn produced a thermos and teabags and Miss Smith a bottle of water. Dafydd had been going to open his own thermos but as Glyn said, once it was open it'd start to go cold; they might as well share his on the way out and Dafydd's on the way back. They all sat in a row on a bench and offered to share their sandwiches too; Miss Smith had Marmite, Dafydd and Gareth cheese, and Glyn corned beef. People stared because they were speaking Welsh: Dafydd heard someone say something derogatory about people from Eastern Europe, and saw the look on Miss Smith's face.

As though in defiance, the journey resumed to the tune Pembroke. Dafydd forgot his inhibitions and his voice soared with the others:

'Rwy'n gweld o bell y dydd yn dod . . . ' Does that mean anything to the others? I see afar off the day coming: do they believe it, that the whole earth will acknowledge God? Maybe they just like the idea of the hilltops rejoicing when the sun rises . . .

They arrived at Kay's house at about three p.m. and were grateful for the chance to sit in her garden for a while. Dafydd left his bag in the horsebox; he couldn't think why he'd bothered to bring the knitting, as he'd been too busy singing even to get it out of the bag. Kay went off to ring Jon who was going to come and help, then offered tea and coffee. Miss Smith was asking Glyn if he sang on every journey; apparently he did if the horses seemed to like it. Most of them did, but there was the odd one . . .

"So how do we get the big piano out?" Gareth asked.

Kay told him that the legs came off, and the pedal mechanism, and they would need to use the trolley from the garage.

Without bothering to wait for Jon they all helped to take the hay out and stack it on Kay's drive, left the younger men to carry the upright piano to its temporary location in the dining-room, then gathered in the pale blue living-room with the grand piano. It looked even larger than Dafydd remembered it.

"We'll need it on its end, to get the legs and things off." Glyn pushed a chair aside; Miss Smith whisked it away before it marked the wallpaper.

"I don't think I'd better watch," Kay said firmly, and left them to it. They heard her playing scales on the upright.

With fascinated horror Dafydd helped them turn the grand on one side, collected the legs and the pedal mechanism, hoping Mrs. Powell's piano tuner knew how to fit all the pieces back, and finally helped them get it onto the low trolley which had been used for moving the locomotives up a ramp into a trailer. Without it he did not think they would have managed to get it out of the house.

There was a long hiatus while he and Miss Smith dragged bales back into the box and covered them with a sheet to make a platform for the piano body to land on: the younger men hauled it in and settled it in place, surrounded it with the remaining bales and sheets and went to tell Kay they were ready for the railway.

They had loaded Juliet and the electric locomotive, and the signal box, when Jon came up the drive at a run.

"He's here! Parked in Anson Drive, just out of sight; the cul de sac opposite. I left my car there because of the horse-box being on the drive. He'll see you leave . . . "

"That's *it*," Kay started. "I'm ringing the police——"

"No, no; there's no need." Dafydd looked at Jon. "We're safe 'til we're ready to go; he can't see what's going into the box, not unless he comes round into your garden.

All we need to do is to stop him following us when we leave. We need a diversion: would you park your car across the road, Jon? Only to distract him 'til the box is out of sight."

"If it was me following you and you did that," Miss Smith remarked, "I'd just go to Borth and wait . . . and of course we're not going to Borth! Or he'll wait for us on the A40 at Gloucester. Is there anywhere else where you can cross the Severn without paying?"

"Could go up to Worcester, I suppose. Let's get it loaded, anyhow; you can look at the road map on the way."

They had got everything in, secured it as best they could, and let Kay have a few minutes alone in the box. Saying goodbye, I suppose, Dafydd thought sympathetically. He turned to Jon. "Are you happy about being a diversion?"

"I don't mind parking across the road," Jon said cautiously, lowering his voice as his mother came down the ramp, "but I need to get his number in case he rams me."

"I don't think he would." Dafydd spoke with more conviction than he felt. "He doesn't want a lot of attention. He's more likely to swerve round you, so we need to distract him properly at the psychological moment."

"We?"

"Yes: I can stand on the pavement or something, stop him driving round you."

"Don't get run over . . . And how will you get home?" Kay looked anxious.

He had already checked he had his pass. "If you can take me to Euston I get free rail travel." (Well, it would use up another box, but it was worth it.)

"Okay, then. We'll give you three minutes to get into position before we start the engine." Gareth cracked his knuckles and stretched. "D'you want me to drive the first stage, Glyn? We're all ready to go, except putting the ramp up. Okay, love? Ready to close up?"

Kay withheld judgement on being addressed as 'love' and said that yes, she was, and she was very pleased with the upright piano, and here was an address sticker, could Mrs. Powell possibly let her know how the grand had travelled, thank you for all your hard work . . .

Glyn was closing the gates across the back of the box, ready to raise the ramp.

"Shall we go?" Dafydd suggested, putting the address sticker into his wallet. "Thank you very much, Mrs. Farrell. See you in Borth, lads! Goodbye."

He and Jon squeezed past the horsebox and crossed the road.

"If I start it up and do a three-point turn across the narrowest bit, backing right up to that tree, and just sit there . . . " Jon suggested. "If you mean it, you can stand on the pavement in front of me, so I can see you."

That made sense. Dafydd reminded him to write the car number down first, and strolled over towards a large laurel in someone's garden, which was in full flower.

Jon started the manœuvre. Dafydd watched the silver BMW. Yes, the driver was the young man who had followed them to Borth. He heard the horsebox start up. The young man started the silver car and began to move forward. Jon stopped, sideways on across the road. Dafydd moved forward a yard or two and stood solidly as the silver car mounted the kerb. He looked the driver in the eyes.

The silver car stopped.

"Move!" the driver yelled, waving his arm out of the window.

"Try 'please'," Dafydd grinned. He and Edith had been right about their shadow: whatever he was, he was not the sort of young man who ran over people.

Jon moved forward, directly across the path of the BMW, and stalled, presumably by accident. Would there be room for the other vehicle to reverse and go round the back? How far had the horsebox got? Dafydd marched up to the silver car's open window and looked the young man in the face. He said: "Take me to your leader."

The young man's eyes widened. He gulped.

"I mean it." Dafydd moved closer. Could he grab the keys?

"Er—he's not going to like it——" There was desperation in the young man's voice.

"That's my problem."

Minnesota Williams went swiftly round the silver bonnet and scrambled in before the young man had recovered sufficiently to lock the doors. He winked at Jon, who was staring in disbelief, and fastened his seatbelt. "Now drive. And no funny business."

The young man seemed thoroughly subdued by the unexpected turn of events. He drove sedately through suburbs; past shopping-centres, streets of modern boxes and huge villas divided into flats. Ten minutes later they drew up outside a pair of black metal gates in a high wall. The gates opened, closing silently behind them.

"Here we are." The young man stifled a nervous giggle. "I'll let him know you're here."

" 'He' is already aware of this, thank you," a voice said drily from the porch. "Mr. Williams, I presume? Do come in."

Dafydd went up the three stone steps, through a white wooden front door and across black and white tiles. It was a big double-fronted Victorian house with sunlight pouring onto the hall tiles from a window above them. The man pacing solemnly in front was slim and clad in black, his grey hair cut fairly short. The young man brought up the rear of the procession. Dafydd glanced round at him and could have laughed aloud at the look of apprehension on his face.

Chapter 9

THEY ENTERED A high-ceilinged room lined with bookshelves, with an array of computer equipment and screens on and above a large desk. The man in black gestured at some padded chairs upholstered in black leather. The first thing you noticed about him was the scar disfiguring one side of his face.

"Please, Mr. Williams, sit down."

"You have the advantage of me." Dafydd was carefully formal, wondering when he would wake up. "Yes, I am Minnesota Williams. Would you kindly introduce yourselves?"

His host took pity on the young man who was close to collapsing in giggles. "James, go and put the car away and bring us some coffee, please . . . no, tea. Mr. Williams prefers tea. Thank you. Now, Mr. Williams. My name is

Richard Cavendish Haddenham. It won't mean anything to you."

"No, I'm afraid not. Mr. Haddenham, I took the liberty of—er—inviting myself here because of this business with the railway. What I would like to know is, why do you want it?"

"Because I like railways."

There was an intensity in the words which made Dafydd wonder if the man was completely sane. He persevered. "Well, I like yogurt, and I don't follow Rachel's Organic lorries around . . . Why this particular railway? Because you've been told you can't have it, or is there a more complex reason?"

The man studied him for a long minute, elbows on the desk, long pale fingers steepled together. Dafydd realised that the eye on the scarred side was glass.

"Does it matter why I want it?"

"Well, yes, it does, to me." Minnesota Williams looked the man straight in the relevant eye. "If you could have any railway at all but you want this one just because you've been told you can't have it, like a spoilt child, then we will do everything we can to thwart you, Mr. Haddenham. We are only a little Welsh village but we are used to having to fight for everything we get, and to tell you the truth I think they are enjoying it." He paused. "But if there is a good reason for all this . . . "

There was another long pause. This time Richard did not meet his eyes, fiddling with something on the desk. At last he asked, quietly: "Do you know what a Comet was?"

Dafydd considered. "An aircraft, I believe. Was it a type of airliner?"

Richard smiled grimly. "It was the first passenger jet. My father was a pilot, a job as glamorous as being an astronaut at the time. He behaved as though he were a hero and immortal . . . Married what they would now call a trophy wife, a very beautiful Latvian girl. They had one child. I was supposed to follow in his footsteps. The only problem was that I didn't want to. I loved railways from a very early age and wanted to be an engine driver like most of the other boys, but when my father found out, I wasn't even allowed a clockwork toy train. I didn't read the Rev. Awdry books 'til three years ago . . . Oh, I had toys. Cars, planes; lots of planes. It didn't help that I couldn't cope with heights. Still can't. But I had to have lessons, and I was just about all right in a dual-control plane, obeying orders, but then eventually I had to go solo. I hoped Mother could persuade him to let me stop, but she said I had to do it, to please him. He'd always blamed her for me being so useless. I don't know what happened; whether I panicked, or blacked out, but I crashed." His hand went up to the scars. "Lost the eye, which of course meant I could never fly again, thank goodness. We had a row. Father said he wished I'd been killed. I said I hoped he would be. Comets were full of metal-fatigue problems because people didn't understand what the air pressure did; lots of them crashed. His never did . . . I told him I'd never wanted to fly, hated it, hated him, all I'd ever wanted to do was be a train-driver. You can imagine. With hindsight I realise I should have walked out, but Mother wouldn't leave him and

I was afraid of what he'd do to her. Besides, I was pretty badly smashed up. Eventually I got a job in computing. Father sneered at me but I'm glad I did; who cares about pilots, these days? But if you understand computers you can do anything." He sighed. "The railway; well, when I did leave home, Father made a will. The family solicitor didn't like it, but Father insisted, and it says something for what he was like that the solicitor met me secretly and told me the terms. I was to inherit everything after my parents died, if it could be proved that I'd had nothing to do with railways."

A long silence. Dafydd shook his head slowly. Such hatred . . .

"When I found that out I knew I could do two things. I could laugh and tell him I'd sooner starve than inherit anything he'd poisoned; there are times when I wish I'd done that. But I didn't know how computing was going to take off, whether it would be enough of a career to give me a pension; I didn't know how well I was going to recover, whether I'd need specialist nursing care when I got older, so I kept completely clear of trains. No pictures, no books, no travelling by rail: it drove him crackers. He didn't know I knew, and he kept giving me railway books and booking me on railway holidays, and I kept saying I wasn't interested, and giving them away . . .

"He died three years ago. I'd hoped he'd die before Mother so I could make it up to her a bit, but she went first: got away from him at last. One of the nurses said that to me openly. So now I'm making up for lost time. I'm too old to train as a driver, and I couldn't even on a preserved line, because of course I'm one-eyed. Can't judge distances or speed. But in one of the magazines I take there was an article about Ken Farrell's railway, so I got in touch with Kay . . . "

"And you tried to buy it."

"Yes. And she said no."

"You didn't explain the circumstances?"

"No! I don't think I've ever told anyone, not even James, as much as I've told you."

"Ah." Dafydd sighed. "So you just offered more and more money."

Richard grimaced. "I admit that was a mistake, but I didn't know what else to do. I was absolutely set on having Farrell's railway. You see, you don't often find things like that offered for sale, and it was a whole railway, not just a loco; it was small enough to fit in a garden, but big enough to drive and feel you were actually *driving* . . . I don't know how to, of course, but there are films on YouTube and I've read books."

"I suppose a driver's experience day would be out, because of your eyesight."

"Yes. And I have fits, sometimes. Since the crash." He scowled. "Something else I don't talk about. Not often, just often enough to prevent me having a normal life . . . Oh, well. So how much did you pay for it?"

"She gave it to us." Dafydd held his breath.

"She——?" He sat with his head in his hands. "I must have really upset her. You're not kidding?"

"No. Did your magazine say why it was built in the first place? Yes, it was for a care home he worked at. And then it closed, so a group of them took it out to fêtes, to raise money for charities. And then the group got older and older, and Mr. Farrell died, and Kay wanted it to go on raising money for charities."

"Oh, I see. Yes . . . Why didn't she *explain*? I'd have been quite happy to store it and help at fêtes even if I couldn't drive in public, if I could drive it on my own property . . . "

Silence.

"You work?" Dafydd asked.

"I run my own computer consultancy company. Buntingford is my sole employee." He pressed something on the desk.

"Most of your work is in London?"

"If you mean, do we visit clients in London, yes, we do occasionally. Quite a lot of what we do can be done by phone, or online. Sometimes we visit companies for a few days. Why do you ask?"

"Because I think you might consider a holiday, at least. In Wales."

"West Wales, by any chance?" An urbane smile.

"West Wales."

Richard Haddenham leaned forward and asked conspiratorially: "Will I have to play bridge?"

Dafydd frowned. "I suppose you could if you want to; I don't know anyone who does."

A broad grin. "Oh, good. I hate bridge. It's more or less compulsory round here. What do you do in the evenings?"

"Well, I do crossword puzzles, gardening if it's light enough; I cycle, I read; there's Bible study at Chapel on Wednesdays and the prayer meeting on Tuesdays . . . I don't really do much in the evenings. But I go out at about six every morning and walk along the beach or the sea wall, fetch my paper if it's not Sunday and go home to feed the cats . . . Ah. I don't have a spare room, not now, so I can't have you to stay; you'd need to book in for a guest-house or self-catering. Would you mind?"

"Not at all." He turned to the computer and tapped keys as James entered the room with a tray. "Yes, Borth does apparently have broadband . . . Thank you, James."

Tea was poured (from a teapot which, presumably, contained teabags) and handed out. James moved towards the door.

"Will you pack for me, please?" Richard Haddenham requested. "We're going to West Wales for a few days."

"Will Sir be requiring his golf clubs?"

Richard hesitated. "No, not this time. Please make a reservation at the guest-house where you stayed on your previous visit. And, Buntingford, I shall be using the passport in the name of Richard Cavendish."

Dafydd opened his mouth to say that they didn't need passports, it was Wales, but realised that it must be some sort of coded message.

James left; Richard settled back in his chair and took a sip of tea. Dafydd applied himself to his own, looking at the bookshelves. There were railway books, some he couldn't classify with titles like *Three Signs of a Miserable Job*, and a whole bookcase of Dornford Yates, Margery Allingham, Dorothy L. Sayers, John Buchan, and Arthur Ransome, all looking as though they were well-read.

Richard put down his cup. "You say you don't now have a spare room? May I ask why?"

Dafydd explained briefly about Sky. "So you see, I need to get back. I left extra food down for them both, but I want to make sure she's all right. And I really ought to tell the others *I'm* all right . . . " He blushed.

"That I haven't dropped you into the shark tank?" Richard grinned. "Feel free to ring them." He pushed a telephone across the desk.

Kay's address sticker was in Dafydd's wallet; he squinted at it, rang the telephone number provided and asked her to tell Jon he was fine, about to leave for Borth, and would explain later. He also rang Miss Smith's house and left a message on her answering service: could she check on the cats, the key was with his neighbour at Anfield; he was fine and would be back as soon as possible.

"Of course, you speak Welsh," Richard commented when he had finished. "It sounds quite attractive—much better than it looks written down. I'd never heard it spoken before. Does everyone in the village speak Welsh?"

"Not everyone. Most of them know a bit, but there are holiday people and people who've retired, and they use English mostly. 'Til I got to know people, it was only the cat I spoke with in Welsh, just to keep from going rusty." He checked the time. "Well, thank you for the tea, and for the explanation—which I shall keep to myself. Do you think Mr. Buntingford could drop me off at Euston, please? I can catch the next train and get back tonight."

"I'm tempted to come with you," Richard said, "but it would make more sense to drive down, then we can talk without anyone overhearing. Would you feel safe in a car with us? After all, we might suddenly stop and throw you into a reservoir with weights tied to your feet!"

"If you were planning that, you wouldn't warn me." Dafydd was beginning to like the younger man. "And I came to London in the back of the horsebox with Napoleon Powell's piano: it can't be any worse than that."

Richard shook his head in amazement. "I am really looking forward to hearing exactly what your side of this is. Don't tell me now; James will enjoy hearing it too. I have a call to take in about an hour but we should be able to leave well before dark. Would you care to come and help me make some sandwiches?"

Chapter 10

THE JOURNEY BACK to Borth took far less time than the journey to London. Once out of the city and on motorways James drove fast and competently; Dafydd, sitting beside him in the front, had been uneasy at first, but soon realised that the young man was probably a better driver than most, his reflexes so quick that he had seen and dealt with potentially hazardous situations before Dafydd was fully aware that there was a hazard at all.

Richard asked for the story of Borth's involvement with the railway and Dafydd obliged, carefully not mentioning where the piano teacher lived (though of course they could no doubt find that out on the internet, as they knew she was Powell), and not naming Esme, Gareth or Glyn.

"Borth sounds more interesting than London," James remarked. "I brought our binoculars; we must spend a day or two at Ynys Hir—and aren't the ospreys due back soon?"

"There're four been seen already." Dafydd had completely forgotten about going up to Cyffordd Dyfi to look for them, what with cats and bicycles and pianos and railways, but it was something he wanted to do. "Monty's back, and Glesni, and I can't remember the other two names. They nest quite close to a railway station: you can stand on the platform and watch, and the trains don't seem to bother them at all. There was a marsh harrier around last month; I don't know whether it's been seen recently, I've not spoken to Bill since the Batter Pudding Festival."

"The what?"

Dafydd explained, playing down exactly how annoying Dai had been, out of loyalty to the man who was now his friend.

Richard gave a sigh of contentment. "I think I'm going to like Borth. James, I don't know what relationship we'd better adopt. Richard Cavendish wouldn't have a manservant, and we're not on business. For once we could simply be us—but if people are going to assume that two men with an age difference of thirty years can't possibly just be colleagues . . . Usually it doesn't matter, but it might reflect badly on Dafydd and he's got to live there after we've left."

"I don't mind chatting up a few local girls." James sounded hopeful.

"Again, Dafydd's got to live there when we've left."

Dafydd wasn't quite sure what they were implying, but said firmly: "You'd be better off being yourselves. Your real selves. Then people can't catch you out . . . who are you, really?"

"Oh, we're Richard and James all right. Marcus Richard Cavendish Haddenham and James Isleham-Buntingford. Sorry, James, I know you hate it, but he's Minnesota . . . We just use different parts of who we are at different times. In the same way that the person who gets down on the floor under a rug to play bears with a toddler isn't the same person who goes to see the bank manager. The DnA, the atoms, are the same; but the clothes, the voice, the demeanour . . . We play parts when we're working, James and I. He's far better at it; he can be a geeky Oxbridge graduate, a harassed young father with a mortgage, or a druggie with barely any English. I tend to be a silly-ass Public School bloke which can work quite well; people despise you, so they aren't as careful with what they say as if I'd gone to the company looking like Bruce Willis. *Die Hard*? Um . . . you know about John Wayne? Right. Do you see what I mean?"

Dafydd thought he did. "So what do you do with your computers?"

"Oh, the usual debugging and so on, but we also do undercover work for big companies. That wasn't what we intended to do at the beginning, but we love it."

Dafydd remembered the shelves of John Buchan and Dornford Yates, thought he could guess the sort of person Richard pretended to be, and the sort of person he wanted to be . . .

They stopped in a lay-by near Newport and ate the sandwiches. There was coffee in a flask but Dafydd said he'd rather not and made do with an apple; they had rather hastily cleared all the perishable food supplies into a couple of cool-boxes before leaving London.

"So how did you manage for railway tickets, coming to Borth?" he asked, when they were under way again.

"Young person's railcard, which of course I couldn't use much on the way out." James overtook a timber lorry. "I knew which platform your train went from at Euston, so I got a ticket to Birmingham on the grounds that if you were going to Scotland you'd probably have gone for a faster train. And then I found out that you two came from Borth because your friend was talking to the girl from Rugby. The conductors are usually decent enough if you go and find them straight away and you're polite and don't jib at paying the full excess fare; it's not as though you're abusive and clearly trying to get away without paying."

"It must still have cost you no end——"

"Well, I recouped quite a bit on the overnight accommodation in Borth." He grinned. "Less than thirty pounds, and a fantastic breakfast. It's a bit dated, Richard, but it'll do for us. I got single rooms—well, the single and a double. He's pretty well booked up, but he says once there's a sea view room free you can have that if you like. I said two weeks initially, bird-watching . . . "

Richard sighed. "I suppose I'll just have to bite the bullet and be a fairly well-off Londoner with a disability that prevents me driving, taking a holiday from the office and paying you to come with me as my driver and general nursemaid. Which is the truth."

There was silence.

"What sort of office?" James asked at last.

"Oh, computers. As usual. It usually shuts people up." Richard sounded happier.

"That, or we get asked to de-frag systems that went out with the Ark," James grumbled. "I've actually had a girl ask me back to her place, and it turned out all she wanted was to get rid of a virus that kept filling the screen with error messages."

Silence.

I don't suppose anyone ever even asked Richard, not with those scars, Dafydd thought compassionately. Poor bloke . . . He wondered how the rest of Tîm Pwdin would react when they found he had invited the enemy into the camp. Siân and Dai and Sandy might understand, and possibly Donald, but he couldn't see Miss Smith being too pleased, or Edith; and as for Marged . . .

"It's no good; I have to ask," he said at last, when they were safely past Abergavenny. "Why did you follow us to Borth? Why were you watching Kay's house? How did you do it? Did you stay there all the time, or what? And if you had followed the horsebox and we hadn't got in the way, what were you planning to do?"

"That's about six questions," Richard pointed out. "To start with, we had a tiny thing trained on Kay's drive, like a C.C.T.V. camera. It was attached to the garden wall opposite, under a coping stone. We'll have to go back and remove it at some later date, James; I took it off the system at our end before we left. When we saw the horsebox arrive James went over in the car to see what you'd do. We knew if you were actually removing anything big he'd have enough time to get into position before you finished loading."

"So what were you going to do when we'd loaded it?"

"Just—follow." James was at that moment following a red Fiesta which was crawling behind a tractor. "Find out where you went, and let Richard know."

"It seemed logical at the time." The older man sounded embarrassed. "Once we knew you were on the scene, it was as though we were living in some sort of thriller. When Kay told me you'd come for it, and I told James, he said: "D'you want me to find out who they are?", and I said yes, so he shot off in the car and ended up leaving it illegally parked in Eversholt Street; he texted me and I sent Felix to get it, in a taxi. He's the grandson of my first landlady, wanted to be a spy when he was a kid. James followed you two to Borth, found out who you were, and to be honest we couldn't believe Kay was serious and you really were having it. Remember, I'd offered her a considerable amount of money, and didn't realise she'd given it to you because you'd use it for charity work; we assumed you'd outbid us, and—if I can be so rude—you simply didn't look sufficiently wealthy! So we set up the device to watch the drive—not the house itself, only the mouth of the drive, in case she found out and was justifiably peeved with us. And the horsebox arrived, and once again James went off to find out what was happening . . ."

"And met Minnesota Williams." James grinned briefly at him, intent on the Fiesta and the tractor. "At that point

I almost wished I'd gone in for accountancy instead! You said you're retired now, but what on earth did you do as a job?"

"Worked for British Railways, mostly," Dafydd admitted. "Not driving. Not anything exciting, either. I'd never done anything exciting in my life until Llinos threw a batter pudding at me and I decided to find out why."

"And now you're making up for lost time, like me." Richard laughed. "Must say I envy you, though, with your cats and your bicycle and this Team Pudding . . . I don't suppose we can very well be introduced, not if they think we're second cousins to Fu Manchu."

"The men who drove the horsebox were hoping you'd try to stop them or something; they were looking forward to having a go at you," Dafydd confided. "What they meant by that I'm not sure, but they're both big lads."

"H'm. Good thing we didn't, then." James shivered. "It was never in the plan to stop you, or interfere with you, but in this I could obviously run rings round a horsebox, so if they'd spotted me following, it would have looked so suspicious they might well have decided to find out why. Nasty!"

Another few miles of silence. James finally managed to overtake the Fiesta and the tractor.

"Perhaps," Richard suggested, "we should drop you, Dafydd, at the station before Borth—or Machynlleth would be better, it's a long walk to Dovey Junction from the car park—so you can get home by rail as they're expecting you to. Then we can quite legitimately meet you on the beach one morning and they needn't know we're anything to do with the railway . . . "

His voice tailed off. James said: "I booked this afternoon from London. The same place as I stayed before. And I was asking about Dafydd and Edith in the pub. I could go home, but you'd have to explain why I booked two rooms."

"The more lies you tell, the worse it is," Dafydd said heavily. "I invited you; I'll be the one they turn on, if they do. It isn't the whole village that knows, just Tîm Pwdin. The best thing to do would be to get everyone together and explain."

He remembered that Richard would be unwilling to explain in full, and added hastily: "I'll call you Richard Cavendish. If you tell them you've never been able to drive a loco because of your eye, so the only way you can is to actually own one, and you'd have been happy to use it for charity fundraising like she wanted, only neither of you asked the right questions . . . "

"And we really have come for bird-watching, too; we can both go on at great length about bar-tailed godwits, so the rest of the village needn't know the real reason," James put in.

"What's your excuse for asking about Dafydd and Edith in the pub?" Richard demanded irritably.

"I don't suppose they'll remember that you did," Dafydd offered, studiously ignoring the fact that Dai had made enquiries about James' activities, which people *were* likely to remember. James was already saying that he'd thought it was Dafydd he'd seen on the train, but as he'd known he wasn't married and the man on the train had been with a woman, he'd thought it better to check before getting into a long complicated explanation with elderly people who were probably deaf.

"And they said it was Dafydd Williams all right: they even said you went to Chapel and only drank leaf tea, so I knew it really was you." He grinned across at him. "Despite the knitting!"

"And how did you know him, before seeing him on the train?" Richard probed.

"I'd worked with him in London once. And as I had some leave due I thought I'd go to Borth and look him up. Go to Ynys Hir instead of . . . name an R.S.P.B. reserve north of Birmingham. I'll look one up on the net when we get there." James glanced at Dafydd again, driving more slowly because of the high incidence of sharp corners. "Have you ever worked in London? If that's going to be the story . . ."

"No. Not in your lifetime, anyway, but no one here would know that." He sighed. He'd forgotten about the knitting, still in his bag in the horsebox. He hoped Glyn had used the thermos, that someone would rescue the bag for him before the horsebox went back to its owners. "Can't you just tell the truth?"

"Would anyone believe it? The cover story's much more credible." Richard sounded pleased. "That was good, James. Well done."

"They might well believe it,' Dafydd muttered to himself. "This is Borth we're talking about, where they invent a batter pudding festival . . . "

Chapter 11

WHEN THEY REACHED Borth, James parked under the sea wall opposite the guest-house. Dafydd got out stiffly, thanked them for the lift and arranged to see them next morning at ten, and left them to deal with the proprietor. It was not far to his own house but after the long drive his back ached and he was glad when he was finally opening his front gate. He glanced up and saw a small brown and yellow face gazing anxiously down at him.

First he went upstairs and spent some time with Sky, putting out more food and dealing with her litter tray, refilling the water bowl. He sat and stroked her for a while, but it felt like a long time since the sandwiches and he went down to talk to Rheidol and heat a tin of soup.

Just as he was about to eat it, the doorbell rang.

He heaved himself out of the chair, muttering, and found Miss Smith on the step, with his bag.

"Come in." He stood aside. "I was just going to have soup. Have you eaten? I can put toast in."

To his relief she said she was fine, they'd got chips after dropping everything off; eat it before it went cold. Mrs. Powell had shrieked a bit about the travelling conditions of the piano, she continued, but it hadn't looked damaged once they'd got it into her house and put the legs back on, and the tuner would sort out the pedals.

"So what happened?" she asked. "You stopped him following us all right: did he damage Jon's car?"

He realised that none of the horsebox party knew anything of what had happened. As whatever he told her was likely to involve a long explanation, he drank the last spoonful of soup and put the bowl in the sink and bread in the toaster before replying.

"Thanks for bringing my bag back. Jon's car was fine. We need to have a meeting of Tîm Pwdin, as soon as possible. I've met Herring-dancer."

"You've met him—the man in the car?"

"No, the man who sent him."

"How on earth——?" She grinned as the toast popped up. "Deal with that first, Minnesota Williams . . . It could only be you! What did you do to him?"

Dafydd scraped margarine onto the toast. "We talked. Um . . . I don't really know what to say. He's called Richard. He *seems* okay, and he seems to have a good reason for wanting the railway, but he might just be a good actor. So I—I suggested he came to Borth, for a holiday. And he has, with the car driver, because apparently he's too disabled to drive himself. They're staying at Min-y-mor. They're coming here at ten tomorrow; I don't know what I'm going to do with them, except take them bird-watching. Miss Smith, we need to watch them, listen to them, find out if he really does mean what he said or if he's just trying to pull the wool over our eyes." He munched for a few seconds. "Now they're here I wish I'd never done it, but at the time it seemed the only thing I could do . . . "

"Calm down." She reached to stroke Rheidol. "I'll organise the others for a meeting, let them know what you've told me."

"Tell Dai first. He might have more of an idea about what to do next."

"I'll email him when I get home, ask him to ring as soon as he picks it up." She was still stroking Rheidol. "So what was his excuse? For all this?"

"Misunderstanding. He says that because of his disability the only way he'll ever drive a locomotive is to own a railway, or have one on his own private land. So he tried to buy Kay's. And he didn't ask why she wouldn't sell, and she didn't ask why he wanted it. She assumed he'd lock it away for his own use and no one else's, and he assumed she just wanted more money than he was offering. And he's told me he'd be quite happy for it to go to fêtes if it was his, even though he couldn't drive it in public . . . "

He finished the toast before she spoke.

"I wonder . . . If we get this right, Dafydd, do you realise you might have found the only person who could afford the insurance and might want to?"

"I thought of that almost immediately when he explained," Dafydd admitted. "But we can't say yes, he can have it, because Kay might be so furious that she wants it back, and we can't expect him to insure it if he doesn't own it."

There was a long silence, during which Dafydd realised that it was raining heavily outside. Rheidol padded away into the hall. Dafydd imagined him curling up on the easy chair in the living-room.

"Tell Dai, tomorrow," he said, at last. "Did Glyn use my thermos on the way back? I hope he did."

"He did. We realised you'd left your bag with us. I didn't know you knitted."

"I hadn't for years. Edith inspired me to start again." He put his hand over his mouth, hiding a yawn.

"At least you're okay." She smiled at him and picked up her umbrella. "I had a feeling you would be, Minnesota Williams."

Despite his tiredness he slept badly, waking at three to hear the rain still lashing against the window. After half an hour he was still awake, so, unenthusiastically, he sat up, put the light on and reached for his Bible.

Five minutes later, he went through and sat in the spare room with Sky, holding her outstretched paw between turning pages.

> *I will lift up mine eyes unto the hills: from whence cometh my help?*

My help cometh from the Lord, who hath made heaven and earth . . .

Such a long day. So much happening. So much frantic plotting and lying, or preparing to lie; so much leaping from frying pan to fire, to a different fire, to yet another fire . . .

He could have died, if James Isleham-Buntingford had been a different sort of young man; if they'd simply been unlucky. Accidents did happen. He could have died, there in that London suburb, and he'd never have seen another sunset, or the way the grass shone in the sunlight, or Sky's kittens . . .

But he hadn't died. No one had died. They'd all been so careful, so alert, waiting for some sort of gangster attack . . . and to the best of his knowledge both Richard and James were harmless. Harmless in that they wouldn't kill, but they were both prepared to lie for fear of not being believed, which was always the most dangerous sort of lie. He'd done it himself; not this time, but too often before that . . .

Why don't I trust You, Lord?

He stroked Sky's white paw with a fingertip.

I claim to love You, but I don't trust You. How much do I trust anyone? I don't feel safe unless I know what's going to happen. I always try to work out what people are going to do next, and You keep putting me up against people who do something completely unexpected . . . I should have learned by now.

Is this why, Lord? Teaching me to trust You? Like Sky trusts me . . . I should wait for You to come and feed me and talk to me, and trust that You're doing everything right, but Sky sits on the windowsill watching for me to come back, and if I let her out she'd go and hunt for her own food like Rheidol does . . .

He doesn't need to. I wish he wouldn't, especially when he catches birds. He doesn't trust me to feed him … Yes, he does. The way he waits by his dish. But he likes to pretend he can manage on his own. Does he resent relying on me? Do I secretly resent being supposed to rely on God?

He had an uncomfortable feeling that he knew the answer to that, but shied away from admitting it.

Was Richard lying when he told me about his family—his accident? Did he invent all that because it was the sort of thing that would make me feel sorry for him? I saw him being at least three separate people yesterday . . .

Play-acting, his mother would have said, and from her that was a worse condemnation than any from a judge in a wig.

Play-acting. Like me being Minnesota.

Like me being the sensible cautious Dafydd M. Williams everyone knew for all those years, rather than ever daring to be Minnesota. What was I so afraid of?

He stroked the little white paw.

"There's a lot I should have done differently, little puss," he whispered. "O, pws fach, maybe there could have been more like you. Forgive me . . . "

He went back to bed at five, woke with a start at nine and hurriedly washed, shaved, and dressed, fed the cats and himself, and washed up. He sat by the living-room window and knitted for ten minutes, then put down the knitting and fetched his binoculars, walking boots and a raincoat. Where should he suggest they go? The young man would have looked things up on his computer, but if not they could go up to Ynyslas. There was the visitor centre there if it came on to rain hard . . . He picked up the knitting and found that he had knitted where he should have purled and vice versa; he pulled out the offending two rounds and by the time he had picked up the stitches and knitted a round correctly, Richard and James were on the doorstep.

They commented on the array of items brought back by Rheidol and displayed on the railings, and asked about Sky. Dafydd made sure the kitchen door was firmly closed and took them upstairs. Sky jumped down off the windowsill as he opened the door and came to greet them. He had taken a tiny sliver of cheese up for her: she fell on it rapturously and rolled at his feet purring.

"She's beautiful." Richard lowered his voice as Sky stopped purring and looked up. "How could people throw her out? Even if she was going to have kittens . . . "

James was crouching, stroking her head. "Have you thought about homes for the kittens?" he asked. "We could probably have one . . . ?" He looked up hopefully.

"Two'd be better," Richard said. "Company for each other."

"I'd not got that far, yet. I've no idea how many she'll have; there might only be one. But yes, I'll keep you in mind," Dafydd promised.

They went downstairs, closing the door carefully, and let Rheidol out of the kitchen. James fetched a cool-box from the car and asked Dafydd if they could put things in his fridge and eat at his house that night.

"I'll cook for you, or not if you'd prefer. We've kept the fruit and stuff like that at Min-y-mor but we can't cook there."

"All right, if you're happy to use what equipment I've got." Dafydd watched as James stowed cheese and milk and various packets, fitting them in round the existing contents. "But I have to go out to Chapel tonight, for seven-thirty. Where did you think of going today?"

In the end they went to Ynys Hir and spent most of the day in one or other of the hides. Dafydd spent quite a lot of the day listening and knitting, picking up his binoculars only when he saw something particularly interesting. James had a notebook and wrote down each species they saw, like a train-spotter; Richard preferred to watch one bird for long periods when this was possible, studying its behaviour. At midday James apologetically asked Dafydd if he was bored.

"Because I'm knitting? No: mostly I don't need to look at the knitting, so I can just sit and listen and look; enjoy it. I don't come out here very often and there aren't many trees near Borth, so to sit and hear all those titmice and the black-caps and the robin . . . it's very special." He reached for the binoculars. "Woodpecker. Just gone behind the broken branch."

James focussed eagerly.

"What's one of those in Welsh?" Richard asked, intent on the pair of bluetits which were picking over the nearest tree.

"Yswidw las. Woodpecker is cnocell y coed."

"And an oak tree?"

"Derwen."

"Do you mind my asking you?"

"Not at all. But some things I may not know the names of in Welsh because I didn't see them first until I was speaking English."

"Hmmm. Which language do you dream in? Sorry, that's rather a personal question, but my mother said once that she never dreamed in English. I just wondered."

Dafydd considered. If he did dream, usually he didn't remember anything about it. "Depends. Who I've been talking to that day, in which language . . . "

To his relief they left in plenty of time to get back to Borth and prepare a meal before his meeting. James cooked two lamb chops, took the meat off the bones and divided it between three, padded out with a few sausages and a packet of green beans. Dafydd had contributed rice and cabbage, and the visitors sat at his kitchen table—he was very glad the bicycle was now in the bwthyn—on a variety of chairs (he'd retrieved the one from Sky's room and brought in the smaller chair from his living-room) and politely waited while he said grace before beginning to eat. Once the chops and sausages had been eaten, with none left for Rheidol (who had materialised hopefully, ignoring the food Dafydd had put down for him), James issued cartons of yogurt and teaspoons. Dafydd produced the packet of sweet biscuits he had hidden at the back of the cupboard. After the meal Richard washed up and James dried while Dafydd made a pot of tea; they took chairs with them and sat in his living-room to drink it. It was all, Dafydd thought contentedly, very civilised . . .

He got up at a quarter past seven and told them apologetically that he really must go to his meeting but they were welcome to stay, and it was a Yale lock so when they went they could just close the door behind them; he wasn't sure how long he'd be but probably an hour or so.

James said he'd go back to the guest-house and watch television. Richard, who had found a book on the Glyn Valley Tramway, asked if he could borrow it overnight.

They all left the house together, rather to Dafydd's relief; he had feared they would be there when he returned and want to talk until the small hours, and although it looked very much as though it would rain, he hadn't cycled for two days . . .

He hurried down to the chapel, unlocked the side door they used on Bible study nights, put half a dozen chairs out in the vestry and waited. After a minute or two he went to the door into the main body of the chapel, opened it cautiously and slipped through.

The building was very quiet, the rows of seats shadowy in the poor light. He had never been alone in this chapel before and found that it was not just silent but filled with quietness, like the warm summer nights of his childhood when you felt the darkness round you almost as tangibly as water.

"Darkness isn't necessarily evil," he said aloud. "Darkness is neutral. You divided light from darkness and saw it was good. All of it . . . Lord, I really don't know what I am doing, but if You will show me I will try not to misunderstand."

After a few long seconds in the comforting silence he added: "Thank You," and went back into the vestry, closing the door.

Four people attended the meeting, to his surprise: all of them were women, which wasn't a surprise. Siân Gilchrist, Mair Blethyn and Carol Williams he knew from the Bible studies, but Alice Brownsword was introduced by Siân: she attended a church in Shrewsbury on Sundays and had orchestra practice on Wednesday evenings. Dafydd greeted her solemnly and hoped his apprehension did not show: she appeared to be at least seventy-five with a no-nonsense air about her as though she had been a teacher.

For a long while they sat and talked. He asked if there were any specific matters they wanted to pray about, and collected a list of international concerns: the Ukraine, the Korean ferry, the schoolgirls abducted in Nigeria and so on, as well as more local topics; children starting a new term, care-workers and the health service in general, people and businesses still affected by the winter floods. He mentioned the Minister's new responsibilities in Furnace and also suggested that they give thanks for the spring, which was making life so much more encouraging now there were leaves on the hedges, and flowers and birds to be enjoyed.

To his relief, when they did pray no one was too formal, highbrow or long-winded, and when everyone seemed to have run out of ideas he suggested that they should say the Grace together. Five minutes later people were putting the chairs back and dispersing. He locked up, tried the door to make sure, and offered to walk Siân home. As he had expected she had so many questions to ask about his trip to and from London that she invited him in for a paned.

"Miss Smith says that Herring-dancer is disabled, poor man, and can't drive?" she called through, filling the kettle.

Dafydd was trying to keep his wits about him and divulge as little as possible. "Yes, he was involved in an accident and lost one eye. He seems to manage well enough; I suppose it might be getting insurance that's the problem."

"Oh, poor man. And why did Kay call him Herring-dancer?" She put down the tray and poured milk.

"I have no idea." Dafydd accepted a cup of tea.

"Do herrings dance? Like the lobster quadrille in *Alice*, perhaps." Siân smiled, imagining it. "Shoals of fish all change direction at once, like a flock of starlings . . . "

"It must mean something to Kay. I went out to Ynys Hir with them today, and they seemed quite ordinary. They came back to my house and James cooked: Min-y-mor does evening meals but they'd emptied their fridge in London before they left."

'What did you have?"

"Chops, sausages; rice and vegetables. Yogurt."

"They sound sensible people." She sounded so like his mother that he wondered if she would have disapproved of his friendship with them if the meal had been more exotic.

"They seem to be, most of the time. They mend computer systems for a living, which must be very boring. Perhaps that's why they sometimes pretend they're living in a detective story." He finished his tea. "Thank you, Siân. Do you know when the next meeting of Tîm Pwdin is? No, I only wondered. Well, good night. And thank you for coming to the prayer meeting."

"Thank you for running it. See you at Bible study."

It was raining by the time he came back from his cycle ride. He had a quick bath, washed his cycling clothes and hung them over the bath to drip, spent half an hour with Sky, almost falling asleep, and went gratefully to bed.

Chapter 12

WEDNESDAY WAS ANOTHER fine day. James and Richard arrived at Dafydd's house at nine, on foot, saying that they thought they might go for a walk on the beach and then up to the monument, and did he want to do anything specific or what?

Dafydd told them to go and enjoy it, he'd be in the garden when they got back if they wanted to come in for a cup of tea. When they had gone he pegged his cycling clothes out to dry, did the week's washing and after pausing for a chat to Sky over a cup of tea, dug some more of the garden. The seedlings on his bedroom windowsill would soon need planting out. The grass was still damp: he would mow it when it had dried.

He collected some of the stones from the demolished wall and piled them neatly in the back lane, wondering how difficult it would be to rebuild the wall. He scraped with his spade and found that the lowest layer was still there. If he asked Richard and James to bring some cement from somewhere . . . ? He'd have to go to a cash-point soon, but if they all went to Aberystwyth or Machynlleth . . . They could go up the Vale of Rheidol railway, perhaps. He couldn't remember when he'd last done that.

"Hi!"

It was James, coming down the lane towards him, Richard following. "Have you had lunch? We got sandwiches for all of us."

Dafydd had not realised that it was already two p.m. He invited them in, put the kettle on, washed his hands and found plates and cups, accepted a packet of cheese and pickle sandwiches and said grace quietly while Richard poured the tea.

"Did you enjoy it up there?" he asked. "Good view, isn't it?"

Richard nodded. "Right across to whatever the hills are at the far side. And the wind farm, inland. We had a look round up there: there's good reception right up at the top, as we expected. Do you remember before the caravan sites were here?"

"Oh, I've only lived here three years. Some of the caravan places go back to the 'fifties or even earlier, I wouldn't wonder. There was a man called Savin, tried to make this a proper holiday place round about 1860, he built the hotel and the houses by the station, but it never came to much."

"I'm almost glad it didn't," James said, to Dafydd's surprise. "It's such a weird little place, as though it's made up of bits of other towns that were left over, all jumbled together. Like a town of film sets. Caravan parks and modern bungalows and little sheds down alleys and big suburban-looking houses and Victorian terraces, and then little slate cottages that look like N gauge in a street of double-O gauge."

"And all of it due to be under the sea again in half a century, we've been told," Richard added. "Except the streets on the hill, presumably, and the church on its hillock, and the intriguingly-named Ynys Tachwedd . . . Why November Island? Or does Tachwedd have more than one meaning?"

Dafydd frowned. "Well, it might. Gorffennaf, July, is gorffen-haf, end of summer." He got up and went into the living-room, came back with a large Welsh-English dictionary. "Now, here we are . . . yes, it's an obsolete word for slaughter; November being the month you slaughter all the livestock you can't feed over the winter."

"Slaughter Island! Would that be a slaughter by Vikings, or other Welsh tribes, or who?" James asked.

Dafydd shrugged. "Do you know the legend of Cantre'r Gwaelod? The Hundred at the bottom of the sea? In Wales, history goes back through time further than you'd think, and the Mabinogion is like the Tain is to Ireland: stories that look as though you can date them to one era, but if you look closely you can see that there are centuries of additions, and the story at the centre of it, the kernel, goes back to the Bronze Age or maybe before that."

"We saw the sunken forest," Richard remarked. "There was bark on some of the trees; you could recognise pines and birches . . . And great chunks of peat washed up, and thick grey boulder clay under that. The trees apparently date from before 1500 B.C."

"Bronze Age, then." Dafydd finished his sandwich. "I seem to remember hearing that what they call the Mold Cape is from that period, not later as they first thought; it's a piece of ceremonial armour made of a hammered sheet of gold. They used to think it was to go on a horse, but when I went to see it exhibited in Wrexham in 2005 they had it on a model of a woman. And then the Battersea shield: that was Bronze Age, wasn't it?"

They talked archaeology over the remaining yogurt and went back into the garden. James offered to mow the lawns; Dafydd thanked him and asked shyly: "Could you fetch me a bag of cement in the car one day, please? Not much, but I want to put the wall back and I can get sand."

"Oh, we can do that for you." Richard went down the path to investigate the remains of the wall. "Wouldn't mind helping to build it, if you don't mind me learning on the job?"

"That makes two of us." Dafydd smiled wryly, feeling some of the washing. He fetched the basket to collect the dry items. "It's supposed to rain all day tomorrow, according to the radio, so I thought you might like to go to a railway somewhere."

"Have to check what's running. Good idea."

Dafydd folded a sheet roughly into the basket. "If you like," he offered, "you can have the use of my washing-machine while you're here. There's no drying-machine so you'd have to pick your day, but you're welcome to it."

"Thanks very much." Richard was scratching at the mortar left on a loose stone. "Tell me, Mr. Williams, how long was it before Borth accepted you?"

He considered, pairing socks. "I don't really know. I go to the chapel, which means I know people, and I use the local shops and the railway and sometimes buses. And I walk, used to walk on the beach every morning 'til I started cycling, and still do if I get the chance. That way you meet the people with dogs, and most of them are all right so you get talking, and if you listen, and seem like their sort of people in what you say, you start to fit in."

James went rattling off round the corner with the lawn-mower before Dafydd could tell him to take it through the house. He'd made a good job of the back grass.

"Where do you cycle to? Just curious, considering some of the hills round here."

Dafydd grinned. "Not up to the monument, I can tell you! Out to the garage at Tre'r Ddol is the latest: community shop it is now, with no petrol, like many of them round here. Five miles each way, and mostly flattish. I was going to do a sponsored cycle ride but it's on a Sunday. Oh, I'd not got any sponsors, it was just seeing could I get fit enough to do it, and I have, more or less, and there's plenty of other things happening."

"We've seen the notices; there's a craft show coming up, and a line dance event and a duck race. I suppose your tourists will be arriving in force soon to support them."

"It'll be good if they do support us but we're all involved, one way or another. It's to raise money for the Syrian refugees——"

Dafydd would have said more, but a familiar figure came round the corner. Dai, who had seen someone mowing Dafydd's lawn, and thought he'd pop round for a chat.

The three stood in the garden, conversing cautiously.

Dai knows this is Herring-dancer, Dafydd thought; Richard knows it's Dai, and we're all being very polite and British . . . Here comes trouble!

"Thought I saw you diving down here, Dai." Marged rested her shopping bag on the wall by the gate. "Hallo Dafydd; glad it's still holding together. How's your refugee? And Gareth wants to know what really happened in London . . . You must be Herring-dancer. Why?"

Richard gave Dafydd a look that said very plainly: Do you know this mad woman?

"This," Dafydd explained, "is Marged Pugh. Her grandchildren's Wendy-house——" He waved at the bwthyn. "Sky's fine, thanks. Gareth helped to drive the horsebox. And what we've all been carefully not saying is yes, this is Richard Cavendish who wanted to buy the railway. And Mr. Cavendish, for some reason Mrs. Farrell called you 'Herring-dancer' when she spoke of you. Unless you know why, we have no idea at all."

"Unless your surname's really Green," Marged suggested. "And we all had a go at anagrams, and it nearly makes 'Eric Handgrenade' but not quite."

Dai said desperately: "Can we go inside for a paned, Dafydd?"

"I might have enough cups . . . Why not?"

He put the kettle on, and went out of the front door to talk to James.

"It would have made more sense for everyone to come to my place," Dai reproached, moving up to allow Donald, Sandy, and Siân to squeeze into Dafydd's living-room too. Dafydd noticed with relief that they had brought mugs. "However, we're here now. Mrs.Gilchrist, Miss Smith, Miss Pickering, Mr. McBain: may I introduce Mr. Cavendish and Mr. Buntingford."

"The villains of the piece," Richard smiled wryly. "Unintentionally; we seem to have given you a good bit of excitement. By the way, how is the grand piano?"

Dafydd admitted that he hadn't yet contacted Mrs. Powell, but Miss Smith told them that although the tuner had removed quantities of hay from the innards, it was all back in working order and already being played by Mrs. Powell's pupils.

"So what exactly happened between you and Mrs Farrell?" Dai asked.

Richard explained that he'd tried to buy the railway and been refused, offered more money and been refused again, repeatedly. James explained that he'd volunteered to follow the new owners, to find out who they were and where the railway would be going to.

"Why? What did you hope to get out of that?" Marged demanded.

Richard shrugged. "I did wonder that at the time, when I found out where James had ended up. I suppose I might have offered to buy a part share in it, to store it for you, or to be the person you went to first if you decided you couldn't cope, but initially it was just—follow that car! Or in this case, train. And then when James reported his findings I'm afraid I just didn't believe you could be buying it. Not if you'd offered anywhere near what it was worth. Unless you had a businessman backing you, and there was no sign of that. So we put Mrs. Farrell's gateway under surveillance, and saw a horsebox arrive. James went over to see where it went, and was—er—hijacked by Mr. Williams."

"And why are you here now?" Marged persisted.

"Tell us what happened in London!" Donald knelt up and was pulled down again by Sandy.

"Later," Dafydd muttered, embarrassed.

Richard looked at James, who shrugged. He addressed Dai. "Okay. We came down here because Dafydd invited us to come to West Wales for a holiday, and to be honest, the way he described this place made me want to see for myself. I'd like to be involved in running your railway, if possible; ideally, I'd like to move down here and run the business from here too, though we'd need a *pied-à-terre* in London. We've been looking at houses today and arguing about how much of our work could be done at a distance."

"I happen to *like* living in London!" James grumbled, grinning at his employer.

"Yes, well, it'll be you that runs the London office. We currently operate out of a big old house in the suburbs, which isn't ideal for our needs; even before this we were thinking of moving to smaller premises, though admittedly not so far from London. I won't be able to help much with the railway on open days, because I have health problems. However, if you'll let me drive it when there aren't any members of the public around, I'll be only too pleased to do as much as I can to help you to keep it here and run it for whatever charities you choose."

There was a long silence.

"Do you suppose Kay Farrell would believe you?" Siân leaned forward in Dafydd's armchair like Miss Marple.

Richard sighed. "Probably not, because once you've annoyed someone that much they have trouble seeing you in any other way, ever."

Donald and Miss Smith and Marged all spoke at once; Dai blushed.

"All right, I know: Mr. Cavendish, it is possible to redress the situation, as I know from experience. If we can ever get you and Mrs. Farrell together, would you be prepared for her to throw a batter pudding at you?"

James Buntingford began to laugh.

Richard grimaced. "I suppose so. And James, I might even need to practice having batter puddings thrown at me, so as to react in a suitably contrite manner . . . "

James flopped back against a bookcase and laughed uncontrollably. Marged got up and picked her way across the floor. She patted Richard on the shoulder on her way past. "You'll do, bach. You'll do. Dafydd, have you got enough milk if I put the kettle on?"

Chapter 13

THE STICKER BEARING Kay Farrell's name and address was still in Dafydd's wallet. He remembered about it during Bible study, and when he got home he found his writing-pad and a pen and sat at the kitchen table to write to her.

He couldn't think of anything to say; or rather, there was so much he could have said that he wasn't sure how to start. Eventually he began by thanking her on Mrs. Powell's behalf for the grand piano, reporting that it was in use for pupils already and much appreciated, and the lady had asked for the address so she herself could write.

After that he made a pot of tea and considered for a long time. It seemed silly to pray for guidance when simply writing a letter, but he did so anyway, and then took the second cup of tea with him into Sky's room.

The tortoiseshell and white cat leapt off the windowsill to greet him and rolled at his feet. She was definitely rounder after a week of good feeding; not fatter all over, but much wider round where her waist would have been if cats had them, her short fur sleek with washing. How many kittens was she expecting? How big were newborn kittens? He'd never seen any . . . When would they be born? Maybe he should tell Kay about her; she was sound on cats . . .

The problem was not how to fill the sheet of paper but how to explain about Herring-dancer. Could he invite Kay to Borth? Not if Edith would feel obliged to put her up. He sat by Sky's box, holding the outstretched white paw as she purred.

At last he made his apologies to the cat and went downstairs again with the saucer and empty cup, and sat down to finish the letter.

I am sorry to have taken so long to write, but things have been happening. When I telephoned to tell you I was all right and going back to Borth, I was in the house of the man you call Herring-dancer. He had a very credible story to explain his actions, but as I did not know whether he was telling the truth I made the decision to invite him to Borth along with the young man in the car who works for him.

The railway is still in storage at Mrs. Powell's until we have cleared space for it at the museum. The local P.C.S.O. *and a friend are working on this in the evenings. It is quite safe at the farm, locked into a shed. Richard and James do not know where it is kept and have not asked about its whereabouts, though they have now met my friends, some of whom you have met.*

Richard says he would be pleased to help with the railway; he is not insurable to drive in the presence of the public but has longed to drive a train since being a child and for various reasons has never had the opportunity.

As far as I can tell Richard seems to be speaking the truth about himself. He has been to watch birds all day at Ynys Hir and genuinely knows about them: James is more of a twitcher but is also keen. They have done some local walks and have looked at what is for sale from local estate agents to see if they can move their business (computer consulting) to Borth. James will then spend time with clients in London if necessary. Richard has offered to help to rebuild a slate wall at my home and James appears to enjoy mowing lawns; he is going to do more for some older ladies when the weather improves. As far as I know they are staying for another three weeks at present, in one of the guest-houses, as I have a cat in my spare room expecting kittens.

How is Minnie? My cats are Rheidol and Sky. Rheidol is a neutered ginger shorthair who brings me odd socks and suchlike from around the local gardens. I put them out on my railings to be collected. Sky is a tortoiseshell and white shorthair, I have had her a week now, she was half-starved when I got her but she is looking healthier and is very friendly. The whole village seems to be looking forward to her having the kittens. They see her sitting on my spare bedroom windowsill and ask after her if she is not up there. She sleeps in an apple box.

We have talked about Herring-dancer (in their absence) and decided that it might be acceptable for Richard and James to help with the railway but not to ever own part or all of it, just in case. The Museum says that they would like to run at least the electric locomotive on the May bank holiday, when the village is doing events to raise money for the Syrian refugees, and some people from the 7 ¼ inch Gauge Society are talking about coming down to see it and talk to the Museum about someone to drive Juliet.

You would be very welcome if you would like to come to Borth. Please call in if you do, my address is as above, and the Museum is at the Railway Station, and although they are not open every day they have an email address and website.

Thank you for your patience with us and I wish you all the best with moving house.

Yours sincerely,

Dafydd Minnesota Williams

He read it through, considered altering a few points, realised that he would have to rewrite it if he did, as crossing out would look bad, decided not to bother, and sealed it into an envelope. He went to the Post Office to post it, on foot.

It was dark and the sea was calm, sloshing about on the other side of the sea wall. When he had dropped the letter in the post box he went up onto the top of the wall and walked all the way back, past Min-y-mor where Richard and James were staying, past his own house, then further, as far as the first of the two distinctive 1930s houses with a semicircular bay. There were a few small boats pulled up at the top of the shingle. Somewhere down there was the sunken forest, and, above the tide-line, the stretch of pebbles where the ringed plovers nested.

It was only when he turned towards home that he realised he had not brought his stick with him and didn't need it. The cycling was doing him some good. He would have to start making meal plans again, if only to ensure that he used the second aubergine before it went rotten: he'd had it a week already . . .

Chapter 14

IT WAS THE Friday before the May bank holiday. Tîm Pwdin plus Richard and James had been busy dusting and polishing the stock and locomotives of Kenneth Farrell's railway before it was displayed at the museum; they had finished on Thursday evening and now Dafydd and Richard were once more battling with his garden wall.

"I suspect some of the best bits are in someone's rockery," Dafydd grumbled, knocking old mortar off a piece of slate with his trowel. "There must have been more than this."

"Or under your shed." Richard sat back on his heels and wiped his face. "Not that I'm suggesting you move it to look! We could go out tonight and hunt for suitable bits down the lanes; there are enough old walls about. I'm not thinking of taking any apart, just removing some of the stones which have already come off."

'We might have to." Dafydd fitted in another flat-edged piece and gazed critically at it. "There's an old cottage I know of that's almost fallen down. But we're well over halfway up, now, and I'm grateful for your help. Shall we go before or after the meal?"

"What are you thinking of having? Before, if it's something solid."

"Salad with rollmops. And batter pudding with tinned peaches in, and custard."

"Pudding and custard for James' benefit: well, he's not back yet, so could we leave him a plate of salad and a note, and do the pudding when we get back?" Richard was tidying up the remaining pieces of slate.

"Why not? I'll wash the lettuce and feed the cats if you put the rest of it out."

Dafydd picked up their tools and went towards the house.

He pulled half the leaves off the lettuce James had bought at the Machynlleth market on Wednesday and left them to soak in salted water, put food out for Rheidol who had been dozing on the wall in the sun, and went upstairs to feed Sky and deal with her litter tray.

Richard came to find him fifteen minutes later. Dafydd met him in the doorway, finger to lips.

"Kittens," he whispered. "Have a look, quietly now, but don't disturb her."

Richard peered cautiously into the apple box. Sky was licking a tiny white shape while a darker one squirmed beside her. Downstairs, someone rang the doorbell.

"That'll be James. I'll let him in," he whispered, tiptoed out of the room and took the stairs two at a time.

Dafydd, intent on the tortoiseshell cat, hardly heard him. Why was Sky so careless? She'd stand on the first kitten if she didn't look out—and her whiskers were stretching forward again, so that would be a third kitten coming.

Who was that in the doorway? He heard Richard telling someone to be very quiet, and then it was Kay beside him, gazing into the apple box with a fascinated smile on her face.

The third kitten was another dark one, and when Sky was licking it dry while the first two tried to feed, he suggested to Kay that they should leave her to it and have something to eat.

Downstairs they found Richard and James making batter and slicing cucumber.

"How many?" James demanded. "Is she okay?"

"Three so far. A white one and two torties or tabbies, I think. She seems fine. I've put food down for her but she probably won't want it yet. Must remember to give her extra water. Mr. Cavendish, Mr. Buntingford, may I introduce Mrs. Farrell?"

There was an unexpected silence.

"Don't tell me you hadn't realised!" Dafydd grinned.

"Didn't give your identity a moment's thought." Richard looked apologetically at Kay. "There've been so many people coming to see Sky and stopping us in the street to ask if she's had them yet, that I assumed . . . !"

"Oops," James murmured in the background, then: "Are you staying to tea, Ma'am? There should be plenty."

"Please do." Dafydd indicated the spare rollmop still in its jar, and the three plates full of lettuce and tomatoes. "Do you eat rollmops?"

Kay said that she did, and if they were sure it wasn't too much trouble . . . They sat in the living-room with James on the floor as there was still one chair in Sky's room and they didn't want to disturb her, and ate the salad, and then James jumped up and said he would make custard and see how the pudding was getting on.

Richard exchanged glances with him, and then said, shyly: "Mrs. Farrell, I'm sorry to have annoyed you so much. Sorry I annoyed you *at all* ; I didn't mean to, but I got carried away, and—well. Sorry. Have you come up to see the railway? They're displaying it at the station on the bank holiday Monday, and we've polished everything and we *think* we've got all the hay out . . . "

"I'm still finding bits round the piano." She smiled. "So—you are the man who kept ringing me?"

He nodded. "I didn't think about what it'd be like for you. But I'm glad it's come here; you were absolutely right. It is a community thing, not for one person to keep to himself—and if I'd had it I doubt I could have driven it without training, and I'd far rather be one of a group of people learning to do it properly, if we can get someone to teach us . . . "

"There's a couple of blokes coming out from Ludlow to look at it tomorrow," Dafydd added. "They can't run Juliet on Monday, but we're insured for the electric loco for one day."

Kay sighed. "I'm pleased. I wish Ken could have handed it over himself, but we didn't have time." She sat up straighter and fixed Richard with a stern stare. "And you say you're content that it's gone to Borth?"

Richard nodded again, and took a deep breath. He said, 'You probably feel quite angry still, and I don't blame you. Er—do you know about Borth and batter puddings? Because James has made one and we didn't put the peaches in it, Dafydd, so that if Mrs. Farrell wanted to throw it at me——"

"W*hat?!*"

"It's Borth's way of dealing with annoying people," Dafydd explained. "It started with the P.C.S.O. You make a batter pudding, cut it in halves, take it to your annoying person and tell them what you think of them, throw half at them, and then share the rest. With custard, and, in this case, tinned peaches."

"You're all absolutely mad." Kay was trying to keep a straight face. "But I must say I'm tempted. Would you mind?" She was looking at Richard.

He said gravely: "Not at all. I'd prefer it if you did. James has been throwing puddings at me for a while, as practice."

"Not in here," Dafydd said, firmly. "We mustn't disturb Sky. Let's go into the back garden."

There were times, Dafydd thought, dolloping custard and peaches into bowls, when he was very fortunate to have understanding or absent neighbours. He went to the door and saw Rheidol sniffing at the scattered remains of the batter pudding, while Richard and James explained to Kay what they were doing with the garden wall. He called them in and sat eating contentedly. Sometimes he had bitterly resented having no family, but now . . . He slipped away upstairs to look in on Sky, came out and found James on the landing.

"How is she?"

"Fine, as far as I can tell. Four kittens, and she may have more yet, I don't know."

"May I look?"

"Of course. She knows you."

He went in and Dafydd saw him sit down very quietly on the chair, then lean over and smile at what he saw in the box.

They're nice people, he thought, making his way downstairs to find Kay washing up and Richard drying plates. He found another tea towel and collected cutlery.

"James is up there with her," he reported. "Four kits. Two dark, two white. They all look healthy so far."

"We'll have to chase that estate agent," Richard remarked happily. "One more weekend should deal with packing up the London house . . . I suspect I'll have to do at least half the City work myself; now James has found out about the surfing he won't want to be away too long, even before we have to dance attendance on a couple of kittens."

"I almost wish I was coming to Wales," Kay smiled. "But I've got Minnie, and the riding-stables, and the piano."

Napoleon Powell's piano, Dafydd thought, grinning. We've had *fun* . . .

James tiptoed downstairs to join them an hour later.

"Five. And she's gone to sleep curled up round them, so I've turned the light off and come down. Wow! Never seen anything born before: they come out in sort of little plastic packets, and she bites it open to get the kitten out. That was amazing . . . Richard, have you asked yet?"

"Asked what?"

"The question everyone wants to know the answer to!" He sat with his arms folded round his knees, grinning up at them. "Why Herring-dancer?"

They all looked at Kay. She blushed.

"Do you have another batter pudding handy? I think it might be my turn now . . . It was a programme on television that my brother used to watch. I don't remember much of it, only the beginning, with a huge foot coming out of the sky and squashing things——"

"Monty Python's Flying Circus," James murmured.

"—and one sketch; someone dancing about like a Morris-man and hitting another man around the face with a little herring: splat, splat, splat, like a mosquito buzzing around. And in the end the other man lost his temper and produced a really huge fish, a pike or a cod or something, and—whack!"

"I'm glad you only dealt your return blow by phone," Richard said courteously. "But if you want to hit me round the face with a fish, I'm sure Sky would appreciate the remains."

"Oh, please!" James joined in excitedly. "I can go to Aber tomorrow and buy a coley . . . "

Dafydd put down his knitting and slipped out into the hall. He would make a pot of tea for them all soon, but first he felt he should report the new arrivals. He lifted the receiver and dialled.

"Siân? She's had the kittens. Five! And Kay's here, and Richard and James . . . they're getting on fine. Miss Smith? No; I was going to ring her next . . . Well, if you don't mind . . . Thank you very much. Yes, Siân, that is an excellent idea! Thank you! I shall go and do it at once."

He wrote out a notice in Welsh and English, thanking people for their concern and reporting that mother and five kittens were doing well, sealed it into a clear plastic bag, and taped it firmly to the railings.

As Siân had said, it was good enough for Buckingham Palace, so it was good enough for Borth.

Part 3:

The White Box of Tynyllechwedd

Chapter 1

"I THOUGHT I'D leave you a week to settle in," Dafydd explained, following Richard up the stairs. "Did the move go well?"

"Better than we expected, but there was only a chain at our end, which helped."

His host opened the door of what Dafydd expected to be a bedroom and ushered him into the office. "It's far more pleasant than being in London, and as we're so high up here we're managing to pick up a decent phone signal without having to have an aerial, though we did have some rather expensive problems with broadband . . . James! When you've finished that check, can we have some tea please?"

The younger man looked up with a start from behind a computer screen, greeted Dafydd and continued with whatever it was he was doing for a minute or so while Richard led their visitor across to a padded bench in the bay window with a coffee table in front of it.

"We usually sit in here even when we're not working, because of the view; downstairs hardly gets any light, because of the trees and the hillside, and if anyone looked through the ground floor windows it'd seem like an ordinary house. We don't have a big sign on the gate saying Cavendish Computer Security, and all the computers and so on are up here, so unless someone knew they probably wouldn't bother to burgle us, but I've fitted a few alarms none the less, to keep my hand in. On a clear day you can see right across the hills, and the sunsets visible from the other side of this floor are amazing. How are the kittens?"

"Growing fast. Climbing, now; they're out of the box and running around the floor falling over their own feet. You must come to see them."

James paused on his way out of the door. "Definitely. Milk and no sugar, isn't it?"

"That's right. Thank you."

Dafydd looked out at the view of hills, hedges and fields and a few neighbouring roofs while Richard sorted papers. "Do you get many birds in the garden?" he asked, noticing a pair of binoculars on the windowsill.

"We've had jays and a woodpecker, and the usual small stuff: titmice and finches . . . Ah, thank you, James."

James put down the tray and sat on the windowsill. "Have you told Dafydd about our mystery? It started two days ago. Like Richard said, we sit in the bay here most of the time when we're not working, and sometimes when we are, and we talk about clients or wildlife or shopping or whatever, and that's the view. We don't stare at it all the time, but it's there. Two days ago people started to park in the road just over that far hedge. There must be a gateway or a lay-by or something; we've not gone to look yet because it's not on our route into Borth. At first we didn't take much notice, but cars and the odd van keep stopping there, and people get out—not always two, quite often it seems to be just one, and occasionally more—and they come back after a short time and drive off again. You notice the movement when the cars arrive or leave. At first we thought it was someone having deliveries, but there were too many; then we wondered about people visiting for a birthday, or if someone was ill, but Richard looked on the map and there's no house there, not even a farm track, and we've timed people and they aren't away long enough to be going anywhere specific that's on the map."

"It's probably something quite obvious," Richard commented, passing Dafydd a cup of tea, "but we can't think what. Any ideas?"

"Thank you. Rare plant? A rare bird might take longer to find . . . " Dafydd shook his head. "Are you going to put one of your little cameras down there?"

"I'm very tempted," Richard admitted, "but it's fun having a problem we aren't obliged to solve; rather like doing a crossword puzzle. We do watch visitors if we spot them arriving, as much as we can: sooner or later we'll see something which gives us more evidence. And I'd rather not put a camera in, not for something like this. If anyone found it we'd be in serious trouble, and we've only just arrived."

"I suggested we built a hide in that tree—" James gestured at the field "—and watched, but we'd need to get permission for a proper hide. I still think we could take a ladder . . . There's a car now. Dafydd, do you want the binoculars?"

Dafydd refused, as he had no idea where he was supposed to be looking at.

"Okay." James took them himself. "Blue roof to the car, two people getting out . . . Lost them. Time it."

"Timing," Richard confirmed. "It's usually about ten to fifteen minutes. They don't seem to be carrying anything; nothing big enough to see at this distance, at least. Usually they don't open the boot of the car, so it probably isn't fly-tipping. And it's too frequent to be sheep-rustling or anything dodgy, so we've not mentioned it to Dai. If it carries on I might tell him, but we've got so much work on that we don't have time to start chasing red herrings."

Dafydd applied himself to the tea, making what he hoped were appropriate comments as Richard explained where they were currently working, and how many of the sites had to be visited in person. It seemed that they pretended to be checking fire extinguishers and escape routes as a reason to be wandering around the buildings, but surely they would have to have some sort of qualification in fire safety? What if the real fire extinguisher-checkers turned up at the wrong moment?

"We might both have to go up to London next week," Richard finished.

"I won't keep you, then," Dafydd said promptly. "You should have said it wasn't convenient."

"Oh, visitors like you are no trouble!" Richard smiled at him, suddenly looking almost as young as his business partner. "It was the woman from the Carnival Committee who was worst: she couldn't quite manage to get to the point and I had a call to take: in the end I had to summon James to deal with her and he managed to get out of her that she wanted our support."

"And even then I couldn't pin her down as to whether she wanted us there on the day or putting money into it." James was suddenly serious. "Coming back now; two of them. Not carrying anything. Timing?"

"Twelve minutes." Richard drained his cup. "Average. Well, I dare say we'll find out, one day."

Dafydd thought he saw movement beyond the distant hedge, wondered which road it was. Did it come out in Glanwern, or further over, maybe at Dôl-y-Bont? He handed over his gift of a home-grown lettuce, wished them well with their computer security work and thanked them for the cup of tea, and was seen out by Richard.

"Come back whenever you like." The tall man opened the gate for him and checked the mailbox in the wall. "You're welcome any time. Seriously, we can always find time for a cuppa and a natter. No sign of the marsh harrier again?"

Dafydd said that he was afraid not, mounted his bicycle, and free-wheeled away down the hill.

Once out of sight, he took a long detour in hope of finding the lay-by. Without a map it was harder than he had thought, but at last he found a point from which he could see Richard's house between the branches of an oak tree. So this was the lay-by: there was no clue as to why so many people should stop there. An assortment of rubbish had been thrown down the steep slope but nothing looked recent. Where did people go when they got out of their cars?

To his surprise the only signs of foot passage were on the uphill side of the road, where trodden grass and footprints in the wet earth of the bank showed that people had gone over an old stile built into the slate wall beside a field gate. He made his way up the bank, skidding a little, clambered up the steps, and peered into the wood. The gate led into a field of sheep but the steps on the other side of the wall went down into the corner of the wood, with a rough path of flattened vegetation leading off between trees and bramble bushes. Reluctantly deciding that he wasn't dressed for detecting, he climbed down and rode back to the village, dismounting for the steepest parts of the route and promising himself a second visit when he had time to explore properly.

He dropped in at the shop on his way past, bought bacon and cat food, and was stowing them in his rucksack when he saw Edith.

"How's the sock coming along?" she asked.

"The first one fits; I'm part way down the leg on the second. Thanks for teaching me. How's Mike?"

She grimaced. "Another trip to Bronglais tomorrow; see if they can stabilise him. If not, it'll be Copthorne Hospital again. Shrewsbury."

"Let me know if you need an escort on the trains."

"Thanks. Mr. Cavendish did say he'd take us, but it's a low car, low to the ground, and I don't know if Mike could get in and out. I don't know how I got out of that Mini of Jonathan's, to be honest, not without a crane!" She smiled. "He's kind, isn't he?"

Dafydd nodded, explained that he'd just been up at the house to visit, and seen the office with its views out over the hillsides.

"Pity it's not a sea view for him," Edith remarked. "But there again, it might tempt him to go down on the beach all day."

"I think he's got quite enough distractions without that," Dafydd smiled, and told her about the cars which kept parking in the lay-by.

Edith shook her head. "Up to no good, I'll be bound. Fly-tipping, maybe."

"I looked. I went that way round coming back, and there was nothing I could see out of place. I wondered if it might be wildlife of some sort: a rare bird, or badgers or something. I might go up and look properly, one evening."

Edith said dubiously that he should be careful, you never knew what people got up to, and went on with her shopping.

Dafydd cycled home, planning. He couldn't go tonight, he had Bible study, but he'd try tomorrow, if it looked like being fine weather. He'd make sure there was no car already there—he'd have to leave the bicycle some distance away—and go and sit in the wood, where he could see without being seen. At least with so many different cars it wasn't likely to be courting couples but, just in case, he'd better have a good route of retreat worked out so he could depart unobserved.

He made bacon sandwiches for tea, finished off a couple of pears which were going squashy, and was about to leave for Bible study when the phone rang.

"Dafydd M. Williams sy'n siarad . . . Hallo, Miss Davies, what can I do for you?"

Edith's niece said that she wanted to talk to him.

"I'm just on my way out; do you want me to call round after Bible study?"

"No, no—will you be in tomorrow? I'll ring you when they've gone to the hospital."

"Is it something secret, then? I don't think——"

"Well, sort of. But it's not a *wrong* secret. It's about the cars you saw. I'll tell you tomorrow. Goodbye . . . "

Chapter 2

HE MANAGED TO concentrate on Jeremiah for most of the Bible study, but when it was over he rode south rather than returning home. For Esme to explain his mystery before he'd got his teeth into it seemed extremely unfair, so he would have to investigate tonight. At least he was not wearing his best clothes—and it had been dry for a day or two.

He locked the bicycle to a gate and walked the last quarter of a mile, seeing no vehicles, hearing only a few, far away. The sky was a clear cold pearly grey, slightly tinged with gold to the west. Swallows flew above him hawking for flies, and presumably there would be bats out instead soon, though not nightjars up here. He walked, found the lay-by, found the trodden path going off up into the wood. It headed single-mindedly to the remains of a building which was a tumble of once-whitewashed slate walls and jagged roof-timbers, then wandered off in a maze of subsidiary tracks which apparently led nowhere. Where should he wait? Should he sit somewhere in the field to watch the lay-by itself, or in the wood beyond the old ruin?

Finding nothing obvious which might have attracted visitors to the ruin, he climbed the hillside beyond it and found a couple of trees to sit behind, spread out the plastic bag which had contained his Bible, because the ground might be damp, and prepared for a long wait. Nothing happened. He read Philippians until he could barely see, and hoped he wouldn't twist an ankle getting back to the road, but the ground round the ruin was fairly clear of branches and stones, and the path the visitors had made would help. If he'd been thinking straight he should have brought the front light from the bicycle, if he could get it un-clipped . . .

Was that a car? It was almost dark. How long should he stay there? The nights were short, but not that short, and the cats would be anxious . . . Well, Sky would be anxious. Rheidol wouldn't care until breakfast was late, and the kittens were still too young to be concerned with anything other than food and warmth. Three torties and a white one: there had been five, but one had died at only a few days old and Dafydd had buried it solemnly in the back garden.

Poor little kit, he thought. Don't know what happened: maybe it was sickly or caught cold, or was damaged somehow before birth because Sky was so thin before I took her in . . . but the others are lovely, setting fair to be right little terrors. Good thing Siân managed to put me in touch with someone with an old big fireguard to spare, so I can block off the doorway, or they'd be all over the house . . . Yes, it is a car, coming up here. It'll be going past, sure to be . . . It isn't!

He sat very still. The engine noise stopped. Doors slammed. More than one person, then . . . Oh goodness, if it is a courting couple, I shall have to go uphill very quietly, like someone stalking deer. I should have looked for a way out while it was light; the fences all seem to have barbed wire in them . . . Here they come. They've got a torch. Up to the gate; coming towards the old ruin—and past it! Help! Keep still and they'll never see you, with their eyes used to torchlight. She's looking at something. Something small in her hand. A book? A compass? What's she saying? The other one's a girl too, with a bag. Going back to the gate; looking at the thing in her hand . . .

"It's all over the place," the girl by the gate announced. "It's the trees . . . What's the hint?"

The response was too quiet for him to hear, but they both went over to the ruin and began to poke about in the remains of a wall where a young rowan tree was hastening the dilapidation. After a minute or two one exclaimed: they crouched by the wall with the torch and Dafydd heard metallic noises, and then almost before he had realised it the torch was bobbing away down the path.

He sat still, wondering what to do. What had they had found?

When the car had gone he picked up the plastic bag, put his Bible back in and went carefully down the hill to the ruin, found the rowan tree, and felt gingerly among the stones. It was too dark to see details and he had no idea what he was looking for. He moved a stone and heard a metallic clink. There! There were stones piled on it . . . It was big, bigger than he had expected, a metal box about the size of three house bricks but not as heavy, with various protrusions at one end. It rattled.

He knelt there for a long minute. In order to get it open and find out what it was he'd have to take it with him, even if he only went down to the first street lamp. Surely more people wouldn't come for it tonight? Find out what it is, first. Then take it to Dai, if it's dangerous, or get up early tomorrow and put it back if it's harmless. He couldn't imagine what on earth it could be if it was harmless; all he could think of was some kind of spies' hiding-place for—what? A gun? Secret messages? But Esme knew about it; something to do with young people; students. Back in the days when the Free Wales Army was active he would have assumed it was something to do with extreme nationalism, but at least that was unlikely . . .

He found what seemed to be a sturdy handle on one narrow side of the thing, and made his way very carefully down the path, over the wall, and back down the road to where he had left the bicycle.

It was impossible to fix the box securely onto the carrier and he hadn't brought his rucksack, so he walked, pushing the machine. It seemed a very long way back. Would the bicycle light be suitable for investigating? He was tempted to try, but by now he was tired and cold. As the road flattened out onto the long main street, he got on and rode one-handed, arrived back too worn out to consider wangling the bicycle into the tiny ex-Wendy-house which was his shed, and brought it into the kitchen. He set the kettle to boil, spread a sheet of newspaper on the table, put the box on it and was joined enthusiastically by Sky, who had heard him return and leapt over the fireguard to greet him. He stroked her and fussed her, gave her a couple of treats and a dish of cat milk—the own-brand sort, which still seemed ridiculously expensive—and put another couple of treats in Rheidol's bowl. He made a pot of tea. Then, at last, he could turn his attention to the box.

It had been roughly painted white but had once been grey or olive-green. There was a folding handle on top, a complicated catch mechanism at one side . . . and, after all its handling, a slug still adhering to the lid. Ignoring the slug, Dafydd fiddled with the catch until it came open, and lifted the lid.

Inside was a clip-lock plastic box and, in a plastic bag, a large soft toy which appeared to be a hippopotamus wearing a necklace.

At least it wasn't arms or explosives, or drugs. Presumably it wasn't drugs. He stared accusingly at the hippo and drank some tea.

Now for the plastic box. The lid came off easily, disclosing a notebook in a plastic bag, two pens, a child's bracelet, a rather attractive coin the size of a crown piece with Celtic knotwork on it, a plastic dinosaur which had a necklace like the hippo's, a pencil sharpener from Lichfield Cathedral, a pencil labelled TITANIC-BELFAST, a doll's hat, some marbles and three football stickers. It was a child's treasure-box . . . but why was everyone so interested in it? Maybe there was some sort of treasure-hunt.

He took out the notebook and opened it. A sheet of folded paper fell out. The book contained a list of names and dates, with a few cryptic comments. The girls had signed themselves SukiSuzette and The Toucan. The first entry read: 'Skulker on the Slope—Roadkill Stew.'

That seemed rather ominous. Wondering if he should have taken the whole thing to Dai and left him to open it, Dafydd unfolded the paper and read:

> *'Official Geocache: Congratulations, you have found it! Inadvertently or otherwise . . . '*

The explanation continued chattily, telling him that it was part of a world-wide game for which you needed to use the internet, and that he was welcome to add his name to the log and to take something if he left something of equivalent or greater value. Above all, he must leave it exactly as he had found it . . .

Dafydd looked at his watch, groaned, put everything carefully back into the various bags and boxes and put the completed geocache by the back door, locked up and went hastily to bed. His alarm was set for six; he moved it back an hour, just in case.

At twenty past five he came downstairs, made a pot of tea, unfastened the tin box and the plastic box, signed the log (shyly, in very small letters) as D.M.W., and took the Celtic knot coin, replacing it with a Churchill crown piece. He fastened the cache again, put it into his rucksack and set out to replace it.

At seven a.m. he fed the cats and sat with the kittens and Sky for an hour, feeling smug. He knew why the cars parked in the lay-by, he'd found the cache; he hadn't taken it to Dai, he'd replaced it. So far so good. He wondered how many more there were around, whether he could find them without using the internet. Who was Roadkill Stew who had placed the cache? Probably a Welsh-speaker, as he'd called the cache Skulker on the Slope, which translated as Llechwr ar y Llechwedd, and the cache had been hidden in Tynyllechwedd wood . . . It would be interesting to hear what Esme had to say.

Chapter 3

"DAFYDD M. WILLIAMS SY'N SIARAD . . . Hallo, Miss Davies. I think I know what you're going to tell me."

"Hi, Mr. Williams. I think it might be people looking for a geocache. They——"

"You're absolutely right; I went up there and found it last night. It was a big metal box with a notebook in it, and lots of other things, and it's called Skulker on the Slope."

"Oh, that's fantastic! I wish I'd been there! What was in it?"

Dafydd paused, remembering the things in order. "A hippopotamus toy with a necklace on, and a plastic box with other things in it. The notebook, and some toys, and a dinosaur with a necklace on, and a rather handsome medal: I kept that and put a Churchill crown in instead. It had Celtic knotwork all over it."

"Ah, here we are. Skulker on the Slope, placed by Roadkill Stew four days ago. Three trackables in it: Hattie the Hippo, Swampmonster and Jeremy's and Alison's wedding geocoin."

"How do you know all this?"

'I'm on the internet. Signed into the website and looked up the caches. Mr. Williams, I hate saying it, but have you got that Celtic knot medal handy? I think it might be a trackable."

"What's a trackable?"

"People put them in a cache and other people take them all over the country—all over the world, sometimes. The hippo started in Bath last month and it's been to Scotland already . . . There's a number on each tag or coin, and you type it into that part of the website and tell them you've got it, and then you tell them where you've moved it to, and someone else comes along and takes it somewhere else. The hippo belongs to a little girl who's plotting all the places on a map. The wedding geocoin was started off at somewhere called Rosebush when the people got married last year, and it's trying to get to Montgomery where they live, in time for their first anniversary in September."

"It's upstairs. Ring me back in five minutes."

Dafydd put the receiver back and went upstairs. The coin did indeed, now he looked at it more closely, have a number printed round the edge. Bother. He'd have to go up there yet again and put it back. But he'd take a rubbing before he did so: it was a beautiful pattern. He sat by the phone and waited for Esme to ring back.

The phone rang.

"Mr. Williams? Oh, call me Esme, please; 'Miss Davies' reminds me of school. Did you find it?"

He read the number to her and she wrote it down.

"Yes, that's it." He heard her hesitate. "Mr. Williams—okay, Dafydd—would you be prepared to hunt for other caches? If I look them up on the internet, and tell you where they are? Because I can't do the looking-for part of it and you can, but I can do the research, which you can't."

"How many are there?"

"Oh, millions. At least two million, I think, worldwide. And quite a few round here, to judge from the map. There's one near the Animalarium, and one somewhere on the sea-front, and one up by Ynyslas, and one at one of the caravan parks . . . they're all different sizes, too; some are only about the size of a film canister, and there are smaller ones than that, apparently."

"Would you mind doing the research?"

"I'd love to! I've always wanted to do this since I found out about it, but I didn't see how I could; there are some which are supposed to be wheelchair-friendly, but most of them aren't. If I could *get* there, there's a whole series of accessible ones along the old railway line that's now a cycle-track; the rules say they have to be a certain distance apart, but there seems to be one every few hundred yards. Would *you* mind looking for them? Don't say yes just to be polite."

"I would be delighted," Dafydd said firmly. "I did sign the logbook as D.M.W.; don't you have to write that down somewhere on the internet?"

"Yes. Dafydd, if we're going to be a team, we need a name. I wondered about that while you were looking for the geocoin. How about Symbiosis?"

"Most appropriate." He grinned. This was going to be fun.

"And—do you mind not mentioning it to Auntie and Uncle?"

Dafydd hesitated. "Why?"

Esme took a deep breath. "They mean well, but—— Oh, sometimes I could scream! They won't let me do anything—I don't have a door key, and I can't go as far as the supermarket by myself 'in case something happens', and they stand on the doorstep watching me when I do go out—just down to the pharmacy—and they tell me off if I'm gone too long . . . Dafydd, I used to teach at a secondary school, and they treat me like a little kid just because I can't walk! I want to go down on the beach but I can't without a bit of help, and they won't hear of it, they can't understand that I just want to lie on the shingle and feel the stones hot under my hands and seaweed crunchy in the sun and——" She stopped, and Dafydd thought he heard a sniffle.

"You feel trapped," he suggested.

"Exactly. I bet they'd think of some wonderful reason why I shouldn't be caching. I just sit there and watch television like an old woman in a care home! Auntie was even trying to stop me cutting the pieces for my quilting in case I cut myself, at one point. Do you have a mobile phone? Then we can text."

He told her that he didn't. "Will they let you go to the phone box by yourself? I can find a big screw-topped jar or something and put it on the wall under the hedge; we can leave messages in it."

"Oh, wow!" Esme sounded suddenly gleeful. "You really are into this, aren't you! That'd be fantastic! When can we start?"

"I'll go out in the next half-hour and place the jar," Dafydd promised. "You do some research and get it written out; see if you can deliver it today sometime. I'll wander past a few times and check . . . and you'd better tell the website that I've got the geocoin: if I find another cache big enough I'll drop it off. Okay? If you think of anything else before they get back you'd better ring me. Thank you, Esme. I'm going to enjoy this no end!"

Twenty minutes later he went for a walk, carrying a bag. He stopped by the phone box and studied his shopping list as a woman with a dog passed, then reached into the bag and brought out a screw-topped plastic jar which had contained Ovaltine, then raisins. It now held a small piece of dry seaweed and a folded piece of paper which read:

Dear Miss Davies,

I hope this is an appropriate container. This is going to be an interesting experiment: I won't tell anyone except Rheidol and Sky and the kittens—maybe you could persuade them to let you visit the kittens one day? Or I could put them in cat-baskets and bring them over, if you think we could ever catch them all again once they got out!

Kind regards, Dafydd M. Williams

He glanced around to make sure no one was watching, and pushed the jar into the hedge beside the phone box so that it rested on the wall but was concealed by the privet. There; he'd done his bit. Now it was up to Esme. He went on down the road, towards the supermarket.

When he returned home he put the margarine into the fridge and the cat food into the cupboard, and went upstairs to sit with Sky and the kittens. Sky landed on his lap almost before he had sat down, the kittens wandering about on the floor looking for her and trying to climb up his trouser-legs. He picked one up, very carefully; it was the tortie with white patches.

"You look like Mavis," he told it. "At school with me; she was very pretty but not particularly clever, poor girl. People would tell her the most outrageous stories, and she used to say 'Ooh, really?' with her eyes wide, looking just like you . . . " He stroked it between the ears with a fingertip and put it gently back on the floor. The white kitten was almost as far up as his knee, needle-sharp claws hooked firmly into the cloth of his trousers, which were starting to show the damage.

"You, my lad," Dafydd told it sternly, "are going to be over that fireguard and falling downstairs before any of the others, though your sisters won't be far behind. And by the size of you you're getting more than your fair share of food already; that, or you take after your father, who must have been enormous . . . "

He winced as the claws dug in again, and stroked Sky's gleaming fur. She would never be a big animal, but a room she could defend as her own, plentiful food and the odd bottle of cat milk had transformed her from the timid creature cowering on top of Becky's kitchen cupboard in Penparcau to this protective mother. She leapt down to lie in a patch of sunlight on the floor and the kittens surrounded her within seconds, clambering over each other to feed. Dafydd got to his feet quietly and left them to it, stepping over the fireguard with exaggerated caution and deciding to make a pot of tea before he weeded the garden.

Chapter 4

TO HIS DISBELIEF there was someone using the public telephone at six-thirty the next morning. He walked on, put half a newspaper in the paper-bank (he was having to ration his recycling, but at least it was a viable excuse to be passing the phone box), and went to read the notice board outside the Community Hall.

There was going to be a talk in Llanbadarn on airfields of the Second World War and another at the same venue on shipbuilding in the Dyfi estuary, which he thought he might try to get to until he realised it clashed with Bible study. There was a felt-making workshop, a new yoga class, and the usual weekly line dancing, exercise for over sixties, mums and toddlers . . . There was also a poster up about the Carnival. He looked away. Why did he always feel guilty about avoiding it?

Because they keep going on about being community-spirited, and everyone helping to make it a good day out—and I really don't like being with crowds of people, even if I know them, or getting involved and looking stupid, especially in public . . .

Previously he had carefully arranged to be on holiday that weekend so as to avoid it completely, but this time he'd not booked anything; besides, he had the cats, and although his neighbour at Anfield (who worked away during the week) was quite happy to feed Rheidol for two nights in exchange for Dafydd keeping his eye on the house for the rest of the year, Dafydd didn't feel he could land him with the responsibility of a female cat who should not be let out and four lively kittens. Well, he could go for a really long cycle ride; go out all day on the train. If he warned Esme maybe she could find him some caches on the road to Machynlleth or Tywyn . . .

He went back up the main street to the phone box. At last it was vacant; the street was deserted, and there was a message in the jar. He sat on the bench to read it.

Hi Dafydd

Thanks for doing this! The first is 'Seaside Special: Borth' which is a nano (smaller than a film canister/ micro) on a notice board by the public toilets. If the warders ever let me out that far I'll be under escort so I won't be able to sign it, but if you can give me a description of where exactly, I can at least see it (or feel it, if it's at the back)! I've printed out some sample logs for you and the description and everything, so you can get an idea of what comes up on the website. If I'm under surveillance (believe me, that doesn't feel like exaggeration some days), I won't print stuff, just take notes and write it up at night in my room. I don't expect I'll be able to get out every day so there's no hurry!

I've printed off the second one too which is 'Prickly Patch' up by the Animalarium, under a gorse bush by the sound of it. Do you have gardening gloves?! This one is a small, which could be any size I suppose, the Skulker was a Regular! (Like coffee shop coffees, where the choice is More than enough, Far too big, and Even bigger!) The nano one said you might need tweezers, if you don't have any let me know and I'll put some in the jar for you.

Did you realise that part of the fun is not letting anyone see you doing it? Non-cachers are called muggles (like the non-magical people in Harry Potter) and muggles have a nasty habit of vandalising the caches or just taking them away and not putting them back.

If you need more information, let me know and I'll do my best. I've done sketch-maps of what the satellite view was on Google Earth, but apparently the cache could be within 10-20 feet of the G.P.S. reading.

Good luck! And thanks so much——Esme.

He studied the maps. It was still quite early so he could have a go at both of them. The Animalarium one first, if there weren't any dog walkers about. He went back up the main street and took the turning by the Health Centre, which led to the church via the fire station where he had met the Dreaded Batter Pudding Hurler, the disused chapel, the cottage by the level crossing, the tip and the

Animalarium. When he got to the Leri, he pulled out the maps again. Yes, that was the river; that was the cluster of buildings. So he needed to go this way, along the river bank, about this far . . . Gorse bushes. Yes, a whole shrubbery of them, golden with blossom though not yet smelling of coconut; that would come when the sun was at its highest. And somewhere under one of the bushes was a Small, in a camo bag.

From the maps it looked like the bush nearest-but-two to the far end. According to the logs it had been found three times in the last week. Therefore . . .

Dafydd strolled along the bank, trying to look as though he did this every morning, and saw a patch of trampled grass and scuffed earth where people had been investigating under the last gorse bush but two. Yes!

He checked quickly for dog-walkers, saw no one and got down on hands and knees in the grass. It must be right in under the branches. He crawled forward, spines catching at his hair, and saw a corner of something green and brown which came loose when he pulled at it. He sat back on his heels and opened the bag, and took out a plastic box half the size of a small margarine tub. The geocoin would have fitted into this one, if he'd brought it. There would, no doubt, be others. He opened the box, found a stub of pencil provided for signing the logbook—which was good, because he'd forgotten to bring a pen—two marbles, a plastic horse-shoe, a hair-bobble, and a little metal brooch of a cat.

He felt in his pocket and brought out an air ambulance trolley token which he'd acquired as a potential swap, took the cat, dropped the trolley token into the box, signed the logbook proudly as 'Symbiosis', and dated it, put the logbook back in the box and the pencil in his pocket, put the box in the bag, replaced it, and brushed the grass back into place as best he could before heading towards the village. There was earth on his trousers, and the snags made by little claws had been added to by a tear: there must have been barbed wire or glass somewhere among the gorse.

Should he try for the second one as well? Would that be being greedy? But Esme couldn't have found the gorse bush one without help, so if the seafront one was accessible it would be kind to let her have a go at it as soon as possible.

He stopped by the pharmacy and checked the second map, then pushed it back into his pocket as a dog-walker passed. The notice board would be easier to find than a particular gorse bush . . . What did the logs say? In the corner, up inside. Of course, that notice board was really three boards, arranged as a triangular pillar on top of a metal pole. Which corner?

He hurried down the road, up the ramp onto the concrete shelf where the notice board stood next to a bench and a litter bin, felt around inside one corner, then had to stop because people came into sight, and stood reading about water quality. When they'd gone he had another go, but then Bill came past with Rosie straining at her leash, and they exchanged a few words . . . and when Bill finally left, someone drew up in a car to use the toilets.

Dafydd loitered, scrabbling around up inside the notice boards, but found nothing. How small was a nano? In desperation he knelt down on the ground and peered up inside the triangle of boards—and there it was, a tiny nub of black, slightly higher than he'd been searching.

"What *are* you doing, Mr. Williams?" someone enquired from behind him, and he almost cricked his neck as he scrambled to his feet.

At least it wasn't Marged; it was Carol from the Bible study group with her terrier.

He opened his mouth to say 'nothing', but realised that was Dafydd aged six thinking for him, and remarked instead: "There's a terrific lot of spiders about this year, have you noticed? I come out in the morning and there are webs all over things, not just gates and the usual places."

Fortunately this was true, though not the correct answer to her question, and Carol said yes, there'd been one from the lamp post to her neighbour's car aerial one morning, and was his house infested with harvestmen?

Dafydd looked blankly at her. "Oh, that's what they're called, is it? Those really spindly spiders? Yes, I've got them making webs all round my curtains, and the more I brush them away the more there seem to be. It must be a good year for whatever they feed on, I suppose."

At last Carol went away. Dafydd reached up inside the corner of the boards, detached the cache and almost went onto the beach to sign it in peace before realising that if he dropped it in the shingle it would be lost for ever. Instead, and with more dog-walkers approaching, he took it into the Dynion and shut himself into a cubicle to sign it.

When he got home he wrote another letter, then collected the second half of the newspaper and sauntered back down through the village towards the recycling bins.

Dear Esme,

I have found and signed both caches. I got a cat brooch out of the Prickly Patch one, which was easier to find than I had feared because there was a path to the right bush! I've pinned it to this letter for you and replaced it with a trolley token.

I was glad I had the brooch for the pin part of it, because when I finally got the nano—they are about the size of a bumblebee and it was magnetic and about six inches up inside the corner of the boards nearest the last house that side—I unscrewed the top and the logbook was about a quarter of an inch wide and tightly rolled up inside and I couldn't get it out until I thought of the pin. I signed it with the pencil I kept from the previous cache by mistake and managed to put it back between dog-walkers—the entire population of Borth *must have come past while I was trying to find it or put it back, including Carol from Chapel who saw me on my hands and knees looking up inside the notice boards and said what was I doing, I carefully didn't tell her but went on about there being a lot of spiders around this year!*

You can get to the notice boards up a ramp, so you might be able to find it by feel; if you knock it off by mistake don't worry, I can put it back for you if you let me know (if I can find it). The magnet is quite strong so you'd have to hit it hard to detach it.

I've not written logs like the ones you provided, you may like to do that yourself if I tell you what happened and you can censor it.

Thank you for this—this is fun! I have a bicycle if you want me to look for caches further away; I also get free local rail travel which may help. Let me know if there are other big/ small ones I could put the geocoin into, otherwise I will put it in Prickly Patch (and replace the pencil).

Kind regards, Dafydd.

Chapter 5

ESME'S NEXT NOTE, which he retrieved at 6 a.m. a day later, had clearly been scribbled in haste.

> *Hi Dafydd, thanks! Well done—logged both. Next 2 are near Ynyslas, one at the end of a footpath and it sounds as though it's under a loose stone at the base of a wall, another small one, and the other's on a fence round a yard, called 'Look Sharp', magnetic micro. Good luck—Esme.*

Enclosed were two sketches, one showing the path and which side of the wall she thought the cache was, the other showing the yard, with a tiny X where the cache was supposed to be.

Dafydd went back through the village, collecting his paper and some milk on the way, fed the cats and had breakfast, made a cheese sandwich and got his bicycle out of the shed. The rubbing he had taken of the geocoin was safely in the top drawer in Sky's room; the coin itself was in his pocket with the padlock and chain.

He cycled out to Ynyslas under a blue sky with gulls calling and a few ponies watching incuriously from the fields beyond the golf course. The first cache he wanted to try for was the one on the fence; he hoped there would not be anyone around to watch him.

The yard was easily found, a small enclosure containing a Portakabin and assorted vehicles and trailers, near the boatyard. The fence consisted of vertical metal railings which had once been painted white, topped with barbed wire . . . no; razor wire. Look sharp, indeed. But no one could reach the wire without something to stand on—or want to—so it must be on the fence itself . . . No, there was a sign, more or less where the X had been on Esme's plan. He leaned the bicycle against the kerb and went towards the notice. It seemed to be plastic; maybe the cache was on the fence, after all . . .

The sign read: WARNING: THIS PROPERTY PROTECTED BY RAZOR WIRE AND ANTICLIMB PAINT; and was made of some sort of stiff plastic. How was it fastened to the fence? He reached through the railings and felt the back of the notice, starting at one end and working along the top. Was that a car coming? Aha, there was something attached to the plastic, a strip of metal—and attached to the strip of metal, something which fell off into the brambles underneath.

Dafydd very nearly swore. He hurried back to his bicycle, and when the car passed was kneeling beside it apparently checking the front tyre. As soon as the car had gone he wheeled the machine closer, leaned it against the fence by the notice and grovelled desperately in the brambles for the film canister. He could see it but couldn't quite reach it . . . and clearly at least one other person had met the same problem because there was a stick lying beside the fence, and not a tree within yards. Another vehicle; he ripped the pump off the bicycle and as the van passed was calmly fitting it onto the valve.

Safety: a few seconds of raking with the stick, and finally the container rolled into reach. He grabbed it, knelt by the bicycle to open it and sign the log—this time he had remembered to take a pen—and hoped no cyclists would appear and offer to help, as yet again he fiddled with the front tyre as a car passed. At last he managed to replace the cache behind the notice, replaced the pump on the bicycle frame, picked thorns out of his fingers and set off with relief for the second cache.

When he reached the start of the path shown on Esme's map it was definitely a footpath, not a bridle-path, so he locked the bicycle to a fence and climbed the stile. The path led towards the Dyfi estuary on an artificial bank which ran alongside one of the drainage ditches. It was long and straight and completely deserted.

He walked steadily, watching a cormorant fly over, hearing oystercatchers and gulls. There were small flowers in the short turf and sheep in the fields. He tried to remember the details of plants which he did not recognise, intending to identify them at home and tell Esme, but after a few minutes he simply walked, enjoying the morning.

The path led under the railway line in a culvert but though it was clearly often underwater he reached the end dry-shod and studied the estuary. There were shelducks at the edge of the field and waders on the mudflats: a redshank and sandpipers, and more birds further away: he had not considered bringing binoculars but thought they might be curlews. Sunlight glittered on the water and a stiff breeze whipped at his hair. Why had he not come out here before? He would have to come back with binoculars and a flower book . . .

Meanwhile, he ought to look for the cache. A wall, she had said, with a loose stone at the bottom of it. The only wall was the stone-built bank which kept the sea back.

He studied the map and slithered down to the fence which kept the sheep from scaling the bank; there were tufts of wool caught in the lower strands of wire. Under a litter of driftwood and dead reeds which had been left after a storm, he found the stone, and there behind it was the plastic box; a clip-lock box containing another, smaller clip-lock box, and about a gill* of dirty water. Dafydd shook out the water and dried the inner box on a spare handkerchief before opening it. The logbook was in a plastic bag and was more or less dry, but a key-ring had rusted and left marks on a toy car. Even before discovering that the logbook had

*A quarter of a pint; five fluid ounces.

not been signed since April he had decided that this would not be a good place to leave the geocoin, not if it was supposed to be reaching Montgomery by September. He signed the log and sat holding it in the sun until it had dried thoroughly, re-packed the box and arranged it neatly under the stone, and sat on the bank feeling contented.

This is the sort of cache I enjoy doing, he thought. No danger of being interrupted; no need to pretend to be doing something else, no need to lie to people if they ask awkward questions . . . That's what I really don't like, but I promised Esme I wouldn't tell anyone. I shouldn't have promised. I didn't realise how difficult it would be to find some of them . . . Oh dear. But I'm not sorry to have done this one, because I'd never been here before and without the cache I'd never have bothered to. Yes, I must come back out here. Maybe on the way back from a cache further out towards Tre'r Ddol, if there are any . . .

At last he got up and began to stroll back down the path, thinking how fortunate he was to live in such a lovely part of Wales. No wonder people came here on holiday, bought caravans or houses and visited when they could . . . Ah. People on holiday. Mr. Norgate at Anfield was all right, but there had been a car outside his other neighbours' house the previous evening, so they must have driven down after work. He wondered how long they would be staying for and whether it was the whole family or only the parents, or only the grown-up children and their friends. But he didn't have them all year and they weren't too bad, really, just louder than he was used to. And he could always go out and walk if they disturbed him.

He retrieved his bicycle and rode back to the village, wrote a note for Esme and decided to deliver it straight away. He walked down the sea wall at first, then saw Dai and Llinos heading for the station and crossed the road.

"Sut dach chi?" he asked. "How are you?" Dai was out of uniform for once, and there was a train due in ten minutes; he fell into step with them as they turned the corner.

"Fine, thanks. Yn iawn, diolch," Dai grinned. "You tell him, Llinos."

Blushing, Llinos informed him that they'd just got engaged to be married, and were going to see Dai's parents in Stone.

"It's in Staffordshire," she added in explanation. "Yn Swydd Stafford. "

"Llongyfarchiadau!" Dafydd smiled. "Congratulations! Pryd dach chi'n priodi?"

"In the autumn, we hope." Dai looked at Llinos, who nodded.

"We can't get married any sooner; I need to sell my house, and Dai's going to have new windows in his, to start with."

"Well, it's a lovely day for a trip. Dydd braf am wibdaith; mwynheuwch! Have fun!"

He left them on the platform and went back down the road, round past the hotel and along the main street to knock at the door of Stretton where Esme was staying with Edith and Mike. Edith answered the door.

"Dafydd! How are you? Come in; would you like a cup of tea?"

"Yes please, if you're making one."

Edith bustled away. Esme wheeled herself into the room and asked anxiously: "What's happened?"

"More gifts from Rheidol for you to put on the windowsill. And my recycling." He handed her the carrier bag and winked. Esme looked inside it, took out the much-folded note and stuffed it into her pocket. As Mike came in, followed by Edith, she held up a small teddy bear and a pink sock.

"Do you mind having them on your windowsill?" Dafydd asked, generally, taking the bag back. "The sock looks nearly new, and the weather forecast said thunderstorms later this week. I wish I knew where Rheidol gets these things from!"

"You could get him a collar with a camera on it, like the cats on that television programme," Edith suggested. "Maybe Richard and James would be able to get one for you."

Dafydd thought that Rheidol was quite likely to come back without the collar, given half a chance, but said yes, that was an idea . . .

Esme grinned broadly at him and asked how his sock was progressing.

"I'm about to turn the heel." A flicker of mischief prompted him to add: "I'd have finished by now if things hadn't kept distracting me."

Esme camouflaged a giggle with a fit of coughing, and had to protest that she was fine, she hadn't choked.

"Maybe you should knit something next." Edith hovered, anxiously. "Gloves, perhaps, or a nice scarf: you say you're bored with quilting . . . "

"You would be if you'd done eight hours solid to get it finished for Cae Hir!" Esme snapped. "And I hate knitting!"

"What's Cae Hir?" Dafydd asked, in an attempt to keep the peace.

"There's a garden on a hillside, down by Cribyn; it was a smallholding and a Dutch family have made it into a garden. It's lovely; lily ponds and clipped trees and all sorts of things—and each year they have a quilt competition there."

"They hang up the quilts outside, between trees," Mike put in, unexpectedly. "With plastic over, if it rains."

"Sounds interesting," Dafydd commented. "How many people enter it?"

"About twenty, thirty a year." Esme looked daggers at her aunt. "And it went there by post, so I wanted to make absolutely sure it arrived in time. I'll start another quilt soon, but I want to think about the design . . . and it would be good to have a change for a while, do something a bit different. Not sewing or knitting."

Dafydd said: "How about bird-watching?" and held his breath, in case that provoked another snap from Esme.

"There's not much comes to the garden," she said glumly.

"You could sketch," Edith suggested. "I've got boxes of lovely postcards you could copy."

Seeing the look on Esme's face, Dafydd leapt in again. "If you *can* sketch, why don't you sketch plants? I keep seeing stuff I can't identify, and if I brought them to you to sketch . . . "

She grimaced. "Thanks, but it's illegal to pick wild flowers. I suppose I could draw florist's flowers, if the supermarket here sells any, or things from the garden. Have you got a book to identify flowers with?"

"Yes, but it's an old one of Mam's. I was going to ask Miss Smith if she could lend me a book. I know: I could bring you a kitten to sketch."

Edith was now looking horrified, and Esme was on the verge of giggling again. Good.

"Or maybe not . . . Next time I do some weeding, I'll bring you a bunch of flowers." He grinned.

"Lovely!" Esme pretended extreme enthusiasm. "Thistles, and bindweed, and ragwort——"

"Dandelions," Mike growled. "And ruddy *ground elder*."

"Mike!" Edith expostulated.

Dafydd applied himself to his tea and almost choked as, behind her aunt's back, Esme pulled a reproachful face at him and made stirring motions.

"Do you have paper and pencils?" he asked, when order seemed to have been restored. "Sketching paper, I mean, and proper BB pencils? Let me know if you run out and I can get you some. I go into Aber or Mach quite often, and Siân usually fits me out with a list of stuff her neighbours need fetched. In fact, I might as well go to Mach on Wednesday; I can get my hair cut, and it's market day."

Chapter 6

AS HE LEFT Stretton on his way to the bottle-bank he noticed that Miss Smith's parlour curtains were open. Get rid of the empty ketchup bottle, first . . . He posted it into the correct slot and turned away, waiting for cars to cross the roundabout by the supermarket.

Miss Smith next. In case she too invited him in for a cup of tea he nipped into the public conveniences by the lifeboat station, and came out to hear gulls screaming angrily: there was a red kite swooping over the shore, mobbed by gulls and jackdaws. Presumably one had found something edible and the kite had decided to try its luck. He watched until the kite gave up and flew away down the coast, went down onto the beach and walked along the shingle bank until he came to the new sea defences, found the gap by the Victoria Inn and ended up on the main street next to Miss Smith's house.

He knocked on her door and while waiting for her to answer studied her tiny front garden for flowers. There was a bush of most un-Miss Smith-like bright pink roses, and a couple of other shrubs in pots, and a mat of something small sprawling at his feet; he had that in his garden, too, and he'd never noticed it except as something to be hoicked out. If he recalled, it had tiny white flowers . . .

"Bore da!" Miss Smith greeted him, holding the door a little wider as Konrad trotted past and went straight upstairs. Dafydd wondered how the black cat managed not to get run over. "Good morning, Minnesota, come in. Dere i mewn. To what do I owe the pleasure of your company?"

"Oh, I'm here on Invisible University business. Busnes y Brifysgol Anweledig." He grinned. "Dw i eisiau benthyca llyfr o'ch llyfrgell. I want to borrow a book from your library."

"Pa fath o lyfr? What sort of book? Paned? Ewch i'r parlwr tra fy mod i'n gwneud y te."

He obediently went into her parlour to wait for the tea and sat down on the old black shiny sofa. The brown-upholstered armchair he left for Miss Smith. One of the bookcases contained natural history, but there seemed to be several shelves of books on flowers so he would wait and see what she recommended. He looked around the room. After Edith's living-room, cluttered with the television and ornaments and photographs, Miss Smith's parlour was almost empty, except for books: there was indeed barely wall space for anything else. There were no photographs, no pictures or ornaments of any kind, and no plants except a large stoneware jar in the corner which contained pale, contorted branches. He thought he remembered plants; maybe she'd put them outside for the summer.

There was a small table in front of the window and a large rug at his feet, not a cheerful bright green like the one in his own living-room, but a dull brown, and although he had never before noticed the fact, the floor was uncarpeted and the floorboards were also painted a dark brown. He turned round to inspect the window wall: the curtains were dark green with a pattern of ferns, the wall off-white. Presumably the other walls were, too. What was the rest of her house like? None of his business.

He stood up politely as Miss Smith came in with a tray.

"So what sort of book do you want to borrow?" she asked.

"A book about flowers." He hesitated. "I do have one, but it was Mam's and the pictures aren't very clear."

"What's it called?" She was scooping her teabag out with a spoon; he did the same.

"*A Flower Book for the Pocket*," he said promptly. "By Skene, I think."

"Mm. Good for its time. Start with this one." She picked a book from a shelf behind her chair. "Can you remember what the flower looked like? What colour was it?"

He frowned. "White, mostly. A little tiny thing, low down in the grass."

"Whereabouts? Dunes, fields, woods?"

"On the sea-bank out by Traeth Maelgwyn."

She held out the book. "That sort of shape?"

"I don't know . . . I don't think so. It was in the grass: I didn't notice any leaves. There was tormentil there, too."

She turned pages. "That one?"

Dafydd looked more closely. "Yes, that's it. White, with purple and yellow. Eyebright: I must remember that. And then I noticed a little plant between the slabs when I was ringing the doorbell; it grows in my garden too."

"Pearlwort. Everyone who's ever gardened has seen it, I think, but only a handful know its name. Why the sudden interest?"

Dafydd shrugged. "I was walking, and I stopped to rest and looked at the grass, and there were flowers I didn't know the names of. I went in to take Rheidol's latest to Edith, and Esme's finished a quilt and is looking for something else to do before the next one; we suggested sketching, and she seems happy to draw flowers but apparently you're not allowed to pick properly wild ones now, so I said I'd bring her a bunch next time I did any weeding."

"We could photograph plants for her but it wouldn't be the same." Miss Smith frowned. "Why have you started taking things to Edith again? Has someone else complained about you using your railings?"

Trust her to notice that, Dafydd thought. "There were a couple of things that looked too good to get wet; a teddy and a sock. No one's complained; I just fancied a chat. May I ask what plant that is? Those branches in the vase over there?"

"Oh, those are shaped by ivy and honeysuckle, would you believe it; it's all driftwood, some out of rivers and some off the beach. Good sculptural shapes." She reached over and pulled out a sample. "Look—you can see where the creepers have wound round the branch and it's grown in a spiral like a narwhal's horn."

"Honeysuckle . . . you wouldn't believe that would be strong enough." Dafydd shook his head. Shyly, he added: "I don't like the idea of that. As though you could sit under a tree and if you fell asleep it might wind round you and—well, squeeze. Like a python."

"You've seen too many science fiction films! It doesn't grow that quickly, and you'd have to be asleep for months, years, before it was too thick to break out of. But yes, I agree with you: there is something a bit eerie about it. And positive, too, if you think about it: the tree keeps growing, and the honeysuckle hangs on but it can't stop the tree growing, it just twists it a bit . . . Do you think Esme would like a couple of these to draw, as a still life?"

"I expect she would. I said I'd fetch a sketchpad for her on Wednesday when I go to Mach, if she wanted. Anything you want me to bring back? I'll ask Siân, too; see if she wants anything."

Miss Smith said thank you, she'd think about it, and drank tea. "How are Sky and the kittens?" she asked, leaning back in the chair and stretching moccasin-shod feet across the rug.

"Oh, fine. Sky's eating me out of house and home, and the little ones are friendly and inquisitive and climbing up things already. You must come and see them. I'm expecting Richard and James tonight or tomorrow; they want to choose two, so they'll be company for each other if they go away. I said I'd look after them if they do both go back to London for more than one night: it doesn't seem to happen much."

"Do you have homes for the other two yet? I couldn't have another one, myself; I just wondered."

Dafydd told her that several people had expressed vague interest, but so far the only definite offers had come from the butcher, who wanted the white tom kitten, and from Richard and James. Miss Smith said she'd ask around and let him know if anyone seemed genuinely keen.

"You must get her spayed as soon as possible," she added, "or you'll end up with another litter."

Dafydd grimaced. "I know. I ought to keep the kitchen door shut because she comes downstairs sometimes now, but I keep forgetting. Oh, and I've had a postcard from Kay: she's settled in well at the riding-stables, and she wants to know if we're planning to run the railway at the Carnival."

Miss Smith said that she had assumed they would, and he'd better ask Richard when he visited because they would know far more about it than she did.

"How did their move go?" she asked. "One of my friends lives near their house and she said there was a huge removals van, almost too big for the lane."

"All right, I think. I went to see them and they work in one of the upstairs rooms with a view out over the hills. They seem to have got everything set up and running very quickly, but then, they know what they're doing . . . The house is like Fort Knox, alarms and remote-controlled gates and goodness knows what: I'm sure they can't really need all that, not out here."

Miss Smith shrugged. "If they're handling other people's confidential information they need as much security as they can get. Do you think they'd mind me joining them when they come to see the kittens? I'd rather hear about things firsthand, and Mrs. Powell has been asking about the railway too."

James and Richard arrived on Sunday afternoon, just as Dafydd was washing up after a late lunch. He had taken a plate of salad out into the garden and sat in the shade for a good half-hour after eating it, simply enjoying the coolness (and the silence from next door: the young people seemed to have gone out). He greeted them and offered tea; James pulled a face.

"This weather? It's so hot . . . thundery, almost."

"Mm. At least there's a breeze out here: I've opened Sky's window, but she must be really hot. Do you mind if I ring Miss Smith? She wants to ask about the railway."

He made tea for himself and Richard, apologised to James for having nothing but water or milk to offer, rang Miss Smith, then ran a jugful of tap water and put it in the fridge for later, collected a kitchen chair and took them upstairs to see the cats. Sky accepted them calmly; the two Londoners sat quietly in the room, allowing the kittens to explore. Dafydd watched for a few minutes, then heard the doorbell and went down to let Miss Smith in. He opened the door and stared at her in surprise before remembering his manners. She grinned.

"It's about all I've got that Konrad hasn't covered in hairs, so maybe it won't smell as threatening."

He followed her upstairs, wondering when, if ever, she usually wore the long dark-blue dress. It was made of a slightly shiny fabric and looked rather formal. Maybe when she was a lecturer she had worn it to official functions.

"May I——?" she asked, gathering up her skirts and stepping over the fireguard, and folding neatly down onto the floor before either of the others could finish getting up to offer her their seats. Sky came over to sniff at her, followed by the white kitten. The two darker torties were chasing each other: one scrambled up Richard's trouser-leg and fell off. The calico tortie was pulling at the lace from one of James' trainers. The white kitten was climbing, leaving a pattern of pinholes in Miss Smith's dress.

"Shall I pass you your cup of tea?" Dafydd asked Richard. "And would you like a cup, Miss Smith?"

Richard said yes, if it wasn't too hot, he'd be careful; Miss Smith said she'd wait.

They talked about the weather, principally the heat; about the new sea defences, whether they would have the effect intended, and how many visitors might have been put off by the mess; about the Carnival which was a month away; and the railway. Several students were interested, and some people from Ludlow had come over to teach them how to drive not only the electric locomotive, but Juliet too; they were hoping to run the steam loco on the Carnival weekend. Dafydd was not so interested in the driving aspect of the miniature railway; he hoped one day they would be able to find a permanent home for it and set up a layout with proper signalling and timetables.

He suddenly realised that someone was talking about cats: he had almost fallen asleep, despite being seated on the top stair. Miss Smith was asking James why they didn't want both the dark torties.

"We'd never tell them apart." The young man hesitated. "Well, obviously we would eventually, because they're almost mirror images, with those half-yellow and half-brown noses, but I do like this little one." He reached down and stroked the calico's head. She looked up at him with her usual expression of innocent surprise and Richard laughed.

"Okay, James, she's yours if Dafydd says so. Pity we can't have three, but . . . We'd prefer two, if possible. Either one of the other girls, as the butcher wants a tom."

"I hope he's going to get it neutered." Miss Smith detached the white kitten gently: it had reached her shoulder. "I love cats, but they're hardly an endangered species. I brought that flower book over, Minnesota, if you want to borrow it. It's on the telephone table."

Dafydd thanked her and explained that he'd been realising how few plants he actually knew the names of, and had decided to rectify the matter.

"I could do with it after you," James grimaced. "It's only when you start digging them out that you realise not all those yellow things are dandelions."

"I know daffodils and roses," Richard admitted, "but not much more than that. Birds are just so much more interesting. There was a young kite around this morning; did either of you see it?"

Dafydd leaned more comfortably against the wall and said that he had; it had been mobbed by gulls and gone away towards the south. Richard started telling them about the family of greater spotted woodpeckers which visited their garden, and he half-listened. He ought to buy squash or something, if James was going to visit . . . Who would take charge of the other tortie kitten? Where would the next geocache be? He thought Esme had said something about one of the caravan sites . . .

Chapter 7

IN CASE HE had not been supposed to mention it yet, Dafydd had carefully not told anyone about Dai's and Llinos' engagement, even when Marged had asked him outright if he had any news. They had been washing up after the post-Chapel cup of tea at the time, and he was pleased that he'd let nothing slip, literally or metaphorically. However, when on Monday morning he saw Dai striding down the road in his uniform, he hurried over to have a word, and found not only Miss Smith but also a family of visitors doing the same.

"Ar eich ôl chi," he protested generally, stepping back. "After you."

"No, no: you first." Miss Smith smiled at the mother, who was trying not to block the pavement with her bicycle.

The father and two children came up to join them, the smaller child sitting in a trailer behind his father's bicycle.

"What do you want to tell me?" Dai asked, briefly acknowledging the two other members of Tîm Pwdin and turning his attention to the tourists.

"We thought we ought to report it," the woman said anxiously, pushing dark hair out of her eyes, "because Rory was out in front of us as usual and he says he saw something. Tell the policeman what you saw, love."

Rory, who was about ten, stopped fiddling with the fastening on his helmet and said diffidently: "There were people in a van cutting a sheep up."

Dafydd, Dai and Miss Smith looked at each other in horror. Dai squatted, bringing his face level with the boy's, and took his cap off. He asked gently: "What was the van like?"

"It was a white van with the door open," was the response.

"The van we saw was white, with two doors at the back," Mother said helpfully.

"A sliding door, like Uncle's!" Rory protested.

"Transit," Father provided.

"No name on the van? I don't suppose you remember the registration?"

Mother shook her head regretfully.

"When and where did this happen?"

"Yesterday morning, at about nine-thirty, in the lanes up there: the van was in a lay-by near a wood; the one by the geocache. We were going to try to find it, but with the van there, we didn't. Rory didn't say anything about a sheep 'til we were quite a way down the road, and when we saw the van the doors were closed."

"Right. So, Rory; these people in the van, did you see how many there were of them?"

He considered. "Two, I think. And the man had knives."

Dai grimaced. 'Okay. Thanks, Rory, you've been very helpful. If you see anything else, tell your parents and they'll tell me."

He stood up and passed the adults a card. "Please, if you see anything else suspicious, don't approach anyone: stay well clear and contact me as quickly as you can on this number. If there are sheep-stealers about they're likely to be dangerous."

He took their names and addresses and wished them a pleasant holiday. When the family had formed up rather self-consciously on the road and started off, he fitted his cap back on and looked round at the others.

"Not good at all, if he really did see that. Butchering a sheep in a van on a back road in broad daylight . . . H'm. She was talking about a geocache: that's a sort of treasure-hunt, I think. Maybe it wasn't exciting enough for the kid. What do you two reckon?"

Dafydd looked at Miss Smith, who said: "Good of them to report it. Some mothers would have told the child not to make up stories."

"Do you think he invented it?" Dai asked.

Dafydd shook his head firmly. "If he had, he would have given a lot more detail and enjoyed the importance of having us listen to him. Instead, he was quite off-hand. I'm prepared to believe him. You'd better get that information passed on as soon as possible. I was only going to ask how it went on Saturday."

Dai grinned. "They liked her: mind you, it wouldn't have made any difference to me if they hadn't! And she likes them. What were you going to ask, Miss Smith?"

"Whether you'd be prepared to take on one of Sky's kittens. You don't have to answer immediately."

"With being out so much, I don't think it'd be fair to have just one. Especially if Llinos gets a job . . . Dafydd, haven't you told anyone? You could have done, but thanks for being discreet! We got engaged on Friday. Went and saw her Mum that night, and went home to see my people on Saturday." He was grinning all over his face.

"Llongyfarchiadau!" said Miss Smith, politely. "Congratulations."

"Thanks. So if there are two kittens, yes, we'll have them. If there's only one left, Phil in Aber's after a kitten for his daughters. They're a good family, they'd take care of it. They had an elderly cat and a middle-aged one, and the old one's just had to be put down, and the girls are heartbroken, and reading between the lines, he and Liz are too. I can put you in touch with him." He sighed and pulled out his radio. "So we have sheep-rustlers. Have to go up there and talk to the farmer, find out who else is missing sheep, how many have gone. Warn butchers and slaughterhouses . . . but stolen animals won't go through a reputable slaughterhouse. No paperwork. They'll end up sold by word of mouth at pubs and boot sales: if meat's cheap, people don't care too much about where it comes from, especially if they're intending to sell it on."

"Another job for Tîm Pwdin?" Miss Smith asked.

"Well, you can keep your eyes and ears open, obviously, but don't put yourselves in danger. Yes, that includes you, Minnesota Williams!"

He grinned at Dafydd. "Bad enough if it's one here or there every six months, but sometimes it's a big well-organised racket, and if they've got a lot to lose . . . You be careful."

Dafydd had been intending to visit Siân anyway, and now there was plenty to tell her. He ended up accompanying her to the supermarket so they could choose a suitable congratulatory card to be signed by the rest of Tîm Pwdin, but unfortunately, there was nothing inspiring in stock.

"You could look for one in Machynlleth on Wednesday," Siân suggested.

Dafydd, who sent very few cards and had no idea why nothing at the supermarket had been suitable, said hastily, "Why don't you come with me? It's market day. I need to get my hair cut, but we can have a sandwich or something in a cafe."

Siân was clearly thrilled to have been asked. He wondered how often she went anywhere. At least Mach was smaller than Aber and the market was not very far from the station . . .

He did not pick up Esme's message until 5.40 on Tuesday morning. He hastily stuffed the roll of paper into his pocket, put the lid back on the jar and concealed it again, and went on down the road. After dropping a couple of empty jars into the correct recycling bin, he crossed the road and sat on the beach reading the message.

Hi Dafydd,

Thanks for that! Under the very noses of the guards! I bet you were awful when you were at school! And thanks for telling Miss Smith, she came round with some driftwood for me to draw. Uncle has brought some plants indoors too—I'm drawing a tomato plant at the moment but two ripened yesterday and we ate them so the composition's changed!

Caches: last one in Borth is behind one of those B.T. *cabinets by Bryn Mawr caravan site. Magnetic micro. The next nearest is in a lay-by right up on the top road, by the look of it, and there's a travelbug in there (or there was when I looked at the latest logs) which wants to go north round the coast. It's a pity the Traeth Maelgwyn cache is so damp. However, there is a cache sort-of near the estuary, at the Dyfi Osprey Project, a box behind a fence post; it might go in there if you can find it, though there have been a few* D.N.F.*s—logs where people say they couldn't find it. I've put sketch-maps in for all these.*

Thanks—Esme

A second sheet of paper read

P.S. *Can't get out to post, so two more—if you are going to Machynlleth there is one in a hedge by the far entrance to the Plas, and one on the footbridge that goes over the Dyfi towards Corris. Small and nano. And there's a puzzle cache where you have to count stones—white ones outside the Co-Op, and you need the date from a big standing stone in a housing estate, and then the number in the Gorsedd circle by the golf course. I'll print the whole sheet if I can.*

Thanks so much—E.

Dafydd was rather taken aback by this letter. At school he had been, if not exemplary, at least acquiescent, and he was annoyed that she had imagined him to have been a naughty little boy. So many caches! Did she expect him to find all of them before contacting her, or what? At least she sounded happier and the sketching had proved successful. But with Siân accompanying him there would be no chance of searching for caches on this particular journey to Machynlleth.

You can't have it both ways, he thought vindictively. Either I can tell people about caching and explain why I want to go to strange places, or I can't, so I can't . . .

He did, however, cycle out to the lay-by on the road to Llandre after the prayer meeting that evening, and succeeded in placing the geocoin in the plastic tub which he found behind a tree. He scribbled a note for Esme to this effect and was quite pleased that someone called Twynnyms had already taken the travel bug. On his way home he finally replaced the pencil in 'Prickly Patch', dropped off the note in the jar, and arrived home tired, hot and with a piece of gorse bush firmly lodged in his left thumb.

He put the bicycle away, set the kettle to boil, became aware of a smell, and sniffed suspiciously. Cat.

Oh dear. Sky or Rheidol? Both seemed happy enough, neither looked the least bit guilty, and he wanted to get the spine out of his thumb. He dipped a needle in boiling water and prodded until the offending object came out—ridiculously small for the amount of discomfort it caused, as they always were—drank a cup of tea, poured another and took it upstairs with him, and had a bath.

He was vaguely aware of rain on the roof at some point during the night, but in the morning it was as warm as ever by the time he got back to the house with his paper. Because he would be escorting Siân he changed into a long-sleeved shirt and tie rather than his usual open-necked Aertex shirt, with the least heavy of his two jackets. He really ought to look for another pair of trousers: it would have been more sensible to go caching in the old pair which had paint on them. Maybe if he darned the ripped pair very carefully it wouldn't show. Perhaps Siân would be prepared to go to a charity shop, or at least to wait somewhere while he did . . .

He put on his best trousers, noticing as he did each Sunday that they were worryingly tight round the waist, and found a belt. Shoes rather than trainers, and a handkerchief: there, he was ready. He put his door keys into his right hand pocket, made sure he had his bank cards and rail-pass, and set off.

Chapter 8

MACHYNLLETH WAS CROWDED, as it always was on market days. Once Dafydd had queued and had his hair cut, he joined Siân, who was sitting waiting for him in the fabric shop with a bag of mending wool, chatting to the assistant. They went up one side of Heol Y Maengwyn and down the other, acquiring items people had asked them to buy, each stopping politely if the other was looking at a particular stall. There were rugs, plants, vegetables, bread, toys, books, fabrics, hardware . . .

Siân stopped at the china stall and chose a bowl to replace one Marged had dropped, and mugs for her grand-children; Dafydd studied the next stall. There were buttons and house numbers made from slate, knitted hats and mittens and baby-clothes, bird-boxes and turned wooden bowls, bags of what looked like multicoloured candyfloss which turned out to be combed, dyed wool, and some ferocious implements which were labelled as felting needles.

He glanced at Siân, who was deep in conversation with the china-seller, and began to ask questions. How long did it take to make felt? How much wool did you need? What did you do with it when you had it? The woman behind the stall—round-faced and quite young, with brown hair in plaits—began to produce samples: brooches and bags, and a picture of blackbirds eating rowan berries which Dafydd would have been tempted to buy if it had not already had a *SOLD* sticker in one corner.

You could also make mats and coasters, she added; hats, slippers . . . if you had enough wool to spare, you could even make linings for things like tea cosies and oven-gloves.

"I'm running a workshop at the school here next Saturday," she told him. "Pictures, this time. Have a leaflet."

Dafydd took the piece of paper, saw the charge and winced.

"That's what things cost, I suppose," he said, realising she'd noticed. "Insurance, and hiring the room . . . "

"And materials, especially dyed wool, and covering the cost if I don't get many people to attend. You have to try to find a balance between charging enough to cover your costs and having some profit left to live on, and not charging so much that people don't come to it."

"Could you teach a disabled woman? She's in a wheelchair and it might be something different for her to do. She quilts, and she's quite artistic."

The felt-maker said she didn't see why not, the venue was suitable.

Siân had joined him. "What are you plotting, Dafydd?"

"Thinking about Esme," he explained. "I wondered if she might like to try felt-making. I'll have to ask her. And I'll buy one of those needles, have a go some time . . . Thank you."

They proceeded down the street. Siân chose a card for Dai and Llinos, to be passed round Tîm Pwdin to be signed. When they had exhausted the possibilities of the market they went into a cafe and, despite the weather, had soup and a roll each. Then Siân said she'd like to look in the antique shops, and did he mind . . .

He came with her into the first shop and looked at the second-hand books. The second shop was so cramped that he said he'd stay outside, did she mind if he went into the charity shop next door . . .

The only trousers which might have been his size were polyester, so he went out again and stood by the antique shop. Siân emerged triumphantly ten minutes later with a heavy-looking bag.

"What did you find?" he asked. "Will it break, or can I carry it for you?"

Siân smiled. "Books; one about William Williams Pant-ycelyn, and some sermons by Christmas Evans. They looked interesting. Have you done everything you wanted?"

He nodded and took the bag. "We ought to catch the 2.56 train; we've plenty of time."

When he got home there was a pile of post on the doormat. He took it into the kitchen and sorted it while the kettle boiled, tearing the clear windows out of the junk mail envelopes and putting them in the bin. It was all junk, apart from a note from Dai, headed Annwyl Tîm Pwdin/Dear Team Pudding, and which went on to inform them that some farmers had already checked their sheep and reported the results: there were none missing, but three farmers had found something very strange: person or persons unknown seemed to have been shearing one sheep and then releasing it back into the field. He was going to contact the tourist family and ask if he could speak to Rory again; Evan Williams was going to lend him a pair of old-fashioned sheep shears to show the child, to see if that was the explanation for the 'knives' he had seen the man using.

I should have noticed that, Dafydd thought, carrying the tea tray into his living-room and sitting down by the window. I should have asked how he knew it was a sheep, and if it was dead . . . You know it's a sheep because it has wool on it, of course, and they must have been shearing it with hand-operated clippers, not the modern equipment, or there would have been a generator to run it and the adults might have noticed the hum. Presumably the people had a dog, a trained dog which could separate out the animal they wanted—— Whoever is that, at this time of day?

He went out to the hall where the telephone was ringing, almost knocked backwards by a sudden strong waft of Cat.

"Dafydd M. Williams sy'n siarad. P'nawn da, Miss Smith. Good afternoon. Sut dach chi?"

Miss Smith said that she was fine, thanks; had he had Dai's note, she'd had it by email, and he'd sent another email now: one of the Aberystwyth policemen had noticed from the map that places where sheep had been shorn corresponded to places where there were lay-bys with geocaches.

"It's some sort of techno game," she added disparagingly. "I looked it up online, and you need a global positioning system device to find where they are. Another one of these modern ideas. Anyhow, Dai thinks that's why no one's caught the thieves: if anyone sees them, they just assume they're looking for the cache."

"They must have a sheepdog, to bring them the sheep," Dafydd pointed out, longing to explain that you didn't actually need a G.P.S. and it was quite fun really . . . He'd have to report all this to Esme. "So it must be someone who knows about farming, and they know how to shear the animal."

"Yes; that's something else Dai said. Apparently the thieves have even been putting the farmer's paint-mark back on the animals once they've sheared them, and with wool fetching the price it does, none of the farmers he's spoken to are really worried, just puzzled. I wondered if it's someone insulating their loft! Wool's very good for that, apparently."

"It could be." Dafydd was putting two and two together at high speed. "Or might it be someone who's refilling an eiderdown, or who does felt-making, or knitting? If it costs quite a lot to *buy* a fleece, even if they're not worth much when the farmer sells them, maybe people have given up picking bits off thornbushes like Mam and I used to, and are thinking bigger! You see sheep wandering about with the fleece coming off in great lumps sometimes, but if there's a mark on the shorn ones, that has to mean someone's doing it on purpose."

Miss Smith said: "H'm . . . Yes, I suppose most of the fleeces commercially available are from rare breeds, or specifically sold for craft-work. You could be right. D'you want me to email Dai?"

Dafydd was still thinking. "Y—es," he said, slowly. "Yes, please do that. And ask him to get in touch . . . "

He went out that evening to Bible study, and having walked Siân home, cycled off to find the magnetic micro cache which was stuck on the back of the B.T. cabinet outside the entrance to the caravan park. Having completed this task quickly, he decided to check on the cache where he had put the geocoin. It had already gone and there was another traveller there, just a metal tag with a loop of chain at a corner, with 'Travel Racer' and a picture of a racing car enamelled onto it. He checked the logbook: someone called Moosebros had left the travel racer, and The Wipeout Kid had picked up the geocoin. He would have to ask Esme where the racer wanted to go next . . . and from now on he would have to travel himself if he was going to find any new caches. Oh well; it was exercise.

He sat on a bank beside the road and wrote to Esme, giving the number of the travel racer and suggesting that she might find out if there were any more on the roads towards Machynlleth, as he would now be cycling. He also added a quick explanation of the sheep-shearing mystery, folded the message and put it in his left-hand pocket, got back on his bicycle and set off down the hill in the dusk.

There was no one in the phone box when he reached it, but there was a silver car parked further down the entry, apparently unoccupied. Dafydd leaned his bicycle against the wall and reached into the hedge for the jar, got the lid off and felt for the contents.

The car door opened and he stuffed the jar back into the hedge as James approached.

"Sorry, Mr. Williams, but I've been employed to find out who's contacting Esme. Her uncle is concerned."

"What!" Dafydd stared. "Does Esme know? You'd better not tell her, or I can see her walking out—or whatever the wheelchair equivalent is."

James shrugged, looking acutely embarrassed. "He's worried she's met someone online who's going to . . . I don't know what exactly he's afraid of for her, but she couldn't do much against an able-bodied bloke with a knife, for example. So what are you doing here?"

Dafydd thrust the roll of paper into his hands. "Read that."

James produced a torch and spread the top sheet on the side of the phone box.

> *Hi, D., well done for Bryn-hir, & your Celtic knot coin's on the move! Enc. maps for two on the coast path small and micro, one small on the track down to Wallog. No hurry! Thanks—E.*

James let the end of the paper go. It rolled up again instantly. He stared at Dafydd.

"*You're* doing it too?" he whispered. "I *wondered* what it was she'd left there . . . "

"You know about geocaching?" Dafydd sighed with relief. "Thank goodness I don't have to explain that part of it. I told Edith about the cars in your lay-by, just after I'd been up to yours, and I got a phone call from Esme later, saying she knew what it was, it was quite safe. We ended up deciding to work as a team. She does the part that needs a computer and I do the part that needs mobility. She's keeping Mike and Edith out of it because this is her rebellion against the way they're fussing over her . . . how you explain that to Mike I don't know, but if his feelings have to be hurt, he's asked for it. Esme's been going crackers, sitting in there—like an old woman in a care home, she says; she got the doctor to tell them she has to go out, for exercise, but they still won't let her go much further than here, not alone."

James whistled softly. "Poor kid," he whispered. "When you put it like that . . . "

"Just how many white slavers does Mike think there *are* in Borth?" Dafydd was still angry on Esme's behalf. "Sorry. Not your fault. So when did you start caching?"

The young man grinned. "A couple of days after you did, by the sound of it. I went out and followed the tracks—there's quite a path, by now—and I got to the ruin, and all the tracks seemed to be concentrating on that tree growing out of the wall, so I was standing on a pile of stones looking at it, and a kid popped up out of nowhere and said: 'Have you found it yet?' "

Dafydd could picture the scene. "And what did you reply?"

"Ah-ha." James tapped the side of his nose. "Like that. And then the kid's parents came up the track with a dog, and the kid says: 'He's not got it yet, what's the hint?' And we all started pulling the rubble about and we found the box—for my first find that was a pretty good one!—and they took everything out and I grabbed the paper with the explanation on, which they were ignoring, and suddenly it all clicked. I'd heard about geocaching, but I'd never thought I could be bothered to do it. It's addictive, isn't it?"

Dafydd was trying so hard not to laugh that he could only nod. "Well," he managed at last, "I found it by hiding near there, the night you told me about the people stopping, and it was so dark I couldn't see what the cachers before me had got, I just heard something metallic—and I found it by feel, *and took it home* because I'd no idea what it was, and when I opened it and read the explanation I realised I'd have to put it back—and then Esme joined forces with me the next day so I went back again and signed it Symbiosis, for both of us."

"Oh wow! How cool is that! Oh, well done, Mr. Williams!" James sounded far younger than his age. "So you're Symbiosis! I thought they must be local, you've beaten me to just about every cache round here."

"What's your nickname?" Dafydd asked.

"The Wipeout Kid." He grinned. "Means I fall off surfboards a lot. Wow, makes you wonder how many more people we know are secretly cachers."

"I won't tell anyone if you don't," Dafydd said gravely. "Esme excepted, of course! Does Richard know?"

James nodded. "I told him today, when we got Dai's email. Something I will say, though, and tonight's proved it: because we're supposed to be stealthy and not get seen, if people do see you it could get very nasty. Mike thought you were an online stalker."

"It was a couple of girls who found Skulker on the Slope before me," Dafydd said quietly. "If they'd seen me lying in wait . . . or if anyone else saw me hiding, watching them . . . I was worried about the lay-by people being courting couples, before I knew, but I'd not thought people might assume *I* was up to no good. Oh dear. I suppose I'll have to operate in the early hours of the morning."

James shrugged. "Just something to be aware of. If you never did anything someone else could misconstrue, you'd never do anything! Well, I can ring Mike and report tomorrow. See if I can make Esme's life a bit easier. Wish me luck!"

Dafydd nodded. "I'll pray. And may I have the maps back?"

"I've not found those yet." James grinned, handing back the roll of paper. "How about we go for one now? Wallog?"

They did so, eventually found the container quite a distance from where the map printout and the co-ordinates suggested, and signed the log triumphantly. James replaced the cache where the G.P.S. app on his phone said it was supposed to be. The Wipeout Kid and half of Symbiosis grinned at each other in the torchlight.

"Have to collaborate again sometime," James suggested. "If you don't have a G.P.S., and there's something you *can't* find without one . . . Here, you'd better have this. It's my mobile number."

"That's very kind of you." Dafydd was trying not to yawn. He pocketed the business card and checked; yes, he still had his keys. "Thanks, James. If you can drop me off where I left the bicycle . . . "

Chapter 9

DESPITE THE LONG day, Dafydd woke in the night and lay half-asleep, wondering what had disturbed him. It wasn't raining; it wasn't too hot, either, for a change. Then he heard the unmistakable sound of a cat singing, down in the garden. Rheidol was still at the foot of the bed. Konrad? Probably not. He went to the window and peered out, thought he saw a dark shape moving down the path. As he was awake he went out to the bathroom and heard Sky scrabbling at the spare room door; he had taken to closing it at night or when he went out, because he had seen the white kitten right at the top of the fireguard one morning.

"Have to find out when we can get you spayed," he murmured. "And what age this lot have to be before they leave home . . ."

Before he went to fetch his newspaper he wrote another message to Esme, explaining that he'd met The Wipeout Kid, who had offered them the use of a G.P.S., and that they had successfully gone out to get the cache on the track to Wallog.

He brought the paper home and sat on a kitchen chair in a patch of shade in the garden to do the crossword, occasionally praying that James would be able to get his point across without upsetting people too much, and wishing Dai would contact him. He had an idea.

By midday he had done his washing, it had dried outside and he had ironed what needed ironing and put it away. He had several ideas by now and still had not seen Dai. That wasn't surprising, because the man had to cover almost all the territory between the north edge of Aberystwyth and the Dyfi, but he wanted to discuss things with someone . . . He wrote everything out neatly and rang Siân.

"It's a good idea," Siân agreed, when he told her that he'd thought Esme might agree to go on a secret mission to learn felt-making and hunt for clues about where the wool had come from, "but I'd already thought of that—and I thought I might go, too; it looked interesting. So I rang up to book two places and the young lady said they'd had to cancel, they needed twelve bookings to cover the hire of the room."

"Could she come here?"

"It needs to be a proper venue, for the insurance. She was quite angry, not at me: she says there's a chain of craft shops that's taken to running workshops like hers, and charging a lot less because of being a big organisation. But she's got another day coming up at the end of the month, at C.A.T.—you know, the eco-place in the hills behind Mach—and she hopes that'll do better. Poor girl. It can't be easy, trying to make a living out of making things by hand."

Dafydd told her that there had been a poster up at the Community Hall about felt-making, and he wondered who was running that one: Siân said if it got a bit cooler she might stroll down and find out.

He thanked her, rang off, checked he had not missed a call while they'd been talking, and went out into the garden. There was a good deal of activity next door, a different car outside, washing going out on the line and loud music. He went indoors again, refilled the cats' water-bowls, sat with Sky and the kittens, hoping they could cope with the music because it was beginning to annoy him. Poor cats . . . He left them to it after twenty minutes, closing the spare room door but leaving the window open a quarter of an inch at the top. He collected his notes, annotated them according to what Siân had said, and found an envelope. He would drop them in at Dai's, and go for a walk on the coast path.

Rheidol was in the back lane when he got home, tail not yet subsided from bottlebrush mode, ears flat. Something had clearly frightened him. The noise from next door had reduced a little, at least. Dafydd unlocked the back door, went in, and thought he heard something coming downstairs. However had Sky opened that door? Or hadn't he closed it, after all? He reached down to lock the cat-flap and found himself facing a slim black cat with four white socks. Male, he thought; quite young. No wonder this place smells of cat: he's been coming in and spraying. Let's discourage him . . .

He went to the fridge and brought out the new plastic bottle of ketchup. Tom Socks was pawing at the locked cat-flap. Dafydd took aim, carefully, and squeezed the bottle hard.

Tom Socks took off like a squib, zooming around the kitchen with Dafydd squirting ketchup at him. When he thought the lesson might have been learned (and before he'd wasted too much ketchup), Dafydd opened the back door and Tom fled, still spattered with ketchup—as was quite a bit of the kitchen. Grinning, but feeling rather guilty, Dafydd watched him jump off the wall and vanish. Poor little Tom Socks—but tomcat was a penetrating and persistent stink that took weeks if not months to fade, and he really didn't want any more visits.

He ran a few inches of water into a bucket, set the kettle to boil for a pot of tea and started to clean up the mess.

As he worked he thought about Esme, and about James. Even if Mike and Edith did let Esme out more, so to speak, most of the Borth caches were completely inaccessible to someone in a wheelchair. Perhaps there would be more suitable ones in Aberystwyth, or Machynlleth, or further along the coast. Without a car—and a car you could get a wheelchair into, at that—she was stuck, reliant on him to bring back the trophies she had worked for. Would the wheelchair fit into James' car, even if the lad asked her to go with him? Would they have to take Edith as a chaperone? How long would Esme be in the chair, anyway?

Edith had said something once about her having been to be measured for a false leg, so presumably it was temporary, but if so, why wasn't she on crutches? Maybe she simply needed more practice at using them; he couldn't imagine there being any space at Stretton for serious walking. And he didn't want to ask, because with him Esme seemed to be able to forget her disability, and he didn't want to remind her.

He sighed, emptied the bucket, poured in some hot water from the kettle and a few drops of washing up liquid, and continued to scrub at the tiles. It was a pity there weren't more caches in Borth.

He sat back on his heels suddenly. What was to stop him making some caches, just for Esme? They wouldn't be real ones, of course, but surely he could manage some form of treasure-hunt? It would have to be sufficiently complicated that she didn't feel patronised . . .

He began to scrub again. At least the kitchen would be cleaner afterwards.

How many clues could he invent? Would it be better to make a trail, with A providing the clue to B, and the contents of cache B being the clue for C, or to give her a list of clues, with a cache for each one? Probably a list, then if one cache was vandalised she could still work on the others . . . and if he put one or two letters in each cache, he could do the clue to the final cache as an anagram. How many containers did he have? Would he need to buy anything? He'd need to get permission from people if he put them in gardens, even at the very edges. What did Borth have in the way of road signs and street names, assuming that he could get hold of enough small magnets? And whatever could be at the end of the trail, and where could he hide that? It would have to be something worth having: chocolate was too cliché-ed, and would be particularly unsuitable in this weather. Might Siân ice a cake for him if he made one, or was Esme one of those women perpetually on a diet? He couldn't remember her seeming to be particularly large. He would have to consider it further.

He had barely finished cleaning the kitchen when the phone rang. It was Dai; could he come round, he had Phil from Aber with him to see the kittens.

Goodness knows what the neighbours will think I've done if they're in uniform, Dafydd thought, putting the receiver back and going straight to the kitchen to close the cat-flap again. I need a notice: *If an answer is required, please knock on back door*. . . I must find out how soon after kittens she can be spayed; maybe Miss Smith would know, or the animal charity shop in Mach . . . but they're still feeding from her as well as eating her biscuits, so presumably not yet.

The two policemen came to the back door and Dafydd let them in, apologising for the terrible smell of cat; there had been a tomcat in, and did Dai know who owned the little black tom with white socks?

Dai said he didn't, it was probably a farm cat from somewhere, and introduced Phil Price, who shook hands with him and followed Dai up to the spare bedroom while Dafydd stayed behind to make sure the door onto the hall was closed.

"I'd forgotten how cute they are at this age," Phil remarked, watching as the calico kitten tried to climb up Rheidol's wicker carrying-basket and fell off, then, turning his attention to the white kitten: "He can't get out of there, can he?"

Dafydd peered round Dai and laughed. "No, they're up and down the curtains all the time now. The window's very stiff, so he won't get through: I closed it down to a quarter of an inch once they got onto the chest of drawers. The white one's been spoken for, and so has the calico: I hope one of the dark torties would be acceptable?"

Phil nodded, and began to take photographs with his phone. "I promised I would, but I'll only snap these two and the mum: if the kids don't see the other two they can't pester for them. Megan's already chosen 'Twinkle' as a name, but Alwen says we should wait and see what it looks like."

Dafydd smiled at Dai. The man seemed sensible enough.

There was a sudden burst of loud music from next door and someone ran upstairs shouting.

"Your neighbours?" Phil asked, gently detaching the white kitten from the top rail of the fireguard and putting him back on the lino, then straightening up and putting his phone away.

Dafydd nodded. "They come in the holidays; usually they're not too bad. I can always go out. Well, let me know which you choose, and when you'd like to collect her."

Dai grinned at him. "And let us know if the racket goes on too late at night; you've more patience than I have, but there are people the other side of them too. Right, Phil; I'll stay for a chat with Dafydd if you don't mind . . . "

Phil left amicably, pausing to stroke Rheidol who was dozing on the slate wall round the garden. Dafydd waved him off, fetched a water-bowl and put it in a patch of shade, and went back to talk to Dai.

They sat in the garden, Dafydd on a kitchen chair, Dai on the path, protesting that he didn't mind, wake him if he fell asleep . . .

"Siân's already rung the felter from Mach," Dafydd began, "and she's had to cancel the course because there weren't enough takers. So that scotches that line of enquiry unless someone goes up to C.A.T. to her course there, at the end of the month."

"Pity; that was a good idea." Dai yawned, covered his mouth with his hand and looked embarrassed. "Sorry—it's the heat. We've heard from most of the local farmers now, none seem to have lost animals they can't account for. Well, one bloke said he'd lost six, but he's notorious for letting his beasts stray, you could get a herd of elephants through some of the holes in his fences and he never seems to get round to fixing them; and there's only been one more with a fleece missing: that was interesting, because it was a coloured animal they shore—or is it sheared? Anyway, it was a brown one, and the woman's quite peeved because she said she kept it all for hand-spinning last time they were shorn and she's run out halfway through a jumper, and she was hoping to finish it from this year's fleece. So we just might have a fleece we could identify. But there's no further manpower being assigned to the case at the Aber station now the results are in: they've got too much else on."

Dafydd nodded. He had suspected as much.

"Your next idea—getting someone to place a geocache in a lay-by next to a field of sheep and waiting—seems plausible, but firstly whose sheep do we use as bait, secondly who's going to place the cache and how long does it take to get known about, and thirdly, who's going to watch for the van?"

Dafydd took a deep breath. "I know someone who's a cacher. I think he'd place it for us if I asked nicely. I don't know how long they take to get published, but I don't think it's too long . . . and surely the rest of the sheep are due to be shorn soon anyway? Most of the ones I've seen have been. So if the thieves want another one or two they'll have to hurry up. I'm sure I can do a few days of watching, and so could James and/or Richard, and possibly the students and Miss Smith, if they aren't too busy."

"They'll have finished exams soon, if they haven't already," Dai agreed. "Well, you go and ask them, and I'll look for a farmer."

"It mustn't be near any other geocache," Dafydd warned him. "They have to be a certain distance apart. You'd have to look that up."

Dai studied him quizzically. "You seem to know a good deal about it! Okay, I'll be tactful and not ask who your source is. Honestly, you lot! The lad at Aber who pointed out the connection was being very secretive, too, but he did suggest that he could go to an Event of some sort and talk to the cachers, warn them what's going on and ask them to keep an eye open. I think that's this Saturday."

Chapter 10

ON FRIDAY MORNING he went round to see Esme, taking a bunch of assorted weeds with him as an excuse. It was still hot and muggy and although there had been a few rumbles of thunder in the night nothing had come of it. Edith let him in and fetched a vase for the plants; Esme looked hopefully at him, but he smiled and shook his head slightly, then began to explain about the wool-thieves.

He was careful to make it appear more of a prank than anything likely to be dangerous, emphasising, when Mike asked questions, that the police had found nothing worth following up. He added cheerfully that a policeman who was also a geocacher was going to an event on Saturday to ask if anyone had seen anything useful, and Dai was thinking of asking people to invent a new cache next to a field of sheep, so that Tîm Pwdin could lie in wait and find out what the registration of the van was.

Esme looked excited at the thought of this; Dafydd went on to say casually that he might go cycling later, possibly up towards Machynlleth, and received a grin in response.

Then, cautiously, he suggested that if Esme could get as far as his house she could see the kittens before they went to new homes, adding that he wasn't sure when that would be, but all four had now been spoken for and he would be glad to know they were someone else's responsibility.

"The oldest one's a calico, that's what they call a tortoiseshell with big patches of different coloured fur. She got up to the top of the curtains last night and was too scared to come down. Her brother went up and down twice to show her how easy it was, but she just hung on and cried until I got up on a chair and unhooked her. I've taken the curtains down, now; she might hurt herself if she falls off because I'm not there to rescue her."

Esme was amused by the story but Edith seemed horrified that he had let them climb up at all, and said that whoever was going to have them would need to train them not to.

Esme and Dafydd exchanged smiles, aware that it was almost impossible to train a cat if it didn't want to co-operate.

Mike cleared his throat. "Well, if you'd like to see them, Esme?"

Esme nodded, but she was looking at her aunt.

"You can't: there's all the kerbs and the traffic—and some of those boys on bicycles go so fast . . . " Edith started.

"Well, she has to cope with it sometime," Mike said grimly. "And I reckon a bicycle would come off worst, eh, Esme? If you take your crutches, you can get into the house all right."

"And if you fall and hurt your shoulder again, who's going to have to look after you?" her aunt demanded.

"If—if it makes you happier," Esme said, clearly making a great effort to compromise, "you can come too. If Dafydd wants you—— Oh, I've said that wrong . . . "

Dafydd smiled. "I know how you meant it. I don't mind. Seriously, you two are welcome, as well, but if you're too busy, or not keen on cats, I can come down and—well, not push you, Esme, not all the way, but be there if you get stuck at a kerb or something. Help when asked to. The kits are upstairs but I can bring them down to the living-room; my stairs are quite steep and the policeman who's having one of the kittens commented on it a couple of days ago, so I wouldn't recommend . . . "

"Oh, that's why they were round at yours!" Edith exclaimed. "Emrys Williams said there'd been Dai and another man at yours, Muriel thought you must have complained about the teenagers in the next house."

"No, no. Just choosing a kitten. So what do you think?"

Edith hesitated, looking at Mike.

"You go if you want to, love." He reached for her hand. "I don't think I could get that far."

"I know!" Esme said suddenly. "You have the wheelchair, Uncle, and I'll use my crutches—and, Dafydd, could you push Uncle? I don't think Auntie could; she finds me a bit heavy."

This effectively silenced everyone.

After a minute of frantically working out who would sit where, and how he could keep the kittens in the living-room once people started opening doors, Dafydd murmured that he'd be pleased to oblige.

"We could get a taxi, if you're set on seeing the cats," Edith said at last.

"Auntie, it's only just down the road! And you don't have to come; I know you don't like animals. I don't mind people looking at me; I'm sure Uncle doesn't. They all know him, anyhow."

"I've been in enough wheelchairs at hospitals," Mike growled. "And this one at least goes forwards . . . Edith, we know you don't want to come. If I go it's not as though she'll be on her own, and Mr. Williams has said he'll push me, so I don't see what the problem is."

"Oh, you go and get on with it!" Edith snapped and marched out of the room. They heard her clattering china in the kitchen.

Esme raised an eyebrow at Dafydd. "No time like the present . . . ?"

"If you're ready, yes. Mr. Davies?"

Mike grinned. He got up slowly, went out into the hall and came back with a pair of crutches. Dafydd suddenly wondered if he had felt as imprisoned as Esme.

"Hop out, lass," Mike smiled at his niece. "And you can shoo all those biscuit crumbs into the bin first, before they end up on the floor . . . that's it. I'll walk as far as I can, and if you get tired, now, you're to tell me and I'll get out. All right, young lady?"

Esme nodded and set off towards the front door.

They processed along the narrow pavement, Mike with two sticks, followed by Esme on her crutches, followed by Dafydd pushing the wheelchair. Other pedestrians had to step into the road: many greeted one or other of them, and Dafydd was impressed by Mike's refusals to stop and talk, when people clearly hadn't seen him for weeks. They got as far as the butcher's before he gave in and sat in the chair: Esme, too, was clearly tiring, so when they reached the hotel Dafydd suggested that they should cross over and sit on the bench.

"The cache is in the notice board," he whispered to Esme as she sat down: she nodded and grinned. After a minute's rest she got up and casually began to feel inside the triangle of boards.

Mike sat looking out at the sea.

"Edith's all right." He sighed. "Means well, but she's not well herself, and won't admit it; Esme was right when she said she finds the wheelchair too heavy. And she doesn't like Josie—that's Esme's step-mam. Well, neither do I. Has Esme ever told you why she's here?"

Dafydd shook his head. Behind them, Esme was unscrewing the lid of the cache.

"Threw something at one of Josie's friends. And wouldn't apologise, so Josie said would we have her. She'd last been to stay when she was ten, before they moved down south. Steve—my brother, I was the eldest and he was the youngest—told me Josie thought it'd be some sort of a punishment for the lass, there being no social life round here."

"At least she can ring her friends, and I suppose she can email, too," Dafydd said cautiously.

Mike nodded. "I reckon she's better off here, despite being stuck in the house. But if she did go out, and fell and hurt herself, what could either of us do? We couldn't even lift her up . . . It's a pity that young James isn't a girl, they could be friends and go out together."

"I think James and Esme are both mature enough to be friends without it going any further." Dafydd felt he was treading on eggshells, not sure what James and Mike had said to each other. "And maybe James knows a nice sensible girl who'd be company for her sometimes." He raised his voice. "Esme, are you ready to go on now? I hope you won't look at the state of my house when we get there; I've not dusted."

He settled his visitors in the living-room, closed the kitchen door firmly, checked the front door was shut, and went up to fetch the kittens. Never having been caught before, they were fairly easy to load into Rheidol's carrying-basket; he brought them downstairs with Sky trotting anxiously behind, asked Esme to reach over and shut the door, put the basket down on the rug and opened the lid.

For a second or two nothing happened. Then the white kitten came out, sniffed at chair legs and vanished under the table. Sky, who had never been in the room either, went to the door and began to sniff too: Dafydd explained about Tom Socks and the ketchup, and by the time he had finished the kittens were all exploring, climbing people's legs and pouncing on Sky's tail and generally being as adorable as anyone could have wished for. Sky finished her inspection of the room and settled firmly on Dafydd's lap.

"May I hold a kitten?" Esme asked, tentatively.

"Of course. Any one in particular?"

"I don't mind." To Dafydd's initial horror she turned over to lie face down in the armchair, slid down to kneel on the floor and turned over again to sit on the rug, leaning against the chair.

"Wish they'd get my leg finished!" she remarked. "It's so awkward without. Come here, gorgeous . . . "

She had picked up one of the dark tortie kittens; it hooked onto her jersey and looked up inquisitively as she stroked it. The calico came to investigate and she picked that one up too. "Which is the policeman having?" she asked.

"One of the dark ones. James and Richard are having the other, and the calico; the butcher's having the white tom," Dafydd explained, yet again.

"I wonder if they'd let me see them sometimes?" she asked wistfully. "They're so persistent: that white one's fallen off you three times now, Uncle, but he keeps trying."

"Doesn't half tickle," Mike growled, but Dafydd saw how gently he unhooked the little claws and was pleased he had suggested the idea.

After half an hour Sky jumped off his lap and the kittens ran to her: she went under the table and they swarmed over her to feed.

"Wow, thanks!" Esme whispered, and rolled over. "That was wonderful. Don't help, please: I can do it myself."

Dafydd watched with respect as she pulled herself up, got her knee onto the armchair and wriggled round until she was sitting properly again.

"I reckon you could manage quite adequately if you did fall," he remarked, quietly. "As long as you didn't knock yourself out."

"I keep exercising, as much as I can." She grimaced. "Three of us used to go to Pilates classes at weekends. Uncle, I bet you could manage to walk as far as the café; we could go in and have coffee or something once a week, and you could talk to people . . . no; take Auntie; she's stuck indoors as much as we are . . . and while you're out I can have a very quick wild party and ring everyone I know on your phone! I wouldn't, but could I ask Miss Smith round one day? Or Dafydd?"

"I'll have to introduce you to James, who's having the kittens." Dafydd glanced at Mike, who nodded. "He works with computers: you know that, from when we were dealing with Napoleon Powell's piano. And since they moved here he's started surfing. He seems a sensible young man; I'm sure your Aunt wouldn't mind if you met him in the cafe sometimes. I don't want to kick you out, but she must be worrying about you: do you want to ring first and tell her you're on your way?"

Chapter 11

AFTER DAFYDD HAD seen them home and escaped quickly before anyone felt they had to ask him in, he went back to move the kittens and Sky back upstairs. Sky ran out into the hall as soon as he opened the living-room door; he gathered up two kittens and took them upstairs in the basket, let them out, left the door open so Sky could join them, and went back for the other two, realising one of the dark torties was at the top of the curtains . . .

By the time he had got the last two kittens into the basket, the first two were over the fireguard and coming downstairs, the telephone was ringing and Sky was scrabbling at the kitchen door. Dafydd took a deep breath and fastened the lid firmly on the basket, left it in the hall, caught the two loose kittens and closed the door on them, took the basket upstairs and released the second pair of kittens, closed the door very carefully on all four and went to find Sky.

"Time to plan all this would have been useful," he told her, scooping her up and carrying her upstairs. "At least the living-room doesn't open straight onto the street, like some people's . . . Now, you were very good with the visitors, but you have to go back in with the kits. I'm sorry it's so hot for you, but you've got water and I've opened the window a bit wider since I took the curtains down."

He managed to close the door before any further escapes were attempted, went down and put the kettle on, and while it boiled rang 1471: fortunately it had been a 'number withheld', so he could have his cup of tea in peace.

Neither lunch nor cycling to Machynlleth appealed, even after his second cup of tea. He sat in the armchair and wondered what Edith had said to Mike and Esme. It had been unfair of them to be so unkind to her, and she couldn't help not liking animals . . . but at least the escapade had proved that both Mike and Esme were capable of coping with brief expeditions. Poor Edith. He hoped she would not take it personally. He prayed . . .

It was only when someone in the next house started singing along very loudly to a pop song that he realised that he had slept. He rubbed his eyes, yawned and looked at the clock. Two fifteen already! It was too hot. He was tempted to go up to bed, but if the young people were going to be noisy he might as well go out: he could set off slowly towards the caches on the coast path.

He strolled through the village, pausing to make notes of house names, street signs, posts and walls and seats where something might be concealed. He was still no nearer finding a suitable prize for Esme's treasure-hunt but had ideas for some of the clues. He went slowly up the hill to the monument, grateful for the seat halfway up, then out onto the coast path. There was a slight breeze coming off the sea, but he was so hot . . . If he wasn't so unfit it'd help, he thought angrily. Why hadn't he stayed in, put up with the racket and darned his trousers? Because sooner or later the noise would have got to him . . .

The path was narrow, steep in places and sometimes edged with gorse, mostly quite manageable, but with the occasional place where the cliff had eroded and people had made new paths a little further inland. He could see walkers in the distance but no one had disturbed the birds on his stretch of the path for a while and he was delighted to hear a stonechat calling from the top of a gorse bush, and to see it briefly before it flew away. There were butterflies too, and bees in the gorse, and he began to relax and enjoy the walk.

He missed the first cache, as he had done on his previous visit, unwilling to wait while a party of muggles threaded their way past the place where he suspected it was hidden. Reasoning that he could find it on his way back he continued, up and down the undulations of the clifftops, watching a pair of canoes in the bay below him and a small yacht further out, finally arriving at the slope down to the odd shingle spit called Sarn Gynfelyn and the stream which flowed into the sea by the farm at Wallog.

The cache was a little further on; he took his time on the slopes, rather surprised by the farmhouse—he assumed that it belonged to the outbuildings further inland —which with its whitewashed wall and iron railings would not have looked out of place in a seaside resort. He looked up at the windows, imagining what it would be like to live there. Lonely, apart from the people on the coast path, with a long rutted farm track between you and the back road and only a couple of other farms in the valley; cold in winter, no doubt, but peaceful and convenient for bird-watching and photography.

Maybe he should take up photography. It would be helpful for identifying plants—he had brought as little as possible because of the heat, leaving both flower book and binoculars at home—and he would like to capture some of the kittens' excesses: the calico kitten and her brother up the curtains, for example . . . How much would a camera cost? These days it was all digital; presumably you could print the pictures somehow, probably though access to a computer. He would have to look into it. Richard would know, or Esme.

He looked along the path in both directions, saw no one too near, and sat casually on a tussock beside a bush. Somewhere under the bush—under all those sticks, probably—was the cache. He pushed the sticks aside and saw something black; a plastic tablet-bottle with a wide neck, wound round with duct tape. He opened it and shook out the contents.

Two marbles, a spinning-top, a railway ticket from Manchester to Aberystwyth dated the previous month, a logbook in the remains of a plastic bag, a football sticker, something plastic which looked as though there should be more of it, and a pencil sharpener. He signed the log, put everything back in the bottle, realised that a couple of walkers were closer than he had thought, pushed the bottle quickly down the side of the tussock where it would be least visible, and sat innocently looking out to sea.

The young man was walking slowly, studying something in his hand; he stopped at the other side of the bush. The young woman pulled out her mobile phone and tapped at the screen. Dafydd tried not to grin: he suspected he knew what they were after. They came closer, looked at the bush, looked at him.

"Are you sitting on it?" the young man asked, grinning back.

"Is this what you're looking for?" Dafydd retrieved the bottle. "It goes under the sticks, under the bush."

"Great! Thanks." The young woman took it and opened it.

The young man sat down on another tussock. "Hi; so who're you? We're Twynnyms: on holiday here from Cheshire."

Dafydd admitted to being half of Symbiosis and asked where they had put the traveller which wanted to go north round the coast.

The young man laughed. "Nowhere, yet: we went to look for the Osprey Project cache and we couldn't find it, and the ones we found in Aberdyfi were too small, so it'll have to wait until we go up to Tywyn."

"D'you want to see it before I hide it?" the young woman asked him. "Only be quick, there's what looks like a school party coming."

Dafydd wished them happy caching and made his escape, glad the weather was dry because some of the slopes would have been treacherous if the dust became mud. He managed to stay a good distance ahead of the children—a Scout camp, perhaps?—and found the other cache without difficulty; a film canister shoved down into the grass by a fence post. He scribbled hastily in the logbook and got it back into place before they came round the gorse bushes. By now he was more than halfway back; he let them overtake at a suitable place on the path and slowed down, sticky and thirsty but pleased that he had found both caches.

He stopped at the monument to compose a note to Esme, then went slowly down the hill, promising himself a bath when he got home. It was by now unbearably muggy: his shirt stuck to him and when he scratched his forehead where something had bitten him, his nails were full of muddy sweat. He stopped at the phone box and delivered the message to Esme, and was still screwing the lid back on the jar when he heard thunder.

About time too, he thought; a storm might clear the air a little . . . More thunder, a few raindrops. Car alarms started to go off as the air pressure changed. Suddenly it was raining hard, sluicing down as though someone had emptied a giant bathtub over the village. His hair was plastered to his head and his shirt to his back, rain running down his face, soaking through his trousers. Thunder again, and lightning almost immediately. Cars splashed through puddles and people were scurrying for cover. He walked sedately, occasionally wiping his face, enjoying it. The gardens could do with it, and if people were hay-making, well, it was sure to be blisteringly hot again in a day or so to dry everything out. As though someone had turned a tap, the rain eased to a thin drizzle and the sun shone; he looked round for the rainbow and saw it between roofs, arching over the hills.

How lovely to live in a country that has weather, he thought, not for the first time. A climate would be boring: I suppose you could prepare for the rainy season if you knew when it was coming, but—I do like weather. The way mist hangs about in valleys, in conifer plantations, and the way you can see rain falling out of clouds several miles away . . . Now I really do need a bath. And possibly even a bowl of soup or something hot to eat. I wonder if Rheidol got caught in that? Or poor little Tom Socks, if he's still about . . .

He could hear his neighbours' music several houses away. He went in through the back door, looked for Rheidol and found him asleep on the green rug in the living-room, put the kettle on and set the water heater, stripped his wet clothes off and left them in a heap on the kitchen floor and went upstairs for a towel and dry clothes. Music thumped and wailed behind the dividing wall.

"Oh, go away," Dafydd said, without rancour, and went downstairs to make soup and toast.

He had a long, hot bath, got into bed and read for a while, gave up when it got too dark, and tried to sleep. The music persisted. Maybe he ought to do something. Have a quiet word tomorrow, when they woke up . . .

Thump thump went the music. He couldn't sleep. People were using geocaching as a cover for stealing wool: how long before farmers refused to give permission for caches on their land?

But that was all wrong, because the caches he'd found had all—except Skulker on the Slope and possibly Prickly Patch—been accessible from roads or public footpaths.

He got up, put the light on and found the pile of messages, maps and printouts which had come from Esme. Yes, one of the printouts contained the information that the cache was easily accessible from the footpath and there was no need to disturb walls or climb fences. Another had a note thanking the local Council for permission to place the cache. Presumably some official had realised that geocaches would bring tourists, or at least give tourists something more to do. That meant that individual farmers had no say in whether a cache was placed just outside the boundary of their property.

What was it that Miss Smith had said, that he'd not responded to at the time because he wasn't supposed to know anything about the subject? Passers-by seeing the thieves' van and assuming it was people caching; that was it. It had been niggling at him ever since, because most people wouldn't know about geocaching and unless they lived very locally and had taken the trouble to find out what was going on, as he had, they wouldn't even be aware that there was a cache to be looked for.

And that meant . . .

Thump, thump, thump in the background. Dafydd yawned, put the papers back on the chest of drawers and went downstairs to make a pot of tea and try to marshal his thoughts. He put the radio on and found a programme of classical music which helped to counteract the thumping, poured a cup of tea and stared, unseeing, at the door to the cwtsh. If people didn't know there was a cache, and wouldn't know what someone was supposed to be doing if they parked there, then it couldn't be an alibi.

So that meant . . .

Surely it wasn't a geocacher who was stealing wool? But if they were seen behaving suspiciously—well, up to the point of actually laying hands on a sheep—they could claim to be looking for the cache.

And the policeman from Aber was going to go to the Event, tomorrow, *and warn whoever the thief was . . .*

What time was it? One a.m.; un y.b. in Welsh, which was short for y bore, meaning in the morning. He yawned. He couldn't ring Dai now. But Miss Smith would probably be awake still, and she could send an email. He hurried out into the hall and rang her, not even having to look up the number because he'd memorised it when they were after the Batter Pudding Hurler.

"Miss Smith yn siarad, what do you want? Beth dach chi eisiau? Dafydd! What's up? Beth sy'n bod?"

"O, dim llawer, ond——"

"Not much? Dach chi'n gw'bod ei bod hi'n un o'r gloch y bore?"

"Yes, I know it's gone one. I'm sorry, but I need to contact Dai before tomorrow morning. This morning. Could you send him an email, please?"

"O'r gorau. Okay. So what's happened?"

He explained his theory. Miss Smith took notes, said she would email Dai straight away and rang off.

Dafydd went back to the kitchen. Here the radio was announcing a jazz programme, and he turned it off. He was instantly aware of thump, thump, thump, punctuated by squeals and laughter. When would Dai read the email? When was the Event due to start? Would Dai be able to contact the policeman in time, especially if he was off-duty? A pity he couldn't go to the Event himself . . . Suddenly he pushed the chair back and hurried into the hall. His jacket was hanging in the usual place and he couldn't remember taking the card out of his pocket . . . Yes, there it was, creased and grubby but still legible; James' business card. Dafydd had never rung a mobile phone before but began to dial, trying not to think about how much it might cost.

"Uh . . .Mh? This is Cavendish Computer Security: you're speaking to James Buntingford."

"James, it's Dafydd. Sorry to disturb you."

"'S okay. What's up?"

Dafydd explained. James agreed that if Tîm Pwdin were going to try to do something about the wool-thieves, it would be a shame to warn the culprit.

"So what's this event, then? Let me get the page up . . . H'm. One at Dolgellau and one at Bont . . . where's Bont? Oh, Pontrhydfendigaid. That'll be it, I should think. Starts at eight a.m. I can go over there if you like; I should be able to take the day off, 'specially for something like this . . . Dafydd, is this a bad connection or is there a lot of noise at your end? Good grief . . . What I'll do is, I'll leave Richard a message and go, make sure I'm there first and can catch the bloke before he says anything to anyone. I'll take Dai's number. I'll be okay, I'll sleep in the car. Done it before. Okay? If you ring me and it goes to voicemail, I'm driving or talking to someone: just leave a message and I'll pick it up a.s.a.p. Any news of the Davieses?"

Dafydd told him that Mike had come over with Esme to see the kittens, but Edith hadn't been at all in favour of it.

"It's a start, poor kid," James sighed. "I wondered if she might like a trackable of her own to watch. I was looking at ones with cat pictures on . . . They had some pink fluffy ones, but most teenagers I've known are more into skulls or manga than fluffy; what do you reckon?"

"That's a brilliant idea!"

Dafydd told him, very quickly, about his plan for a treasure-hunt, adding: "If you can get me one, that would be a good prize. A normal cat-looking cat, if they do them. She used to teach at a secondary school, so she's hardly a teenager."

James whistled. "Ouch. No wonder she's sick of being shut in. I'm looking forward to meeting her, when it happens. Right: I'd better get off. Thanks for ringing."

Chapter 12

AT SEVEN O'CLOCK HE woke to hear the telephone. He stumbled downstairs to answer it, thinking it would be Dai, but to his surprise it was Esme.

"Dafydd! I hoped you'd be in—I've had an idea!"

"You'd better tell me, then." He sat down on the bottom step.

"These wool-thieves; I couldn't sleep last night, and I thought if they've been to the caches to case the joint first, they'll have signed the log. So if Dai tells us which the relevant caches are, I can look up the list of everyone who's been there and that gives us a short-list!"

"Good idea," Dafydd said, already thinking that if the thieves had planned to be up to no good, surely they wouldn't have signed the log to prove they'd been there. "I'll ask him."

"And I looked up how much wool is worth, and they're right: most sorts aren't worth much at all. The official British Wool website says the maximum farmers can get for Welsh no. 1 wool is 81p per kilo, and 76p for Welsh no.2, whatever that means. Then I looked up how much a fleece weighs, and it's only about three kilos on average. And then I looked up another site to find out how much it costs to have a sheep sheared, and people come over from Australia and New Zealand to do it professionally; they can do a whole sheep in a minute! The Wool Board do training courses for people in this country who want to learn. It costs about a pound per sheep to get it sheared."

"That's less than one pound fifty profit per fleece, and then only if they get the maximum price for the wool. So why are woollen clothes so expensive? I suppose there's all the processing, and presumably nylon is cheaper to produce." Dafydd shook his head.

"Yes, and the farmers have to sell all their wool to the Wool Board if they have more than three sheep, or they did seven years ago when the information was posted. It says it's a non-profit-making organisation, but anything with staff can't possibly hand back all the money they get for something . . . Apparently lots of small farmers shear their own sheep, to save money, but then I suppose it might not be as tidy a fleece as a professionally cut one, so it wouldn't be worth as much. It doesn't seem fair at all. So no wonder they aren't all that bothered about one fleece disappearing, especially if they don't have to shear the sheep!"

"H'm . . . Well, thank you for that, Esme. I left you a message last night in the usual place: I did the two on the coast path. Met Twynnyms at the farthest one; a young couple from Cheshire. I'd better go; Rheidol will be through the door soon if he goes on scratching like that. He wants his breakfast."

He had fed the cats and himself, washed, shaved and spent some time with Sky and the kittens, and had woken up sufficiently to think about revisiting a few locations to see if his ideas for treasure hunt caches would work, when the phone rang again.

This time it was Dai, who said yes, he'd passed on the email and had been talking to Donald and Sandy, the students from Dol Wen. Siân had told them about the sheep-shearers and they'd suggested that the thieves might also have been stealing fleeces from flocks where sheep were free to wander, such as the area round the Abergwesyn pass; it was a narrow road with cattle-grids at intervals and the sheep were often standing on the road itself. Someone who parked at a good vantage point could probably catch a sheep and shear it without being seen, as there never seemed to be much traffic about.

Then he'd rung a farmer from the church he attended in Aberystwyth, who had suggested that moorland sheep would have harsher, dirtier and less valuable fleeces compared with those from breeds kept in lower-lying fields: the man had reeled off a few breed names, but none had meant anything to Dai.

"And he said," Dai continued, "that if we want to use one of his fields, he has two on back roads with biggish gateways—no actual lay-bys, but fairly wide gateways where people could park. And although he's sheared all his already, he knows people who keep rare breeds and he said he'd tell them about the plan and see if anyone was prepared to lend out their sheep! He said it'd probably be okay as long as we could make sure there was 24-hour surveillance. So I'll put the grid references through your letterbox later today and you can talk to your contact."

"It's James Buntingford," Dafydd informed him. "He said there was no harm your knowing . . . and Richard knows he does geocaching, too; he's gone to the Event at Bont today but you could email him directly. Dai, I don't suppose you happen to have the grid references for where the fleeces were stolen from? Because there might be some common denominator . . . "

"Great minds think alike, and, as my Nan used to say, fools never differ! I've been round to them over the last few days, and the most obvious thing was ease of access: one's got a bridle-path gate, two had the gate fastened with string, and the rest were the draw-latch sort. None of them was padlocked or wired shut, but then, not many are round here. Don and Sandy said they'd be happy to do night duty, and they think they could rope in some friends."

"I'll do dawn 'til whenever," Dafydd offered. "If your friend lets us, Richard and James could rig up a C.C.T.V. camera covering the gateway, and then the only reason to have humans there would be so there's an actual witness—and someone to ring the police, or the farmer, and shut the gate or whatever else is necessary."

"We can do a rota once we've got the cache set up, and the sheep. And Sandy's going to the felting workshop today in Mach. No, not the one that was cancelled; the one run by the shop in Aber. See what it's like."

That reminded Dafydd of the felting needle he had bought. When Dai had rung off, he checked what he had in the way of food, made a shopping list and put it in his rucksack along with Miss Smith's flower book, his binoculars, a water-bottle and a couple of carrier bags, and went out on his bicycle. He rode to the start of the Traeth Maelgwyn footpath, locked the bicycle and enjoyed a leisurely walk, occasionally stopping to identify a plant or bird, or collect tufts of wool. He had wondered if he should ride out to Machynlleth, but it was still too hot and the main road, when he reached it, seemed very busy. He dropped into the community shop at Tre'r Ddol and bought bread, fruit, a lettuce and a packet of tuna sandwiches and took the lower back road to Dôl-y-Bont. He paused to eat the sandwiches, looking at a field of sheep. Yes, now he was actually looking at them properly, these were different from the ones out by Traeth Maelgwyn. These were bigger animals, with black noses and black eyes like pandas, and black knees. He wondered how the wool differed, found some snagged on a thorn tree and compared it with what he had collected earlier. It was a little longer, with none of the harsh thick hairs that looked more like whiskers than fur. How could he have lived in rural Wales for at least seventeen years of his life and still know so little about sheep?

He went back to Borth slowly, collecting wool as he went. When he got back he made a pot of tea, put a couple of inches of lukewarm water into a bucket and added the wool. His neighbours were making a racket again. He also added three drops of washing up liquid, and was gratified by how dirty the water already was. Carefully not wringing, rubbing or doing anything else that would have shrunk a woollen garment, he sloshed it about for a minute or so, left it to soak while he drank the tea, rinsed it carefully and wondered how to dry it. His mother had used an old lace curtain with the worst tears darned. Dafydd went upstairs and looked in the airing cupboard for inspiration, found an elderly pillowcase and pegged it onto the line with the wool inside. That would have to do, and in this heat it should dry before nightfall.

He went back indoors where it was cooler, poured another cup of tea and went up to sit with Sky. She shot past him as he opened the door and vanished down the stairs. Had he closed the kitchen door? He couldn't remember, and as he clearly had no chance of catching up with her, he stepped over the fireguard and let the kittens swarm over him.

After half an hour he shut them in carefully and went downstairs. Yes, he'd left the door ajar and the cat-flap open. Bother. Where had she gone? What if she got run over, on the road or the railway? At least the kittens were eating biscuits now, and could lap from a saucer . . . Nothing he could do, beyond leaving the cat-flap open for her and food in the kitchen. Kicking himself for his carelessness, he set off with a notebook for a second mooch round the village. He had thought of a cryptic clue for a cache . . .

Sky had still not come back by the time he went to bed that night. He gave the kittens plenty of biscuits and water, gave them a stone hot-water-bottle wrapped in a towel to cuddle up to if they were cold (which seemed unlikely, but you never knew), and tried to trust that everything would turn out for the best.

At six on Sunday morning he was woken by Rheidol leaping off the bed and rushing downstairs. Dafydd followed almost as quickly, fearing that Rheidol would try to drive Sky away and there would be a fight, but found Rheidol in the kitchen glowering at the cat-flap, while Sky sat on the kitchen windowsill, tapping daintily at the window.

He lifted down the washing up liquid and the jar he put silver foil into and opened the window for her, speaking soothingly. "Tyrd i mewn, 'te. Come in, then, you dreadful little cat . . . Cath fach ofnadwy . . . " Then: "Oh, I see! Dwi'n gweld, mae cariad efo ti! You've got a boyfriend!"

Tom Socks was sitting by the wheelie-bin, as smugly as Sky. Dafydd shook his head at him and closed the cat-flap in case Sky tried to get out again, fed Rheidol, emptied a pouch of wet food into a bowl and waved it under Sky's nose, then set off upstairs. He opened the door of her room, placed the food on the lino a good distance inside the fireguard, and watched as she leapt nimbly over the barrier and began to eat. The kittens welcomed her rapturously. He shut them all in and went down to open the cat-flap.

On Sunday afternoon the young people in the next house went out and Dafydd slept for several hours. He woke as a train passed going north, and heard Sky scratching at the door of her room.

"No you don't, lass," he said to the closed door, and went downstairs to find a banana to eat before he went to the evening service.

Alice Brownsword was already waiting at the chapel when he arrived for the prayer meeting on Tuesday evening.

"I wondered if I could ask you to help me with something?" she began. "I know you always dash off straight afterwards, so I came early."

Dafydd grimaced. He had been going to find geocaches, of course. Had it been that obvious?

"You see, my neighbour moves to Tywyn tomorrow," she explained. "Everything's packed, indoors, but the place hasn't sold yet and she's asked me to dig things up from the garden, to put straight in the garden of the place she's going to. Her nephew and his wife have been there for a year but they've not done much with the garden, and he says he'll work from home. I know it's an awful cheek, but I wondered if you'd be prepared to help dig things up."

As they regularly prayed about her shoulder and back problems, Dafydd could understand why she was not prepared to do strenuous gardening. He agreed to be ready at eight and was pleased to hear that tools would be provided.

He had not been aware that Alice lived near Richard and James on the hillside overlooking the valley of the Leri. She parked her small red car in her own drive and they went along the lane to the next gateway, each carrying a plastic washing-basket. Dolwyddelan was a suburban-looking house with the front door down a side-branch of the gravelled drive, pleasant enough but with nothing to recommend it architecturally. The removals lorry had arrived and people were carrying things out of the back door. Once past the vehicle, Dafydd looked around at the garden and frowned.

"How much of this is hers?"

"Oh, all of it. That's partly why she's moving. When her parents were alive they used to keep the whole place immaculate, but as she got older she let the further parts of it go and now she's reduced it to just these three beds and the borders along the drive. It's a shame, but I can understand it."

Dafydd looked at the nearest flowerbed. Fuchsias, Michaelmas daisies, some miniature roses, a hebe, hydrangeas . . . "What does she want us to take?" he asked, with trepidation.

"A couple of hellebores, a clump of the Michaelmas daisies, the love-lies-bleeding, some of the apple-mint and the fennel, and as many of the vegetables as we can. She was going to hang on until October, but she had another mini-stroke, and everyone agrees she'd be better off in the granny-flat as soon as possible."

Alice put down the basket and pulled a pair of gardening gloves from her pocket. "Do you want some? There should be a few pairs in the garage with the tools, but I don't know whether they'll fit you . . . "

"I'm rather enjoying this," he admitted to Mrs. Acton, when she came out to ask if they wanted tea or coffee and to see how they were getting on. "I know it's spoiling what's here, but—knowing you're going to enjoy it in Tywyn . . . "

"Yes!" Mrs. Acton smiled. "And when you know there's a definite end to it, like digging out a really long bramble, there's a great sense of satisfaction."

Alice murmured something about rescue archaeology and offered to come down to the house and carry the tea, and was there a tin bath or something they could use? "What do we do about the runner beans?" she asked. "Leave them? They're well up the bamboos."

Mrs. Acton gave Dafydd a suddenly wicked smile. "I'm sure you'll be able to unwind them, if you're careful."

He managed not to let his jaw drop and smiled back. "Challenge accepted . . . "

Chapter 13

THAT AFTERNOON, AS a reward for dealing with the runner beans, he finally went to Machynlleth to look for the caches. First he called in at the Animal Sanctuary charity shop, acquired a squeaky toy mouse for the kittens and picked up a leaflet about neutering cats, then tried on three pairs of trousers at the Hospice charity shop and bought one, bought a sausage roll from a market stall, and went back to his bicycle to go in search of the caches.

He had never before needed to use the new footbridge over the Dyfi and while the modern design did not impress him the bridge was clearly appreciated: he was passed in both directions by numerous cyclists and for almost ten minutes stood gazing thoughtfully at the river, aware of exactly where the cache was but unable to retrieve it without being seen doing so. At last he grabbed it, went a little way up the track to sign it, and then had to wait for a chance to put it back. To his relief he managed not to drop it into the undergrowth, and set off for the next, the puzzle cache concerning the stones in the town.

The stones outside the Co-Op. were partly concealed by hoardings and building work, but he counted what he could see, then followed Esme's map to the standing stone which was, incongruously, in the middle of a tiny island of turf surrounded by modern houses. He copied down the information he needed and went on up the road past some very noisy dogs to the golf course, climbed the hill in a cloud of flies to where he could see the Gorsedd circle, and, despite the flies, ate the sausage roll and drank most of the water he had brought with him. It was impossible to count the stones from a distance because the bracken was so high, so he went downhill, walked round the circle counting, wrote down the answer and went slowly back to his bicycle.

The last cache she had suggested was at the opposite side of the town, a box in a camouflaged bag poked in at the bottom of a hedge. Of course, they would need a box—or a film canister—to make the cache by the field of sheep. Presumably James had thought of that. Would it be acceptable for him to go and find it if James had placed it, or would that be cheating? If he hadn't seen where they put it, it wouldn't be cheating . . . At last the dog-walker had passed; Dafydd stooped and dragged the bag out of its hiding-place, took it to a bench and opened it.

Cliplock box, logbook in plastic bag, blunt pencil, pencil sharpener . . . He tucked the cache out of sight under his rucksack and sharpened the pencil. What else? A plastic dog, a huge paperclip, a biro, a soggy packet of tissues (he took these out, meaning to drop them in a bin), a card declaring that the Fifth Shrewsbury Scout Troop had found this cache, and a geocoin with a flag enamelled onto it; Dutch or French. Dutch, to judge from the wording on it. He slipped it into his pocket and annotated the logbook.

Should he cycle back and have a go at the Dyfi Osprey Project cache? He wouldn't mind seeing the ospreys . . . Regretfully, he decided against it. It was too hot to cycle ten miles on a busy road with, quite probably, no cache to be found. If James ever found it, he'd have a go; get off at Cyffordd Dyfi and walk to the Project and back, take binoculars and a sandwich and make a day of it.

Meanwhile, if he didn't hurry he might miss the train.

On the journey back he wrote a report for Esme, peered out of the window at Cyffordd Dyfi and saw only the nest-platform without any visible ospreys, remembered that he'd not heard how either the Event or the felting had gone, and decided to visit Siân before he went home.

There was a car outside Siân's house, and he hesitated, not wanting to disturb her if she had visitors. Which number did the students live at? Well, it was probably that one, with a big Scottish saltire hanging up in one of the bedroom windows.

He knocked at the door and Donald answered.

"Mr. Williams! Dewch i mewn—come in. Sandy! Dafydd's here."

He was ushered into the living-room and sat on a low-backed sofa with a black woven throw draped over it.

There was a box of driftwood in the middle of the floor and only one curtain up: the other was in a heap on the coffee-table with pins in as though someone was hemming it.

Sandy placed a mug of tea in front of him and said how nice to see him, did he like ginger biscuits, she'd made some yesterday and if there were any left . . .

He did, and there were: they sat munching contentedly while Sandy finished hemming the curtain, then Donald fetched a chair from the kitchen and hung it in place.

"That looks better than those purple striped ones," Sandy said firmly. "Honestly—the fabric had roses in some of the stripes, and one had the header on with the roses the right way up, and the other didn't. How could *anyone* live with that, once they'd noticed?"

"Well, it took you over a year to notice!" Donald grinned. "So, Mr. Williams, how's the detecting? Have they got permission for the cache yet?"

Dafydd explained what he knew, and asked how she had got on at the felting course.

Sandy pulled a face. "It wasn't all that good, unfortunately, because I'd have really liked to learn. There were loads of handouts, but they were all laminated and she collected them back in. I did photograph a few bits on my phone without her noticing, but we found out when I got back here that it was all copied and pasted directly from someone else's web site! We made a coaster and watched her do stuff, and had a go at a big piece of felt with spirals on it in different colours, but for what it cost I'd have liked more to take home with me. Someone said could we have the special needle and foam pad we'd been using, and she said yes, it cost six pounds, and she had little bags of coloured wool for sale too at three pounds each, and a book on how to do it, that was twelve ninety-nine . . . It was all like that. Anything beyond the absolute basic coaster cost extra, and we didn't even get a drink mid-morning; there was a machine in the lobby, so most of us didn't bother. It was really all a marketing exercise for her shop, which might have worked if it hadn't been so expensive and if she hadn't been . . . I don't really know how to describe her. Sophie Marston, her name was. And she sneered, the whole time. As though she was used to teaching A-list celebrities in Paris and someone'd made her come to a mosquito-ridden swamp in the middle of nowhere and teach half-wits. And the poster went on about how eco-friendly it was, but when someone asked about dyeing she said you had to use chemicals to get decent colours, and she had a flip-chart and used loads more pages than she needed, and at the end she just stuffed them all in the bin!" Sandy lifted her hands helplessly. "More to the point, she didn't seem to understand what I meant when I asked what sort of sheep the wool was from, so I said where did it come from, quite slowly. in. words. of. one. syllable, like that, because she'd really got to me by then, and she swung round away from me and started shouting at someone for using the needle dangerously, and I bet they weren't. So I came home and told Don, and he said write how you feel about it and save it as a draft, and as soon as we've found out who's stealing the wool, send it to the head office of the chain . . . and I'm going to send it, because all right, it was a lot cheaper than the other workshop, but considering what you got for it, it was an absolute rip-off."

Dafydd shook his head. "No wonder it cost so much less than the other course, and the other woman had to cancel hers because there weren't enough takers . . . No, thanks; they were very good biscuits, but I'd better not have another one. I ought to be going home. Could you find out about this chain of craft shops on the internet? If they're all like that, surely someone else has complained."

Donald finished his tea and put the mug down. "I'll go and check."

When he got home there was an envelope on the hall floor: a message from James, who had come round while he was out.

> *Hi, Symbiosis, this is the travel-tag cat you wanted. Cost about £3 but I got several different and they threw one in free so no need to pay for it. Event went well, got loads of litter picked up and met some ace people. Checked out hiding-places and drafted cache pages for two sites, one was too close to the final for a puzzle cache so I sent the other one in, asked for it to go live on a Friday night. Nothing yet. Cache already in place—small, screw-top tub covered in duct tape, a few dead leaves stuck to it—they'll probably come off when it's handled, but hey. Meeting your other half at cafe tomorrow at ten! Can we visit the kits again sometime? The Wipeout Kid*

Dafydd inspected the travel tag, which was in the shape of a cheerful tabby cat with the unique trackable number on the back, and puzzled over 'your other half' for at least a minute before realising that it meant Esme. Well, well. At least she was being allowed out. How would she get on with James? None of his business . . .

He checked Rheidol was out in the garden, put his new trousers in the basket to be washed, locked the cat-flap and closed the kitchen door, and went upstairs to give the kittens their toy mouse and read the leaflet, which was annoyingly vague about timescales. He folded it into a paper aeroplane and threw it gently towards Sky, who leapt and brought it down with worrying efficiency. Once she went out, there'd be no birds left in the neighbourhood . . . He sighed and continued to work on the treasure-hunt. The neighbours were being noisy again and he needed to speak to Siân before he went much further.

At six on Thursday morning he went solemnly through the village, placing his caches. Some were simply slate pebbles from the beach with two letters painted on one side; some were dog name-tag holders which he tied onto railings or branches. There was a tablet-bottle hidden behind a drain-pipe and a small plastic tub which had contained hummus under a couple of stones at the end of a wall, and (the one he was most proud of) a zip-top plastic bag attached to a piece of button thread which was tied round one of his own garden railings, so that the bag hung down on his side of the garden wall, hidden by a clump of marguerites.

By the time he had finished it was almost eight so he rang Siân. As he had hoped she was awake, and fortunately she was happy for him to place the final cache in her garden, on top of what had been a dustbin store in the days before wheelie-bins and on which she now kept several pots of geraniums.

"Ask Esme to leave the clues in place," she requested, "because I'd love to have a try! All right, I know where the prize *is*, but I'd like to find out how to get there . . . And what's the prize going to be?"

Dafydd hesitated for a split-second. "A little enamelled picture of a cat," he told her. "Like a key-ring. I hope she'll like it."

When she had rung off, he sat down at the kitchen table and carefully made a second copy of the clues. He sealed one into an envelope, wrote 'Miss Davies—Stretton' on it, put it into a carrier bag along with the travel-tag in a tub which had once held baking powder, and put it by the front door. It would make sense to wait until ten before placing the final cache and delivering the envelope. He fetched his torn trousers, and the toffee-tin where he kept needles and thread, and began to darn them. When he'd finished, he would have a go at felting.

Chapter 14

"I'M SURE I saw Sky sitting on a wall when I went past the Post Office on Saturday evening," Miss Smith greeted him.

Dafydd moved aside to let people into the Spar. "You might well have done. She dashed past me and I'd left the kitchen door open; she was gone all night, and at six there she was, waiting for the window to be opened, and Tom Socks by the wheelie-bin: 'See, I brought her home!' "

"What it is to have a teenager in the family!" Miss Smith grinned sympathetically.

Dafydd sighed. "I'm still trying to keep her in, of course, but I wouldn't be surprised if she has more kittens. I got a leaflet yesterday from the Animal Sanctuary shop in Mach, but it didn't say how soon after kittens she could be spayed."

Miss Smith changed her shopping bag to the other hand. "I'll look it up for you, if I remember. And I'll ask around, see if anyone owns Tom Socks. I expect he's a stray."

He delivered the instructions for the treasure-hunt, carefully didn't peer into the cafe to see how Esme and James were getting on, delivered the final cache and, with Siân's enthusiastic help, concealed it under an upturned flowerpot. She asked him in for a cup of tea; Dafydd grinned.

"Yes, please. I'll give Esme a head start on the clues, but you can have your set tomorrow and when you get up to my end of the village you must come in and have a paned with me. Now, I had a go at felting this morning; I'll leave my efforts with you—be careful of the needle, it's a vicious thing, all hooks—and maybe Sandy could show us how she was taught. The needle came with a leaflet but I'm not convinced I've got it right. The wool I'm using is bits and pieces I found when I was out walking; I washed it and picked all the thorns and dead beetles out of it. If I find any more I'll bring it over."

Siân set the kettle to boil and examined the shapeless mass of felt. "What's it meant to be?" she asked.

Dafydd shrugged. "That's part of the problem. I didn't have a specific shape in mind, so I just kept prodding, and got a blob."

"If you make a smaller one and put it on top, it might make a snowman," Siân suggested. "Or a small blob and then two flattish wings and a tail, for a bird . . . Well, if you really aren't bothered, I'll try to make it into something. Some of this wool is mostly kemp: that won't felt, will it?"

"Kemp is the stiff, thick fibre? No; it doesn't seem to. There were two sorts of sheep, the little ones down by the sea which had kempy fleeces, and some bigger ones inland which had black noses and eyes and knees, with no kemp at all."

"Welsh Mountain, or some sort of cross, and Kerry Hill, by the sound of it," Siân pronounced. "Don't look so stunned! When Ieuan worked at Welshpool I used to go to the livestock market with the children, to see the animals. Shall we sit in the garden, or do you think it'd be cooler in here?"

When he left Siân's to go home it seemed to be hotter than ever. The town was full of strangers in shorts and sleeveless tops, with small children in pushchairs and older children carrying bodyboards. He went back along the beach which was at least wider than the pavement, the grey pebbles too hot to touch under the merciless sun. How could people bear to lie on the beach for hours at a time, like so much bacon under a grill? And how could people possibly want to eat beef-burgers and chips, this weather? He had intended to have lettuce, tomatoes and cheese for lunch, but didn't feel at all enthusiastic about it. Maybe it was because he had no outstanding projects to work on, or because he was fat and unfit, but all he wanted to do was sleep . . .

He went up onto the sea wall, crossed the road, went down the back lane and heard his neighbours' music growing louder as he approached the house. Rheidol was half-asleep on the lawn in a patch of shade, but opened one eye as Dafydd unlocked the back door.

There was a fly buzzing against the kitchen window and the wet food he had put out for Rheidol that morning was mostly still there. Dafydd picked up the bowl and saw fly eggs yellow among the meat, fetched a plastic sleeve which had been round some junk mail and tipped in the food, tied off the top and dropped it in the wheelie-bin. Rheidol was feeling the heat, too. Was anyone feeding Tom Socks?

He washed the bowl carefully, put a handful of cat biscuits into it and put it in the garden, then refilled the water bowl.

Food . . . He opened the fridge, saw nothing he felt like eating, drank most of the cold water from the jug and refilled it, wondered about bread, found that the edge of each slice had mould on it. Bother. He should have kept that in the fridge. He'd eat in the evening. He closed the cat-flap, closed the kitchen door and went upstairs to see Sky. It was so hot. He lay full-length on the landing, watching the kittens through the fireguard. It wouldn't matter if they got out; he'd closed all the doors . . .

A car drew up somewhere outside. Doors slammed. People ran up and downstairs shouting. Dafydd slept.

When he woke it was evening, the sun beginning to set over the bay. People were being loud in the house next door and the spare bedroom was deserted. Where had Sky taken the kittens? He got up stiffly and investigated: the whole family was curled up in a heap on the mat in the hall. Well, at least they were all there, and he wasn't likely to use the front door. The noise from next door went on and on. Dafydd went up and moved the fireguard aside to make it easier for the kittens if they decided to return to the spare bedroom. The music went thump thump thump. Well, thought Dafydd, trying to be fair, it's no louder than usual, and they've probably got their windows open, even if I haven't, and at least I *have* slept . . . If they're making a night of it I might as well go for a walk.

He crept into the kitchen without disturbing Sky and filled his water-bottle. Bother, he'd not fed the cats yet. He poured biscuits into a pie-dish and put it down quietly in the hall, then closed the door again. There was still water upstairs. He pushed the kitchen door gently to check it was closed, took the rest of the packet outside, locking the door behind him, and refilled Rheidol's bowl, put the empty packet on the doorstep with a stone on top to be recycled later, and set off.

As usual he went north, towards Ynyslas. There were still people on the beach, on the golf course, on the sea wall. It was a little cooler now that he was out of doors and he walked steadily. The tide was going out, the beach gleaming gold in the sunset where it was wet. He walked on and on, past the last breakwaters, up the long sweep of beach towards the Dyfi estuary. Now he was alone except for the odd dog-walker. The sun set. The afterglow was enough to see by, and when he got to Ynyslas there were pools left in the sand by the receding tide. Temporarily forgetting about weaver fish, he took off his trainers and socks, rolled up his trouser-legs and paddled. The water was warm in the pool, icy when he left it and stood at the edge of the sea. If I'd brought swimming trunks and a towel, he thought, I could have swum . . . but I'd be daft to, so close to the estuary and alone, at night, with the tide still going out. He could hear the engine of a boat, far away. A bird called once and was silent. Redshank? He yawned widely and realised he was still very tired.

He walked back towards Borth in the shallow water, and when there was more gravel than sand underfoot stopped to put his trainers back on. His feet were gritty and uncomfortable, and he sat on the first breakwater to shake out his trainers and socks and brush bits off his feet. He tied his laces again and sat still. There was a faint breeze which didn't seem to make any difference, and insistent music interspersed with a booming amplified voice, probably from a caravan site. He went along the path at the edge of the golf course until the music was a whisper in the background and sat down, leaning against a fence post. It was still too hot. Poor Esme, stuck indoors; poor Mike, too, and anyone else who was ill or couldn't do anything to escape the heat but just had to survive it . . .

He opened his eyes, aware that his back and neck ached. He must have slept. What time was it? Just gone two a.m. There was a thin sliver of waning moon in the sky, a few house lights still on in the village when he stood up. He walked, his joints stiff. The tide had turned but the sea was still a long way down the beach, and he could hear the thump of music if he listened for it, though now it was part of the environment and his ears had tuned it out as they had the sea. What was that? A car door, perhaps, or a house door closing. He walked on and on, feeling sticky and light-headed and slightly unreal, as though the village were a painted backdrop and he might be walking anywhere, across a desert or through a city, or on the moon . . .

He was almost home, music still thumping out from his neighbours' house, louder as he drew closer. A door opened, spilling light and sound into the night, shrill female voices raised in argument. Dafydd walked past, on and on past the Post Office, up to the first houses on the west side of the road. He crossed the green and sat on the wall looking out to sea. He felt as though he could fall asleep again quite easily, and at least here it was quieter.

So as not to fall asleep again, he went down cautiously onto the shingle and watched the dark, calm water. Occasionally light caught the waves and he could tell it was moving. What was that, down by the new sea defences? A seal? Maybe a dolphin; there were dolphins in the bay. He thought he saw the dark shape again. Maybe it was someone swimming. If I had the courage, he thought, that would be me: it must be lovely and cool, with the cold water all round you . . . Why do I never do things like that? Why am I always so *sensible*?

Because I see the potential danger. I don't want to be thoughtless enough to make people have to rescue me, or find me drowned and washed up one morning, and I certainly don't want to be shouted at for a reckless young fool by someone who sees me doing it . . .

Had there been anything there at all, out in the dark water? If so, it was probably a young person. A surfer like James, maybe, or one of the teenage boys who loitered with their friends because they had nothing better to do. But teenagers seemed to do things in groups, and this person was alone. It definitely was a person; as he watched, the swimmer stood up in the shallows and walked up the beach, for a split-second crossing a strip of light from a window before being lost to sight behind the nearer houses. A woman? But why shouldn't a woman do something like that?

Best of luck to her, he thought enviously. I wish that was me, Dafydd Minnesota Williams . . . Why am I always Dafydd and never Minnesota?

Right, I am not going to put up with any more of that racket, I am going to tell them to be quiet, and then I shall go to bed and *sleep* . . .

His fury carried him most of the way home. A taxi passed him, heading south. His neighbours seemed to have turned the music down considerably, so he felt there was no point in complaining. There was a car outside Anfield, so his neighbour on the other side was at home: maybe Mr. Norgate had said something to them. Whatever the reason, Dafydd was grateful for the peace. He let himself in, locked the door, slipped cautiously into the hall in case Sky was still there, closed the kitchen door, went upstairs and ran a cold bath, the water a little deeper than he usually had it. He stripped and stepped in. It was so cold that he hesitated for a long minute.

Just now, you were wishing you'd gone swimming. The sea wouldn't be any warmer. He lay down, gasping with the shock, made himself lie there until the water began to feel a more comfortable temperature. Shivering, he got out without draining the water, rubbed himself briskly with a towel, closed the bathroom door behind him so the kittens couldn't fall in, and lay on his bed with just a sheet over him. Already he was beginning to feel too hot again but at least he was clean.

By five a.m. the temperature had dropped. He half-woke, felt for the blanket he had discarded and pulled it over himself. Something cawed on the roof above him and he heard the machine-gun rattle of a magpie in response.

Crows versus magpies continued at full volume for half an hour, and as Dafydd was now thoroughly awake he got up, fed the cats and went out. He left the bathroom door closed and the water still in the bath for future reference. He might even borrow a hose and siphon it out to water the garden . . .

Chapter 15

"THIS IS THE hide," Richard explained, gesturing in the direction of a pile of plastic-wrapped bales. Everybody turned dutifully to look. "Most of it is made out of bales, but there's a bit of framework inside to support the roof tarpaulin so that if we do get rain it'll run off and won't just make a lake on top. The reason for this is partly to keep the surveillance team dry, but mostly to keep the equipment dry. We've set up two cameras in the hedge, ten feet either side of the gateway. They're magpie-proofed, rain-proofed, and as well-camouflaged as we can manage, and the cache is described in the instructions as being at ground level so no one should be looking up. If you're interested, there's still the remains of an arc scraped in the mud outside the gate from when we were checking the camera coverage. If you come up two at a time and sit in the hide I'll show you how to operate the cameras. They're fairly standard battery-powered C.C.T.V. cameras with as high a definition as we could get. We wondered about making them dependent on movement, but if they picked up every dog-walker and pigeon and flying carrier-bag there'd probably be no memory left by the time the target arrived, so they're manually operated . . . Good question, Don; we ran a cable in a length of heavy-duty plastic pipe under the line of the gate itself. It's buried about three inches deep, and it's designed to withstand being driven over by tractors and so on. When we've finished here we can either dig it up completely or just take the cable out, depending on what you want, Mr. Williams."

Yet another Mr. Williams, thought Dafydd. This one was the farmer, Dai's friend from church. They followed Donald and Sandy to the back of the hide where a pair of kitchen steps led up to a gap between bales, and waited while the students were shown how things worked. Dai and James were loitering at either end of the lane, ready to give a warning if anyone approached. He'd carefully avoided being shown where the cache was: it was called In Low Places and was already hidden, though apparently it hadn't been published yet.

At last Donald and Sandy came down and he climbed solemnly up the steps, followed by Marged who had refused to be left out.

"So we sit here . . . and this is . . . ? Right. But we can see the gateway on the screens; I thought it wasn't switched on yet?" She turned to address Richard, who was standing on the steps behind them, almost pushing Dafydd off his seat in the confined space.

"It doesn't record anything 'til you switch it on, no, but there should be an image visible all the time on each monitor, so you know if there's anything worth recording. To start recording you press this button, and to stop, you press it again. If someone enters the field and comes towards the hide, pull the steps up if you haven't already, and fill the space with the board that's behind Dafydd; you should have plenty of warning, if you're awake. And that takes me to the next item . . . This will be very important, especially when the target arrives. No, it's not a toy, though it does look a bit cheerful: it's a mobile phone, one of the very simple ones they sell for use by vulnerable people, hence the big buttons on it. At night you'll only have the faint light from the monitors to see it by because the hide isn't light-proofed. I've rigged up an aerial in that tree over there so you should never lose the signal: it's your panic alarm. If the target arrives or something else happens and you need to contact the police urgently, this is linked directly to Dai's phone. If you press the CALL button, his phone will ring . . . but then you can talk to him if you need to, which is what makes it better than the usual panic alarm they give elderly people. Yes, Marged, we did think about what happens when it's Dai in here on watch! He'll have his own phone with him, so he'll use that. This is for the rest of us."

Dafydd climbed down the steps and hoped he'd never be rostered with Marged. How warm would it get, in the hide?

At least the bales were wrapped in pale green rather than black. Miss Smith and Mr. Williams climbed in and Richard began to explain everything again.

"He sounds like Q from the James Bond films," Marged remarked. "I was expecting him to say: 'This is the rocket-launcher, and this is the machine-gun . . . ' "

Dafydd shook his head. "He seems to have thought of everything. I hope he has. If we did have to call Dai, urgently, how long would it take him to get here? Or—I don't want to call them the real police, but you know what I mean."

Marged was rubbing mud off a stockinged ankle. She said: "Well, you're the one who runs the prayer meetings. You'd better put in a word for us."

They began to man the hide there and then, Donald and Sandy taking the first watch, with Miss Smith and Richard due to take over at ten p.m. James was expecting the cache to be published at any moment and Dafydd had said that he'd take over from the night watch at about four on Saturday morning and stay until ten, he was quite happy to do it by himself. He was wondering whether there would be any chance of bird-watching whilst on watch: presumably as long as he watched the monitors too no one would complain.

Marged dropped him off by the Spar and he decided to walk down and check the jar behind the telephone box. There were two messages. One explained that his Dutch geocoin was simply travelling round Europe, so he could put it anywhere, the final part of the puzzle cache at

Machynlleth seemed to be by a fence near the Gorsedd circle, and here were some caches round Aberystwyth for when he next went in that direction.

The second message came as rather a relief: he had been hoping Esme wouldn't feel patronised by his treasure hunt.

Hi, D., got your envelope—planning first expedition tomorrow! Checking Streetview for possible hidey-holes—will leave everything in place for Mrs. Gilchrist, she's a good sport doing it this weather! J. explained very circumspectly about In Low Places and I said I'd ring you when it went live—don't suppose it'd be fair for you to get First to Find! (Second?!) Thanks—E.

Of course, he'd posted the other copy of the clues through Siân's letterbox that morning. It would be interesting to see how they got on. He'd already thought of a few refinements which it was too late to include . . .

He went on down to the supermarket and bought some yogurt, and went slowly home. If it got any hotter he'd have to dig out his sunhat. At least he wasn't going bald; his hair was thick enough to keep most of the sun off. If it was going to be another hot day, how much washing was there to be done? He was looking forward to wearing the new trousers.

His first session of watching proved to be eventful. He had allowed plenty of time to reach the farm, lock his bicycle and walk up the field to the hide in the half-light; as a result he was twenty minutes early and stood for a while watching the small flock of Llanwenogs. A good thing they hadn't been shorn yet. Poor things, they must be so hot. But wool was supposed to be a good insulator, so perhaps it kept the heat out.

When he announced his presence at the hide, Richard told him that James would be along soon and meanwhile he'd give Miss Smith a lift home. They left and soon he saw someone coming up the field at a trot. Fitter than me, Dafydd thought ruefully. And at least forty years younger, which helps . . .

They sat in silence, listening to the few birds still participating in the dawn chorus. Then, unbelievably, they heard a motorcycle approaching.

"Cacher," James breathed. "It must've gone live."

"I won't watch," Dafydd whispered back, and closed his eyes tightly so as not to cheat.

He heard footsteps and repeated rustling, silence, more rustling, footsteps and then the motorcycle leaving.

James nudged him as he opened his eyes. "Go on—you go and get it! Go quick, before someone else comes!"

Dafydd needed no prompting. He scrambled down the steps and was opening the gate before he realised that he'd not read any descriptions of where the cache was hidden. Bother . . . But James had said it was a tub covered in tape and dead leaves, and it was at ground level . . . and there was a trail in the dew, and a broken twig, and a few bits of dead leaves on the grass—— Yes! There it was, about two yards along from the gate-post, stuffed into the gap between hawthorn trunks and half-buried in leaf litter. He pulled it out, getting thoroughly scratched in the process, got the lid off and signed the logbook, dropped in the Dutch geocoin, pushed the log in and was screwing the lid back on when he heard a vehicle in the distance.

Quick, quick; cache back in place, scrape a few leaves over it, through the gate, close the gate very quietly, hurry across the field . . . Help, was he too leaving tracks in the dew? Nothing he could do about that now. Up the steps, into the hide, James holding both thumbs up, and already on the monitors a car drawing up in the gateway.

James produced a pad of paper and scrawled: "Well done—will txt E 2 log it."

Dafydd reached for the pad, and wrote: "Put in Dutch geocoin."

The newcomer was standing in the gateway looking at his G.P.S. device, then his phone, then back at the G.P.S. He walked a few paces in the wrong direction, swung round and walked straight towards the cache, grovelled for it, and signed it. James must have seen me doing the same, Dafydd thought, suddenly feeling uncomfortable about spying on the man, but it wasn't as though they were recording the images . . . He wasn't sure if that made it any better. The man got back in his car and drove away.

James produced his mobile phone and began to text Esme.

"I'll tell her about the trackable," he whispered. 'Well done—are you always that good? That was less than two minutes!"

"He'd left a trail in the dew and leaves on the grass," Dafydd whispered back. "Ought I to go out and try to disguise the tracks I made in the field?"

"Might be a badger or something. They shouldn't be looking over the gate, not if they've read it properly." He was simmering with suppressed excitement. "I am so glad they found it, and it wasn't *too* easy—who was the first one?"

"Roadkill Stew, I think. His writing was a bit faint."

"I'm longing to go out and see who the third guy was," James admitted, "but that would be stupid. I'm so glad I was here to see them! And another car—hope he's not too disappointed."

They waited, but the car drove straight past without stopping.

We're mad, thought Dafydd, settling back against a bale. Absolutely crackers. But it's fun, and other people obviously think so or they wouldn't be coming to look for it. If we borrowed a G.P.S. gadget maybe we could place a cache, Esme and I . . .

There were three more visitors before the end of their shift, including a carful of children who were audibly disappointed at not being the first to find it, and someone in a campervan. On seeing this vehicle James and Dafydd watched the monitors closely, poised to begin recording, but the woman searched for the cache, signed the log, replaced the tub and drove off without even glancing over the gate into the field.

At ten to ten Llinos and Marged came to take over: Dafydd climbed out of the hide rather stiffly and grinned at Llinos. "Have fun."

"It's gone live," James told them quietly. "Six visitors so far, and I bet there'll be more today."

"Oh, bother," Marged murmured. "And I've brought my knitting . . . "

James suggested that Dafydd should put the bike in the back of the car and drop in for a cuppa before he went home, so he could see the logs so far on his computer. Dafydd said he'd be fascinated, but he really mustn't be long because of the cats, and ten minutes later was peering at a list of three logs, including one by Symbiosis. Roadkill Stew had indeed been first to find: his log explained that he'd expected to be too late but the logbook had been completely empty on his arrival, adding: 'Thanks, Wipeout Kid, for the certificate, and happy caching'. The third finder appeared to be Milo Vedig: Dafydd wondered if he was a vet, which was milfeddyg in Welsh, and if so how he balanced an addictive hobby with a demanding job. Like James did, presumably: the young man was already reading emails on another computer while he drank his tea.

Dafydd thanked him and rode home, collecting his paper on the way, fed the cats, prevented another escape bid by Sky, and realised that if he was working the same shift on Sunday he'd be late for Chapel. Bother. Oh well, he wouldn't be going to James' again, and he wouldn't be going quite so far up the main street: he shouldn't miss too much of it.

He still had all that water in the bath. If he was careful not to slosh it everywhere, he might as well use it to flush the toilet. He'd just have to make sure the kittens didn't get into the bathroom for a few days.

Chapter 16

AFTER A WEEK the novelty of manning the hide had worn off and people were beginning to drop out. Marged said that if someone was ill she'd be happy to do it, but she'd done about as much plain knitting as she could cope with. Dai was working and could only really watch on his rest days, and Richard had to go to London for a meeting with clients, but the students, Miss Smith, James, and Dafydd manned the hide, with Llinos occasionally watching with Miss Smith or Sandy. Dafydd was usually with James or on his own, which pleased him because he had time to think.

There had been fifteen visits to the cache, some by local people and some by tourists; another travel bug had been left, attached to a small toy elephant which belonged to a school in Devon, to be picked up almost immediately by a Girls' Brigade from Birmingham.

There had also been several visits to the gateway, mostly by vehicles looking for somewhere to pass on the narrow road, once by someone exercising a dog and once by a van driver who threw three bags of litter into the gateway and added a pile of carpet off-cuts.

"We recorded it," Miss Smith had reported indignantly, "and once we get the wool-thieves—if we do—we ought to hand the recording over to the Council. It took us ages to pick everything up, and some of it was mouldy."

Dafydd climbed up into the hide, waved goodbye to Don and took a banana from his rucksack for breakfast as he would be going straight to Chapel. Don had asked, as had everyone at some point, how long they should keep watching. They knew that James thought they should keep going for a month, but Dafydd couldn't see there being many people left to man the hide by then. It was difficult to decide because, as one might have expected, nothing relevant seemed to be happening. He ate the banana, wondering how long it would take Esme and Siân to finish his treasure-hunt. He must have made it too difficult; either that, or they were rationing themselves . . .

He tucked the banana skin into a pocket of the rucksack and measured the correct length of wool. He had taken to knitting, like Marged, and had already done the leg part of two more socks, using the bright green and yellow wool from Aberdashery. Edith had lent him two huge safety-pins to keep them on until he got round to turning the heels, and he was about to cast on for the next sock, which was going to be dark blue this time, at least to start with. Nothing on the monitors, and when he'd come up the field the sheep had been calmly resting under the hedge: the field had such a slope on it that if the animals were at the bottom it would be quite possible to think the field was empty. He began to cast on, counting stitches. Forty-three, forty-four, forty-five . . . Was that a car?

No, it was a van. He scribbled 46 on the notepad and watched the monitors. A white van drew up and the woman who had been driving got out. A man joined her with a slim border collie which jumped up at him and ran to and fro excitedly until he spoke to it. The man opened the gate and went into the field, followed by the dog.

When he called to the dog and it began to run away from him down the slope, Dafydd pressed the button to start recording, hardly able to believe his eyes. The man went further into the field, calling to the dog, moved back towards the gate as it came back up the slope driving the sheep in front of it. Man and dog separated one sheep from the rest; the woman opened the side door of the van and let down a ramp, stood at one side of it. The man stood at the other and the sheep was driven up the ramp into the van. The man followed with the dog, pulling the gate shut, the ramp was drawn up and the door closed.

Dafydd blinked. He had not imagined that it could be so quick an operation. Wake up, you idiot: this is real. What's the number plate of the van? Minnesota Williams peered at the monitors and wrote it carefully on the pad, realised that the light on the recording device was still red. Was it working? If it wasn't . . . He grabbed the panic alarm and hit the CALL button hard, scrambled out of the hide and hurried across to the gate. What had Marged said when they were talking about the panic alarm? You're the one who does the prayer meeting . . .

"Help!" he gasped, glad that God didn't demand formality. "Do something—please!"

Where could he hide? There was an elder tree in the hedge by the latch-post of the gate; he squashed himself back into the branches and heard the door of the van open, a metallic scraping, hooves on something hollow, the gate opening . . .

As the dog barked, Minnesota Williams stepped out in front of the young man and grabbed for his collar. "I arrest you in the name——"

The young man gasped and twisted away; the dog jumped up at him, still barking; the van revved and lurched away, gathering speed, and the sheep bolted down the lane in the opposite direction. Minnesota caught at the man's jacket and held on.

"Okay, okay; you can let go," his captive protested. "We've got to get that sheep back in the field before it's run over. Nell!"

The dog ran after the sheep, managed to get in front of it by going up a bank and drove it back towards them. Minnesota and the young man had opened the gate and stood across the road; the sheep swerved into the gateway and ran away down the field. The young man closed the gate and stood against it with the dog at his feet.

"So what happens now?" he asked.

"It's on film," Minnesota informed him. "We've been waiting there for a week with cameras, and the police are on their way."

"Oh well. As long as you get her, too. That's why I stuck it so long, because at least I knew I wouldn't harm the sheep, and if she got someone else to do it they mightn't be so careful . . . " He sighed. "Nice flock of Llanwenogs; hope that one's all right. It was going a bit lame just then."

Minnesota was rapidly becoming Dafydd once more. He hesitated. "So why did you do it at all? How do you come to be working with her?"

"For her," the young man corrected. "It's a craft shop, and she was sent over here to turn it round because what worked in Guildford and Cheltenham wasn't working in rural Wales for some reason. So apparently she sacked all the local staff and tried to take on people like her, but that didn't work and she was losing money hand over fist, and she got rid of the next lot of staff when they'd done their month's trial and tried to run it with one older woman to mind the shop and her doing the workshops, and I was looking for work and saw a card in the window and, not knowing any of this, I thought give it a go . . . Well, I had to wait for her to come back from the workshop she was doing, and the woman behind the till was half-asleep so I went round the shelves and tidied things up a bit, noticed how much she charged for stuff, offered to make the woman a coffee an' she said okay, so I went in the back and looked at the stockroom, washed the mugs, made the coffee, tidied up a bit in there too; the sink was vile an' I'd been in a chippie once an' done my basic food hygiene . . .

An' the woman locks up at five on the dot an' leaves me on the step, hoping this Sophie is going to come back and doesn't go straight home. Well, she got back at five twenty, an' I could tell she was in a temper. Snapped at me what was I hanging about for, so I said I'd come about the job, could I make her a coffee while she restocked the bags she had with her. An' she grudgingly let me. An' when she came in the back she noticed someone'd been tidying, an' she said was that me, so I said yes, I'd done stock control in a newsagent. So after a bit more of me being helpful she said come for a pizza and I'll interview you. And I looked her in the eye and said I hoped she was paying, I'd been out of work for a month and I was sleeping on a mate's floor. An' she said she'd got a fiancé in Colchester, but I could stay with her if it was absolutely clear that I wasn't to come near her, and I said, uh, okay, er, pizza?"

He bent down and stroked the dog's head. "Well, when she got round to the interview—an' I'd seen how she treated the staff at the pizza place and if I'd not been desperate I'd have walked—she asked all the usual stuff, an' then she started asking more about the farm. I was brought up on a farm near Cardigan, see, an' Tad-cu—that's my Grandad . . . " He looked at Dafydd, who nodded, and continued: "Tad-cu took it on when Da did away with himself, 'til he got too ill and had to sell up. An' I helped out at another farm for a bit, but Mam married a bloke from Wem and we moved over there and it was too far to go, considering it was unpaid work, an' I tried to get work round Wem but I couldn't, an' I'd had to leave Nell at the farm—they'd let me train her, working with their sheep—

so when I left school I moved out, got a job near Carmarthen, an' went back to the farm when I could an' asked to work there for my keep but they wouldn't, so I went back for Nell that night and went right down to Pembroke, looking for a job with sheep . . . "

He sighed again. "Anyhow, Mizz Marston liked that I knew about sheep. An' she said the shop was going under, she was cutting all the corners she could, an' could I get wool for her? Fleece? Go out an' catch a sheep and take the wool off it. And I thought, wait a minute: I don't like this . . . but if I don't do it, some clumsy druggie will do it for her, an' they won't have a clue about how to catch a sheep or shear it. So I said yeah, okay, but it doesn't come off the sheep clean in little plastic bags, and she said I could do the washing and dyeing too if I was going to be clever. I used to wash it in the bath at her flat. Spin-dry it, then finish it off in the back of the shop. Dye it at the shop, too, after hours."

"How many sheep did you shear for her?" Dafydd asked.

He shrugged. "About twenty, thirty. I knew we had to get in there before the farmers sheared them; we've been all over. Long Mountain, Llanidloes, you name it. Pick out the cleanest-looking sheep, check the wool's not got weak spots—if the sheep's been ill the wool breaks—then shear it and mark the sheep, skirt it, wash it, dye it . . . "

"Why were so many near geocaches?"

"Because we had to check the access for the fields, and that was a good excuse to be there. I'd done some caching ages ago with school. Sophie would park up an' I'd have a quick look as I was getting out, check how the gate fastened, what sort of sheep, then find the cache an' sign it. I signed them all as Little Nell. Sometimes she'd park up a bit further down the road too, an' I'd take Nell for a walk, see if I could see anything in the field. Like those Llanwenogs; they've been under that far hedge both times. You wouldn't believe how many caches are next to padlocked gates or empty fields. And I was also hoping we'd get caught," he added, very quietly. "I'd have gone to the police myself, only I didn't think anyone would believe me . . . There's a car coming."

Dafydd recognised Dai's car with relief.

"It's Dai. Local P.C.S.O. Helped set this up. What's your name? I'm Dafydd. Williams."

"Aled." The young man scowled. "Jones. Don't say it or I'll thump you."

"Same goes for you. I'm Dafydd Minnesota Williams. He's Dai Laffan."

He went towards the car as it stopped. "Dai? This is Aled. He's got the most interesting story to tell you, and the person we really want is Sophie Marston. I guessed as much, from what Sandy told me, but now we ought to have proof."

Dai grinned at Aled, who was holding Nell's collar in case she jumped up.

"You three had better get in the car and we'll go down to the farm. James is coming over any minute to collect the recording."

"I hope he picks up the notebook with the registration in it," Dafydd remarked, getting into the back seat with Aled and Nell. She took the opportunity to lick his face. "And my knitting."

Dai dropped him off in the village an hour later, in good time for Chapel. He combed his hair surreptitiously in the alley, took off his jacket and inspected it for leaves and insects, put it on again and went towards the white-washed building which always seemed rather too large for the village. One day, he thought, pausing on the threshold, it'll be full of people who want to hear the Gospel preached. Not by a celebrity preacher, either, just someone ordinary who's close to God, like Siân's Ieuan was . . . At least our Minister *can* preach. Why don't people come to hear him? Maybe they don't know; more than likely they don't care. But it's a good sign, I suppose, that young Aled did his shearing early on a Sunday morning when there'd be fewer people about, even if more of them would be in bed than in Chapel . . .

"You're early!" Marged remarked accusingly, handing him a hymnbook. "Deserting your post?"

Dafydd shook his head. "Tell you later."

He sat down in a pew and wondered what would happen to Aled. If he was telling the truth he deserved to be given a chance to hold down a proper job, preferably with sheep . . . Would Dai and Mr. Williams and the police think the same? Was there anything he could do for Aled? Maybe he was already doing it . . . He opened the hymnbook at random and a sheet of paper fell out. It was the hymn they had sung in the horsebox on the way to London to fetch the piano: *Yr Arglwydd yw fy Mugail da.* He murmured the words under his breath and sat praying silently.

Lord, there's plenty of potential in young Aled. Give him a chance to find You, to find a proper place to live and a proper job he can take pride in. Give him the humility to take You up on it . . . Oh Lord, forgive him, and may others be as merciful as You . . .

When the Minister announced that he would be preaching on Ezekiel 34, Dafydd felt comforted. It seemed an appropriate answer.